Kiss of the Jewel Bird

MERCER
UNIVERSITY PRESS

Endowed by
Tom Watson Brown
and
The Watson-Brown Foundation, Inc.

Kiss of the Jewel Bird

A Novel

Dale Cramer

MERCER UNIVERSITY PRESS | Macon, Georgia

MUP/ P504

© 2015 by Mercer University Press
Published by Mercer University Press
1501 Mercer University Drive
Macon, Georgia 31207
All rights reserved

9 8 7 6 5 4 3 2 1

Books published by Mercer University Press are printed on acid-free paper that meets the requirements of the American National Standard for Information Sciences—Permanence of Paper for Printed Library Materials.

ISBN   978-0-88146-525-9

Cataloging-in-Publication Data is available from the Library of Congress

For Lori Patrick

midwife to this work

Also by Dale Cramer

Sutter's Cross

Bad Ground

Levi's Will

Summer of Light

The Daughters of Caleb Bender

Paradise Valley

The Captive Heart

Though Mountains Fall

Acknowledgments

Kiss of the Jewel Bird evolved over the course of seventeen years, first appearing as a short story titled "Under Fortune's Wing," written in 1996 for an online writers' forum, and subsequently published by *Eureka Literary Magazine* in 1999. But the idea wouldn't go away; it just kept growing. I always felt the concept had the makings of a grand fable, so in 2007 I wrote the first draft of a novel. Since then, off and on between other projects, I've gone back to it more times than I can count, reworking, rewriting, adding, subtracting, tweaking, and refining. I nearly have it memorized.

Speaking of the forum, I owe a lot to Elise Skidmore and her minions, who provided a safe haven for a host of fledgling writers, many of whom have since found success in publishing.

Karen White was one of them. An extraordinary writer and a woman of grace and wit, I'm delighted that she took time out of her busy schedule to read and endorse this work. Despite huge success, Karen openly admits that she is, and always has been, envious of my typing and punctuation.

It was also in the old Compuserve forum that I first met Lori Patrick, who has since become an outstanding freelance editor. A kindred spirit, Lori has been a constant source of encouragement and help with all my books, even writing the back cover copy for several of them.

One of the biggest patrons of my writing career has always been Larry McDonald. He and I have worked together for over forty years, watching each other's backs every step of the way. In recent years he's provided me with work whenever I needed money, and let me write when I needed to write. He also does all the photography for the books and the website, and listens patiently while I prattle on about works in progress.

But as indispensable as these people are, there's no doubt that my greatest supporter has always been my wife, Pam. She paid the bills while I wrote the first few novels and has provided real-time feedback during the writing of the last few. I could not have done any of this without her.

I'm also grateful to my friends Bobby Johnston and Charley Corva, who freely offered priceless insights into psychologists and their trade, as well as read early versions of the manuscript and helped me navigate some of the finer plot points.

During the long evolution of this novel a number of people (more than I can name, but they know who they are) have read various versions, offering insight, advice, and encouragement. I owe them a debt of gratitude, for each of them has had a hand in this, the finished product.

Some are born knowing who they are, and some never learn. A few, a tenacious few, discover themselves only by a process of elimination. They must first learn who they are not.

—Crito

Chapter 1

> History tacks and yaws at the secret heart of a gale, and every Ishmael plucked afterwards from a slack sea proves inarticulate, fervently biased, or an outright charlatan. What can we finally *know*?
>
> — *Atlantis Requiem,* Fletcher Carlyle

The *New York Times* called it a "brilliant fury" when Fletcher Carlyle slaughtered a chicken on the hood of a BMW in the middle lane of Central Park West, but then they'd never been able to write about him without using the word *brilliant*. The front-page photo was the Holy Grail of the paparazzi, the first Carlyle sighting in two years, a sensational shot—sunlight glinting off the butcher knife in his raised fist, wild eyes burning through rivulets of greasy hair, teeth grinding against themselves. The crystalline image even captured the downy white feather snagged in his beard and the faint comet of blood across that threadbare bathrobe. Like all things Carlyle, there was something almost biblical about it. The wrath of God. Moses gone mad.

He was unconscious when they wheeled him through the doors of Weatherhaven in the icy blast thrown by the rotor wash of a departing helicopter. Strapped to a gurney and heavily sedated, he slept for the better part of two days.

On the afternoon of the third day, Toma took the author by the shoulders and steered him into Anton Kohl's office, where he collapsed into the leather armchair opposite the psychologist's desk. A copy of *Atlantis Requiem* lay facedown on Kohl's desk—Carlyle's first novel, the book that catapulted him into international stardom just six years ago. The jacket photo stared up at Kohl, begging comparison to the man in front of him, a pale, doughy caricature of the sharp, confident face on the back of the book. Gone was the immaculately tailored English-wool suit, supplanted by a standard white Weatherhaven uniform—stained, wrinkled, misbuttoned. Vacant eyes peered out through a tangle of hair in the general direction of a small fabric snag, a strand of wheat-colored yarn unraveling from the antique Persian rug.

Kohl clicked his pen and made a careful note on a blank legal pad lined up precisely with the right edge of the blotter: *Find someone to repair rug.*

He clicked the pen again and laid it down, perfectly parallel with the pad, then folded his hands to keep them still. His hands, if he let them, would pick up the pen, and after a while he would find himself absently clicking it, a nervous habit he was determined to break. Experience told him to wait, to let the patient come to him. There were signs. Carlyle's chart noted a massive hematoma on the right hip where he'd been slammed to the pavement by the police, but until today he had seemed unaware of it. Today, he walked with a pronounced limp.

Today, he was feeling something.

The attendant lingered by Carlyle's chair, watching. Toma was a giant, a Samoan behemoth, but he could be counted on to be as gentle as the patients allowed him to be, and Kohl trusted his instincts. Normally, Toma would have left the room immediately and closed the door behind him, but when a patient with a history of violence emerged from a vegetative state, the first few moments could be tense.

The doctor cleared his throat. "Mr. Carlyle."

No response.

Toma smiled. "Patience," he said, or perhaps, "Patients." Either way, his meaning was the same. Leaning down, he put three fingertips on Carlyle's shoulder and shook him lightly.

"Come on, you," he rumbled. "Wake up."

Carlyle's head turned slowly, and he stared without expression at the fingers touching his shoulder.

Kohl made eye contact and gave the attendant a small nod. Toma stepped out the door and closed it softly. He would remain just outside, alert. Should Carlyle turn violent there were two panic buttons in the room, one on the desk and one under the lip of the table by the counseling chair, either of which would bring Toma running.

Gathering up folder and tablet, Kohl rose from his desk and walked softly across the room, then lowered himself into the chair facing Carlyle where there would be no obstruction between them. He laid the manila folder on the little Queen Anne table and kept the legal pad in his lap.

Leaning forward, he tried again. "Mr. Carlyle."

"What?" A low rasp, but clear enough. A response. An opening.

Kohl waited a beat. "Good afternoon, Mr. Carlyle."

The author lay low in the chair, his shaggy head resting against the back. Slowly, gripping the studded leather ends of the chair arms, he pulled himself upright and then collapsed forward, dropping his head into his hands, fingers entwined in his hair.

He stayed that way. Kohl waited nearly five minutes in complete silence. Neither man moved.

Patients.

"How are you feeling today, Mr. Carlyle?" He clasped his hands a little tighter, resisting the urge to pick up the pen and click it.

Patience.

Carlyle's breathing deepened. Finally, with a sigh, he gripped his hair in his fists and pulled himself upright again. His hands dropped into his lap as he slumped back in the chair, oblivious to the fact that his dirty hair remained absurdly peaked in the middle. He didn't seem to have the energy even to hold himself erect, but for the first time his sunken eyes glared at the doctor. A dusty voice crawled out of a deep well of fatigue.

"Where am I? What is this place?"

"You're a guest of Weatherhaven Institute, Mr. Carlyle. My name is Dr. Kohl. I'm a staff psychologist."

"Weatherhaven. The nuthouse in the Hamptons?"

Kohl suppressed a grin. "Well, not exactly, but close. We're actually rather well hidden in the interior of Shelter Island, in the heart of the bay formed by the eastern forks of Long Island. And we prefer 'mental health facility.'"

Carlyle took two or three slow breaths before he spoke again. "How'd I get here, and why am I wearing this prisoner getup?"

"Mr. Carlyle, when you had your...*episode* on Central Park West, you were wearing only a bathrobe. You carried no identification, and under the circumstances the police mistook you for a homeless person. According to the report, you offered significant resistance."

A deliberate understatement. One of the policemen required nine stitches.

"Even after you were placed in restraints you were apparently uncooperative and incoherent, which is why, as a matter of routine, they sent you to Roosevelt. By then you were in such a state that the attending saw no choice but to sedate you. Fortunately one of the nurses recognized you—a minor miracle considering how much you've changed in the last two years. The hospital called your publisher, their lawyers got involved, and you were flown here by helicopter."

"Huntsman-Wisner had me sent here?"

"Yes, but please understand they were doing you a favor. Ordinarily you would have been held for three days at Roosevelt for mandatory psych evaluation and then, most likely, transferred to Bellevue."

"But there's that pesky Nobel thing."

Interesting self-image.

"Well, yes, I imagine that may have influenced the attending psychiatrist to circumvent protocol. Mr. Carlyle, the public doesn't know you're here, and we're very discreet. In fact, if the photographer hadn't been on the scene when it happened, the entire incident might have been suppressed."

"Am I under arrest?"

Kohl fidgeted for a second. It was mostly a matter of semantics. "We like to think of it as being in our care, Mr. Carlyle. Under our protection. However, you are required to remain here, at our discretion."

Carlyle rolled his head to one side and stared out the window between the imposing mahogany bookcases at the far end of the office. A naked maple branch scratched at the glass, swimming in a brittle wind. Spring was just around the corner, the recent snow flurries and harsh winds merely winter's exit lines.

"*At your discretion*. In other words, I ain't leaving here until you say so." Carlyle seemed to focus on the branch for a minute, but then he gathered himself. He drew himself upright and forced his attention back to the doctor.

"All right. What do you want to know?"

"It really doesn't matter. Why don't you just tell me about yourself? Begin anywhere you like."

"You don't want to know about me. Tell you the truth, which is something I don't hardly never do, you wouldn't believe it anyhow."

Kohl rearranged himself in his seat, confused. It wasn't what Carlyle said that threw him, but the way he'd said it. For the last two days, Kohl had pored over every scrap of information he could gather on Fletcher Carlyle—articles, interviews, video clips. Though he'd always sounded vaguely Southern, Carlyle's accent in the interviews had been subtle and rather genteel. The man sitting across from him spoke with an unvarnished drawl and gave the impression of a lowborn Southern redneck. The difference was striking. The faint possibility of multiple personalities flitted across his mind.

"Mr. Carlyle, really, I just want us to get to know each other, to establish trust. You can tell me absolutely anything without fear of judgment. I'd like to know whatever you care to tell me about Fletcher Carlyle."

"See…that right there is the problem, Doc. You don't even know what you're asking. You want to know about Fletcher Carlyle, read the tabloids. Carlyle's just a face on a magazine cover, a two-minute yack on a late-night talk show." His bleak eyes leveled on the doctor. "And he's dead."

More of the pronounced Southern drawl.

Carlyle leaned forward in his seat, glaring. "Cut to the chase, Doc. You want to know about the chicken."

Dr. Kohl picked up the pen, clicked it twice, laid it back down.

"Would you *like* to talk about the chicken?"

Carlyle winced as he shifted his weight from the injured hip, scratched at his beard, and stared at his grimy fingernails as if he'd only just noticed them.

"Might as well. I got nothing to lose, now. But it's a long story, and before I get cranked up I want you to know I ain't crazy. The plain truth is, what happened to me ain't in any of the books you studied in that Ivy League school, Doc. I'm pretty sure you can't even imagine it."

His eyes leveled on the doctor and Kohl held the stare. Very few people knew what Anton Kohl was capable of imagining.

"I assure you, I will listen with an open mind."

Carlyle sighed deeply. "Well, I reckon that's as fair an offer as I'm apt to get." He took a minute to collect his thoughts, then said quietly, "The whole thing started in Georgia, seven years ago."

Dr. Kohl made a note—*seven years*. The files didn't go back that far. Prior to the publication of his first novel, Carlyle's past was a mystery.

"Georgia." Echoing the patient, drawing him out.

"North Georgia, in the Appalachian foothills. You don't know, do you? You don't know none of it."

"I'm here to learn."

"Yeah, well, learn this first—I ain't Fletcher Carlyle."

Dr. Kohl scanned his files. The patient's identity had been established beyond doubt.

"All right. I must admit you don't *sound* like Fletcher Carlyle."

Slowly, the patient straightened his back, raised an eyebrow, and struck a dignified pose.

"I'm perfectly capable of assuming the *role* of Fletcher Carlyle when necessary," he said, and suddenly his voice and style matched his interviews. "I'm Fletcher Carlyle's face. I'm his body, his bank account, his autograph, his public persona, but I'm not Fletcher Carlyle. My name is Richard Frye."

"I see." Kohl spelled out the name on his legal pad. "So Carlyle is a pseudonym? That's surprising."

Carlyle rolled his eyes slightly and slumped back into himself. "Listen, Doc, if that one's a jolt you're gonna need a seat belt before I'm done."

"Well, it's just that we have no record of it. It strikes me that to have maintained that level of secrecy while living so completely in the public eye for the last six years is remarkable."

"We took some pains to keep it that way. We had to."

"Why?" Kohl jotted the word *We* on his pad, followed by a question mark.

"Because it ain't just a name, Doc. Fletcher Carlyle is a fictional character built from scratch to go with his literary panache." He spat the word *panache* with a smirk, as if he were mimicking someone. An enemy, perhaps. "Every bit of it—the name, the look, the attitude, the language, every stitch of clothes, every pompous pose, all them highbrow one-liners—it was all part of his plan."

"Whose plan?"

"The CHICKEN!" Carlyle roared.

The sudden eruption caught Kohl by surprise. His fingers wrapped around the lip of the little Queen Anne table and found the edge of the panic button, just in case. But the burst of anger ebbed quickly, and when Carlyle regained his composure there was a note of apology in his voice.

"It was all his doing."

"The chicken."

"Right."

Kohl would have spotted a lie. There was not the slightest glint of pretense in Carlyle's eyes or body language. The man clearly believed what he was saying. Here was the heart of Carlyle's delusion, and he had laid it on the table matter-of-factly, without fanfare.

"Look, Doc, I know it sounds crazy, and I got no way to prove it now that he's dead, but at least check it out. I know you got people. All I'm saying is check out Richard Frye, and then you tell *me* which one you think I am."

Patience. Kohl wanted to dig further, but he was a cautious man and he had already witnessed Carlyle's volatility. To confront his patient's delusion at this point would run the risk of alienating him. Anyway, the *source* of the problem was more important than the delusion itself.

"All right, we'll do that. It would help if you could give me some background, fill in some of the blanks. Mundane things like, for instance, where you went to school."

Carlyle looked at him a little sideways, and now there was a hint of mischief in his eyes. "If you had to guess, what would you say?"

"Well, from what critics have said about your work—the depth of historical detail, fluency in a number of languages, the uncanny grasp of political nuances among vastly different cultures—I would guess maybe Oxford or Cambridge. The linguistics alone…you're obviously well educated. So where *did* you go to school?"

"Calhoun."

Kohl blinked. "I'm sorry, I'm afraid I'm not familiar with Calhoun. Is that a liberal arts college?"

"No, it's the high school I dropped out of. Richard Arlis Frye. Calhoun High School. Northwest Georgia. Now *there's* a fact you can validate."

"You lived in Calhoun?"

"No, I lived in Squalor."

"S…*squalor?*"

"Yeah. My old man was an independent cuss with a weird sense of humor. When I was a kid there was an old guy named Fergus who lived just down the road, and he liked to tell folks we were living in squalor. So Daddy talked a couple of his hunting buddies on the county commission into putting up one of them little green signs—*Squalor Unincorporated*. He said, 'Now old Fergus lives in Squalor, too.' It ain't a real town; it's just a wide spot in the road. Calhoun was the nearest town."

Another note. "Okay. What did you do for a living?"

Carlyle broke eye contact and his jaw tightened. Kohl waited patiently. The maple branch ticked against the windowpane.

"Carried mail. Rural route out of Calhoun. Dead-end job. Depressing."

"I see. Do you think you suffered from depression?"

Carlyle ran a hand over his face, pulled his bottom lip down with his palm and held it there for a second, thinking.

"If you're talking about, you know, *clinical* depression, I don't know. I don't even know the definition. I was just frustrated, that's all. I never aimed to drive up and down the same dirt roads every day for the rest of my life, stuffing mail in boxes. I always figured I could do better. It ain't the kind of thing you dream about when you're a kid."

His voice trailed off and he fell silent for a few minutes, his eyes wandering among the books lining the shelves, dusting his memories. Drifting, losing focus.

"What *did* you dream about as a child?"

Carlyle's eyes dropped away from the bookshelves and a little sadness came over him.

"Believe it or not, I wanted to be a writer. That's the truth. I loved to read, even when I was little, and books took me away. I could go anywhere I wanted to in a book, and I was a natural storyteller my ownself. Mama said I got it honest, that I was a born liar like my daddy."

"Your mother accused you of lying?"

"Nah, she just meant I could spin a yarn. It was kind of a tradition in our family."

"I see. A storyteller. So you've always had aspirations."

"Wouldn't call 'em aspirations exactly. It's just that there was lots of times I'd read a book and see something I thought I could've done better. When I was a kid I daydreamed about being a writer the way other guys dreamed about being Big League ballplayers."

Kohl nodded appreciatively. "And you made it happen."

Carlyle pressed his palms against his eyes and twisted, grimacing. His shoulders shook. A low chuckle grew and swelled into outright laughter and then degenerated into a fit of coughing. When he finally gained control he gave Kohl a devious sideways glance.

"Oh, this is gonna be good." His voice deepened slightly as, once again, he assumed the persona of Fletcher Carlyle. "You're picturing a literary prodigy honing his skills, preparing his magnum opus."

Kohl's head tilted and his eyebrows went up, a kind of ocular shrug. "Well, I can certainly imagine it would take years to develop and refine such a talent as yours."

Another chuckle. "Depends on the teacher, but that's beside the point. I dreamed about it, but like most folks I didn't *do* anything about it—least not till about eight years ago."

"I see. Why did you wait so long?"

"If you knew my old man you wouldn't have to ask. He was a shade-tree mechanic, and he come from a long line of sharecroppers, pulpwooders, bootleggers and such. Half our clan couldn't read or write, and a lot of them thought Arlis Frye was uppity on account of he wore shoes in the summertime."

"Arlis was your father?"

"Yeah. Got my middle name from him. He was a good man, even if Mama couldn't make him go to church."

"So your mother was a religious person?" Another point of potential conflict.

"Oh yeah, big-time. Never cut her hair, not once in her whole life, because the Bible said. Kept it up in a bun and wore a full-length dress all the time, even working in the garden. Tall, skinny, raw-boned woman with steel eyes and a backhand quicker'n a copperhead. She wouldn't abide foul language, and she was death on drinking and gambling, but we loved her anyway. She was as decent a human being as I ever known, in spite of her religion."

"But your father was not a religious man?" Kohl noted all this on his pad.

"Hard to say. I think he believed all the right things, he just didn't much like church. I expect I understood him a sight better than Mama ever did, mostly because she never went hunting or fishing with him. Thing is, Daddy was a self-made man. Before he got married he saved up enough to buy a little piece of land with an old cotton storehouse on it—a big long thing with two-foot-thick stone walls and a high-beamed roof. He put a door on it, cut some windows in it, and they lived there for three years while he worked at the gas station. When somebody needed a house or a barn tore down he'd take the job for salvage, clean up the boards and bricks and stack them in that cotton storehouse. When he got enough lumber he built a house, from fieldstone pillars to roof shingles, every stick of it with his own two hands, working at night and holding down a job at the gas station all day. After they moved into the house he cut three big bay doors in the side of the cotton storehouse, poured a concrete floor and made a garage out of it. Went in business for hisself. I can't remember a time in my whole life when my old man didn't smell like mineral spirits and axle grease. There was always grease under his fingernails, ground into the cracks in his hands. He worked hard to feed his family, and he was proud of it."

Digging a finger in his ear, Carlyle said, "Where I come from, you don't go around daydreaming about artsy crap when there's work that needs doing. A man makes a living with his hands. He fixes cars, digs ditches, plows a field, swings a hammer—whatever it takes. In that house, if I'd said I wanted to be a writer it would've been like saying I was going to Hollywood to be a movie star. It would've been a slap in my daddy's face, like I was better than him. Like I thought I was too good to work. We just didn't think that way."

None of this was what Kohl expected. He could easier imagine the urbane Fletcher Carlyle teleporting in from Venus or springing whole from a lotus flower than growing up shoeless on Tobacco Road. It was an impossible contradiction.

Chapter 2

> Adrian Ott fought his way into the world the very night his father's whaling ship fought its way round the Horn. At first light, though oceans apart, his father and mother ruminated on the same truth: great gain lay only beyond dire trial.
> — *Atlantis Requiem*, Fletcher Carlyle

Kohl focused on the most glaring absurdity. "Your education. You really never finished high school?"

A shake of the head. "Dropped out in my senior year, got a job sacking groceries at the Winn-Dixie in Calhoun, got married. I was in love."

This, too, was news. "You were married? We have no record of a Mrs. Carlyle."

"*Frye*, Doc. Try and remember that. I don't know how, but I managed to stay married to Raye Anne for seven years. She was the only girl ever gave me a second look—leastways the only one with all her teeth—and I was the only guy ever offered her a way out of that hellhole she grew up in. I was a bit on the homely side in those days, and Raye Anne was hot. *Lord*, she was hot. Took second runner-up to the Corn Queen in the Floyd County Fourth of July parade when she was seventeen."

"I take it you're divorced now?" Kohl asked this while spelling out the name *Raye Anne Frye* on his pad.

"That's right."

"What happened?"

"Long story, but being raised the way she was I don't think Raye Anne ever really got what it meant to be a wife. I knew she was kind of loose when I married her, but I figured I could break her of it. Never did."

"She left you?"

"No, I was the one that left. I moved back in Mama's house and let Raye Anne have the trailer. She had nowhere else to go except back to her daddy's place, and I wouldn't wish that on *nobody*. I guess I still felt sorry for her. She told me later, after the divorce—and I guess you'd have to know Raye Anne to understand she was kind of apologizing—she said, 'Richard, you just can't believe everything you hear. There's folks'll tell you I slept with every boy in the county, and it's a filthy lie.' Then she kind of shrugged and said, 'I slept with *most* of 'em....'"

A sad smile came into Carlyle's eyes. "She was the only one ever called me Richard. There was this loudmouth in the ninth grade started calling me Dickie, and it stuck. After that, everywhere I went I was Dickie Frye. I reckon Raye Anne had her faults, but at least she called me Richard."

"You never had any children?"

"No. Thank God."

"Is she still living in...Squalor?"

"More'n likely. She don't know."

Kohl blinked. "She doesn't know what?"

"About Fletcher Carlyle."

"Your ex-wife doesn't know you're Fletcher Carlyle?"

"No. None of 'em do. To the folks around home, Dickie Frye was a mail carrier that went nuts and disappeared seven years ago. They probably half expect me to come back toting an AK-47."

"So you began writing in secret while you were still living in Squalor."

"Yeah. After I left Raye Anne. I don't know, maybe the writing was a kind of therapy. That was a real bad year."

"Because of your divorce."

"That was a big part of it, but it was just one thing after another, that whole year. First, my old man died. One evening he was out in the garage working and he didn't come when Mama clanged the dinner bell, so she went looking and found him lying on the creeper up under Cleve Wright's Crown Vic, dead. Stroke, they said. He was fifty-two."

"I'm sorry. So you lost your father, and then your marriage ended shortly thereafter."

"Yeah, a few months later. I moved back home to look after Mama, but mostly she looked after me. A rock, that woman was. She said God gave her Arlis, and God took him home in his own good time. Anyway, that was when the writing started."

The writing started. Passive voice, a fairly common ego defense.

"So, you actually did write."

"A little, yeah, but it was just baby steps…not like what you're thinking."

At least he acknowledged the writing. Progress.

"Why don't you tell me a little more about that. What made you decide to start writing at the age of…"

"Twenty-six."

"Yes. Why then?"

A long sigh. "It was an accident, mostly. Mama kept the radio on all the time in the house, tuned to a gospel station, and she was hard of hearing so she kept it cranked up to where it rattled the dishes. I couldn't take more than five minutes of that before I'd have to slip out to the garage where it was quiet. When my old man died he left behind a half-built '57 Chevy he'd been tinkering on for years, and I'd go out there and pretend to work on it. Truth is, there was a computer. The year before Daddy died, a buddy of his talked him into getting one so he could find classic car parts on the Internet. He never got the hang of it, but the computer was still there on his desk amongst a pile of old bills and yellow receipts with greasy fingerprints on 'em. So when I needed to get away from Mama's radio I'd go out to the garage and fire up Daddy's computer and plink around on the Internet. That's how I come across the writers' group."

"I see. Tell me about this writers' group."

"Bunch of amateurs, wannabes. In the beginning I just went out there every night and logged on to see what they were up to. They'd write short stories and then talk about it on a kind of message board. Worst bunch of liars I ever seen in my life."

"What do you mean?"

"Well, they were *supposed* to be writing fiction, but most of them just flat didn't know how to tell a proper lie. They couldn't help it—they were Yankees, most of them. Look, Doc, any Southern boy knows if you're gonna tell a lie, you tell it *big*. It's the polite thing to do."

"Polite. How so?"

Carlyle rested his chin in his hand for a minute, thinking.

"All right, I'll give you an example. Me and Daddy used to hunt deer every winter. So we're sitting around the campfire one night, me and him and Uncle Early and a couple old boys from Mama's church, and after a few sips of Uncle Early's home brew Daddy says, 'Boys, did I ever tell you about taking that big buck off of Pine Ridge on my bicycle?' Now, Daddy didn't even own a bicycle, but he told this big long story about how his truck blew a U-joint and lost a drive shaft right when the big bucks were in rut, so he left the house at midnight, riding this bicycle up to Pine Ridge, hoping he could get to his tree stand before daylight. Make a long story short, he said he shot a ten-point buck that morning right after sunup. He hung that deer on his bike with its front legs draped over the handlebars and its hind legs straddling the rail, and lit out for the house. But he was so wore out from being up all night he got about halfway home and fell asleep. When he woke up, he said him and that deer were still on the bicycle, and they were turning into the driveway of the house. He claimed that deer had come to, got his hooves tangled up in the pedals and drove that bike all the way home.

"Now, my old man could tell that story a whole lot better than I just did, but the point is, by the time he got done those old boys were laughing so hard they were crying. Daddy told it for the truth, and never cracked a smile. He was a gifted liar."

Kohl stared. "I'm afraid I don't see—"

"No, I don't reckon you would. Thing is, if Arlis Frye had quit that story without waking up that deer, it would've been like he was trying to get folks to fall for something stupid—making fools of them. But soon as those cloven hooves hit the pedals those old boys knew they were being entertained, and that's a compliment. See, Doc, when it comes to a lie, the difference between a insult and a compliment is a matter of pure magnitude."

"Interesting. I never thought about it that way."

"Lots of folks say the reason there's so many good writers from the South is because they pick up a kind of poetic rhythm from being raised on the King James Bible, but it ain't so. Truth is, people in the South know a good lie when they hear one, and a lie ain't good if it ain't *big*. So I logged on to the message board and gave those Yankees a few pointers. 'Course, I couldn't resist spinning a yarn or two of my own, and they ate it up. Folks on the forum loved those stories, crude as they were, and before I knew it I was hooked. It got where I spent every spare minute out in the garage huddled over a keyboard thinking I was the second coming of Mark Twain."

Carlyle paused then, and a darkness came over him.

"That's where I was the night the storm hit," he said softly. "I know now, it wouldn't have made any difference—I've told myself that a thousand times—but I still can't help feeling like I should've done something. If I had gotten her out of the house and into that stone garage she'd still be here."

"Your mother?"

"Yeah. It was a big old broad-shouldered bear of a storm, one of them brawlers that comes tearing down out of the hills in late spring, slinging lightning bolts, drumming on the roof and moaning around the eaves, making the rafters pop and groan. But there wasn't anything I could do about it, so I just kept pecking away at the computer in the garage."

Kohl squirmed a bit. Lightning, among other things, made him nervous. "You didn't unplug the computer?"

"Nah. Wouldn't have been no great loss, that old computer *or* the stories. Anyway, all at once it seemed like the storm got organized. Right after the lights went out I heard a sound like a train chugging up a grade, and then it got *loud*. I'm telling you, if you ever hear that sound you know exactly what it is. The door blew off before I could get out, and something knocked me halfway across the garage, slammed my head into the sandblaster. Last thing I heard before I passed out was a tumult of old dry lumber tearing and snapping.

"It was quiet when I come to, except for a hard rain on the tin roof. There was a couple sheets of tin peeled off the roof of that old stone building, but that's all. Mama's house was gone. The little six-room clapboard house I grew up in, the front porch with the old cane-bottom rockers where my folks used to sit of a evening and wave at cars, even the tire swing in the front yard was gone, along with the oak tree that it hung from. I went running down there in the pitch-dark, and when the next streak of lightning lit the place up I saw I was standing in soft, fresh-plowed dirt right about where the living room used to be. Everything was gone, roots and all, and Mama with it.

"We got the family together and combed the woods and fields for a solid week. The first couple days, tough as she was, I kept looking for Mama to come storming out of the woods half naked and madder'n a wet hen, but she never did. There was pictures and clothes and wallpaper and splintered wood and broke dishes strewed over corn and soybean fields, across two creeks and a ridgetop, but we never found Mama. Not a trace. I couldn't help thinking about what she used to say all the time—what she always *told* us was going to happen. She got called up."

Kohl jotted terse notes as quickly as he could.

"And this occurred how long after you moved back home?"

"'Bout six months."

He stopped writing, laid his pen down, and looked his famous patient in the eyes. "That must have been terribly traumatic. You lost your father, your wife, your mother, and your childhood home all in less than a year?"

Carlyle nodded grimly. "Yeah, I was starting to think Job was a bit of a whiner."

"That's a lot of upheaval for one man in so short a time span. How did you cope?"

"All I could do was keep on putting one foot in front of the other. Mama's church turned out and set up chairs, had a memorial service right there where the house used to be. The tornado took everything but the clothes on my back, so I went and bought a few things and moved into the garage. Had to put a new door on it and hook up a water heater. There was already an old refrigerator out there, and somebody give me a little microwave and a coffeepot. Living there wasn't half bad once I got used to it. Didn't have a whole lot of choice anyway because I couldn't afford better. I'd just got on with the post office, and what little money I had went to buy a used mail Jeep with right-hand drive."

"What about the insurance money from the house?"

"They didn't have no insurance. Daddy wasn't the sort to pay for insurance on something he figured he could replace with his own two hands. I could've sold some of the land I guess, but the thought never crossed my mind. Even after the house blew away, it was still home."

"So you took up residence in the garage."

"Yeah, me and the cars—my old man's '57 Chevy, the Jeep I delivered mail in, and a raggedy Mazda left over from my marriage. That old cotton storehouse kept me warm and dry. I didn't really need no more than that."

"Did you continue writing?"

"Well, yeah, such as it was. The writers' forum was called Section Eight. Nice folks, friendly and helpful. Most days, after Mama was gone, I'd pick up a six-pack on the way home and just sit there till bedtime pecking away at a story. I had nothing else to do. That stuff wasn't much good, though—that's why I didn't tell nobody about it."

"I see. You didn't feel your early efforts were up to contemporary professional standards."

"No, I mean it was *lousy*. Writing takes practice, like singing. I knew from the forum that a beginner don't always know how bad he sounds, but I guess all my reading gave me an ear for it. I knew my writing was bad, it's just that back then I couldn't tell you why."

Kohl flipped a page in his pad, comparing dates. "You started eight years ago?"

"Right. About a year before I left."

"Remarkable," Kohl whispered. Something didn't add up. It made no sense at all that a man with no formal education could start from scratch, alone in a garage, and go from "lousy" to a Nobel Prize in a few short years. Carlyle's rise to prominence in the literary world had been meteoric. Critics used words like *luminous*.

"You must be a very quick study."

Carlyle waved him off. "You still don't get it, but you will. I've learned patience, if nothing else. Thing is, I really did enjoy that time, all alone with my little stories. Bad as they were, they were mine. Those stories were the only thing I ever created out of my own head, and I couldn't get my fill of it. Once I started writing I just couldn't *not* do it. You wouldn't think a childhood dream would have such a hold on a man—to be a writer, to see my name in the bookstores."

"*Your* name. Richard Frye."

"Yeah, that was the dream." There was a note of bitterness in his voice.

"Would you rather I called you by that name? Oh, but wait…" Kohl flipped a page, scanning his earlier notes, confused. "Did you tell me you preferred Dickie?"

Carlyle's whole body tensed. His eyes narrowed, his fingernails bit into his knees, and his nostrils flared, rage bubbling near the surface once again.

Kohl's hand edged closer to the panic button, but again the rage faded quickly.

Carlyle broke eye contact and ran his fingers through his dirty hair as if mildly ashamed of the flash of anger. "No, I don't care. It don't matter now."

Dr. Kohl waited a beat, letting the moment pass, and made a mental note to avoid the name Richard Frye for a while. For whatever reason, it appeared to be linked to Carlyle's rage.

"So tell me," Kohl said, in an effort to steer the author back into calmer waters, "what was the impetus behind such a startling improvement in your writing skills?"

Carlyle smiled, met the doctor's gaze again. His eyes held steady.

"The chicken," he said.

Chapter 3

> "The proud speak of destiny, the humble of serendipity. The difference, I suspect, is God's own secret."
> —Adrian Ott
> *Atlantis Requiem*, Fletcher Carlyle

It would be years before Dickie Frye would know whether the day he met the chicken was the best day of his life or the worst, but it definitely started badly. When he woke up that morning his alarm clock was flashing midnight in a sunlit garage. The power had gone off again during the night.

Absorbed in his writing the night before, he'd stayed up later and drunk more beer than he meant to. Jumping out of his cot, he yanked on yesterday's shorts, grabbed his glasses off the desk, and downed a handful of aspirin for the hangover. Then he snatched an over-nuked breakfast burrito out of the little microwave on top of the filing cabinet and jammed it into his mouth while pulling a T-shirt over his head, which led to simultaneously staining his shirt and blistering the roof of his mouth when he tripped over his shoelaces and skinned both elbows on the concrete floor.

Then the Jeep wouldn't crank. It hated him. The Jeep had seemed reliable enough at first, but he soon figured out that it was only biding its time, waiting for an opportunity, a moment of weakness. If he was five minutes late for work or ten miles from nowhere with a dead cell phone, the Jeep would quit on him, every time. When he turned the key this particular morning, it made a noise like a coffee grinder. The starter was shot. The Jeep, since he was running late, decided not to crank.

So he took the Mazda. With a duct-taped taillight, a muffler held together with baling wire, two slick tires, and a hundred and sixty-two thousand miles on it, the seven-year-old forest-green junker was his last resort. It would be tough delivering mail out of the Mazda, but he'd done it before.

In spite of everything, he almost made it to work on time. He was only six clicks late punching in, but the postmaster, a bug-eyed ferret everybody called Hitler behind his back, wrote him up anyway. That's the kind of day it was.

He had to sit in the passenger seat of the Mazda, straddle the console with his left leg so he could work the gas and brake, and then steer with his left hand while juggling a tray of mail. By noon his leg was cramping and the outside temperature was bumping close to a hundred, but he didn't dare turn on the air conditioner because the engine would overheat. Once or twice every summer a high-pressure dome squatted heavy on the ridge country, and for a few days the wind died and the temperature hit triple digits. This was one of those weeks.

He tied a Rebel flag bandanna around his head, let all the windows down, opened the sunroof and toughed it out. Twice he got stung by wasps, who always got frisky in hot weather, and then he gashed his index finger trying to pry open a mailbox after some delinquent stove it in, probably with a baseball bat. But the real corker, the absolute cherry on top of the day from hell, was what happened to Root Hollis's dog. Powder was a slick, muscular, hyperactive Weimaraner who'd been put on earth to protect the Hollises' mailbox from Dickie Frye. If the dog was anywhere around, he'd attack Frye's Jeep like a possessed wolverine unless Root was there to stop him. Root Hollis, a redheaded, freckle-faced kid, was the only one who could control the dog, and he was Frye's little buddy because Frye handled the mice for him.

An enterprising nine-year-old, Root had worked out a deal with Odd Lester the Bird Man, a recluse who lived back in the woods in an ugly green house way up on the ridge where he raised hawks to sell to falconers. Odd Lester needed a steady supply of live mice to feed his birds, and Root Hollis figured out a way to trap them, live and by the dozen, around local barns and woodsheds. About once a week he'd bring an old cake tin—punched full of air holes and alive with the nervous skittering of tiny feet—down to the mailbox and hand it off to Frye. Frye would put the tin behind his seat, and later in the day he would deliver it to Odd Lester up on the ridge. The next day he would return Root's cake tin with money in it. It was against post office regulations, and Frye didn't make anything from the deal. He only did it because he liked the kid.

Neither boy nor dog had been around for the last week. The last time Frye had encountered Powder, Root wasn't there to hold him back. The dog charged the Jeep and lunged into the window with such force that he nearly got a piece of Frye's right arm. Then he hung there for a minute, snapping and snarling, clawing at the door with his big hind feet, trying to climb inside. Frye finally managed to dig the pepper spray out from under the seat and give the dog a good long blast full in the face. He might have overdone it a little; the last he saw of Powder, he was doing backflips across the pasture, break-dancing and snapping at his own left ear.

Today the dog was nowhere in sight, but Root was back. He was waiting with his cake tin when Frye's Mazda pulled up to the box.

"What's up, young'un? Reckon them hawks'll eat cooked mice?"

Big gap-toothed grin. "They'll be all right, just keep 'em in the shade." Root held out the cake tin. Frye stuck it under the seat and handed the boy his family's mail.

"Sorry I don't have no gum with me today, partner. I left it in the Jeep. I'll get you tomorrow, okay?"

"Sure. It's all good." The kid wiped his nose with the back of a hand—the one with the mail in it.

That gap-toothed grin reminded Frye of his own dental deficiencies. He grinned at himself in the rearview mirror. His front teeth were a bit rabbity, and the gap didn't help. Two of his bottom teeth had broken off in a drag-racing wreck a few years ago, and one of his incisors had a brown spot in the middle of it. His friends said he had "Bubba teeth."

His glasses had fogged again, and there was a drop of sweat in the middle of the left lens. He pulled off bandanna and glasses, wiped the glasses with the dry tail of the bandanna, then swabbed his face with it and put the glasses back on. Clumps of damp brown hair stuck to his face. He needed a shave, and his mustache was getting bushy. Not exactly the square-jawed leading-man type. The mustache only accented his lack of a chin. And the hot weather was making him think maybe he was getting too old to wear his hair down to his shoulders.

"Haven't seen you in a while, Root. Where you been?"

Root's smile got wider. "We went to my aunt's for a few days. She's got a house on Lake Weiss."

"Cool! Tell you what, kid, a lake sounds like the place to be on a stinkin' hot day like this." Squinting at the shimmer of heat over the red-dirt road, Frye rubbed absently at the throbbing wasp welts on the back of his neck. Glancing around, he still didn't see the dog anywhere.

"You take Powder with you to the lake?"

The kid's smile shattered like glass and he shook his head, staring at his tennis shoes. "Powder's dead."

"Aw, *no*! What happened? He get run over?"

Root shook his head again and looked back up the road as if he expected to see his dog loping over the hill, tongue hanging out.

"'Bout a week ago he went crazy and Daddy had to shoot him."

Frye's face flushed even redder as the news collided with the memory, and he knew instantly what had happened. He could see the tragedy unfolding in real time, right in front of him—the dog rolling and flipping and tumbling, foaming at the mouth, snapping wildly and making those gurgling noises. Madness and a face full of pepper spray looked an awful lot alike. He could hear the breeching of that old Mossberg, the shell sliding in. The blast. He just sat there in shock for a minute, and when he looked up at Root's face he knew one thing for certain: the truth would not do. It wouldn't do at all.

"I'm awful sorry to hear that." He really was. At least that much was true.

He drove the remainder of his route in stunned silence, a kind of mourning, not for a dog he didn't get along with in the first place, but for a redheaded kid that he liked a lot. He finished up at the post office, clocked out without a word to anybody, and forced his baked Mazda through palpable heat waves toward Adairsville. He had called around, and the parts place down in Adairsville was the only one this side of Atlanta with his starter in stock. It would be another hour before he could make it back home to his garage sanctuary with its noisy window-unit air conditioner and a fridge full of cold beer.

He picked up the starter, but on his way out of Adairsville he fell in behind a chicken truck. A grunting old flatbed piled high with little crates of White Leghorns on the way to the poultry-processing plant, the truck was doing about ten miles an hour on the winding macadam road.

With no place to pass, Frye settled back, stewing in the pungent miasma of a truckload of nervous chickens and a brown cloud of diesel exhaust. Little white feathers fell like snow, drifting in through the sunroof and the windows. He wasn't going fast enough to run the air conditioner or even for the windows to do much good. The guy on the radio said the temperature had now reached a hundred and two, a new record for the date. Simmering in his own sweat, Frye fished a cold beer from a cooler on the passenger seat. Normally he made it a rule not to drink until he got home, but this was an emergency.

As he tilted his head back for the first long pull on the beer bottle, his eye caught a movement at the top row of crates on the back of the truck. Looking closer, he could see that two of the bars were broken from one of the little cells, and one of the inmates was trying to break out. The chicken had pushed its head through the gap and was struggling to free a wing. Frye leaned forward against the steering wheel, watching. When the chicken finally worked a shoulder past the bar, he popped out of the crate like a cork under pressure.

Frye expected the bird to fall straight down to the road, so he hit his brakes hard. The last thing he needed right now was another dead animal on his conscience, even if it *was* headed for the processing plant. But the truck had picked up a little speed plunging down a steep hill. The wind curling over the top created a backwash that caught the bird and slammed it up against the crates, then dropped it neatly on the rear bumper of the truck where, by some miracle, it stayed. Now completely free, the chicken just squatted on the bumper, occasionally shaking its head as if to clear it. For a mile or two the bird sat there half dazed, staring back at Frye.

All at once the chicken gathered itself, wobbling a little as it worked for a foothold on the steel bumper, then jumped straight up in the air, flapped a time or two and came down right through Frye's open sunroof, letting out a loud squawk as it crashed into the headrest of the passenger seat, then bouncing back and tumbling down into the floor under the dash.

Frye opened another beer and kept plugging along behind the chicken truck, glancing back and forth from the truck to the lifeless pile of white feathers on the floor of his Mazda. The feathers stirred, puffed out suddenly, and then relaxed. A red-combed head popped out of the pile. The chicken righted itself, then flapped and clawed and worked its way up onto the top of the blue plastic cooler in the passenger seat, next to the open window.

He expected the chicken to jump out the window and complete its escape, but it didn't. It just turned around and hunkered down, watching the road ahead like it was the most natural thing in the world for a chicken to ride shotgun in Dickie Frye's Mazda.

"Tell you what, pard—you're one tough bird. I ain't going to rat you out. You got yourself this far, I say you deserve to make it. You can ride along till after that truck turns off at Pelham Road. Fair enough?"

The chicken's head swiveled toward him, nodded sharply, and turned back to the window.

Frye dropped a tire off the shoulder, then jerked the wheel too hard and fishtailed twice before he got straightened out. That little red-crested head faced the front and never even twitched. Dickie Frye was a fairly astute observer of human behavior, not to mention that his mother had always kept a coop full of laying hens out back, so he also had a working knowledge of chicken behavior. There was something very un-chicken-like about this bird.

His cell phone rang. Unclipping it from his hip, he checked the screen. Raye Anne.

"'Scuse me, I gotta take this," he said, then put the phone to his ear and grunted, "What?"

"Richard! Hey, Babycakes, I just hadn't heard from you in a while and I wanted to make sure you was all right."

"Yeah, I'm just peachy, Raye Anne. I'm happier'n a dead pig in the sunshine. What do you need?" He spit a small feather. Raye Anne only called him Babycakes when she wanted something. As a matter of fact, she only *called* him when she wanted something.

"Well, it's just, you know my new car? The top won't close right, and you was always so good with cars and stuff I wondered if maybe I could just get you to look at it?"

This was classic Raye Anne. Two weeks after he left her she'd taken a job washing hair and doing nails at The Clip Joint, the hair place in the strip mall at the heart of Squalor. The Clip Joint was owned by Talbot Bonniface, as was the Hot Spot Tanning Salon, the drive-in theater, and the used-car dealership out by the interstate. The latest rumor said he was thinking about opening a Piggly Wiggly. There were no real secrets in a place like Squalor, so when Raye Anne started working for Talbot Bonniface and then bought a three-year-old Sebring convertible from him, Frye heard the rumors. He asked Celice what was going on, but she wouldn't say. Celice ran The Clip Joint and knew everything about everybody, but in the dividing up of friends at the end of their marriage, Celice had remained with Raye Anne. She wouldn't confirm anything about Bonniface, though there was a story going around that was too funny to keep quiet. It had to do with the spiked heel of an alligator boot getting jammed in the closing mechanism of the convertible top on Raye Anne's Sebring. Frye was pretty sure somebody other than Talbot Bonniface was in the back seat with her the night she broke the roof, which would explain why she was slipping around now, trying to get her ex-husband to fix it before her regular boyfriend found out about a casual fling.

"Babycakes?"

"I'm still here. Raye Anne, darlin', why don't you take that car back to Bonniface? I'm sure his mechanics can fix it."

He'd known Talbot Bonniface since they were kids. Other than quarterbacking the football team to their first winning season in a decade and dating all the cheerleaders and half the band, Talbot had done nothing to distinguish himself, but in the intervening years his gift for wheeling and dealing had made him the richest man in Floyd County. To anybody from outside, this distinction would have been right up there with being the finest nuclear physicist in Shakerag, yet for anybody born and raised in Floyd County it was a large thing. These days Talbot drove around in a red Cadillac with a vanity plate that said "QB-7." Frye was pretty sure the man had never even heard of Leon Uris, and he wasn't about to tell him. To Talbot Bonniface, QB meant quarterback, and 7 was his number on the high school team. Bonniface was rich, but not particularly bright—everything

Raye Anne wanted in a man. Her catching such a prize between wives was a gift from heaven.

"Oh, I get it," she said. "You still think I'm going out with him."

"Who, Bonniface?" Frye turned to the chicken and mouthed *Buttface*.

"Look, Richard, I done told you I am not romantically involved with Talbot, and I swear I don't know what you got against the man. He's nice."

"Yeah, he's a prince." It was Buttface who'd tagged him with the nickname Dickie in the ninth grade.

"I can hear you rolling your eyes, Richard."

"You *heard* that? Wow."

"And anyway, Celice told me what you said about Talbot being arrogant and self-centered."

He smothered the phone against his chest and whispered to the chicken, "She left out swaggering buffoon." Then, to Raye Anne, "Baby doll, I swear I never told her that. I don't know *how* she found out."

There was a long pause before she answered.

"You just don't like him because he's successful."

"That ain't true, Raye Anne. I'm *jealous* of him because he's successful. I don't *like* him because he's a arrogant, self-centered, swaggering…hello?"

He lowered the phone, stared at it for a second, cocked his arm to hurl it out the window, then changed his mind and banged the steering wheel with it, snarling an admirable string of obscenities.

"I *hate* it when she does that."

After the words were out, it dawned on him that he was talking to the chicken again. There was a kind of compassion implicit in the way the chicken tilted its head and looked at him when he spoke, and Frye emptied his craw without really thinking about it. Maybe it was the heat, or maybe it was the sea of troubles in which Richard Frye found himself drowning, alone and far from help, but somehow he found it soothing to talk to the chicken. The bird was actually a pretty good listener. It seemed genuinely interested in what he had to say, and a White Leghorn, unlike most of the humans he knew, would not take his heat-addled rantings and run breathless to feed them into the small-town rumor mill.

He railed about Root Hollis's dog and how he never meant to kill it. In a softer voice he spoke of his marriage and how he never meant to kill that either, but given that he couldn't even keep the Jeep running, maybe sapping the life out of everything around him was his unique gift. He ranted about his dead-end job, and Hitler, the psychotic postmaster who, as luck would have it, seemed singularly impervious to Frye's gift for killing things. He griped about living in a small-town fishbowl where every drink a man took and every fistfight he got into was subject to public scrutiny and judgment, the kind of place where a man's caste was pronounced by the time he graduated high school, and sealed, immutable, never to be revoked or forgotten. A loser in his youth was a loser for life.

The chicken truck's engine whined as the driver downshifted and slowed, the left turn signal flashing. Pelham Road was coming up, and with all the windows down Frye's car was already steeped in the putrid aroma of the processing plant. The chicken in the passenger seat squatted lower, melting into the top of the cooler and even ducking his head a bit.

"Don't you fret," Frye said. "I'll never let 'em take us alive."

The chicken's eyes followed the truck as it turned off, watching thousands of its cellmates trundle down the home stretch toward death row.

A half-mile later Frye slowed the Mazda and pulled into a narrow gravel road leading back to a fenced-in natural gas pumping station in a pine grove. He got out, went around to the passenger side, and pulled the chicken out through the window. It didn't seem to mind him picking it up. He carried the chicken a ways down the gravel drive before putting it down, just to make sure he wouldn't run over it when he left.

"Look here," he said, pointing, "if you'll go about a hundred yards through them woods you'll come to a farmhouse—Granny Odum's place. She's got a yard full of laying hens, so you'll fit right in. You can live a long happy life there if you keep an eye out for stray dogs and coyotes."

But as he turned and trudged back toward the Mazda the chicken flashed past him, flapped a couple times, launched itself precisely through the open window, and settled back on top of the cooler. It tensed when he picked it up again, but it didn't peck at him. Once more he started down the drive with it, and then, on second thought, went back and raised the windows.

This time he put the bird down a little farther away. Big mistake. The chicken outran him again. Leaping and flapping, it clawed its way up over the hood and down through the open sunroof, landing neatly on top of the cooler. Then it put a foot onto the dash and craned its neck, reaching for something in the middle of the ceiling. Frye heard the hum of an electric motor, but by the time he realized what was happening the sunroof was already closed.

He lunged for the door, but again the chicken was too quick. It jumped down onto the driver's seat and pecked at the buttons. The door locks *thunk*ed into place.

Frye tried the door handle four times before he convinced himself that what he had just seen was real. The chicken climbed back up onto the cooler and stared at him through the window, head tilted, beak gaping.

The engine was still running, the keys dangling from the steering column, but he couldn't get in. He reached for his cellphone and then paused, staring into space.

"Right. Who do I call, and what do I tell them? I got locked out of my own car by a chicken? I don't think so. My life's hard enough."

Fisting sweat from his eyes, he leaned close to the glass.

"Listen, pard, it's a hundred degrees out here. In about ten minutes you're gonna be a *baked* hen. You really want that?"

The chicken craned its neck and twisted a knob with its beak, turning on the air conditioner.

This changed everything. With the A/C running full blast and the car idling, in less than fifteen minutes the tired old engine would overheat and seize up. It was a matter of simple economics; Richard Frye couldn't afford a new engine. He braced his palms on the roof, but snatched them back when it burned him. Hands on hips, he leaned down to the window.

"Okay," he said, speaking slowly and enunciating, the way he would talk to any foreigner. "You win. Unlock the doors and I won't put you out. You can go home with me."

The chicken didn't move. The head tilted, the beak parted, and Frye could just hear a long, soft "Baaaaaa-ack."

"Look, I promise," Frye said. "You got my word on it." He even crossed his heart. He stood up straight, jammed his hands into his pockets, and sighed, staring at the white sky. "I'm negotiating with a chicken."

It was then that he heard the *fa-chunk* sound of the doors unlocking and the hum of the windows sliding down. The chicken nestled on top of the cooler, staring calmly out the front.

Frye climbed in, turned off the air conditioner, opened the sunroof, and pulled back onto the road. It was three or four minutes before he could even make himself *look* at the chicken.

Chapter 4

> "What you call *evil*, Adrian, I call expedience. It is so much simpler not to believe in any cause greater than my own."
> —Oscar Solarte
> *Atlantis Requiem*, Fletcher Carlyle

Dr. Kohl jotted notes occasionally while Carlyle spun his tale in a detached, trance-like state, as though he were reading from one of his manuscripts, for the most part ignoring the doctor. He talked for nearly an hour before the present crept upon him. When he became aware of himself his voice trailed off and he stopped, once again fixated on the rug.

"You think I'm nuts."

Kohl laid his pen down atop nearly three pages of neatly printed notes, initial observations that would lead him to the right questions about Carlyle's past. So far Carlyle had made it easier than expected. Therapy was rarely as simple as movies and television made it appear, but as guarded and hostile as Carlyle had been at the outset, once the dam broke he seemed incapable of *not* talking. All Kohl had to do was listen patiently while the author opened these startling windows into his own mind.

"Please don't be concerned with what I believe, Mr. Carlyle. I'm not here to judge you. My job is to help you return to complete functionality. I'm on your side. You're quite safe here." He was careful not to overdo the disarming smile.

"Safe." Carlyle smirked, shook his head. "Right."

The session with Fletcher Carlyle exhausted Anton Kohl. When the shadows lengthened and the day began to dim, a familiar sense of dread crept over him. It came to him every day at the same time like a great silent cat, stalking him, inching on its belly through the tall grass, its tail twitching, halting, coiled to pounce. He passed the time with noting and filing and a hundred other mundane chores, but trying not to think about it only made him think about it more. Sooner or later he would have to get in his car and drive home. And to get home, he would have to cross Shelter Island Sound.

On the ferry.

He was standing at the desk and packing his notes into his briefcase when Colin rapped lightly on the doorframe, then came in and closed the door behind him. Dr. Colin Fenn, at age thirty-two, had achieved a professional reputation on a par with Kohl's, but privately he still exuded the boyish enthusiasm of a college freshman. His dark hair was a little too tousled, his sport coat a little too casual. As far as Kohl knew, he didn't own a tie, he rarely wore socks, and he usually kept the top two buttons of his shirt undone. Colin literally rubbed his hands together in anticipation as he plopped down in the same chair where Kohl had sat when he was listening to Carlyle.

"Okay, out with it, Eeyore! What's the great Fletcher Carlyle really like?"

Kohl's thumbs fidgeted with the latches on the edge of his briefcase, flipping them up and down, up and down. He'd seen this coming. He and Colin had often consulted each other in cases like this, where a patient had been referred to the practice for evaluation without a specific therapist being designated, but never without the patient's permission. There were strict rules, and Anton Kohl did not break rules. He pressed the intercom button.

"Marlene, did you have Mr. Carlyle sign the authorization form on his way out?"

There was a smile in her voice when she answered. "Yes, Doctor. You may consult freely."

Breathing a small sigh of relief, he turned to his colleague. "It's an interesting case, Colin. I think we can rule out schizophrenia—I believe he knows who he is. The strange thing is that he's not who *we* thought he was."

"Really?"

Kohl explained about the pseudonym, the public persona that accompanied it, and the drawling redneck who appeared to be behind it all.

"He also volunteered a rather elaborate fantasy about the chicken," Kohl added.

"*The* chicken? The bloody-butcher-knife, front-page-of-the-*Times* chicken?"

"The same. Or so I assume."

"He just *gave* you this? Fletcher Carlyle opened up and dropped the chicken in your lap, just like that? Like I've always said, it's better to be lucky than good."

"Well," Kohl said, unconsciously snapping and unsnapping the briefcase latches, "he clearly has anthropomorphic delusions involving the bird, and I'm fairly certain we'll find this chicken at the apex of his divergence from reality. As unlikely as it seems, at this point I'm leaning toward multiple personalities."

"Right—assuming dissociative identity disorder actually exists. So what now? You gonna have the boss prescribe medication, or just dig around in Carlyle's sandbox for a while?"

The slightly condescending tone did not escape Kohl's attention, though it didn't merit a rebuttal. Colin had always considered Kohl's approach pedestrian and pedantic, but it worked; he got results. He picked up his briefcase and turned toward the door, refusing to take the bait.

Colin blocked his path, held his hands up. "Look, Anton, I really don't care how you handle Carlyle, but you're not acting like yourself. I can see it. What's got you rattled?"

"Rattled?" Kohl tried to cover.

"Rattled, yes—highly technical term I learned in my residency at Pilgrim State. You can't hide from me, Anton. I know when something's eating at you. What is it?"

In spite of his flippant air, Colin didn't miss much. He was dead serious now, the flippancy all but gone.

There was no point in trying to be evasive. Kohl took a deep breath. "Carlyle is convinced, utterly convinced, that this chicken of his was possessed of human intelligence, that it communicated with him. There's something about the way he tells his story…it just doesn't seem to be fabricated. It bears none of the earmarks of a lie or a fantasy."

Colin shrugged. "Nevertheless, it doesn't sound like a particularly outstanding delusion, especially from a patient known for his ability to create fiction. Why would that bother you?"

"I don't know. Some nagging instinct tells me there is something very wrong here. Some inconsistency that I can't justify. I can't quite put my finger on it."

"Yeah, well, that's what we do. We help our patients rectify the inconsistencies in their thought processes."

Kohl shook his head, looked away. "Maybe the inconsistency I sense is not in his world. Maybe it's in mine."

In spite of himself, a look of concern crept onto Colin's face. "That happens sometimes—it's an occupational hazard. Fletcher Carlyle is very convincing, so some part of you starts to think maybe there are more things in heaven and earth than are dreamt of in your psychology. Is that pretty close?"

His eyes held Anton Kohl firmly. His words tiptoed around the edges of dark secrets. Kohl swallowed hard, nodded. "Something like that, yes."

Colin put a hand on his shoulder. "I'm always here, Anton. Anytime you need a reality check, I'm here for you. Come talk to me. We'll work it out."

"Thank you, Colin," he said without looking up, and went out the door.

Weatherhaven Institute lay at the very heart of Shelter Island, on high ground well away from the water, and like most of the older structures on the island its dominating feature was its lack of ostentation. The main building—containing only a few offices, a discreet dormitory, and a small but extremely well-equipped medical clinic—was the only building of any kind larger than a cottage. It began life in an earlier century as a clock factory. But the business failed, the building fell into disrepair, and for years it was used as a stable. In 1923 a Wall Street millionaire bought the place and reshaped the stables into a splendid summer hideaway. During the Depression the building fell to ruin for a second time, but after the war it was resurrected yet again to become an exclusive hotel. When the hotel owner's manic-depressive wife committed suicide, he donated the entire twenty-acre complex to a private foundation with the sole provision that they would make of it an institute for mental health.

Even that august structure, with its ivy-laced stone walls and slate roof, had been renovated so often that the cumulative effect of small additions made it seem significantly larger inside than out. The building was laid out roughly in a square, though the profile was broken by a number of jutting wings half hidden among majestic old oaks and maples, its corners mounded with flowering shrubs, softened by cedar and spruce and an occasional weeping willow. Manicured walking paths wove among steep-roofed shingled cottages and immaculate gardens with little isolated sitting spots, granite benches tucked into shady, private nooks. The pastoral setting and the hundred-year-old architecture combined to create an atmosphere of peace and safety, somehow managing to be impressive without being imposing. This, coupled with Weatherhaven's remoteness and its reputation for discretion, combined to make it a preferred accommodation of the rich and famous. The closely guarded client list included a number of front-page politicians, heiresses, and movie stars whose lives had gotten too large for them.

The entire property was ringed about with a twelve-foot-tall hedge, dense and impenetrable, and reinforced on the inside by a ten-foot, spear-tipped wrought-iron fence. The security gate, kept closed at all times and manned by two armed guards, sat back around a curve in the hedge where it could not be seen from the road. There were weekenders from New York who had owned cottages on Shelter Island for years and still did not know of the Institute's existence.

The one great drawback to Weatherhaven, for Anton Kohl, was its location. It was on an island. He could not bring himself to buy a home there because he did not love the idea of living on a spit of land surrounded by water. He could work there, on the highest point of the island, behind hedges and stone walls, but he could not live there. Shelter Island was simply too small for him, and most of the houses on that forested bit of rock had been situated, if there was any way possible, facing the sea. He knew he could not sleep, could not eat, could not live with the water so close at hand, commanding his view. When he set out to buy a home, no place on the island was far enough inland to suit him.

The South Fork of Long Island, while still technically part of an island, at least had the advantage of enough landmass to prevent him from seeing the ocean every time he looked out a window, yet the only way on or off Shelter Island was by ferry. He could be safely inland on the South Fork and away from the water in twenty-five minutes, tops, but he had to endure the ferry ride to do it.

Water everywhere. Dark water. If it weren't for Weatherhaven Institute, Anton Kohl would rather be in Nebraska.

Leaving the office, he settled himself into the driver's seat of his Volvo and, as was his habit, fastened his seat belt before he inserted the key. As if his heartbeat were somehow connected to the ignition of his car, his pulse quickened when the engine cranked. He drove, as always, precisely the posted speed limit, stopping to look both ways before he pulled out from the hedges onto the road. Long before he reached the ferry landing he put on a Bach CD and tried to think of something else, tried to hear something besides the rushing in his ears that sounded for all the world like rumblings from the throat of a great, dark cat.

By the time he reached the ferry a tingling sensation had spread across the tops of his thighs, like bees buzzing under the skin. His breath ran quick and shallow, and more than once he had to tilt his head back to pull in a long, deep breath. When he became conscious of his rapid respiration he focused and slowed his breathing intentionally—inhaling through the nose, deliberately, slowly, making his belly swell. One, two, three, four seconds, and then he let it slip out his mouth, smoothly and evenly.

He repeated the process, putting a forefinger against his neck to check his pulse. He waited his turn at the ramp, distracting himself by carefully monitoring his breathing and heart rate as he pulled up onto the deck of the ferry and stopped precisely where the flagman told him. Fifteen cars, always—three rows of five, unless there was a dump truck or a motor home. He shut off the engine, then turned up Bach and reclined his seat back, slipping down in it until his line of sight was confined to the interior of the Volvo. His own tight little world.

The ferry lurched heavily as it pulled away from the dock, then swayed gently from side to side with the rolling of the waves. Again, he drew in a deep, deep breath, held it momentarily, and let it out slowly. Repeated it. He closed his eyes and took himself away to stand on a mountain of rock. Arid, solid rock.

Even then, despite all the techniques at his command, he could not forget. He couldn't entirely make it go away. The dark waters of Shelter Island Sound swelled and rolled. He would not look, but he knew it was there. It was always there.

Waiting.

By the time the ferry tied up at North Haven and Anton Kohl eased his car down the ramp onto solid ground he realized he'd been holding his breath, forgetting to release it until he almost passed out. He had not done that in months. But his pulse rate slowed as he put the water behind him, and his breathing had returned to normal by the time he pulled into the drive of his home fifteen minutes later.

It was an old house but lovely and solid, in the middle of Southampton, next to a charming little vineyard. Built by a shipwright named Grantham nearly two hundred years ago, the two-story, three-bay Federal-style house still had its original porch all the way across the front, the roof held up by four Ionic-capped columns and edged with intricate egg-and-dart molding. The interior was still solid, the woodwork as well crafted and ornately detailed as the outside, with fireplaces upstairs and down. It was more house than he needed, living alone, but he felt safe in it. Best of all, in a corner of an upstairs bedroom he had found the names of two children crudely carved into the floor, underlined by the year 1836. Apart from the sheer solidity of the place, one of the names scratched into the floor was what had convinced him to buy the house. The first name was Trent; the second, Emma. When he saw the name his heart quickened. Emma. Not the same girl, of course, but finding her name there was like an omen, almost like having her blessing on the house. She would approve.

Once inside, he dead-bolted the door, put on a worn vinyl recording of Vivaldi, built a fire, lit the burner under the teapot, turned on the lamp, and sat in his favorite reading chair by the fireplace. Jarvis the cat leaped into his lap, and his insistent purring put a final calming touch on the day.

Only then did Anton Kohl feel almost safe.

He opened *Atlantis Requiem*, determined to make himself read it. Though he often spent his evenings reading, Dr. Kohl's professional requirements were such that he rarely read fiction; apart from the classics, most of the books lining his shelves had something to do with psychology, except for the ones stashed away in the lower cabinets. Those had nothing to do with anyone's psychology but his own.

Before Carlyle became a patient Kohl had actually read none of the man's work. Like everyone else in the western hemisphere, he knew the name and was aware that Carlyle's novels had spawned two of the biggest-grossing movies of all time, but he hadn't seen the movies either. Now that he had interviewed Carlyle, his professional curiosity forced him to read the book.

Atlantis Requiem was indeed striking, but certainly not what he expected. Captivated immediately by Carlyle's fluid prose, he fell into the story so completely that he forgot himself. When Jarvis leaped up onto the end table beside him, he managed to snap out of his reverie in time, barely, to keep an untouched glass of merlot from tipping over. Only then did he glance up at the antique German mantel clock, astonished at the hour. Nearly midnight. Four hours had evaporated as easily as if he had been dreaming.

Following his usual routine, he laid out his nightclothes, turned down the bed, and showered, but through it all he couldn't evict Carlyle's literary voice from his head. How real it seemed, how immediate, how unlike anything he'd ever read. The man wrote with such authority, such complete confidence in his own storytelling prowess, such easy grace that the words seemed to fall away and leave the reader *living* the novel. But as Anton Kohl brushed his teeth for exactly three minutes and twenty seconds, then put on his pajamas, buttoning all six buttons of the freshly ironed shirt, he couldn't help comparing the voice in the novel to the man slumped in the studded leather armchair in his office.

Unless Carlyle was a gifted actor in addition to his other talents, the contrast was utterly irreconcilable. The answer was likely to be some kind of dissociative disorder, but what could have split Carlyle in two? And perhaps more important, which was the real person? Had Frye invented Carlyle, or was it the other way around?

Even after he switched off the bedside lamp and pulled up the covers, Anton Kohl still saw before him the hollow eyes of an angry, broken man, and that dusty voice came to him as clearly as if the author were still sitting beside him. He tossed and turned for an hour before finally drifting off, haunted by four words planted in his mind by Fletcher Carlyle himself.

"I ain't Fletcher Carlyle."

Chapter 5

> "From dirt he came and to dirt he returned, clawing and protesting, spewing inanities with his dying breath, a single wave in an endless surf, collapsing unseen on a moonless shore. Eternity scoffs."
> —Oscar Solarte
> *Atlantis Requiem*, Fletcher Carlyle

Carlyle's next session was four days later. In the meantime, Dr. Kohl checked on his patient every day, marking a slow but steady improvement. He still brooded, still chose to remain silent most of the time, but now he at least granted the attendants a grudging yes or no when they asked him a question. Lately, he'd even been eating regularly.

Carlyle did have one minor setback when, on the day before his second meeting with Kohl, he turned violent. The attendants brought him a dinner including a Caesar salad topped with strips of grilled chicken. Carlyle went into a rage and flung the whole tray against the wall. He never stated the cause of the outburst, but Kohl added the incident to his notes and, on a hunch, had the nutritionist remove chicken from Carlyle's menu altogether.

By the time Toma escorted him into Kohl's office for his next session, Carlyle had cleaned himself up a little—shaved off the beard, washed his hair and pulled it back into a ponytail. Though his shoulders still slumped and his eyes remained downcast, he looked much better. Some of his color had come back.

Kohl seated himself with pen and pad in the other chair.

"Good morning, Mr. Carlyle."

No response. The eyes were sharp, though they made no effort to even glance in the doctor's direction. The set of his jaw said he intended to keep his distance. Kohl had seen this often enough. Occasionally a kind of remorse would set in when a patient felt he had revealed too much, too soon, to a virtual stranger—a crisis of trust. Under the circumstances Kohl thought it best, today, to steer the dialogue away from the chicken if possible. He knew the end of the story. The key had to be at the beginning.

"Mr. Carlyle, the last time we met you spoke briefly about your father. Would you like to talk more about him?"

Carlyle's eyes moved. Just his eyes. They settled on the doctor.

"I said pretty much all there was to say. He worked, that's all. When he wasn't working in the garage he was mending fence or fixing something. If he didn't have mechanic work he was out horse trading or picking up odd jobs, always looking for a way to make a nickel or save one."

"Did you have a decent relationship with him?"

A shrug. "Yeah, me and him got along fine. He taught me how to hunt and fish, how to get around in the woods. One of my earliest memories was him showing me how to kick the heart of an old rotten pine stump to get lighter wood. There's a streak in the middle that's all full of turpentine—won't rot, and it's so hard you can't drive a nail in it with a two-pound hammer, but you can kick it out of the ground if the stump's soft enough, then bust it up and use it for fire starter. When I was little I spent a lot of time digging out lighter and selling it. When I got big enough he taught me most of what I know about cars. In the spring we'd go fishing."

"You enjoyed that?"

Carlyle's eyes drifted, remembering. "I miss it. It's been years, but when I was a kid, sometimes we'd camp out by the Coosa River or on some little cove at Lake Weiss. We'd put out trotlines and sit around a campfire half the night swapping lies. Those were good times."

He looked like he wanted to say something else. Kohl waited.

"They were decent folks, Doc. If you're looking for abuse, there ain't any. There's no skeletons in the family closet. No incest, no drugs, no drunks—well, no *mean* ones anyway. We had our fights like everybody else, but never a knock-down-drag-out. Just normal growing-up stuff."

"What did you fight about?"

Carlyle rubbed his newly shaved cheek, glanced out the window. It was a heavy, overcast day.

"The usual. Grades and stuff. Mama always claimed I was brighter than what my report card said. Truth is, my mind wandered—I was a daydreamer. She thought I was just lazy. Mama worked hard as Daddy did, raising a garden, cleaning house, and she did a good bit of charity work with her church friends."

"I see. You brought up religion once before. Was the church a major influence in your home?"

Carlyle gave him a wry sideways glance. "You ain't from the South, are you? Mama was Baptist to the bone. *Regular.*" He knifed a hand in front of him to accent the word. "Sunday morning, Sunday night, Wednesday night, she drug me to church. Sunday was the only time she didn't work, except to cook. She said folks shouldn't eat at a restaurant on Sunday afternoon because it caused other people to have to work."

"She felt that was wrong?"

"It was a *sin.*"

"I see. Do you feel she was too judgmental?"

"No, I think she was a good woman doing the best she could. Where I come from, church was just what folks did on Sunday. Especially poor folks."

"Would you say you were poor?"

"No, we just didn't have any money."

"You didn't feel deprived?"

"No. We were country folks, no worse off than our neighbors. Poor is relative. Besides, my folks did right well compared to *their* folks."

Kohl crossed his legs, propped his cheek in his hand. "Tell me about your grandparents."

Carlyle laughed. He leaned forward in his chair and looked down at his shoes. "Yeah, maybe you're right. Maybe that stuff will help you understand where I come from. Maybe it'll show you just how different I am from Fletcher Carlyle."

He rested his elbows on his knees and dropped his face into his hands, covering his eyes. He didn't say anything else for a minute or two, but right when Kohl was about to prime the pump he started talking again, through his hands.

"My grandfather on my mother's side was Brandyce Pugh. They called him Brand. He grew up on a little farm right across the Alabama line where his clan scratched out a living in the cotton fields since before the Civil War. When he was thirteen his granddaddy died and left him seven goats. Brand was proud of them goats—first time he ever owned anything. But he went off to the field one morning and left his goats penned up with a bad-natured six-hundred-pound hog. When he got home that evening that hog had killed five of his goats—he'd *eaten* two of 'em. Brand bowed up, got the shotgun down and stomped out the back, aiming to kill that hog, but his daddy stopped him. It was cotton-picking time, still way too warm for hog killing, and they couldn't afford to waste the meat. Brand got so mad over it he packed a tote sack and left—just headed east and walked till the mad wore off, which, for Brand, was a far piece. He ended up working in a gristmill up by Rome, and he never went home again. Thirteen years old. He could barely read and write."

Kohl was still taking notes after Carlyle stopped talking. When he finally looked up, Carlyle was watching, waiting for him to catch up.

"Granny Pugh—my mother's mother—lived with us for a few years after Brand died. I remember her fairly well. She used to get up before daybreak and make biscuits. I remember her scrubbing floors with lye and singing old gospel songs nobody knows anymore. Wore them cotton print dresses all the time, and you could smell the *old* on her. She was the one used to tell me stories."

"What kind of stories?"

Carlyle's gaze drifted toward the window, toward the only horizon he could see. He shook his head.

"Can't recall a whole lot, but I do remember they all had heroes. She made up stories about the kind of folks she knew—dirt farmers, mostly—except they did grand things. I remember this one, about a big old dumb boy who went off to war and ended up liberating a whole country because he didn't know it couldn't be done. The locals knew he was dumb but they saw he was true, so they followed him anyway. When I was a kid I'd sit up against Granny in the front porch swing for hours, just listening. There's something fine gets handed down in times like that. I don't mean just the stories neither, but whatever it was I don't believe I could put a name to it.

"I don't know much about my granddaddy Frye because he died when my daddy was just a boy," Carlyle said. "They say he was kind of a hothead. He got to feuding with some old boy at the paper mill, and one night after he got a couple drinks in him he took his pistol and went down to the mill. Nobody really knows exactly what happened, except that a boiler blew up and killed both of them. Best they could figure, a stray bullet hit the boiler. Later on they found his pistol in the rubble with a couple bullets missing, but that's all anybody knows."

"Interesting," Kohl said, and jotted *Family history of violence* on the pad. "That was your paternal grandfather?"

"Yeah."

"But your father wasn't prone to violence?"

"No. Well, I mean, Daddy had a temper, and he could pitch a fit with the best of them, but it wasn't in him to hurt anybody. I remember when I was about twelve I broke the axle in his truck. *Lord*, he raised Cain—rolled and tumbled and kicked up gravel, run Granny off and hard-cussed a Jehovah's Witness, threw a skillet at the mule, threatened to turn the electricity off and join the Foreign Legion, shot a buzzard and went in swimming, but he never laid a hand on me."

When Kohl regained his composure he said, "Mr. Carlyle, you do have a gift for hyperbole. Do you have any brothers or sisters?"

"No."

"So you're an only child and your parents are both dead."

"Yeah, that's about it. But you know what, I'm okay with it. My folks had a good full life, and they were happy in it. They wouldn't have asked for any more than what they got—and nobody lives forever." Then he added softly, "*Almost* nobody."

"Almost..." The doctor echoed the word, hoping Carlyle would go ahead and reveal what was behind such an odd qualification, but the author suddenly withdrew. He sat back, an intentional retreat, and draped his head over the chair back to stare at the ceiling.

"Long story." Carlyle's head came back level—just his head—and he crossed his arms. "And I can see it's a waste of time, telling you about the chicken."

Kohl put on his most accommodating face. "Again, Mr. Carlyle, you really don't have to convince me of anything. The things you tell me will only help us—you and me, together—to open your life like a book and show us what's really there. Whatever you say will inevitably be cathartic for you and revealing to me. As we agreed, I may occasionally consult with a colleague, but everyone here is bound by laws of confidentiality. Nothing you say will be ever be repeated outside this office."

"Right. You want me to trust you."

"Frankly, we're not likely to accomplish much unless you do."

Carlyle uncrossed his arms and leaned intently toward the doctor.

"Then you're going to have to trust *me*, Doc. We ain't getting anywhere talking about how I was raised. You got to listen to me, and you got to have a open mind. I ain't making this up, none of it. I'm trying to tell you the straight-up honest-to-God truth. Considering where I come from, my life was pretty normal, if there is such a thing, until I took up with that chicken."

Kohl took a deep breath, clicked his pen. "All right, then. By all means, let's talk about it."

Chapter 6

> Libraries overflow with the rantings of triumphant warriors. Human decency, whose manifestations are unspectacular and hardly newsworthy, goes largely unreported.
> —*Daughters of the Nephilim*, Fletcher Carlyle

Richard Frye took the chicken home on the passenger seat of his old Mazda because he said he would. His word, even to a chicken, was his word.

He had left the garage doors up that morning, but it didn't help much in this heat. There was no need to keep the place locked during the day; he didn't own anything worth stealing, and a thief would most likely get in anyway if he wanted to. Besides, he figured anybody who came into this dump would take one look around and leave a donation. He opened another beer and turned on the exhaust fan to at least move the hot air around a bit. The chicken stayed on top of the cooler in the passenger seat, watching. When Frye really paid attention, it seemed the chicken's eyes were following the beer bottle in his hand.

Maybe he was thirsty. Frye raised the bottle, a question.

The chicken nodded, let out a soft squawk, and hopped out the window.

Unscrewing the lid from a mason jar, Frye ran it full of tap water and put it on the floor. By the time he straightened up, the chicken had skittered past the hulk of the '57 Chevy and started pecking at the water. He drank half a lid before the growling of a dog interrupted him.

"That'd be Bubba," Frye said. "Yard dog from the neighbors' farm."

The chicken looked up at Frye and, very intentionally, pointed with his beak to an engine hoist against the wall. Frye picked him up and perched him on the arm of the engine hoist.

"Well," he said, now almost eye to eye with the chicken, "I kept my word, bird—I brung you home. Now I gotta go put a new starter in that Jeep. I'm leaving the bay doors up. If you want to take your chances, have at it, but I'd keep an eye out for Bubba if I was you."

He took a ratchet set from a workbench and the new starter from the trunk of the Mazda and went to work. A minute later he came back and got a beer out of the fridge. Five minutes later he dropped the empty bottle in the garbage and got another one.

A bushel of professional-grade profanity, three busted knuckles, roughly a gallon of sweat, and five beers later, the job was done. Wiping his greasy, bloody hands on a rag, Frye turned the key. The Jeep fired right up. He shut it down, slammed the door, and spat on the hood as he passed.

While he was putting away his tools he noticed the sun had finally dropped below the treetops. The exhaust fan had done its work, making the garage at least bearable, and now that the sun was going down the creaking old air conditioner might actually have a fighting chance. After turning the window-unit A/C on high, he closed the bay doors to cut down on the bugs. As he passed the engine hoist he noticed it was empty, the chicken nowhere in sight. He knelt down and looked under the Chevy; not there either.

Good riddance, he thought, and was heading for the refrigerator when he heard a scratching sound from the toilet stall. Then the toilet flushed. The chicken trotted out from under the stall door, loped across the floor, leaped and flapped up to the desk, and vaulted precisely onto the arm of the engine hoist.

The spring on the stall door screeched as Frye pulled it open and looked inside. Nothing out of the ordinary, nobody hiding in there to play a prank, just a grimy sink and a toilet with water still swirling. He took his steamed glasses off, wiped them on his shirttail, put them back on, and stared at the chicken. He wanted another beer but thought better of it. Maybe he'd had enough. He went out back for a shower to clear his head.

His father had built a lean-to tin roof on the back end of the garage and poured a rough slab under it for his air compressor; he couldn't stand the screaming noise inside the shop. When Dickie inherited the garage and was forced to turn it into a living space he discovered, once he cleared out the piles of old seat cushions and greasy boxes of used parts, that there was room enough for a water heater and a washer and dryer out back under the lean-to. While he was tying the plumbing into the water heater, it was a simple matter to add a showerhead. It worked out nice. Standing in one spot under the lean-to, he could drop his dirty clothes in the washer, take a shower, and then put on clean clothes straight out of the dryer. He'd nailed a hand mirror to the post, for shaving. A man living by himself could arrange things for pure convenience.

The shop had cooled a degree or two by the time he showered and went back inside. He was hungry, so he took a TV dinner from the freezer and tossed it in the microwave, and then it occurred to him that the chicken probably needed to eat, too.

But the chicken was asleep, roosting comfortably on the engine hoist next to the desk, head retracted. Frye opened a can of corn, poured it cold into a cereal bowl, put it on the floor by the desk for the chicken, and sat down in front of the computer with his Salisbury steak and mashed potatoes.

When he double-clicked a word-processing file labeled MY BOOK, the first page of his novel spread itself across the screen with a musical *pling*. It was like magic, the way it calmed his bruised soul. Alone in his garage with the cicadas chanting the heat out of the summer evening, for a while Richard Frye forgot that he was a wilted, incompetent, raggedy old loser of a letter carrier who killed his friends' dogs and lived in his daddy's garage.

In those hours, he was a writer.

The first thing he did was check the word count to see precisely how much of a book he had already written. Twelve thousand and change.

"Not a whole lot of words," he said aloud, "but they're mine. And it's a start."

He wasn't sure where he was going with it, but it was about two brothers, one of whom was a soldier on his way home from the Middle East. Frye had quit writing the night before in the middle of a sentence, and now he fell into the rhythm easily, finishing the sentence without hesitation and tapping away at the keyboard as if he'd been doing it all his life. The next time he glanced at the digital alarm clock by his cot, three hours had passed.

He looked back over what he had written. It was decent enough, he thought, but now he was stuck. His soldier's plane touched down at the airport, taxied to the terminal, and that was where Frye got stuck.

He wrote, *The airliner pulled into the nose notch and came to a stop.*

It was lame. The sentence just lay there, but for the life of him he couldn't see anything wrong with it. He'd been to the airport a time or two and watched the planes ease in until the muff-eared guy in the orange vest crossed his light sticks and they stopped. That's all they did: they pulled in and they stopped. It was right, as far as it went, but it didn't *live*. Resting his chin on his forearms, he sat motionless for a long time, thinking. He'd felt the same dissatisfaction plenty of times before, and he still didn't know what to do about it. Something was missing, and he knew only that it was important. It mattered. The words didn't come to life. They didn't turn into pictures. They didn't live and breathe on the page, but he couldn't figure out why.

A small ceramic ringing sound caught his attention, and he raised his head to see that the chicken had gotten down from its perch to peck at the corn in the bowl on the floor.

"Guess I woke you up, huh?"

The chicken raised its head, nodded, went back to eating. Or maybe it wasn't a nod, maybe it just raised its head to swallow a grain of corn, the way chickens do. Lots of times, growing up, he'd seen a yard bird throw its head back and worry down a baby snake the same way.

"So tell me, chicken, what's wrong with my writing? What do I have to do to make it get up and dance? What's the difference between me and Hemingway, huh? Just tell me. I can take it."

The chicken stopped pecking and gave him a long blank stare.

"Yeah, that's what I thought. You don't know either."

He read the sentence out loud.

"The airliner pulled into the nose notch and came to a stop."

Something nagged at him. Something on the edge of his memory, some niggling little thing he'd heard in a radio interview with some famous writer spoke to him now: *It's in the verbs.*

"Verbs," he muttered, out loud. He picked up a pencil and tapped it against the words on the screen. "Pulled. Came. *Verbs.*"

Sitting and staring at the sentence, he wracked his tired brain for better verbs, but nothing presented itself.

"Pulled is okay. I mean, what else can you say, right? But the other one—*came*—that's lame. That's the trouble. That one needs beefing up." He looked down at the chicken again. "Twain called it a second cousin. It ain't the right word, but what is? What, exactly, does an airplane *do* when it stops?"

He double-clicked the word *came*, highlighting it, then just sat and stared at it until he realized he needed to go to the bathroom. Grunting up from his chair, he dropped his little frozen-dinner tray in the garbage and shuffled off to the plywood john in the corner of the garage to empty his bladder.

When he came back from the john the chicken was up on his desk, pecking at the keyboard.

"HEY!" Frye bolted the last couple steps and knocked the chicken off the desk. It hit the concrete hard, and rolled up under the '57 Chevy.

No one else knew about this manuscript, and there were no copies. He hadn't backed it up anyplace, so if this insane yard bird messed around and deleted it he'd have to start all over again, from scratch. He stood there for a minute, breathing heavily, watching a feather drift across the floor next to the car, then turned and leaned over the desk to see what damage had been done.

And there, in place of the verb *came*, was a new word. The sentence now read, *The airliner pulled into the nose notch and* **curtsied** *to a stop.*

He straightened up slowly, staring into space for a long moment, his mouth hanging slightly open.

"*Curtsied*. That's what they do. That little dip, down and back. That's exactly what they do."

A motion drew his attention to the floor. The chicken had waddled out from under the car and was watching him. Their eyes met.

"Aw, man." Frye shook his head. "What *are* you?"

The chicken didn't move, just watched. Nor did it back away from Frye when he bent down, lifted it from the floor, and sat it gingerly on the arm of the engine hoist.

"Tomorrow," he said softly. "I can't deal with this tonight, okay? I'm too ragged out to even think about it. I'll leave the air on in the morning and keep the doors down so the dogs and cats can't get in. You'll be safe. I'll put out some food and water, and tomorrow when I get home from work"—he nodded at the computer on the desk—"we'll talk. You and me. But right now I just can't...." He squeezed his throbbing head between his palms.

"I gotta get some sleep."

Chapter 7

> If inspiration is the father of art, surely solitude is her mother.
> —*Daughters of the Nephilim*, Fletcher Carlyle

"You all right?" Carlyle leaned forward in his chair and touched a fingertip to the doctor's knee.

"Yes, I'm just listening," Kohl said, jolting himself out of his reverie. Part of him really had been listening, but he was distracted by the maple branch whipping against the window in great wide swaths. The coming of spring always brought weather fronts to lash the island with gusty and unpredictable winds—nothing serious, according to the latest reports, but a matter of some importance to a man whose home could only be reached by ferry. Kohl had been half listening, and he chuckled now, replaying Carlyle's story in his mind.

"What's funny?" Carlyle smiled with him, apparently not offended. His mood had lightened considerably.

"I don't know." Kohl rearranged himself in the chair to better face his prize client. "Just the idea, I suppose. This chicken of yours is fascinating, to say the least."

"You ain't heard nothin' yet."

"I want you to know I'm greatly encouraged by your openness, Mr. Carlyle. The more I know about how you think and how you've dealt with things in the past, the more likely we'll be able to ascertain the source of your recent difficulties."

Carlyle shrugged. "The cause of my recent difficulties was the chicken."

―――――

The day the chicken launched itself into his car—into his life—had been a long, hot, wearisome, incredibly frustrating day, and yet when Richard Frye finally went to bed that night he couldn't sleep. The word kept typing itself across the screen in his mind.

Curtsied.

He wanted to explain it away, to tell himself maybe he'd had too much to drink, typed the word himself and simply didn't recall doing it, but he couldn't deny what he'd seen with his own eyes. The chicken did it, and he couldn't make it come out any other way. His thoughts tumbled and leaped like puppies as he rolled in his blanket, and his mind would not slow down or look away long enough for him to find sleep. When the blue LED digits clicked over to 5:30 he slipped out of bed and dressed quietly so as not to awaken the chicken.

The bird was still perched right where he'd left it, asleep on the engine hoist. It seemed to telescope into itself when it slept, legs and neck virtually disappearing. Frye put two soup bowls on the desk—water and corn—then stood for a minute staring at the floor under the engine hoist. He expected to see a mess but, except for a few feathers, there was nothing. No black-and-white splotches.

"This afternoon," he said to the sleeping chicken, "don't go anywhere. We gotta talk."

For the first time in a long while, Richard Frye got to the post office early. He cased his route, loaded his Jeep, and in spite of brutal heat for the fourth day in a row, drove his route in record time. He was back home by two-thirty in the afternoon with a bag of chicken feed in the back of the Jeep.

When he crossed the garage with the feed sack on his shoulder, the chicken looked up at him from the desk. It was standing in front of the keyboard, and on the screen was Frye's manuscript.

"Good afternoon," Frye said, with a formality that seemed absurd, given that he was talking to a chicken. "Been reading?"

The chicken nodded.

He laid the bag of chicken feed on the dusty hood of the '57 Chevy and raked sweat from his eyebrows with a thumb. The garage was a sauna, even with the window unit running all day. He nodded toward the computer screen.

"So, what do you think? Of my book, I mean."

The chicken worked the Alt button with a long middle toe and made a series of commands. Frye's manuscript disappeared and a blank document popped up in its place. The chicken pecked at the keys with surprising rapidity.

It is crap.

Frye shifted his feet, stuck his hands in his pockets, and looked around like he thought he might find a rebuttal written on the walls.

"What do you mean, crap? It's a first draft; I ain't done with it. And it's only thirteen thousand words, give or take. I'm just getting cranked up."

The chicken typed again in a flurry of staccato clicks, head jerking back and forth, beak striking keys. Frye moved closer, adjusted his glasses, and read over the bird's shoulder.

Stilted dialogue, purple prose, unconvincing MC, hackneyed plot, point of view problems.

Frye straightened up, scratching his sweat-damp head, at a loss for words. Part of him was enthralled with the idea of having a conversation with a chicken, but another part of him was infuriated by the frontal assault on his writing. In the end, the sheer absurdity got the better of him.

"But apart from that it's pretty good, huh?"

It is crap.

Frye collapsed into the desk chair, crushed but laughing. He rolled himself to the side just a bit so he could see around the chicken.

"Let's just back up one or two squares," he said. "First, I'm having a little trouble warming to the idea of being critiqued by a White Leghorn, okay? Second...who are you?"

It would appear you are correct: I am a chicken. From the fact that I was destined for the packaging plant, I would deduce that I'm roughly three months old.

"Well, yeah. I could have figured that out for myself. That's not what I meant. Are you...have you got a name?"

I have had many names. You may call me Crito.

Reading from the screen, Frye said the name "Critto" as if it rhymed with ditto.

Pronounced CREE-toe.

"Ooookay. So...where you from, Crito?"

Everywhere. Nowhere. I was last a child's parakeet, an utterly useless bird. I drowned myself in the water dish to escape.

"Okay, wait. Listen, you're gonna have to give me a little background here, pard. I mean, I ain't never talked to a chicken before and it's a little tough to wrap my brain around it."

The chicken cocked its head, one black eye looking over a shoulder at Frye. He held the stare for a minute, and Frye knew, somehow, he was being measured. Whatever the test, he must have passed, because the chicken turned back to the keyboard and began to type.

I was once a man, not unlike yourself, but without the silliness and confusion. Long ago, in Sumer.

Frye shook his head, frowning. "Sumer. I remember reading about that in school. Fertile Crescent, four or five thousand years ago, right? But that's ancient history. It ain't around anymore."

The birthplace of recorded history, but it has long since passed into legend. Sumer, in its glory, fell, as did I. I was cursed, and remain so to this day.

"Cursed. Okay, now I got it. Fairy-tale stuff. A wicked witch turned you into a chicken."

I was cast into an ibis. This body is only the latest vessel. There have been many.

"All right, I'll play. If you don't mind me asking, what did you do to get yourself cursed?" He was slowly adjusting to the idea of carrying on a conversation with a chicken, though he half expected to wake up any minute. In a straitjacket.

I slaughtered a peacock.

"A peacock. That's it? You killed a peacock? I don't know, man. Seems a little harsh."

Justice, like most philosophical concepts, is relative.

They talked into the evening, Frye asking questions and Crito typing his answers, often cryptic and hard to understand. Eventually, Frye became aware that he was hungry. He rose from his desk chair, stretched, and sauntered over to the fridge.

Staring into the freezer, dreading another TV dinner, Frye said absently, "Man, wait'll the guys at work hear about this. I got me a talking chicken."

Crito selected the entire transcript and hit Delete. The text disappeared, leaving only a blinking cursor in the corner of a blank page.

"Aw, man, what did you do that for? I was gonna print it out."

You must tell no one.

Frye came back to the desk, read the words and said, "Nobody?"

No one. If anyone learns of this I will say no more. I will become an ordinary chicken, mute, and you will appear quite foolish, or insane. On this point there will be no compromise, no second chance.

"But why?"

First, for your own good. People do not love what they do not understand. If this were Salem you would hang. Times change, people do not. Second, I will not be subjected to public scrutiny, or worse, a laboratory. Tell no one.

Frye stroked his weak chin, weighing Crito's odd condition carefully. That one black eye stared back at him. The chicken meant what he said, and besides, people already thought Dickie Frye was nuts. His life, thus far, had been nothing but an unbroken string of failures and disappointments. Of mediocrity. And now, out of nowhere, something entirely magical was happening to him and a world of possibility had opened up. It didn't take Dickie Frye long to figure out that silence was a small price to pay.

"Okay. It'll be our little secret."

The chicken held the stare, unmoving.

"Oh, listen," Frye said, reaching for the bag of chicken feed. "I brought you some grub. Is this okay?"

Swill. Worse than insects and worms.

It hadn't occurred to him that an unusual chicken might have unusual tastes.

"All right, then. What can I get you? Anything you want."

Fresh fruit—mango, preferably, and kiwi, though I will accept domestic fruit if necessary. Whole wheat, raw, unground. Long grain brown rice, slightly undercooked. I like a touch of scotch in the evening, preferably Aberlour single malt, sixteen years old. Failing that, any of the Speyside whiskeys will do. And I will need cigarettes—Dunhill, if you can find them.

In a matter of seconds Crito highlighted this last paragraph and sent it to the printer—his grocery list—then deleted the entire text again. As the printer began to hum and click he jumped down from the desk, trotted over to the john, and ducked under the door. In a moment, the toilet flushed and he trotted back out. Stopping in the middle of the floor, he glanced up at Frye and gave his head a quick, purposeful jerk in the direction of the car. His meaning was clear.

Richard Frye picked up the grocery list from the printer, folded it, and stuck it in his shirt pocket. Then, with a final bewildered shake of his head, he grabbed his car keys off the desk and headed to the Jeep.

Two hours later he put three sacks on the desk.

"You got expensive taste, pard. I had no idea. Nobody in this part of the country ever even heard of Aberlour. I went four places and finally ended up with this. Will Chivas do?"

He placed the bottle of scotch carefully on the desk. Crito, who had been reading something on the Internet, suddenly pulled up a blank document and began typing.

A blend. Passable for cooking, perhaps.

Next, Frye put an old hubcap on the floor and poured raw wheat into it from a brown paper sack. "I found this in a health-food store outside of Cartersville. Kind of place where they cater to nut-jobs who grind their own flour because they think everybody's trying to poison them."

Everyone IS trying to poison them.

Frye shrugged. "Whatever, man. What do you want me to do with this fruit?"

Crito leaned back, nodded toward the hubcap with the wheat in it. Frye laid a mango and a kiwi on top of the wheat.

"And the cigarettes! Dude, I went to a cigar store and they said the only place you're gonna find Dunhills is in the duty-free shop at the airport—a two-hour round trip. You'll have to make do with these."

He opened a pack of Virginia Slims, tapped one out and rolled it in his fingers like a pencil. "I figured they'd be easier to hold in a beak. Oh, and you're gonna love this."

He pulled a brass object the size and shape of a hockey puck from the sack, sat it on the desk, and pressed the edge of it with one finger.

There was a small snap and a blue flame popped up from the center of the disk.

"See, you can light it yourself. Is that cool or what?" He was quite proud of having figured out on his own what sort of lighter could be managed with a chicken claw.

Crito waddled over, took the cigarette in his beak, pressed two toes delicately on the edge of the brass puck, and lit up. Frye pulled a large glass ashtray from the sack and placed it on the desk next to the keyboard.

"Look, I, uh…I don't need to tell you there's flammables in here, do I?"

Crito shot him a look that answered his question, and went back to whatever he was reading on the Internet, tilting his head to keep the smoke out of his eyes.

Frye waited a minute or two, arms crossed, toe tapping, but being ignored by a chicken was not something he could endure for long.

"Will there be anything *else*, sir?"

Dropping the cigarette in the ashtray, Crito pecked once at the bottle of Chivas and gave Frye a purposeful stare.

"I thought of that, too." Frye pulled a shot glass from the sack. He opened the Chivas, poured a short one, and put it down beside the keyboard.

It was almost dainty, the way the bird nipped at the scotch. His head quivered and his neck feathers puffed out briefly, but Frye couldn't tell whether he was delighted or disgusted. The chicken looked up at him and jerked his head toward the chair. Frye took a seat, then rolled himself to the left to get away from the smoke.

Crito grabbed the mouse in his claw, clicked to Frye's open manuscript, and dragged over a paragraph, highlighting a description of a sunrise. For a moment Frye thought he was about to be complimented on his writing, but a second later Crito selected the color palette and changed the color of the text in the paragraph. To purple. 'Nuff said. He flew through the whole manuscript and turned seven or eight paragraphs purple. When he was finished, at the end of the manuscript he typed his terse commentary.

It is a sentence, Rembrandt. Communication first, art second.

He took another drag from the cigarette before he stubbed it out, then hopped down to the floor and began pecking at the wheat in the hubcap.

"Well there you are, boys and girls. Today's lesson is purple prose." Frye popped a John Prine CD into the little boom box on top of the filing cabinet, bellied up to the desk, and went to work.

―――――

After Carlyle went back to his dorm room, Colin dropped by Kohl's office to catch up on the Carlyle saga.

"I'm still not certain exactly what happened to him, but whatever it was he seems to be rebounding quickly," Kohl said. "He's getting stronger every day. I'm going to move him to a cottage. He's clearly no threat, to himself or anyone else. I suspect the violent episode with the chicken in New York was isolated, an aberration."

"You sure?" Colin dropped himself into the patient's chair, where he draped a leg over the arm, then pulled a racquetball from his pocket and began bouncing it off the ceiling. "There's no particular rush."

"I think there is," Kohl said, and he swiveled sideways in his desk chair, one elbow propped on the desk, clicking his pen. "He needs to feel less confined. We also need to get him some decent clothes. He hasn't mentioned it, but Fletcher Carlyle is known for sartorial elegance. Did you know *GQ* picked him for one of America's ten best dressed three years ago? He's got to be tired of the uniform, and there's a tailor in Sag Harbor who can outfit him nicely."

This was not uncommon treatment for the caliber of clientele normally found at Weatherhaven. Most of them were accustomed to being pampered.

"Okay, so what's next?" Colin asked, still pinging the racquetball off a carved ceiling panel, clearly aiming for the small recessed light in the center.

"I'm recommending a hi-res MRI." Since Kohl was not an MD he couldn't order the test himself, but the psychiatrist on staff could order the scan on his recommendation.

Colin stopped what he was doing, his brow furrowed. "Why? What are you looking for?"

"A lesion in Broca's area."

"You're losing me. What's Broca's area got to do with Carlyle?"

"It's the languages, Colin. That's the one thing that bothers me the most. Marlene had our people run a background check on Richard Frye, and everything we turn up corroborates his story. Frye was born and raised in northwest Georgia, never went to college, and never displayed any unusual abilities of any kind, apart from a certain facility with Bondo. Seven years ago he left everything behind—just walked away and was never heard from again. Less than a year later, Fletcher Carlyle exploded onto the literary scene in New York. I've listened to him very carefully, for hours, and I'm convinced the man I'm talking to is Richard Frye, not Fletcher Carlyle."

Pulling out a bottom desk drawer, Kohl retrieved a heavy book from it and handed it to Colin—a hardcover copy of *Daughters of the Nephilim*.

"Have you read this?"

Colin took the book, scanned the cover, opened it to the first page. "Yeah, but it was a couple years ago. Why?"

"Because I don't believe the man I've been talking to is capable of this. Look at the pages I dog-eared—there are six of them. The man who wrote this knows Sanskrit, Aramaic, Farsi, Hebrew, and some Mesopotamian dialect I've never even heard of. Richard Frye couldn't possibly know those things."

Colin flipped to a couple of the marked passages, gave them a cursory glance and shrugged.

"Anything's possible. You can find it all on the Internet, including dead languages. Besides, a lesion in Broca's area tends to cause aphasia. Speech *deteriorates*."

Kohl shrugged. "Not always. There have been isolated cases of enhanced comprehension. A few years ago there was an article in the *Journal* about a patient out West somewhere—San Francisco, I think—who spontaneously began speaking fluent Italian without having studied it. Hi-res MRI finally found a small lesion."

"Listen, Anton, you know as well as I do, when you see hoofprints, think *horse*. I can't believe a man of your experience is chasing zebras."

"Right or wrong, there are things I have to rule out."

Colin rose from his seat, stowing the ball in his jacket pocket, and slipped the book onto the corner of Kohl's desk.

"Well, you go ahead and order the scan if it'll make you feel better, but you won't find anything. What you're dealing with here is a dissociative disorder. You've just been talking to the wrong guy. Fletcher Carlyle is in there, trust me."

"But, Colin, even if there *are* multiple personalities—and I'm not entirely convinced there are—how can any of them know things that Richard Frye has never learned?"

"I don't know," Colin said, and he laughed that easy laugh of his. "Maybe one of them has a brain lesion."

Chapter 8

> In the invincibility of youth a man sees fear and names it cowardice. Over time his bravado yields to the exigencies of property, and fear becomes discretion. In his later years he may even call it wisdom.
> —*Of an Angry God*, Fletcher Carlyle

Before he pulled out of his parking space Kohl plugged Wagner into the CD player, but when he got a glimpse of the waves shattering against the pilings of the ferry landing he changed to Vivaldi. No sense adding to the Sturm und Drang.

But despite the increased rocking of the ferry, the crossing bothered him less than usual. When he laid his seat back and closed his eyes, Emma came and filled his mind. Perhaps it was the rough sea that triggered the memory of her. Emma loved the beach, but for her own reasons. For most girls the beach was a place to stretch out in a carefully chosen bikini with headphones and a book, a land of cocoa butter and boys. Emma never sunned herself, choosing instead to walk the beach for miles with a camera around her neck, her lens constantly combing the sand and the horizon for surprises. For Emma the sea was the soul of romance and the beach merely a precipice, a place where she could touch the edge of possibility, where she could literally hear it calling to her. Emma, with her pale skin, did not go down to the sea for anything so frivolous as sunshine and boys. She went for the rumble of the waves, the cry of a gull, the allure of that faint gray line where sea and sky merged at the edge of the world.

For Anton Kohl, even when they were young, the sea was a dark and fearful thing, seething with hatred, the mother of countless hidden perils. Brooding. Waiting.

He'd known Emma since high school. *Twenty-five years.* The time lapse made him cringe, made him tilt the rearview mirror to look at the slick scalp that had once been covered with wavy hair. Such a short time ago. He had shared a study hall with Emma in the tenth grade, where he helped her with her algebra and they became friends for life. She was warm and funny and human, and he could talk to her for hours about anything, about nothing, or not talk at all. She didn't seem to mind that he was a nerd, and she saw a side of him no one else saw, which he sometimes thought was the only thing keeping that side of him alive. Emma's auburn hair, pale, lightly freckled complexion, high cheekbones, and Roman nose rendered an odd kind of beauty that Anton never mentioned to her, thinking—*hoping*—that he was the only one who saw it.

He was fairly certain he was the only one who saw her eyes the way he did. They seemed ordinary at first glance, a mixture of gray and green with little highlights of yellow he could only see if he looked really close, but her eyes were deep. In Emma's sea-green eyes he saw trust and love and hope and laughter, but he also glimpsed all the other deep, cold currents running like a river through a woman's soul, and he could not look long into her eyes because it felt like falling, and left him with an ache in his chest. They were the best of friends but, alas, only friends. He was too painfully shy to ever risk their friendship by exposing his feelings to her.

He wondered, even now, if she ever knew. As a psychologist he had become a keen observer of body language, but to his knowledge Emma had never shown the slightest indication that she was aware of his feelings. Or had she?

There was that time in their junior year when he had almost asked her to the prom. Emma was always a bit flighty and, like most beautiful women, had disastrous taste in men. She and Anton saw each other in school every day and talked on the phone nearly every night, but though they had been lots of places together, they had never been on anything like a date, so Anton practiced his approach for weeks. He memorized the exact words he would use, and he dared to dream that she would respond in kind, that she would admit to having the same feelings for him. But on the very night when he had made up his mind and screwed his courage to the sticking place, she showed up at his house beaming, all aflutter over having been asked to the prom by some jock on the football team.

It was this moment, strangely, that absorbed Kohl as he lay back in the reclined driver's seat of his Volvo while the ferry pitched and waddled through the swells. He remembered, now that it was too late, having let just the edge of a yawning cavern of disappointment creep into his expression in that moment, when she told him who had invited her to the prom. Thinking about it now, through a lens of twenty years of trained observation, he was sure he remembered a response, a widening of the eyes, the suppressed shock of sudden recognition. A sadness had flitted across her face, however briefly.

He could have said something then. He could have told her of his own intentions, and, who knows, maybe she would have tossed aside her football player and accepted him willingly, gracefully. Perhaps both their lives would have gone differently.

But he said nothing, and the moment passed. He congratulated her. He helped her pick out a dress.

He found his own date for the prom, a girl in whom he was mildly interested, and for a time his high school love life paralleled Emma's. They would talk about boyfriends and girlfriends when they were together. He resigned himself to being friends for life, and then she went away to Penn State and he went to Yale. For a while they kept in touch—the odd late-night phone call and sometimes a note scribbled on a greeting card that would arrive on no particular occasion. That, too, tapered off after a couple of years.

He saw her once or twice in those rare times when they were both home from school, but she was always dating somebody, and she spent her summers in high adventure, usually out of the country. She Eurorailed her way through the pensiones and youth hostels of Paris, Prague, Brussels, and Madrid one summer, spent the next drinking wine and ouzo on some sun-bleached island in the Aegean, and the next camping in Nepal. She sent him pictures occasionally, sometimes with a note, sometimes just pictures. Horizons. Emma's world was wide, and she would not be confined to a corner of it.

A hopelessly serious student, Anton didn't get out much.

The instant she graduated college, Emma married her first husband. She sent Anton a personal note in which she actually wrote the words, *I'm marrying my first husband*. Another man might have dismissed it as an unintentional gaffe, but not Anton. He laughed and cried at the same time, it was so Emma. He was invited to the wedding, but the fact that the ceremony was to be held in Maryland was enough of an excuse; he sent his regrets.

He saw her again a couple of years later. His father, burdened with his mother's medical bills, couldn't assume any more of Anton's student loans by the time he reached graduate school, so Anton took a part-time job in New Haven watching a boiler, turning dials, writing down numbers. He liked it because he was alone and there was a lot of downtime when he could study. It was there, when he went out for a sandwich one night, that he ran into Emma.

She had trimmed down. She wore heels, which made her taller than Anton, and an expensive suit. She carried herself with the willowy grace of a woman in full. Her auburn hair had grown long and rich, hanging in a neatly trimmed line across her back. Anton wore dirty coveralls and smelled of diesel fuel. Emma suggested they have dinner, for which she paid, and then she held his arm while they walked across the park, back to his job. Emma took off her shoes and strolled barefoot with him on the moonlit green, talking in shorthand, laughing often.

With her arm in his and her high heels dangling from slender fingertips, she told him about her brief first marriage to an ego-driven stockbroker who cheated on her. But she said she had learned from the experience, that she'd taken him to the cleaners in the settlement. Now she was married to a corporate lawyer in New Haven, and she seemed to think this one might work out because she stayed on the road half the time, working on writing assignments for *Newsweek*, and they rarely saw each other. Coming from Emma it made a kind of sense. At first, Anton found himself basking comfortably in the instant renewal of a deep and easy friendship. Thinking about it now, he could still feel the warmth of her arm in his, her perfume mingling with the smell of fresh-cut grass. He could feel the summer breeze through his coveralls and see the way the full moon dappled the grass through the maple and elm trees.

But there had been something else that night, a brief glimpse in a flash of moonlight, the merest suggestion of regret in her eyes—a wistful glance down the road not taken.

He asked for her phone number. She lived right there in New Haven. He thought he might call her at night, sometime when he was bored at work, and they could talk. Just talk.

Her answer was too long in coming.

"No," she said softly. "I don't think that would be such a good idea."

She didn't look at him as she said it. He saw only the side of her face, and it was drawn, strained. She had misunderstood. She thought he wanted to *meet* her at night, that his interest had taken an illicit turn. She had judged him by his dirty coveralls and suspected a kind of desperation. He saw that they had, after all, grown in different directions, become different people. All these things he saw in the profile of her face, the tightening of her jaw.

The misunderstanding stung him deeply, so he made no effort to explain. They parted company, and he made no attempt to see her or talk to her again. Even now, he could picture the curve of silky auburn hair across her back, the forward tilt of her head, the slump of her shoulders as he let her walk away.

He had seen her only once since then, about ten years ago, during the short span when Kohl himself was married. He'd met his wife, ironically, on the tennis court at the club. Much younger than Anton, his wife was everything he was not—a social butterfly, ambitious, acquisitive. Their marriage was doomed from the outset, her need for more always at war with his need to be safe and secure and methodical. In the end, she left him for a stage actor.

But it was during his brief marriage that he ran into Emma in Manhattan while he was in town for a conference. In the busiest city in the world, they both happened to be standing on the same street corner, hailing the same cab. When it stopped they turned and looked at each other to decide whose cab it was, and only then did they realize they were not strangers. They laughed. They hugged. It turned out they were going the same way, so they shared the cab.

Emma had changed yet again. Her auburn hair had been cut short and spiked. Wearing a loose muslin shirt over a tank top with khaki cargo shorts, hiking boots, and wool socks, and lugging a huge one-strap canvas thing that looked more like a duffel bag than a purse, she had acquired a rugged outdoorsy look—except for that pale skin. Emma had never been able to tan. On the way uptown she told him she had shed her second husband, the corporate lawyer in New Haven, when he stopped coming home at night. She said she never really learned whether he was having an affair or if he was just in love with his work; she left him when she realized she didn't care one way or the other.

From the way she described the man, Kohl couldn't understand why she'd married him in the first place, but then he'd always known that Emma had terrible taste in men. Self-destructive. It was easier to judge then, when he was still mostly oblivious to the fault line in his own marriage.

At the time of their encounter ten years ago, she was writing for *National Geographic* and living with a man named Enzo, an art dealer she'd met in Paris who kept an office and an apartment in New York. All these things spilled out in a breathless rush during a ten-minute cab ride uptown, but Anton Kohl wouldn't remember most of what she said because as soon as she got into the cab, she took off her sunglasses.

Those eyes. He looked into those sea-green eyes and clutched the edge of the seat for fear of falling. And then he looked away, withdrew, because they reminded him of a moonlit night in New Haven when she had misunderstood. Misjudged.

"It's a shame Enzo is out of the country for the week," she was saying. "I know he'd love to meet you. But give me your number and we'll have dinner anyway, just you and me."

He ached, torn between those eyes and the residue of that night in New Haven when she had wrenched his heart from his chest.

"No," he heard himself say. "I don't think that would be such a good idea." He couldn't look at her.

She backed away wide-eyed, clearly confused, a little hurt, a little stunned. The cab lurched. Horns honked.

"What's wrong, Anton? Have I done something? Said something?"

He hadn't the courage even to return her gaze, let alone tell her the truth. He just shook his head.

The cab pulled to the curb. She got out and stood beside the open door, digging through her monstrous purse. With two fingers she handed cash to the cabbie, then shouldered the bag and dropped a business card on the seat.

Leaning down, one hand on the roof, she said, "Call me sometime, Anton. If you want." She waited a few painful seconds and added, "Please." Then she closed the door and was gone.

Two minutes later he wished he had not said those words to her, and he wished he had not let her go, but by then she was lost in the crowd. It was perhaps out of shame that he never picked up her card from the seat.

———

By the time Emma faded from his memory, Anton Kohl was pulling into the garage in the backyard of his safe old house by the vineyard. Because of her, the afternoon passage of Shelter Island Sound had been less traumatic than usual, despite rough seas, and yet he wondered now, as he went upstairs and knelt down and ran his fingertips across the name etched into the floor by some long-forgotten child, if such lasting regret was fair toll for the easing of one fretful passage. Deep down, he knew. His own life had taught him that the two were related: lingering regret was fear's child.

Chapter 9

> Burn his house, salt his fields, cover him with boils, and he will accept his lot meekly. Such is life; he knew it all along. Yet make him whole again and he will fret endlessly, like Malchus, forever glancing over his shoulder and pawing at that unblemished ear.
> —*Of an Angry God*, Fletcher Carlyle

Four days later Carlyle stood quietly gazing out the window at the end of Kohl's office, hands clasped behind his back. A steady rain had settled in that morning and showed no signs of letting up. Water dripped from the buds that had begun to appear along the branches of the maple tree; crocuses and jonquils had sprouted here and there like little periscopes, advance scouts of spring.

"I like the new digs," Carlyle said without turning around. "I guess that was your idea."

"Yes. I thought you'd be more comfortable in a cottage." Kohl sat in his usual chair, legs crossed, pad and pen in hand, waiting.

"Right. By 'more comfortable,' you mean you finally figured out I wasn't apt to stab anybody."

"Mr. Carlyle, I assure you I never—"

"It's all right. That's your job, I guess. I'm just glad to be out of that cell."

"It's not exactly a cell."

Carlyle turned to look at him. "It felt like one. It was a right *pretty* cell, with the wallpaper and drapes and everything, real comfortable, but I couldn't come and go without a guard. Even the toilet said it was a cell—all one piece, seat molded in. I guess y'all were worried I'd lay my head on the edge of the bowl and bludgeon myself to death with the lid."

Kohl smiled. "You've been here for two weeks, Mr. Carlyle, and I'd say you've made considerable progress. I wouldn't move you to a cottage unless I was sure you were ready."

After taking a seat in the leather armchair opposite the doctor, Carlyle didn't say much. He glanced at the window again, and several times Kohl noticed him popping his fingers, something he did unconsciously when he was uneasy.

"Are you all right?" Kohl asked. "You don't seem quite yourself today."

"Aw, I'm okay. It's the weather, I guess. Been stuck inside all morning with nothing to do."

"Is there something I can get for you? I was thinking perhaps you could use a laptop, in case you feel like doing some writing."

Carlyle snorted, flopped back in the chair with a smirk. "No. I expect my writing days are over."

He didn't elaborate. Clearly, it had been the wrong suggestion for Kohl to make, pushing his patient in the wrong direction. Carlyle seemed more depressed than before.

"It also occurred to me that you might want something to wear other than the whites. There's no rule, you know—you don't have to wear them. I was wondering if you'd like for us to send someone down to your apartment in New York for some of your clothes. I can arrange that if you wish."

Carlyle looked down and gave his white uniform a lingering appraisal. "No," he said, and his voice was cold and hard. "I don't want anything from there."

"I thought perhaps one or two of your suits—"

"*No*. I don't want the suits, I don't want the socks, I don't want a paper clip, I don't want *nothing* from that place."

"All right." Kohl jotted a note on his pad. The apartment in New York was apparently more important than he had realized. "There's a fine tailor in Sag Harbor. I'll have him come out tomorrow and take your measurements if you like."

"No thanks. Can't we just go to a store?"

This surprised Kohl, but he adjusted quickly. "I hadn't thought of it. It's just as well, actually, because we need to make a trip to the South Fork sometime next week anyway, if you feel up to it. I'd like to have a test done at a hospital, but I'll clear my calendar and schedule the hospital for the afternoon. That way you and I will have the entire morning to do some shopping. Would you like that?"

Carlyle's sideways glance betrayed a fair amount of suspicion.

"What kind of test?"

"Just a routine MRI to rule out some things. Nothing at all to be concerned about. I prefer not to leave anything to chance."

A nod. "All right, whatever. I really am getting a little stir crazy, and I gotta admit it'd be nice to be able to wear real clothes for a change."

"Excellent. I'll have our medical staff send over some forms for you to sign, and I'll make the necessary arrangements."

"Where's Toma? They let me come over here without an escort today."

"The escort is no longer necessary. You can move about freely."

"Oh. I just kind of missed him, that's all. You know, it was Toma that took me to the cottage yesterday, gave me the nickel tour. We hung out for a while and talked."

Kohl smiled. "That's good. What did you talk about?"

"Religion."

"Really? His or yours?"

"Neither, really. You know, he was born and raised in Samoa. Came over here to play college ball, blew a knee—"

"Yes, I'm familiar with his background."

"Well, it turns out we got something in common. His granny was a storyteller, like mine. She was a *matai*, a tribal chief—unusual, Toma said, because they don't normally let women be chiefs. Anyway, when he was little she told him stories about the old ways, from back before the missionaries came. According to Toma's grandmother, I have an *aitu*."

Kohl squinted in thought. "I'm not familiar with the term."

"It's the spirit of a dead relative. They show up in all sorts of animals, even trees. Toma said he don't believe in such, but his granny put a lot of stock in it. Most of his family still leaves little gifts and food at odd places to keep the aitu happy. He said the last thing you want to do is piss one of them off, because an angry aitu can cause all sorts of problems. Toma said they can make you sick—even though he don't believe in it."

Kohl clicked his pen a couple of times. This sort of mysticism made him nervous. He did not wish to believe there were entities behind every bush, in every dark place.

"Do you think your chicken carried the spirit of a deceased relative?"

Carlyle shook his head, rolled his eyes. "Lord, no. Crito was no kin of mine, I'll guarantee you that. I just like talking to Toma, that's all. He don't get all uptight like some folks do, talking about Crito. It was kind of refreshing."

"That's good," Kohl said, feeling the mild sting of accusation. He hadn't been aware that Carlyle had picked up on his nervousness. "We want you to feel at home here. It's good that you've found someone whose company you enjoy."

Kohl looked over his notes from their last session.

"The last time we talked, I believe you were about to tell me how this chicken influenced your writing. Would you like to talk more about that?"

"Influenced?" Carlyle shook his head. "Doc, you still don't get it."

Reading a particular comment in his notes, Kohl laughed out loud.

"What's so funny?"

"I'm sorry. I'm not laughing at you, but you have to admit it's a bit odd to think of Fletcher Carlyle writing the beginnings of *Atlantis Requiem* late at night in an old garage in a place called Squalor under the tutelage of a cigarette-smoking chicken with John Prine playing in the background. I've read the book myself, and seriously—"

"That ain't what I was working on."

"It wasn't *Requiem*?"

"No. Whole different book. This was before that." There was something Carlyle wasn't saying, and his voice had taken on a hard, defensive edge.

Kohl decided not to push. Better, sometimes, to change the subject. "So. If I'm understanding you correctly, you believe this Crito was reincarnated a number of times, always as a bird. You know, this is not an entirely new theme in Eastern mythology."

"Yeah, but this ain't no myth, and he wasn't always a bird. He was a man, *trapped* in a bird."

Kohl wrote *imprisoned* on his pad, followed by a question mark. A possible indication of a terrible guilt looming over Carlyle's past.

"Yes, I remember that. You said someone put some sort of a spell on him?"

"I guess that's one way of saying it. And it's perpetual, which is to say, according to Crito, when his host dies he just migrates into the next nearest bird. Any kind of bird—young, old, male, female—but always a bird. And he remembers everything."

"So this is why you refer to the chicken as 'he,' even though it was clearly female."

"Yeah. I also think it had a lot to do with why he was so glad I brought him home with me. That body-jumping thing."

"I don't understand."

"Well, if he hadn't been able to get away from the chicken truck he would've ended up in the poultry plant."

Kohl stared blankly.

"The *slaughterhouse*," Carlyle said.

Kohl tilted his head and squinted, searching for a point. Logic simply would not hold—as if logic were applicable.

"But, Mr. Carlyle, if I understand correctly, you're saying that when this chicken expires his consciousness merely migrates to another bird. Why would he be afraid of being killed?"

"Okay," Carlyle said, spreading his hands, "put yourself in his place. The instant you're dead, you pop into the head of the next nearest bird, right? Now, imagine yourself on an assembly line of execution."

"Oh my."

"Horrifying, ain't it? And painful."

"Dying?"

"No. Death was nothing new to Crito, except that he felt all the panic and terror of his host. But then it was over, and on to the next one. He said dying was a little disorienting, but reentry was excruciating. Can you imagine being put through that a thousand times in one day? That ain't too far from Mama's definition of hell. Be enough to drive you nuts."

Kohl managed a nod of appreciation. He identified, perhaps too closely, with Carlyle's assembly line. Endless cycles of stark terror and massive adrenaline were the hallmarks of his own daily experience.

The author turned sideways in his seat and hung a leg over the arm. Tapping his knuckles against his lips, he studied the budding maple branch for a minute, as if gathering his thoughts. He seemed, finally, to be relaxing.

"I'm telling you, man," Carlyle said pensively, "Crito would've done anything to stay out of that poultry plant. I don't know for sure, but I suspect that was why he decided to help me, at least in the beginning."

"You mean, help you with your writing."

"Right, but I mean, why me? He could have moved on without saying a word. He didn't always let folks know about him—he *chose* who he would show hisself to. 'Course, sometimes there weren't any people around, but sometimes he stayed away on purpose. He told me once, the best time he ever had was when he was a condor on the West Coast back before the white man came."

"So there were times when he avoided human contact entirely, and other times when he sought people out." Kohl flipped back a page, looked at his notes. The things Carlyle projected onto his imaginary chicken were useful clues to his own psyche, whether he knew it or not.

"Oh yeah, definitely. Crito picked me. What I never could figure out is *why*—unless he just thought he owed me for keeping his butt out of the slaughterhouse."

Kohl thought carefully about his next words. They were risky, because they could validate Carlyle's delusion, but he felt compelled to bolster the man's self-image.

"Perhaps he saw something in you."

Carlyle searched his eyes warily. "Like what? Despair?"

A chuckle. "I was thinking something more noble. Kindness. Generosity. Courage, perhaps. Honesty. Or humor. Maybe he just...*liked* you."

"To tell you the truth, I never thought of that. It don't seem likely. He was kind of ornery most of the time, and the stuff he did was...well, confusing. I mean, look, Doc, I got to know that chicken pretty good. Crito knew everything, and I'm telling you he never did nothing without a good reason. So how do you explain what he did to me?"

"I'm hearing anger. Do you feel that the things that have happened to you in the last six years are *bad* things?"

"Why, *hell yeah*!" Carlyle's face contorted and shook the words out as his hands opened and his arms spread wide. "I'm in the nuthouse, in case you didn't notice!"

"But, Mr. Carlyle, it seems to me you're focusing only on the negative. You completely overlook the fact that you're a Nobel Prize-winning novelist and a very wealthy man."

Carlyle sighed, and his face dropped into his hands. "Right. I keep telling you, Doc, that wasn't me. It was Fletcher Carlyle."

———

Crito's writing lessons continued into the fall. The first month passed in late nights spent rewriting and rewriting and rewriting; Frye added nothing new. He learned, but slowly.

It is not merely a matter of saying things differently, Dickie. You must learn to see things differently. You must learn, first, to see deeply, and then to convey clearly. Cross-reference the images in your mind's eye. Compare men to trees, and trees to animals. Think not of the thing itself but the impression it gives, the metaphor.

And if the work itself was frustrating, Crito's reading list was even worse. He had Dickie Frye reading Shakespeare and Proust, expanding his vocabulary and challenging his thought processes.

Because he'd always been a reader, Frye thought in the beginning that with the right kind of training it just might be possible for a redneck like himself to become a reasonably competent wordsmith, but it was more of a challenge than he expected. Crito blasted him daily, in words as hard as cannonballs, over fine points of writing and esoteric aspects of construction that Frye never knew existed.

These are only fundamentals, Dickie. You have a very, very long way to go.

In the beginning his meager progress fanned the embers of a long-dormant dream into a white-hot lure of tantalizing possibility, and Dickie Frye, wanting to be someone, *anyone*, other than who he was, took the bait. It became a mission. An obsession. He began spending every spare minute reading and writing.

Frye kept his word and told no one more than half the truth. It was all right for his small circle of friends to know he had a pet chicken in his garage as long as they didn't know the chicken was smarter than all of them put together, but it was not easy maintaining a half-truth. To protect the lie, Frye began pushing people away.

The first casualty was his buddy Tiny Colquit. For the last year or so, Tiny had been in the habit of coming by once in a while, usually on Tuesday night, just to hang out, drink up Frye's beer, and tinker with the '57 Chevy. He loved that car and had private aspirations of someday owning it. Sooner or later, everything gets sold. Tiny—who was six-four and two-eighty—was a first-rate mechanic. Sometimes he'd bring his brother Dunk, who was even taller, but skinny. Dunk loved to experiment with the paint gun, though he usually made a mess of it, especially when he'd been drinking.

Tiny and Dunk dropped by one night, about a week after the chicken arrived. Frye told them about the chicken in carefully measured half-truths. He said he was driving home from work and saw the chicken fall from the back of a truck, which was true, but then he told them he'd picked it up and brought it home because it was hurt and he felt sorry for it. His mother had kept chickens, which they already knew, so he said he'd made the bird a kind of pet because it reminded him of his mother. The truth would not do. After a reasonable amount of harassment over Frye's pet chicken—*"Crito? What kind of froufrou name is that? You ain't turning into a twink, are you, Dickie?"*—both of them seemed to accept the idea. Tiny owned a few laying hens himself, but he would never have let them in the house. Crito, for his part, stayed out of sight most of the evening, and eventually retired to his engine hoist.

Frye's friends made him nervous; he'd rather have been working on his manuscript, and the hazing he took over the chicken didn't sit well. After a few beers Dunk was in a mood to paint, so Frye found some interior frames and other parts that wouldn't show when the car was finished, hung them up on wires right next to the engine hoist where Crito was sleeping, and turned Dunk loose to paint them. Dunk was sporting a carefree golden buzz, so it was pretty much inevitable that sooner or later his overspray would hit the chicken and wake him up. Crito let out a squawk of bitter complaint.

Dunk apparently thought it was funny because he turned the gun full on the chicken and gave him a short burst. Crito flapped and cackled and hit the floor in a wobbly lope, looking for a place to hide. Dunk, cackling now himself, lit out after him with the paint gun. The chicken was quick, but Dunk managed to paint his backside black before he could escape under the toilet stall door, past the reach of the hose.

Frye blindsided the idiot, knocked him up against the wall and snatched the paint gun away from him, then threw the Colquit brothers out of his garage and told them not to come back. Ever.

Afraid to put turpentine on Crito's backside, he just let the paint wear off. In a week it was all gone except for one feather that remained black. He thought at first it was just stubborn paint, but after another week passed he noticed there were three or four black tail feathers. Very odd, for a White Leghorn.

Chapter 10

> The forging of a proper blade requires a thousand bits of hard-won knowledge, none of which is worth a whit if one cannot read the coals.
> —*The Forge*, Fletcher Carlyle

The preacher from his mama's church came by one evening, wanting to know how Frye was getting along since his mama "you know...went to be with the Lord," and why Dickie hadn't been to church lately. Brother Emmet was wearing his usual short-sleeved white shirt with a necktie that didn't make it past his ample belly. He took a slow stroll around the inside of the garage and stopped in front of Frye's desk, arms crossed on top of his stubby tie. At first he just stood there with a slightly quizzical look in his eye, staring at the chicken perched on Frye's engine hoist, but after a minute his gaze dropped down to the desk and landed on a half bottle of Chivas Regal, a not quite empty shot glass, and a lit cigarette in an ashtray brimming with butts. The whole place stank of cigarettes.

"I never seen you smoke before," Brother Emmet said, his tone thick with disapproval.

Frye picked up the Virginia Slim and took a drag before he stubbed it out. "Yeah, I picked up some bad habits lately," he croaked, fighting a powerful urge to cough. "Things have been kinda tough."

Brother Emmet peered at him over the top of his black-rimmed glasses. "I know you been going through some mighty hard times lately, son—after what happened to your mother and all. But the devil's a deceiver, and you've chose a perilous road. Liquor and tobacco will only make your troubles worse. It's faith that makes us whole."

According to Uncle Early, the preacher was not above taking a nip of home brew himself on occasion, but it was not Frye's place to bring it up.

"Yes, sir," he said, with just the right note of downcast penitence. "I aim to do better."

He walked the preacher out to his car and stayed there for a long time, leaning back against the warm metal, arms folded, giving Brother Emmet his full attention, but in the end he realized things had changed. His comfortable little small-town world had crumbled like day-old corn bread when Crito showed up, and since then he'd had to rethink everything he ever thought he knew. The universe was broader and deeper and more complex than he *or* Brother Emmet ever imagined.

———

Crito was pecking at the keyboard when Frye came back in. He didn't even look up. Frye's manuscript was on the screen, so he stood behind the chicken with his hands in his pockets and followed the commentary. Something was different. Normally, Crito dropped his nasty notations right in the middle of sentences, bluntly highlighting point of view errors and flowery prose, but now he was indulging himself with a lengthy diatribe in the white space at the bottom of the manuscript. The whole thing was even more snide than usual, but the last paragraph was a slap upside the head.

It is time you took your writing beyond the third grade, Dickie. By now my average protégé would be well into the development of a style, and far more consistent with authorial voice. While your writing has improved somewhat, this particular story lacks scale and scope. Your MC marches in and out of scenes spouting wooden, predictable dialogue with the grace of a mannequin. Scrap it and begin anew.

Frye took a big deep breath, and something in him cracked.

Maybe it was because he was a little embarrassed by the sudden intrusion of the preacher, or maybe it was just the long-term stress of having to lie to everybody. His friends were gone, and it was a hard fact that the only person he ever actually talked to anymore was a chicken. Maybe he really was crazy.

Whatever the cause, he couldn't take it anymore. He'd spend a week going through the manuscript fixing things, and then Crito would crack on him for something else. It never got easier. After climbing a tall hill, he would reach the crest only to find a taller hill in front of him. No matter how hard he worked or how much he learned, things only got deeper and more complicated. He would *never* be able to live up to Crito's literary standards because they kept changing; the blasted chicken kept raising the bar. Dickie Frye was through. He'd had enough. In the end it was the merest puff of wind—the crack about the mannequin—that pushed him over the brink.

He went off like a hand grenade.

"Listen, pal, who are *you* to say what's good and what's not? Anyway, how do I know you ain't making it up as you go along? You sit here all day smoking cigarettes, nibbling on mangoes, and dreaming up ways to drive me nuts! What gives you the right?"

It has been said that knowledge is power. It is not so. Power lies in the judicious *use* of knowledge. I have freely offered you the fruits of my experience, but if you are unwilling to assimilate it, perhaps you are better suited for the delivering of mail.

"It ain't that I don't want to, Crito. You just expect too much. There's no way I can do what you want. It ain't happening. I'm *never* gonna get it. Every time I get up you knock me back down. I can't do it! *I'm not you!*"

Nor have I asked you to be. The focus of my effort has ever been to discover and enhance your own voice.

"You're not listening. *What you're asking is way too big for me!* I CAN'T DO THIS!"

The chicken cocked his head. One black eye studied Frye, hard, for several agonizing seconds, a frightening appraisal. Slowly, deliberately, Crito turned back to the keyboard and typed his answer.

It is not a matter of doing, but of becoming. For any man, becoming who he was meant to be is an odyssey fraught with trial and sacrifice, utterly impossible until he learns to deny himself, to jettison the weight of all the petty baggage he believes defines him. Most lack the courage, and settle for lives of quiet desperation. Perhaps I have misjudged your resolve. I had hoped to spare you a time in the desert, but in the end a man must choose his own way.

Frye's eyes narrowed, wary. "What in the Sam Hill are you talking about?"

Fearing we might come to this place, I have prepared a contingency plan, an alternate route to your destiny, though far more circuitous.

Behold.

Crito moved the mouse—at which point Frye noticed his right claw had turned completely black—and a document spread itself across the screen. This was something new, something Frye had never seen before. Crito stepped aside, pecked a cigarette out of his pack, lit it, and sank down on the end of the desk, waiting.

Fletcher Carlyle's head draped over the back of the chair, his eyes fixed on the ceiling. He didn't say anything for a few minutes.

Kohl waited patiently, but Carlyle didn't move. After a while the doctor said, "He wanted you to read something? Something you didn't write?"

"Yeah." Carlyle's head came up and a thin smile crept into his eyes. "And it was *huge*. Out of habit, the first thing I did was look at the word count—over a hundred thousand. I scrolled down through it, reading a line or two here and there, and Doc, it was *incredible*. Absolutely brilliant. Sharp and confident, never a wasted word. When I got to the end of the manuscript I saw it wasn't finished; it just left off in the middle of a sentence."

"And you believe the chicken wrote this himself?"

"Yeah, while I was at work. I guess he was pecking at the keyboard all day long and then hiding it before I got home. I didn't have a clue."

"How did you feel about it?"

His eyes drifted as he remembered. "Truth is, it 'bout killed me. All the hours I put in, all the nights I wasted trying to learn the basics, and all of a sudden I'm looking at pure genius, this thing of beauty staring back at me from my old man's greasy computer screen like a diamond in a dog's ass. It just proved what I already knew—I was *never* gonna be able to do that."

Carlyle's emotions were real, his passion convincing. There were moments when Kohl almost wished he could believe in this crazy story, but the real world was frightening enough. For the sake of his own sanity, Anton Kohl simply couldn't afford to admit the possibility of possessed chickens, of transient souls.

"I want you to think very hard, Mr. Carlyle. There must have been something familiar in it, something you recognized."

"No."

"Nothing in it struck you as, perhaps, something you had thought about before but never quite put into words? Maybe a familiar phrase?"

Carlyle shook his head firmly. "Nothing. I skimmed through it for an hour, reading bits and pieces. Doc, this was miles beyond anything I could've done—or anybody else, for that matter. I never seen anything like it, and at the time I didn't recognize a word of it. But *you* would. There wasn't a title yet, just 'Chapter One' at the top of the first page, and then the words, 'Truth, like light, may be bent to any purpose, even to chase the shadows from the road to oblivion. But know this: every injustice, in its time—'"

"'—will come home,'" Dr. Kohl said, finishing the quote. "The opening lines of *Atlantis Requiem*."

"Yeah. The now-famous last words of Adrian Ott, right before they put the hood over his head."

Kohl caught himself clicking his pen, stopped, laid it down.

"You're saying the chicken wrote *Atlantis Requiem*?"

A grim nod. "I was there, Doc. I'm just telling you what I saw."

Kohl removed his glasses and rubbed his face with both hands. Then he froze for a second, pulling his hands away and blinking at Carlyle.

"The others too? *Daughters of the Nephilim*? *Of an Angry God*?"

"Yep. All of 'em."

Chapter 11

> Let a man live long enough and he may retrace his steps to find a truth he once held tightly, abandoned somewhere in the labyrinth of adolescence: We are all as little children.
> —*Of an Angry God*, Fletcher Carlyle

The day of Carlyle's "field trip" came a little over a week later. It turned out to be a fine, crisp, clear morning, warm enough for the author to wear only a gray Weatherhaven-issue cardigan over his institutional whites, yet cool enough to be invigorating. A perfect spring day. Dr. Kohl had asked him for his sizes and offered to order clothes for him so he wouldn't have to go out in public wearing his whites. Then, when he discovered their sizes were the same, he even offered to loan his patient some of his own clothes from home. But Carlyle refused.

He looked the doctor up and down with a critical eye. "No thanks. That whole professor look…I don't think so. Seriously, Doc, I'd kind of like to pick out my own stuff, okay? You don't know how long it's been. This is important to me."

Kohl smiled. "All right then, we'll do that."

Though such an excursion could have been handled by the staff, Kohl cleared his calendar for the day so he could do it himself. It was a bit of a risk for Kohl, taking Carlyle out in public, especially in his own car, unescorted, but it was a calculated risk. The author had been at Weatherhaven for nearly a month and, apart from his first few days at the institution, had shown no signs of rage. Despite his unshakable delusions about the chicken, Carlyle had made steady progress toward being a fully functioning, rational human being.

Personable, in fact. Toma and several of the other attendants had gone out of their way to tell Kohl they actually liked the man, a relatively rare phenomenon among the fallen stars whose bruised egos routinely lashed Weatherhaven like winter storms. Carlyle was courteous and appreciative to the cleaning lady, complimentary to the chef, and he seemed to have made a lifelong friend of Manolo, the old Cuban groundskeeper who was always out clipping and weeding and fertilizing and planting somewhere on the grounds when the author went out for his morning walk. In the beginning, Carlyle would just stop and sit cross-legged on the grass, hanging out with the gardener for an hour or so, telling old jokes and prodding Manolo to talk about what it was like growing up in Cuba. After the first couple of weeks he started pitching in, over the old man's objections, and working right alongside him to help with the clipping and weeding and fertilizing and planting.

"It's good therapy," he said to Manolo. And it was.

"Meester Frye, he iss a goo' man," Manolo told Kohl one afternoon. With deep sincerity lining his leathered face, he wagged a finger and added, "No loco."

Carlyle was in good spirits when they pulled up to the ferry landing.

"Been looking forward to getting out and seeing this island for the first time," he said.

Kohl knew from experience that the presence of a passenger helped to quell his anxiety, and he tried to keep up the small talk even as his legs began to buzz.

"In all the time you lived in New York, you've never been out east?"

"Nah. I been all over the country on tour, but never out to the Hamptons. I reckon it's common knowledge that for the last two years I didn't even leave the apartment. Feels good to get out." His head turned constantly as he drank in the sights.

Slowly, deliberately, Kohl eased his car forward onto the ferry. When the flagman patted his hood, he put on the emergency brake and killed the engine. He could feel his heart pounding as he waited for the ferry to pull away from the landing.

Carlyle peered ahead, across the stretch of open water toward North Haven. "Is this the only way off Shelter Island?"

"Yes, I'm afraid so," Kohl said, relieved that his voice didn't crack. His mouth was very dry. Twice he put his hand down beside him, out of habit reaching for the button to recline the seat, but he managed to stop himself. When the ferry's engine rumbled and they left the dock, his knuckles went white on the steering wheel. He forced himself to relax his grip a little when he realized Carlyle was watching him, but there was nothing he could do about the thin beading of sweat on his bald head.

"You ride the ferry every day?"

"Twice a day." Kohl tried hard not to sound nervous, but this time his voice did crack, just a little.

"You look pale. Are you all right?"

Kohl had been fixated on the back of the car in front of him. He turned now to face Carlyle, forcing a smile, feigning a lightness he did not feel.

"I'm fine. The ferry always makes me a little nervous, that's all. But let's talk about you. You were telling me about the chicken writing *Atlantis Requiem*."

Carlyle chuckled. "Little tough to swallow, I expect. I told you from the git-go you'd never believe me."

"So, did you continue with your *own* writing after that?" The question sounded innocent enough, but Kohl had a hunch this was the critical juncture in Carlyle's dissociative disorder.

Peering at the low profile of Gardiners Island off in the distance, Carlyle didn't respond right away. Dark memory moved across his face like a cloud shadow, and he didn't make eye contact when he finally answered.

"Nah, not really. I made a pass at it once in a while, but…no, not really."

There was something he wasn't saying.

"Was Crito still helping you with it?"

"No, but a few weeks before Christmas he wrapped up *his* book. I remember the first time I saw the title *Atlantis Requiem*. I read it straight through when he was done with it. A masterpiece—I knew it even then. But I still didn't know what he had in mind to do with it, so I asked him.

"He said he had a proposition for me. I guess in my gut I knew what was coming—sort of. I mean, not even a chicken would go to the trouble to write a thing like *Requiem* without wanting to publish it, and I knew Crito couldn't get her done by hisself. I don't care how smart he is, there's limits to what a chicken can do. Turned out he wasn't nearly as limited as I thought, but you still can't put a chicken's face on a book jacket. He needed a human to play the author."

Fascinating. The bigger picture was beginning to emerge. "And you agreed to this?"

"Not at first. I mean, who's gonna believe Dickie Frye wrote *Atlantis Requiem*? Turns out he didn't want me to be Dickie Frye, he wanted me to be somebody else. To hear him tell it, if I stuck with him he'd have me farting through silk. He said I would 'walk in starlight and dine with kings,' but first I needed to go through some changes, that I had to 'cultivate the appearance and manner of a man worthy of this work.'"

The droning of the diesel engine dropped an octave, and the ferry pitched forward slightly. A minute later it was tied to the eastern dock, and Kohl cranked the Volvo, relieved to be crawling back onto dry ground at North Haven. He took a deep breath and tried to put the terror behind him. It definitely helped, having a patient along. Carlyle's presence was a much-needed distraction and, if he was honest about it, something of an inspiration. The man was as excited as a child by the prospect of a simple day out, a joy that Kohl found refreshing.

"The thing is," Carlyle said as the car bumped down the ramp and onto the pavement, "why me? That's what eats at me, even now. *Requiem* is a masterpiece. Why me? When I asked him, all he said was, 'Why *not* you?' He told me to think of him as my genie. You know, rub the bottle and he'd grant my wishes. Or, he said, I could think of him as my teacher, but at the end of the day they were different sides of the same coin. Little twerp was impossible to understand sometimes."

They were driving down a narrow road between the tall hedgerows of North Haven. Hedges slid past for half a minute before Carlyle added pensively, "He told me the only other option was that I could stay Dickie Frye and forget the whole thing, that he'd wipe the hard drive and check out. Now *that* I couldn't believe, to think that anybody would just delete *Atlantis Requiem* without a second thought. I told him it'd be a shame and a disgrace, but he pointed out that time itself wasn't the same for him, that a few months' work in amongst a thousand lifetimes was nothing. I reckon that was true enough, from his point of view."

They swung left at the roundabout and took Ferry Road across the arched concrete bridge that emptied out into the heart of Sag Harbor. The Yacht Club and Long Wharf already boasted a sizable flotilla of sailboats and cruisers, a promising sign so early in the season. Quaint, old-fashioned storefronts lined the raised sidewalks—boutiques, a bike shop, a bookstore, souvenir shops, places to buy art or jewelry or pottery—all of them carefully maintaining the weathered, nautical look of the old whaling port. Many of them were closed this time of year, especially on a weekday morning, but there were signs of life. Shopkeepers here and there were already loading in their spring wares, sweeping out winter's cobwebs and bracing themselves for the coming tourist season. Up at the far end of the street, away from the water and traffic, sat a bright yellow, ornately carved Victorian house with a mansard roof. A small, tasteful sign swung from wrought-iron hooks in the front yard.

PORTSIDE GENTLEMEN'S APPAREL
ESTABLISHED 1912

Kohl pulled into a parking spot in front of the place and both of them got out, but Carlyle stopped and laid an elbow on the roof, his face screwed into a frown. He dug a finger in an ear and said, "Uh, Doc, this ain't exactly what I had in mind."

Kohl stared at him over the roof of the car. "Oh, but they're very good. I'm sure they'll be able to—"

"Sorry, but I'm just not into gentlemen's *apparel*," Carlyle said, lacing the last two words with a trace of sarcasm. "I already told you that. I don't want to be hardheaded or anything, but I believe I'd a whole lot rather just go to a store."

"Well, Portside *is* a store—"

"No, I mean like a superstore." Carlyle's fingers drummed on the roof of the car. "You know, a place where a guy can pick out a pair of Wranglers and a T-shirt, some tennis shoes. Off the rack. *That* kind of store."

"I see," Kohl said. His forearm, resting atop the door, was starting to tingle. He knew what was coming. In a minute his arms would begin to burn and itch, like sunburn. He could literally hear the rush of blood, the pounding of his heart. It didn't make sense, even now, but he knew from experience that he could rationalize all he wanted at this point and it would make no difference. The adrenaline was already flowing, flight reflexes already firing. He ducked into the car, fastened his seat belt, gripped the wheel, and took a deep breath.

Carlyle got in beside him, closed his door.

"Doc? Are you okay?"

Kohl nodded, exhaled through pursed lips. "Just give me a minute."

Carlyle waited, watching intently. Kohl didn't dare make eye contact; it would have only made matters worse. After a few minutes he rested his forehead against the cool leather at the top of the steering wheel. He took several long, slow breaths, strictly controlled, and his heart rate began to slow.

"All right," he finally said, without raising his head. "There's a place like that in Riverhead. We can go there. I can do this, I know I can. It's an hour's drive from here, but we have all day. It's okay."

It was not okay, but he would not say that to a patient. The words he spoke had to fight their way out through a gauntlet of images in his head, pictures of wrecks and storms, of getting lost, getting mugged. Fear, fire, foe, flood. So far from shelter, without a plan, anything could happen.

He threw back his head, took a deep breath, and forced a weak smile.

"It's okay. I'm all right now. I'll be fine." One more deep breath. "Let's go to Riverhead."

Anton Kohl had mapped out the entire day. He'd thought it all through, down to the minutest details about how long they would spend at the clothiers, where he would park, what walking route he would take to give Fletcher Carlyle a proper tour of Sag Harbor without actually going too near the water, precisely where they would eat lunch, how long it would take, what he would order, how much to tip the waiter, and precisely how long it would take them to drive down to Southampton Hospital afterward with plenty of time to spare, in case of traffic. Scrapping his entire plan and taking off to Riverhead would try his soul, and he knew it.

But there was no point trying to explain. People who didn't live with such anxiety could never understand it, couldn't relate. He cranked the car and backed slowly out of the parking place. As he put the car in drive and began to pull forward, he glanced at Carlyle's seat belt receptacle. Empty. Neither of them said a word, but Carlyle saw the look, pulled the belt down, and snapped it into place.

Most of the time Carlyle was too busy sightseeing to notice Kohl's angst. From the glass harbor full of sailboats resting at anchor to the quaint little cottages all tidy and tight, everywhere Carlyle looked he saw a postcard. Kohl drove on resolutely, at last managing to loosen up a bit when he had driven far enough into the South Fork to hide the sea from sight.

"It's nice out here," Carlyle said. "Everything's so...*perfect*. It's beautiful."

He was right. Kohl hadn't noticed, but Sag Harbor was at its peak of color. The trees were beginning to leaf out with eye-popping new green. The forsythia was mostly finished blooming, but the tulips and columbines were in full bloom, and the azaleas were beginning to show pinks and whites in the shadow of wine-colored Japanese maples.

"Most of these places have been meticulously restored," Kohl said. "They're small because they're two hundred years old, most of them, preserved from the days when Sag Harbor was a whaling port, but they've been bought up as summer cottages, renovated to pristine condition and retrofitted with all the latest amenities. It has become a rather fashionable neighborhood."

"Yeah, it's pretty. I can see why the high rollers from New York would want to own a piece of this."

Kohl kept his eyes on the road. "An interesting observation, coming from you. You don't consider yourself among the moneyed elite of New York?"

Carlyle contemplated the question, the smile fading from his face. "That was the problem, Doc; I was never *among* anything. The people you're talking about—the ones with serious money—they got their own little world, their own rules, their own way of seeing and thinking, their own language. I can be *around* those people for a minute or two if I'm real careful, but I don't *belong* there. I don't belong anywhere."

Kohl came to the end of a block, braking to a complete stop at the corner. He looked both ways twice before pulling ahead, though it was a four-way stop and there were no other cars in sight.

"So, why don't you tell me a little more about these changes, this metamorphosis Crito wanted you to go through?"

Carlyle settled in, apparently even more comfortable riding in Kohl's car than sitting in his office, and began to talk. Anton Kohl, for his part, was glad to have the calming influence of Carlyle's voice.

Chapter 12

> War was personal in those days. The victor in single combat saw the rolling of the eyes, felt the death rattle in the tang of his blade. In those days, the man who declared the war rode at the head of the column.
>
> —*Daughters of the Nephilim*, Fletcher Carlyle

Stunned by his first reading of *Atlantis Requiem*, Dickie Frye got himself a beer and bellied up to the desk in his greasy chair.

"What kind of changes are we talking about?"

First, a name. You will need a name appropriate to the work, and then we will create a man befitting the name. You must leave your old life behind.

Frye tugged at his mustache. "You mean quit my job?" To be honest, that thought didn't particularly bother him.

All of it. Dickie Frye will cease to exist. We must leave this place.

"Oh, I don't know, man. There ain't much left here, for sure. I mean, everybody thinks I'm crazy as a bedbug, but this is home. I was born and raised here, and I can count on one hand the times I've been more'n fifty miles from this spot. Squalor's the only home I've ever known. To just up and—"

The paths diverge. Fame and fortune, or Dickie Frye. You must choose.

He got up from the chair, stretched, and walked slowly around his father's pet Chevy, running his fingers through his hair. The dust lay deep on the dull yellow paint. He stopped and drew a question mark on the hood with a fingertip, thinking. Nothing worthwhile ever came without a price, but Crito didn't know what he was asking. It was one thing to play this bizarre game in the privacy of his own ramshackle garage, but it was a whole other thing to abandon everything he'd ever known and fling himself into the wider world with nothing to cling to but the outlandish promises of an ornery, scotch-drinking, chain-smoking chicken.

"I got an errand to run," Frye said, shrugging into his coat and raising the bay door behind the Mazda. "I think better when I'm driving."

This was true, and he actually did have an errand to run. He had to deliver a tin of mice to Odd Lester the Bird Man. Root had given him the cake tin that afternoon, but the Christmas rush had him so overloaded he'd forgotten about the mice under his seat. Remembering them now, he figured it was as good an excuse as any to go for a drive and think things over.

What Dickie Frye longed for, what he yearned for as he backed out of the garage was just one redeeming memory of the place where he'd spent his entire life. *Show me one bit of good*, he thought, like God poised to strike Sodom, *and I'll stay*. All he wanted was a memory, a nostalgia, one heartwarming snapshot so achingly beautiful that he could not bear to see it shrink in his rearview mirror, nor leave the place that had granted him such a gift. He was looking for an anchor. Going down the driveway, he glanced across the bare scarred dirt where his childhood home had stood, the house gone without a trace. He drove through Squalor, past the gas station and the beauty shop, the nail and tan place, but they meant nothing to him. None of the memories those places evoked was worth keeping, especially now that his ex-wife worked at the beauty shop.

Yet he had to admit, when he was being honest with himself, that he still had fond memories of Raye Anne, who made the name Richard sound like music. He knew, too well, that it was both her greatest strength and her greatest weakness that she could make a man feel so like a man. He was in no hurry, so he drove over to Calhoun and down the dark street in front of the high school where he'd first met her, past the football field and the bleachers under which he'd stolen his first kiss. But in the end, high school had not been kind to Dickie Frye. Apart from Raye Anne there was nothing in those years that he cared to remember, and a great many things he'd rather forget.

And then he passed down a residential street decked out in the tacky splendor of the season, where every house glittered and twinkled, where the lights of Christmas poured from all the eaves and dripped from the branches of trees, where motorized reindeer grazed on front lawns while heavily laden sleighs waited, and Santas waved—all of them carved in lights. Millions of little white lights.

Raye Anne loved Christmas lights. Once or twice every December she'd get that childish look in her eye and make him drive her around half the night, gawking at the lights. The end of the evening, always, was a trip up to the ridge. There was a road along the ridgetop and a logging trail running out between the pines to an unofficial overlook where he could pull his car right out to the edge. From there they could see every Christmas light in the valley. On a clear night the view was spectacular.

The first time Raye Anne made love to him was in his car up at the overlook a few days before Christmas. He definitely saw lights that night. They both remembered the occasion with such fondness that they reenacted it frequently, even after they were married. They'd be in a crowd someplace at Christmastime when Raye Anne would put her lips close to his ear and whisper warmly, "Let's go look at the lights, Babycakes." He always knew what she had in mind, even before he saw the gleam in her eye. It was a special event, a ritual they reserved only for each other, once a year, at Christmas. Even now, after everything that had happened between them, the memory of it washed over him in a great warm wave.

He had to go up the ridge road anyway because Odd Lester the Bird Man lived there, but once he was on the ridge he decided on a whim to drive out to the overlook. It would be a little strange, going there alone, but the lights of the valley would still be there, and somehow he suspected it might be the very sight his soul needed in that moment.

Out of old habit he turned off his headlights when he swung onto the logging road. Headlights on top of the ridge were just as visible from below as the Christmas lights were from above, and Charley Eberlein—Squalor's one policeman—kept an eye out for them. Frye should have known better. It shouldn't have been such a shock to him when he came out of the trees into the bright moonlight at the overlook and almost ran into the back end of Talbot Bonniface's red Cadillac.

But it did surprise him, so much so that he suddenly flipped his lights on—his brights, like a prison tower spotlighting the back of that red Cadillac.

And then Raye Anne's face popped up from the back seat, staring wide-eyed into his headlights. Her hair was all wild and in her face, her lipstick smeared. She grabbed a handful of platinum and pulled it aside, trying to squint past the lights, but after a few seconds she gave it up; her head submerged and there were flashes of white as she tried to scramble into her clothes.

For a few brief seconds Frye seriously considered flooring it and ramming them over the edge of the cliff, but outrage melted quickly into a puddle of tired regret, and he put the Mazda in reverse. He never even got out of his car, and he was certain that Raye Anne didn't know whose lights had blinded her.

When he got back out to the ridge road, Frye noted that he hadn't seen any headlights in his rearview mirror. Apparently, Raye Anne and Bonniface had seen his taillights through the trees and decided he was not Charley Eberlein after all; they could get back to work.

But now that he'd had time to think about it, the second wave of anger hit much harder than the first. He stopped, cut his lights off again, then turned his car around and crept back toward the overlook.

This time he stopped well short of the Cadillac, back in the dark shadows at the edge of the pines, and kept his lights off. He stepped out of his car quietly and pulled the tin box from under his seat, smiling in the moonlight. There was nothing in the world more horrifying to Raye Anne than a mouse.

Bonniface's head popped up and he barked in alarm when the door opened, but Frye was too quick. He flicked his wrist and a dozen startled, disoriented mice sailed into the back seat, tiny frightened claws skittering and scrambling for cover. Running as fast as he could in the dark, from behind him he heard Raye Anne cut loose with an end-of-the-world wail. He stopped and turned around for a few seconds to watch.

She flung herself out of the car in naked panic, then bounced to her feet and ran screaming, dancing and slapping at mice that had long since abandoned ship.

But she ran straight toward the cliff.

Talbot Bonniface, ever the athlete, piled out after her, chased her down, and tackled her before she could kill her fool self. Frye cranked up and spun the Mazda around, but not before Bonniface got a good look at him. He was herding Raye Anne back to the car when Frye's headlights swept across him. There was murder in his eyes. Talbot the football hero was not accustomed to being humiliated.

Frye was almost home when headlights appeared in his rearview mirror and swelled rapidly, closing the gap way too quickly. A half-mile short of his driveway the red Cadillac blew by him and cut him off, forcing him off the road. For a fleeting second he thought about ramming the car, but for all his faults Dickie Frye appreciated a fine car. It was, after all, a brand-new Cadillac, and the car hadn't done anything to him. He skidded to a stop on the side of the road.

Bonniface, wearing only a pair of boxers and a T-shirt, dragged Frye out of his Mazda and proceeded to beat him unmercifully, cussing and kicking and spitting the name Dickie with every other blow. He did an admirable job. Bonniface had a little gut on him these days, but he could still throw a punch. He might very well have killed Dickie Frye if Raye Anne hadn't pulled him off, but then, before she got in the car, Raye Anne herself came back and kicked him one good time in the ribs. The last thing Frye saw from his final resting place in the ditch was that lighted rectangle sporting the letters QB-7, and then he got hit in the face by a shower of gravel slung by the Cadillac's tires as Buttface screeched away with his ex-wife.

―――――

Crito was sitting on the corner of the desk when the Mazda pulled back into the garage. Frye closed the bay door, flung his coat on the fender of the Chevy, staggered over to the desk chair and collapsed into it. His left eye was swelling shut. Pressing a palm against it, he became painfully aware that the biggest decision of his life was about to turn on anger, jealousy, and despair.

"I want to bury him," he rasped, licking blood from a split lip. "I want to shake the dust of this place off my feet and go make a fortune. Get me out of here, Crito. I don't care what it takes, I want you to make me bigger than Elvis and richer than God, and after that I want to come back here and kick some ass. I want to run Buttface out of business and wreck his life. I want to do a Monte Cristo on that ignorant son of a bitch. I want to stomp him into the ground and leave him bleeding in the ditch like he done me—him and Raye Anne and Hitler and all the other no-good sons of bitches in this hick town. Tell me straight—can you do that?"

Crito nodded sharply, no hesitation.

"All right, then. I'm yours," he croaked, and found that one of his good teeth was loose. "You just tell me what to do."

Oblivious to Frye's distress, Crito clicked a couple of times, opened a document on the screen and printed it out. It was a mock-up for a query letter, a pitch to an as-yet unnamed agent, for *Atlantis Requiem*. The closing said *Yours*, and well below that, leaving space for a signature, he had typed a name.

First, learn to sign this name with a flourish.

"*Fletcher Carlyle*. What kind of name is that?"

A big name, larger than life, perfect for what we are about to do. A literary name that will one day be a household word. I have already made certain arrangements. A birth certificate will arrive in the mail next week, the foundation of your new identity.

Frye's right eyebrow peaked and his mouth skewed a little bit sideways.

"Pretty sure of yourself, weren't you? And anyway, how'd you manage to get a birth certificate for a name you just made up?" He felt a serious twinge in his side when he talked, possibly a cracked rib.

I did not make it up. A Fletcher Carlyle did live, once. I had only to take advantage of a befuddled bureaucracy.

"But how?" Frye was holding his ribs, staring at the phone on the desk when it hit him. "Email. You've been *busy*, haven't you?"

The Internet is a beautiful thing. One of my more useful creations.

"Right. I guess you put the idea in Al Gore's head."

Crito ignored this last, typing more instructions.

I will arrange for an apartment in New York, and transportation. We leave in two weeks. Tell no one.

"Two weeks?" Frye waved the letter at him. "You ain't even going to hear back from that agent in two weeks, let alone find a publisher."

The query letter will not go out until both the manuscript and Fletcher Carlyle are ready. In the meantime we have much to do.

Crito proceeded to spell out exactly what he had in mind—the whole beautiful, grand, audacious plan. If they could pull it off, Dickie Frye's wildest dreams were about to be dwarfed by Fletcher Carlyle's reality. And since success depended largely upon Crito's writing, it was never really in doubt.

Chapter 13

> "Stand down, Mr. Ott. I am master of this ship, and I alone decide her course."
> "Aye, sir. And do you command the wind and sea as well?"
> — *Atlantis Requiem*, Fletcher Carlyle

Kohl listened as best he could, but he was divided, planning his route to Riverhead on the fly, feverishly following his mind's eye down the road past the Shinnecock reservation, through a narrow neck of land between two great bodies of water, and into the town of Hampton Bays, where he would pick up the highway that ran northwest into Riverhead. He'd been there before. It usually didn't take more than an hour, even in traffic, but the path was perilous. He did not drive it every day as he did Ferry Road, and he wasn't sure he remembered all the hazards. Completely apart from the threat of oncoming vehicles, any one of which might swerve and slam into him at any moment, there was water everywhere—saltwater bays, freshwater ponds, bridges over brackish inlets and creeks, the inner reaches of cattail swamps. He drove well under the speed limit, his eyes flitting back and forth, both hands gripping the wheel.

Halfway to Riverhead a motorcyclist got impatient with Kohl, found an opening and ripped past him, engine screaming. Swerving away from the racket, Kohl dropped two tires off the shoulder.

Carlyle could take it no longer. "Look, Doc, uh, I don't want to offend you or anything, but would you like me to drive?"

He'd obviously been paying attention, not that Kohl's anxiety was hard to spot. He flinched at every passing car, held his breath when he crossed a bridge, and winced at his rearview mirror every time he came to a red light for fear the car behind him wouldn't stop.

"You can't drive. You have no license."

A shrug. "Not *with* me, but—"

"You don't understand. If I let you drive, then I have to worry about police. It would only make matters worse."

It was about then that the tire began to waffle, apparently punctured when they ran off the road. Kohl pulled into the parking lot of a furniture store, breathing deeply, methodically, fighting off full-blown panic as he shut down the car and turned on the emergency flashers. His hand shook as he pulled out his cell phone.

"What are you doing?"

"Calling Triple A."

Carlyle laid a calming hand on his shoulder. "Easy, Doc. You just need to chill for a minute. Put away the phone and pop the trunk. I'll take care of the tire."

Kohl blinked. "You can change a tire?"

"I'd hate to think I couldn't."

Kohl's voice came out a little high and frantic. "But it's quite possible both of the right-side tires are damaged, and I only have one spare. What will we do if the other one—"

"We'll burn that bridge when we come to it. Look, there's no way I'm gonna sit here and watch somebody else change a flat. For an old redneck, it's a point of honor. Anyway, I'm dressed for it." He said this while pinching the front of his Weatherhaven shirt out from his chest. "Relax, Doc."

Kohl put his phone away and popped the trunk. He had to admit it was a comfort having a mechanic around in an emergency, but while the Nobel laureate changed his tire, Kohl stood by the car envisioning the jack collapsing, then visualizing the remainder of his route into Riverhead and trying to plan precisely what he would do once he got there. It was hopeless. There were too many variables.

They did manage eventually to find the superstore without any new disasters. Carlyle stretched and yawned ostentatiously as he strolled through the doors and grabbed a cart. "Now *this* is what I'm talking about."

The cavernous store spread out before them in all directions with no apparent boundaries. Kohl followed meekly to the men's department, rubbing palms against the tingling in his arms. Carlyle went straight to a vast wall of denim and started thumbing through a stack of carpenter jeans. When he found his size he tossed three pairs into the cart—*without even trying them on*. He bought a half-dozen T-shirts, some boxers and socks, two hooded sweatshirts, a brown canvas coat, a pair of cheap sunglasses, and a Yankees baseball cap that he immediately snugged on his head, tag and all, with a satisfied grin.

"Crito hated the Yankees," he said, admiring himself in the mirror next to the rack of hats. "He said only Philistines rooted for Goliath."

Next, he tried on a pair of athletic shoes and some hiking boots—both of which ended up in the cart. In less than thirty minutes they were in line at the checkout counter. Kohl hadn't said three words the whole time. While they were waiting, he looked at his watch repeatedly.

"You know, we might still be able to make our reservation at Chez Rubin."

Carlyle glanced at him, a little too sideways. "I ain't eating there."

"At Rubin's? Why not? It's a small, out-of-the-way place—excellent menu, but the lunch crowd is very casual. Really, it's one of the finer restaurants in Sag Harbor."

"Yeah, *that's* why. Is there a McDonald's around here?"

Kohl tried to hide a pained expression. "Yes, I, uh…I believe I saw one just up— are you *serious*?"

"Yep. I want me a couple double cheeseburgers off the dollar menu, with a little paper envelope of fries and one of them cardboard apple pies." His hand drifted out unconsciously as he spoke, and a faint light came into his eyes as if he were seeing a pleasant afterlife. "I want to tap my own Coke."

As soon as they checked out, Carlyle went into the bathroom to change clothes. Kohl stood outside the door, squirming. Fear, fire, foe, flood.

Carlyle came out of the bathroom wearing the whole package—hiking boots, carpenter jeans, T-shirt, hoodie, sunglasses, and Yankees cap. He'd funneled his hair through the back of the cap.

"So how do I look?"

"Well, I have to admit you look comfortable, as if you belong to those clothes, and under the circumstances it's probably good that you don't bear much resemblance to Fletcher Carlyle."

"That suits me just fine. Oh, and now that you mention it, why don't we ditch that name."

"Which?"

"Carlyle. Fletcher Carlyle's dead, Doc. I ain't him, and I don't want to be, okay?"

Kohl nodded. "All right, then. Shall I call you Mr. Frye?"

"Call me Richard."

———

Kohl's anxiety ramped up near the red zone the whole time they were in the superstore, settled back down a bit when he reached the relative safety of his car, and then spiked again when Frye insisted they park the car and actually go *into* McDonald's.

While they were waiting in line Kohl studied the menu, rehearsing what he would say. When it came his turn to order he said clearly, "I'll have a Number One combo, Diet Coke." Distinct, unambiguous, well thought out. It would generate no confusion or delay. His credit card was already in his palm.

Then Frye changed his mind. He stood there hugging himself and gazing up at the menu board for nearly a minute.

Kohl's arms tingled. His stomach knotted. People were waiting in line behind them, staring.

"I tell you what, I think I'll have the Double Quarter Pounder with cheese combo," Frye mused.

The pimply kid in the paper hat started to ring it up, but Frye wasn't finished.

"Uh, could you hold the onions? Them little diced onions are bitter. Easy on the ketchup, and extra pickles, please."

Bees crawled under the skin of Kohl's legs, buzzing. He began to sway and twist like a child in need of a bathroom.

The paper hat nodded, the kid punched a couple of keys, and Frye said, "Could I get a vanilla shake in place of the Coke?"

Unfazed, the paper hat nodded again and more buttons got punched. Kohl couldn't take any more. He shoved the credit card in the kid's face—just reached right over the top of the register and shoved it at him. Kohl's mouth was open, his breathing sharp and shallow.

"You all right, Doc?"

His cheek started twitching, which didn't help matters. "I'll be okay. But would you mind terribly if we just get our food and eat in the car?"

"Yeah, sure. Whatever, man."

Picking at his lunch in the quiet of the car, sequestered in the McDonalds parking lot, Kohl's anxiety abated—somewhat. Frye took a mammoth bite of his Quarter Pounder and sighed with pleasure. "You wouldn't believe how long it's been. So talk to me, Doc. Seriously, what's going on with you?"

There were boundaries. Rules. A counselor was not allowed to discuss his own issues with a patient, but Frye had seen too much. If he didn't give the man some kind of answer, he would supply his own. Kohl set his Diet Coke in the cup holder on the console.

"I just...I get a little nervous sometimes, that's all. It's nothing, really." Kohl took a dainty bite of his burger and tried to act normal, but he didn't feel the part. He was, in fact, a long way from normal, but the truth would not do.

Frye watched him closely, amplifying his anxiety.

"Doc, what I saw at that clothes place in Sag Harbor this morning, and what I saw just now—I ain't seen a face like that since Raye Anne found a possum under the couch, and all you were doing was ordering a burger. I thought you were fixing to have a panic attack."

Frye just wouldn't let it rest, but Kohl couldn't tell him anything, and in the end the ethical dilemma only fueled his angst. Everything fueled his angst. He found it increasingly hard to resist telling Frye about himself, if only to break the cycle and relieve the stress. But maybe there was a middle ground. Frye was the one who had brought up panic.

"Have you ever had a panic attack?" Kohl managed to ask this almost calmly.

Frye shoved three fries in his mouth, thinking, and then talked while he chewed. "Maybe, I'm not sure. I used to have this tricked-out Mustang—that thing was cranking close to six hundred horses. Took it drag racing one Saturday night down in the bottom, where we had a quarter-mile marked off in a straight stretch of Benton Church Road. Up against Tommy Varnum's Camaro, I forgot I had a load of wheels in the trunk. When I hit third gear, the front end come up and she floated like a playing card. Cartwheeled. Strewed pieces of that car over a hundred yards, and I ended up trapped in the wreck, upside down in the creek, gas pouring everywhere. Didn't know if I was gonna burn to death or drown. I got a little panicky *that* night. When that thing was airborne I think I might've even grayed out for a second, I'm not sure."

The mere thought of being trapped in a car upside down in a creek made sweat pop on Kohl's forehead, and his voice shook a little.

"Yes, that would be panic. Now, let's assume we're talking about a person with anxiety issues—not me, but a hypothetical person."

"Right. Hypothetical."

"A person with anxiety issues would have to deal with panic constantly. I suppose you could turn down the intensity a bit from your insane car-wreck scenario, but the physiological panic process and its effects—the rapid heart rate, increased respiration, cold sweat—those are all things a person with an anxiety disorder may encounter a dozen times a day for any number of reasons, all triggered by insignificant things that a properly functioning nervous system should be able to handle easily."

"You're kidding. Why can't you…why couldn't *he* just, like, snap out of it?"

"It's not that simple. It has to do with the production and release of certain chemicals in the body—valves and switches. You can't just rationalize it away. Some aspects of anxiety are manageable with training—neural synapses can be retrained to a degree, and certain drugs can be helpful—but over time the patterns become part of the actual physiology of the brain."

Frye's brow furrowed in concern. "But, Doc, I know for a fact a guy can unlearn fear. You gotta face it—'Stare it down,' my daddy used to say. You didn't get no sympathy from him. My old man would've told you to wear kerosene socks."

"Kerosene *socks*? Is that supposed to help for anxiety?"

"No, but it'll keep the ants from crawling up your legs and eating your candy ass." Frye laughed out loud at his own joke, and it did ease the tension a bit. "My old man never got tired of that line. He was the kind that believed in teaching a kid to swim by throwing him off the dock. When I was little I was scared of the dark, so he left me alone in a deer stand in the middle of the woods at four in the morning. It worked. I unlearned my fear of the dark. You just gotta face it."

"It would be nice if it were that simple, Richard, but it's not. Environment plays a role, of course, but at least part of the disorder is hardwired, hereditary."

Frye shook his head. "Really? Walking around scared all the time? Looking for trouble around every corner? How can a guy live like that?"

"Well, routine is helpful. A person with generalized anxiety disorder would want to stick to a routine and avoid variables. He would tend to stay in safe, predictable surroundings—his workplace, his home. With proper medication he could function out in the world, but only with varying degrees of difficulty. It would help immensely if he could plan every step. He wouldn't like surprises."

"Like an unscheduled side trip to Riverhead," Frye said, thinking out loud while he peeled back the paper for another bite.

"Hypothetically, yes."

"And people are born with this? They put up with it all their lives?"

"Yes and no," Kohl said. "Onset varies with the individual. An anxiety disorder doesn't necessarily have to be caused by anything in particular, but there are cases in which, after an uneventful childhood, a traumatic event in early adolescence triggers it."

Frye's head tilted and he frowned. "Like what?"

Kohl wrapped the remains of his burger in napkins, laid it aside, and draped his wrists over the steering wheel. Right or wrong, talking to Frye had helped. Catharsis was good, but it was against the rules. What Frye was asking went far beyond the hypothetical, and Kohl could not make himself go there now, at least not while he was so far from home.

"I can't go into that. I'm sorry, I just can't."

It wasn't that he didn't want to. In fact, there was nothing he wanted more at the moment, but there were boundaries. He had already stepped too far across the line.

"I'm sorry, Doc. I didn't mean to pry." The sympathy in his voice was real.

Kohl couldn't even look at him. He leaned his forehead against the wheel and spoke in a whisper.

"How do you do it, Richard? Where do you find the courage?"

Chapter 14

> The secret of the legendary Damascus steel, the finest blade steel ever forged, is lost to us today because we do not know what was in it. Its strength was in its impurities.
> —*The Forge*, Fletcher Carlyle

Southampton Hospital lay near the south shore, a half-hour's drive from Riverhead. Kohl avoided the expressway and stuck to the blue highways despite an endless string of red lights. Once near the hospital, his nerves calmed considerably. He'd been to Southampton Hospital dozens of times during his tenure at Weatherhaven, so he knew the ropes—the personnel, the procedures, the probable wait times, and the best waiting rooms. He even knew which magazines he could expect to find.

After they checked in and filled out the paperwork, Kohl grabbed the corner seat, situating himself between Frye and a lamp table strewn with magazines. There was only one other person in the waiting room, a hollow-cheeked, deathly pale woman sitting directly across the room with a colorful scarf tied around her head and huge sunglasses covering half her face—probably here for radiation treatment. Fortunately she kept to herself, quietly flipping through a travel magazine.

Richard Frye wanted to know why he was having an MRI, so while they waited Kohl explained his theory about the possibility, however remote, of a brain lesion that would enhance linguistic capabilities.

Frye snorted with laughter.

"You're chasing rabbits again. I ain't crazy, Doc, and I don't have a brain tumor. But it's *your* time we're wasting, and apart from being in a hospital I'm having a ball." Then the smile faded and he looked Kohl in the eye. "Mark it down, Doc—there's a day coming when you're going to figure out that you owe me an apology."

"Mr. Frye?" A woman in scrubs stood in the open door with a clipboard. When Frye got up out of his chair, she glanced at Kohl, checked her clipboard, and said, "Are you Dr. Kohl?"

He nodded tentatively.

"You're welcome to come back with him if you like."

Half-lit rooms marinated in gamma rays, radiation ricocheting from walls and ceilings, heavy machines clicking and whirring, technicians hiding behind lead barriers.

"No, thank you," he said, crossing his legs and picking up a magazine for emphasis. "You go ahead. I'll wait here."

Despite his familiarity with the hospital and the nearly empty waiting room, Anton Kohl couldn't make himself comfortable. Anything could happen in a waiting room—strange people might want to talk, an unruly child could spill grape soda on his suit, the sprinklers could go off, there could be a fire, a power outage, a vengeful ex-employee with an assault rifle...*anything* could happen.

A Boston Pops medley of Beatles tunes drizzled from the ceiling, and Anton Kohl sifted through the magazines on the corner table beside his chair. He needed something to keep himself occupied so he wouldn't think about the gaunt, sickly woman across the room. Her Aztec print skirt broke sharply over skeletal legs.

She laid aside her magazine and began to stare. He refused to look at her, but he could tell she was staring at him, just sitting there with her hands resting on the arms of her chair and those unblinking sunglasses locked onto him like a radar dish. He began to feel the tingling in his legs. He turned a page in *Auto Trend*, lowering his head just a touch so that he couldn't see her, even peripherally, and pretended to concentrate on the article wrapped around the metallic blue Mini Cooper.

She must have moved quietly because he never heard her get out of her seat. That long Aztec skirt just appeared in front of him, two feet away, swaying gently, sandals and bright red toenails peeking from underneath.

He looked up. Her pale, blue-veined hands gripped the points of a knit shawl hanging from narrow shoulders.

Fighting the urge to scratch at his arms and legs, Kohl heard himself croak, "Yes? May I help you?"

She smiled sadly, and said nothing. Moving like smoke, like empty clothes twisting on a clothesline, she lowered herself into the chair beside him. He looked away to return his magazine to the table, and when he turned back around she was leaning on the arm of his chair, still smiling that sick smile and violating his space in a most unnerving way. Up close, he now saw that she was not bald, as he had thought. A few wisps of auburn hair escaped from the edges of her scarf.

"Hello, Anton," she said softly, and recognition hit him like a bus. When she removed those strange sunglasses, vertigo compounded his anxiety. He began to hyperventilate. His vision narrowed to a tunnel, and the tunnel poured him out into those bottomless sea-green eyes.

He was never quite sure if he completely lost consciousness or only went right to the motley gray edge, but for a time he felt himself drowning in a dark, noisy sea. Surfacing, the first thing he heard above the roaring was a voice, whispering, close by.

"Anton."

The storm quieted, and a bit of light made it through. A geometric pattern coalesced in the center of his vision, turquoise rimmed with coral.

"Anton."

A woman's voice. Thin arms held him. Pale hands clutched his head to her breast, his round glasses askew. The geometric pattern, he now saw, was part of a skirt draped over a thin leg, inches from his face. He became aware of a pain in his side, the thinly padded arm of the chair gouging into his ribs. Slowly, he pulled himself upright.

"Are you okay?" she asked.

He nodded, straightened his glasses, and then carefully, reluctantly, looked into her eyes.

"Emma." In that moment it was all he could muster, a heroic effort. There was deep memory in those eyes, and an honesty that laid him bare.

"How've you been?" she asked, and he saw only now that there was kindness in those eyes, too. Kindness, from the one dying.

"I've been well, thank you." His usual complaints seemed paltry under the circumstances. "And you?"

Her eyes rolled a bit, the tiniest facial shrug. "I've been better, but I have also been worse. Today is today."

"Cancer?"

She chuckled. "No, Anton, cancer is boring—you should know me better than that. Shrapnel, on the other hand.... It happened two years ago, on assignment for Reuters. Ironically, it was a sliver from an *American* rocket that scrambled my insides and took out a few feet of intestine. I'm here for yet another barium party."

"I am so very sorry," he said, and meant it. He was sorry for so much more, but at the moment he could only feel; he could not think. Memories darted and swooped like barn swallows out of a boiling dark cloud of emotion, and he could not capture them.

"It's been a long, hard, lonely battle, Anton, and I'm tired. I'm so tired. I've had to stay close to the doctors for the last two years, couldn't go anywhere or do anything—too sick most of the time anyway—and it's sapped the life out of me. I don't like being an invalid. I'm still young, and there's a lot of the world I haven't seen. So what are *you* doing here?"

"A patient of mine," he explained, careful not to mention the name, even to Emma. "I brought him down for an MRI. I'm on staff at Weatherhaven, up on—"

"Shelter Island, yes, I've heard of it. I've been living at North Sea for the last five years."

He had driven through the village of North Sea often. It was on the South Fork, maybe ten miles from Weatherhaven and less than five from his house. She had been so close all this time.

"Enzo?" he asked, sensing that Enzo was missing from the equation. They could still communicate in shorthand, even after all these years.

The sad smile came back as she turned aside. "We were married for a little while, but it turned out Enzo's frequent junkets to Paris weren't all business. He was keeping house with a model named René."

"He had a girlfriend in Paris?"

"Boyfriend, actually. René was a man. Sort of."

"*Pardonnez moi.*"

"*Pas de quoi.* An inconsequential faux pas compared to the impressive constellation of blunders I've survived." And then she added, "So far."

"I'm sure you'll have ample time to make many more egregious errors," he said, but without conviction.

She saw through the platitude and shook her head. "My candle burns at both ends, it will not last the night."

"I know you better than that," he heard himself saying. "It would take more than one little rocket to do you in."

She looked at him then with the same fondness he'd known when they were young. "Dear Anton. You don't know how many times I've thought of you in the last two years. I've missed you. You were always my safe place."

He didn't know what to say. He'd wanted to be so much more than just a safe place for Emma, but in the end he had chosen to be safe himself, to avoid the risk of rejection. Even now, *especially* now, he could not say these things to her. He said nothing, and cursed his silence.

The nurse reappeared in the door with her clipboard.

"Emma Lansing?"

Her maiden name. For Emma to reclaim her maiden name in her forties was a statement. She didn't intend to change it again.

She rose, too quickly, then swayed and put a palm to her cloth-bound head. Anton leaped to his feet and grabbed her elbows, shocked at the sheer thinness of her arms.

"Are you all right?"

"Yes," she said weakly, and turned those eyes on him. "Anton…if you're not here when I come out, call me sometime, okay?"

"I will." His hands tried to follow her as she turned to go with the nurse. As soon as she left, the bees came into his legs and he sank heavily into the chair, his hands still cupped, remembering the feel of those elbows. It might have taken a guided missile to prove it, but even Emma was mortal. He saw the light going out of those sea-green eyes, pupils fixed and dilated, and wondered if he would call her. If he could find the courage.

He did not know how long he sat with his face in his hands, his glasses dangling from between his fingers, before Frye's voice intruded from above.

"Dr. Kohl, you ready to go?"

He looked up, knowing he could not entirely hide his confusion and despair.

"Yes. I suppose."

"You okay? You look a little gray around the gills."

"I'll make it. Just another of my…moments."

———

As Frye shoved open the heavy glass front door of the hospital, Kohl fumbled in his pocket for the car keys.

"Listen, Richard, I know this is highly irregular, but I wonder if you would mind driving us back to Weatherhaven? Could you do that for me?" He held out the keys.

"Sure. Be glad to." Frye took the keys almost too eagerly. The baseball cap and sunglasses made his grin look a little too cavalier, a little too Richard Petty. "What, you decided you ain't afraid of the police anymore?"

Kohl shook his head. "I'm just too tired to care."

He was, in fact, drained. In his entire life, Anton Kohl had never felt so utterly exhausted. He couldn't focus, couldn't think straight.

"You know what, let's not even go back to Weatherhaven this afternoon—I can't face that ferry two more times today. My house is on the way, and I have a spare bedroom. Let's just take the evening off and go back in the morning. I'll call the office and let them know." Again, it was highly irregular, taking a patient to his house, but this was no ordinary patient.

Still, Kohl had surprised himself. It wasn't that he'd bent the rules by checking out a patient and taking responsibility for him overnight; he had, after all, spent the day with Richard Frye out in the real world and was completely satisfied that the man was not a threat to anyone. The man was competent, and perfectly capable of taking care of himself—perhaps more capable than Kohl. What surprised Anton Kohl was his own spontaneity.

He had made a decision on the fly.

Chapter 15

> Elaborate deception is not at all uncommon in nature, but in every case it serves one of two purposes: to eat, or to avoid being eaten. Only man employs deceit in less noble pursuits.
> — *Atlantis Requiem*, Fletcher Carlyle

Over a dinner of pasta salad and baked salmon, Kohl prompted Richard for more details about the transition from Dickie Frye to Fletcher Carlyle. He told himself he was looking for the point of fracture where the alter ego was born, but beneath that he knew that most of all, he was personally in awe of the kind of courage such a leap required.

"It's been bothering me, Richard. Such a complete change. How does a man walk away from everything he knows and never look back? Were you really that upset about finding your ex-wife in the back seat of another man's car?"

"Nah, not really. I mean, I didn't much like getting the crap beat out of me, but just for the record I wasn't all that bent about catching Raye Anne with another man. It ain't like it was the first time *that* ever happened, and anyway we were divorced."

His voice was light enough, but his face darkened and he broke eye contact.

"It was the Christmas lights. That was always something special, just between me and her. And she took *Buttface* up there."

This, Kohl could understand. The things that bound two people together were rarely the things one might expect.

But then Frye took a deep breath, shoved the regret behind him in that abrupt way of his, and moved on with his story.

"It was freezing cold the morning we left," he said, picking over his pasta salad, obviously not fond of it. Kohl had made a pot of tea in place of the wine he would normally have with dinner, and it appeared Richard Frye didn't care much for hot tea, either.

"I stayed up half the night making sure we didn't leave anything behind. I burned the paper copies in the wood stove, moved all the text files to a flash drive, and wiped the hard drive clean. Way before daylight I cranked the Jeep and left home with nothing but the coat on my back, a pocketful of cash, a flash drive, and a cardboard box."

"You drove your mail Jeep all the way to New York?"

"No, Crito arranged for a driver. I left the Jeep in the bus station parking lot and got in the back of a Civic with Florida tags. Crito had it all planned out, right down to the weird note I left on the seat of the Jeep. I tore a sheet from a spiral pad, and in great big shaky letters I scrawled against the grain, *Gone to the Middle East. Somebody has got to end this madness—Dickie.*

"Crito said the note would convince people I wasn't kidnapped or murdered or anything, just nuts. Anyway, the driver brought me some different clothes, and on the way to New York I shaved the mustache, cut my hair, and tossed my old clothes in a dumpster behind a convenience store in Virginia. Late the next day the driver pulled to the curb in the Lower East Side of Manhattan and let me out in front of a gray building that looked like a million other gray buildings. Before he drove off he told me to knock on the door under the stairwell and get a key from the super, which I did, and then I carried my cardboard box up four flights of stairs to my new home."

"So that was your plan from the outset? Move to New York and establish a completely new identity?"

"Crito's plan, not mine. Like I said, I ain't never traveled before. I never been that far from home in my life, but I was willing to do whatever it took to get out, to be somewhere else, to be some*body* else—anybody but Dickie Frye. Doc, surely by now you can see I couldn't've come up with something like this on my own. Not in a million years."

Within a week of arriving in Manhattan, Fletcher Carlyle had a New York driver's license and a MasterCard. Not only could he *get* absolutely anything in the city, but he could have it delivered. Clothes, food, mangoes, organically grown wheat, Dunhill cigarettes, beluga caviar, even sixteen-year-old Aberlour single-malt scotch was no problem. A phone call summoned a new computer to his doorstep, another got broadband hooked up, and Crito went to work.

The makeover was a long and complicated process as, bit by bit, over a six-month period, Dickie Frye disappeared and was replaced by Fletcher Carlyle. First, Crito lined him up with a plastic surgeon and a dentist. Within a month he had himself a beautiful full set of perfectly even, impossibly white teeth, and shortly after that they removed the bandages from a manly new chin. Crito kept him on a strict vegetarian diet and signed him up at a local gym, where he lost fifteen pounds the first month and begun firming up nicely. He didn't care much for the diet and exercise regimen, but seeing the changes Crito had already wrought, he decided to grit his new teeth and do it anyway. Having a personal trainer helped a lot. Three times a week he went to a speech therapist, who set about doggedly scraping the hillbilly off of his Southern accent.

Next, Crito found a reputable eye surgeon and made an appointment for LASIK surgery. The glasses disappeared forever. A professional stylist worked a miracle with his hair, giving him a distinctive look that exuded, in the words of the hair guru, "a relaxed and unpretentious dignity." When he reached his ideal weight Crito sent him to a tailor, who decked him out in the first of an impressive wardrobe of perfectly fitted and very distinctive English wool suits.

Clothes make the man. **This look will become your trademark.**

"Amazing." The newly created Fletcher Carlyle admired himself in the full-length mirror on the back of the bathroom door, overwhelmed by the complete transformation worked on him in a few short months. "Mind-boggling. My own mama wouldn't know me from Adam's house cat."

Mind the accent, Joe-Bob, Crito typed, and then let out a curiously loud squawk.

"Ba-GACK!"

Carlyle turned from the mirror to see what had happened. An egg sat wobbling on the edge of the desk. He picked it up, still warm, and held it up to the light. Before he thought about it, he asked a stupid question.

"Did you do this?"

Crito gave him a look, then typed.

It cannot be helped. This infernal body is, after all, a chicken.

Six months after they arrived in Manhattan, a contract came from Fletcher Carlyle's newly acquired agent, who said he would be happy—*elated* was his actual word—to represent *Atlantis Requiem*. Confident that he could place it quickly, he wrote that he wanted to meet with Mr. Carlyle in person at his earliest opportunity, and gave several phone numbers at which he could be reached. Crito spent an entire day coaching his protégé on what could and could not be said before he was finally allowed to make the call.

"*Atlantis Requiem* has the ring of destiny," the agent said, and he managed to say it with enough hubris to be utterly convincing. "We are going places, Mr. Carlyle. You and I will storm the literary bastions of New York and shake them to their core, I guarantee it."

Crito listened in on the conversation, typing out Carlyle's answers in real time.

"I would be delighted to meet with you," the fledgling voice of Fletcher Carlyle answered, in an accent that, while still Southern, was now more Shelby Foote than Gomer Pyle, "but I'm afraid it will be at least a week. Prior commitments, you understand."

The young agent agreed. Fletcher Carlyle's first public appearance, his first real test, would be at a trendy little restaurant just off Fifth Avenue.

The agent's name was Micah Erlanger. Slightly plump, red-faced and cherubic, Micah perched at the edge of his seat, leaned over the table, and gestured constantly with his hands as he raved about the book. Four years out of college with a master's in English lit, Micah had paid his dues in minor positions with two major publishing houses in New York, and then, with the frighteningly unbridled enthusiasm of the uninitiated, launched his own literary agency. *Atlantis Requiem*, he said, was his first great discovery.

Fletcher Carlyle, for his part, exuded a confidence and poise commensurate with his talent.

Confidence is key, Crito had said. **Above all, meet success as an equal, like an old and trusted friend.**

Dickie Frye sat watching from the sidelines, from the back of his own mind, thunderstruck by what he saw happening. He liked it. He liked it a lot. In his life as Dickie Frye, he had seldom been granted even ordinary respect; adulation and awe were completely foreign to him. He had to constantly remind his rebuilt face not to reflect the childlike wonder he felt inside. There would be no fist pumping, no dancing on the table. Fletcher Carlyle was charming and elegant, a man who knew his wines, knew how to order in the finer restaurants. He was a man in full control of himself, able to bear life's vicissitudes with dignity and grace.

When the lunch with Micah Erlanger was over a yellow cab dropped Fletcher Carlyle off in front of his apartment building, but it was Dickie Frye who bounded up the steps two at a time, whooping.

———

While Richard Frye sat at Kohl's kitchen table talking, Kohl took the dishes to the sink, washed them, dried them, and put them away. He never used the dishwasher because he usually ate alone and didn't mess up enough dishes to bother with it. Besides, he didn't trust the machine to clean his dishes thoroughly. The house cooled as darkness fell and a fresh wind washed over the South Fork. Despite numerous renovations and a central heating system, Kohl's house was still old and drafty. Frye insisted on building a fire.

Kohl sat facing the fire in his wing chair, a cup of tea on his lap, once again so caught up in Carlyle's story that he had forgotten himself. Questions dipped and dodged through his mind, but they were not the questions of a psychologist.

"He actually laid eggs?"

"Yep. One a day, just about every day after that." Frye stood at the hearth warming his hands behind him. "Normal, for a hen. What was not normal was that, over the next few months, Crito's legs, feet, tailfeathers, and head all turned to solid black, except for that red crest. Never known a White Leghorn to do that."

"Could have been a dormant gene," Kohl said absently. "Not that unusual. So tell me about the money. Where did the money come from? I gather it wasn't yours. You said he was able to move funds about over the internet, but it had to come from someplace."

Frye shrugged. "I don't know. He never said much about it, and I didn't know enough about the computer to follow what he was doing. It just showed up in Fletcher Carlyle's account, and there was always plenty of it. He said something about offshore investments—left over from a former life, I reckon."

"From a previous incarnation, I see. Now, as I recall, you told me he'd been around for roughly five thousand years?"

"Right."

"And he'd had contact with people on numerous occasions in past lives."

"Yeah, quite a few, as a matter of fact."

"Well, Richard, playing the devil's advocate if I may, it seems to me that surely a person with his vast education and talents would have made his mark on history before now. It begs the question—why have we not heard from this Crito before?"

Frye took a seat in the other wing chair, an odd smile on his face. He leaned toward the doctor and spoke quietly, as if he were sharing a secret.

"What makes you think we haven't? How do you know there ain't a *dozen* Fletcher Carlyles in the history books? A *hundred*."

Dr. Kohl took a sip of tea. "You're suggesting he might have been behind other historical figures? People whose names I might recognize?"

Frye scanned the rows of classics on Kohl's shelves. He stood up, plucked a leather-bound volume from the shelf, and showed it to Kohl.

"Poe. They told you in school that Poe wrote 'The Raven.' Wrong. It was the raven who wrote Poe. And that's just one drop in a real big bucket."

"There are others?"

Poe went back on the shelf—in the wrong place, Kohl noted—and after a quick scan of the rest of the books, Frye sat himself cross-legged on the floor in front of the bottom cabinet and pulled the doors open. Kohl squirmed in his seat as Frye examined the private cache, leaning close to read the spines of the books in the dark lower cabinet, his hands propped on the corners of the open doors, talking absently as he browsed.

"Think about it, Doc. How many giants in history went from rags to riches overnight for no apparent reason? Or the other way around. Did you know Alexander the Great carried a guinea hen with him on his campaigns? Napoleon kept a caged finch in his field tent—he said it was for depression. Van Gogh had a pet owl. Dylan Thomas sometimes walked around with a crow on his shoulder. Howard Hughes had a cockatoo, until he wrung her neck. The man went hermit for the same reason I did."

"But those men were not all writers. Are you saying this Crito is trained in other disciplines?"

"Look, man, five thousand years is enough time to master a *lot* of disciplines." Frye pulled a thick book from the cabinet, an exhaustive history of submarine technology and warfare, and thumbed through it as he spoke. "Aren't you a little suspicious of da Vinci? You ever wonder how one man could be that good at so many different things? Renaissance man, my ass. The Mona Lisa was painted by a stork—it ain't no wonder she couldn't keep a straight face. Ever ask yourself how Beethoven wrote the Ninth when he was stone deaf? I'm willing to bet you never heard about the trunk full of stuff some GI found in an attic at the end of World War II. There was a piece of sheet music in there with the original score of the Ninth, except it looked like Braille—all these neat little holes punched in the paper in place of notes."

"You're telling me Beethoven's Ninth was composed by—"

"Woodpecker." Frye tossed this off casually while flipping through the pages of another book he'd pulled from the bottom cabinet, this one a comprehensive guide to scuba diving.

"Surely not."

"Yep. And what about Robert Stroud?"

Kohl shook his head. "Who?"

"Birdman of Alcatraz."

"Ah. Yes, of course."

"According to Crito, they actually met in Leavenworth. Seriously now, what are the chances a guy like that—a semiliterate drug addict, meaner'n a pit bull—could make himself into a world-renowned ornithologist? How does a ignorant con with a history of violence get to be a big-time bird doctor?"

"I'm guessing…with help from a bird?"

"From a sparrow, actually, who got his attention by scratching the word 'water' in a grimy sink."

Frye pulled out another book, a pictorial of marine life in the flats between the tides. "Speaking of water," he said, "every book in this bottom cabinet is about water, one way or another. Oceans, rivers, lakes, diving, submarines, marine life, Cousteau and sons—here's one on free-diving competitions where these lunatics hold their breath for like eight minutes and go down hundreds of feet in the ocean. There's even a book about noodling."

Kohl chuckled. "Yes, where *other* lunatics poke their arms into holes and crevices in muddy river bottoms hoping to get bitten by a forty-pound catfish."

"Collecting these books seems like a strange hobby for you, Doc. From the way you acted on the ferry I figured you were *scared* of water."

The man did pay attention.

"Terrified," Kohl said, nodding toward his secret cabinet. "That's why I bought the books. I know the life story of every American submarine ever commissioned, their victories and tragedies, mysterious disappearances and narrow escapes. I can tell you the depth of the water where the *Wahoo* was lost in La Perouse Strait. I know how many men escaped from the *Tang*, and why the others didn't make it. I know why the *Squalus* sank, how many men were rescued from it, and the technique used for the rescue. Over the years I've armed myself with every piece of information I could find, and still I shudder at the mere sight of dark water."

Frye looked up at him then, and his gaze pierced Anton Kohl's shell. "Why?"

Kohl couldn't answer. He even caught himself putting a hand over his mouth.

"It's about what happened when you were a kid, ain't it?"

The doctor nodded thinly, the hand still clamped over his mouth.

"So tell me about it."

For whatever reason, he wanted very much to talk, to tell Frye what happened. He'd come to like this man, perhaps even admire him, considering all he'd been through and how well he seemed to be adjusting. Richard Frye possessed a brave and resilient spirit, but sharing his own dark secrets with a patient was strictly against the rules. Anton Kohl firmly believed in rules, and the story that prompted Frye's probing questions went straight to the heart of that same issue—the question of whether or not the universe punished those who ignored the rules. It was an ethical dilemma, and Kohl suddenly realized he was leaning toward breaking the rules. He wanted more than anything to share his secret, this once, with a man who knew no such fear.

"It's all right, Doc." Frye made a point of looking elsewhere and speaking softly. "We got nothing but time. I'm a good listener, and I promise whatever you say won't leave this room. Tit for tat, you know?"

The doctor smiled, acutely aware of the role reversal. And then he decided, with what passed for spontaneity in Anton Kohl's mind, to put his reservations aside and tell Richard Frye exactly what happened in the summer of his twelfth year.

Chapter 16

> In every age of man, every culture, every continent, the toll for new territory is the blood of pioneers.
> —*Of an Angry God*, Fletcher Carlyle

It happened the summer his mother nearly died, after relatively minor surgery. They never told Anton what the surgery was for, only that it was "female trouble"; in those days they didn't burden children with specifics. But something went wrong, and wrong again, and before they knew it her condition turned grave. There were certain words Anton remembered from that time that explained much now, though he had not understood them then. Words like *septicemia*. All he knew at the time was that his mother was very sick. His father, a kind and thoughtful man, soft of hand and voice, began to spend all his time at the hospital, and because he felt he had overtaxed the goodwill of his neighbors and friends in constantly asking them to attend to his twelve-year-old son, he made the decision to ship Anton off to Aunt Lyda's home in South Carolina. The boy would live there for nine weeks, most of which was spent in the company of his cousin Derek.

Derek, in Aunt Lyda's words, was a pistol. Anton, even then, was a reticent, bookish boy, born to parents who had married late and treated their only child like an adult almost from birth. Derek was his polar opposite, even physically. While Anton's hair was dark and his skin very white, long days roaming about in the South Carolina sun had left Derek's hair white-blond and his skin bronzed. Anton was thin and small, and though they were the same age, Derek was three inches taller, square-shouldered and athletic, full of a confidence born of discovering the world on his own. Aunt Lyda was always busy with housework and two younger daughters, and her neglect meant freedom for Derek whenever he was not in school. His world was wide and full of wonders, and he feared nothing.

He was good with his hands, too. With a little help from his father he had built a small, ungainly, rectangular rowboat from scraps of lumber and plywood, caulked the seams, and coated it with red marine paint that he found in the garage. Using paddles of oak slats torn from a pallet, he and Anton took the boat out on the pond behind the house anytime they wanted, unsupervised, for they were both good swimmers. It leaked a little, but not more than they could bail with a coffee can. Slowly, Anton became a pirate, second in command to his swashbuckling cousin. Before dark every evening, Derek and Anton would pull the boat from the pond and drag it up to the house, standing it always in the same place against the wall—directly under Derek's second-floor bedroom window.

Late at night Derek and Anton would slip out the window. Using the boat and its seats like a ladder, they would escape into the night to see what mischief they could find. They found plenty. Staying to the shadows and dodging headlights, they prowled the neighborhood, spying on Tony Brock as he made out with his girlfriend in the back of his dad's Impala at the dark end of the lane behind the pond, stealing watermelons from Mr. Canterbury's garden, and once even peeping at Melissa Purcell when she was getting ready for bed. Anton had become a spy.

But their best and biggest adventures were of a pyrotechnical nature. Anton, who read a lot and remembered most of it, mentioned casually to Derek one afternoon that he knew the formula for making black powder from common household ingredients. Derek, characteristically, set about gathering the ingredients, along with a makeshift mortar and pestle that consisted of a thick ceramic bowl and the head from a broken ball-peen hammer. Anton took a hacksaw and cut a short length of copper pipe, beat one end flat with a hammer, drilled a hole for the fuse, then created a fuse by rolling damp yarn in black powder. Once he had filled the pipe with homemade gunpowder, he beat the other end flat to make a cheap but effective pipe bomb. Anton had become a weapons expert, and when the Melnicks' mailbox—handcrafted and painted to look like a Swiss chalet—disappeared in a great cannon blast of flame and smoke, he became a terrorist.

His conscience bothered him a little, but not that much. Derek, proudly unrepentant, said maybe now Mrs. Melnick would learn not to be so quick to scream at the neighborhood kids when they cut across her precious zoysia lawn.

One of the things Derek and Anton loved to do on a hot summer afternoon was ride bikes into the pond. There was a high bank on the side near lovers' lane, with a hill leading straight down to it so that a boy on a bike could get a good flying start. Derek built an inclined ramp out of scrap lumber right at the edge of the bank for added lift. It took Anton the better part of an afternoon and a litany of colorful dares from Derek to get up the nerve to try it. Time after time he watched while Derek flashed down the hill, leaning over his handlebars, furiously pumping the pedals, and sailed, screaming, up and out over the brown water, kicking the bike away in midair and plummeting twenty feet into the pond. He was Derek the Reckless, Derek the Indestructible, Derek the Beautiful. He would pop to the surface waving a fist and shouting in triumph, then promptly dive down into the murky depths to retrieve his bike for another go-round.

Anton would never admit it in front of his hero, but the flying and plummeting didn't bother him nearly so much as the murky depths. The runoff from new construction in the neighborhood in recent months had contributed tons of silt to the pond, turning it brown and impenetrable. Underwater, Anton couldn't see his hand in front of his face. The thought of swimming down into the cold darkness and groping blindly in the silt for his lost bike terrified him. He had always feared dark water. There was evil waiting down there in the cold darkness. Waiting for a chance.

But Derek's taunting eventually proved greater than Anton's fear, and he flew. On his first attempt he flew even higher and farther than Derek, perhaps because he was lighter, but also perhaps because he was driven to prove himself. If he was going to die, so be it, but he would die spectacularly. It took four tries before he could force himself all the way down to the bottom to retrieve his bike, but eventually he swallowed that fear, too.

And then Anton's mother made what the doctors called a miraculous recovery. He heard the news from a jubilant Aunt Lyda as soon as she got off the phone. In a week, he would be going home.

It was a typical July afternoon in South Carolina, heavy heat without a breath of wind, the kind of day when a boy could only be happy wet. Feeling a sudden urgent need to make the most of the remaining days, Derek and Anton spent the afternoon flying their bikes into the pond. By then Anton's sunburn had peeled away and left him as brown as Derek, and while he had not yet acquired his cousin's physique, he had obtained a bit of the swagger. The pointless screams he launched at the sky as he kicked away from his bike high above the pond were those of pure youthful abandon.

Late in the afternoon, filled with a good kind of fatigue, Anton sat hugging his knees on the bank while Derek took one last flight. Aunt Lyda had already stepped out on the back porch a few minutes earlier and shouted for them to come to supper.

"One last time," Derek said. He made a point of saying it, so it didn't surprise Anton when he plunged into the pond and didn't come up. It was a favorite trick of Derek's, and he had pulled it on Lyda so many times that she was fed up with it. He would flail at the water and pretend to be in trouble, then go under and disappear. But Derek could hold his breath for more than two minutes and had a remarkable sense of direction. He could swim halfway across the pond and come up under a shrub overhanging the bank, or under the overturned rowboat where he would watch and wait. If anyone panicked and charged into the water to save him, he'd pop out of hiding and ask what all the fuss was about.

When Derek disappeared, the rowboat was maybe forty yards away, in the direction of the house, upside down and listing to one side. Anton knew there was a pocket of air underneath it, where Derek could hide and breathe for several minutes.

After five minutes of silence Anton grew nervous, but he wouldn't let Derek get the best of him.

"Not funny!" he shouted, in the general direction of the overturned boat. Then, a minute later, "I've seen this before, Derek. Come on, let's go! Your mother *said*."

But Derek didn't appear.

After twenty minutes Anton could take it no longer. He dove in and swam out to the boat, but Derek wasn't there. By the time Anton reached the house he was breathless and sobbing.

125

Lyda wiped her hands on her apron and walked calmly down to the lake, cupped her hands around her mouth, and yelled, "You better get up here this *minute*, young man! Don't you *make* me come down there!" Then she stalked back to the house, muttering something about how tired she was of this crap.

Derek still didn't appear.

Later, after dark, even the county scuba divers with their high-powered searchlights couldn't find him.

He floated up two days later, fifty yards down the bank in the wrong direction, still holding fast to the tip of a blown-down pine. He was white and bloated, his eyes and mouth still wide with shock and surprise. They counted eight thick, brown water moccasins wrapped around his limbs and the limbs of the pine, and they were aggressive, as if the firemen were intruding. The firemen had to fight them off with the paddles before they could pull the body into their boat.

Anton's parents brought him home to Massachusetts and took him to a therapist, who helped him tremendously. Anton was, above all, a creature of reason, and with the help of the therapist he was able to reason away the guilt, or most of it. In the end it was clear that Derek's actions had led to his own demise, through no fault of Anton's. It was Derek who had ducked under and glided over to the bank to trick him. Once he had swum into the boil of snakes, no action of Anton's, hesitant or not, could have saved him.

But no words from the therapist, or anyone else, would ever shake young Anton's conviction that he had been right all along. There were demons waiting in the dark places, waiting to spring like a trap upon the proud. The heedless. The incautious.

Chapter 17

> Triumph is sometimes the death of genuine revolution. The usurper often becomes the greater despot.
> —*Daughters of the Nephilim*, Fletcher Carlyle

Neither of them spoke for a long time. Frye sat cross-legged on the floor, pretending to look at a book about an undersea habitat experiment, intentionally avoiding eye contact. He may not have understood his own need for a moment of silent distraction, but Kohl did. It was a fine point of masculine etiquette, a granting of space and respect.

"That's brutal," Frye finally said, a mere whisper. "It ain't no wonder…"

"Ah, well. I imagine losing your mother in a tornado was equally traumatic."

"Apples and oranges. Anyway, I wasn't a twelve-year-old kid at the time."

"That's true," Kohl conceded. "But years of therapeutic practice has taught me that everyone has a story. Everyone. Sooner or later every house weathers a storm." *Or a stray rocket.* "Some are just built stronger than others, that's all."

The fire was dying, the room quiet. They sat staring at the fire for a long time before Kohl suddenly realized how utterly exhausted he was. It had been a long and eventful day.

"I'm afraid I'm going to have to turn in. It's well past my bedtime."

Frye smiled. "Creature of habit."

"You have no idea."

The next morning, over a breakfast of fresh fruit and whole grain oatmeal, Frye picked up the story of Fletcher Carlyle right where he'd left off the night before. Kohl imagined it was out of kindness that Frye never mentioned Derek, or the snakes, again.

Micah Erlanger proposed Carlyle's manuscript to three publishers, and within weeks all three expressed interest.

Micah called, bubbling with good news. "I tried to tell you, Mr. Carlyle. What publishers want is a good book, and *Atlantis Requiem* is without question the best book I've ever held in my hands."

In the end, the newly formed publisher Huntsman-Wisner won the contract, not because they posted the highest bid but because Fletcher Carlyle himself insisted on it. Micah was puzzled by Carlyle's vehemence—it was as if he knew someone at Huntsman-Wisner, though he never said as much—but the agent had already learned to respect Carlyle's instincts. Huntsman-Wisner was formed by the marriage of two competing houses, which had been struggling to survive on mid-list literary offerings in a shrinking market, though the merger offered them only a temporary reprieve unless they could find the right manuscript to put themselves in the black. In *Atlantis Requiem* they saw one of those rarest of finds, a story with tremendous appeal for both the literati *and* the great unwashed. So firm was their conviction that they decided to go all in and risk everything in pursuit of it.

Huntsman-Wisner gave Carlyle a half-million-dollar advance without so much as a blink, creating enough of a splash to ensure that the trade magazines would pick up the story and give the book an incalculable boost in its infancy.

Micah believed they would have gone even higher if necessary—not that he wanted to, as there were risks on both sides—but it spoke volumes about their confidence in the manuscript. The only sticking point was the movie rights, which Micah ended up splitting with them. The publisher wouldn't say it during negotiations, but they were betting the house that *Atlantis Requiem* would head for the stratosphere.

Within a week, news of Carlyle's windfall raced through the media like a windblown prairie fire.

Over the next six months the people at Huntsman-Wisner put *Atlantis Requiem* through the wringer. A team of artists designed and refined and tweaked the cover to perfection; the marketing department put together an impressive campaign involving a twenty-city tour and a long list of radio talk show appearances; and an editor worked with Fletcher Carlyle to smooth out whatever small inconsistencies he found in the manuscript. Most of it could be handled through email, but sometimes the editor called. He was a bright young man whose insecurities emerged only when he kept bringing up his MFA from Columbia, in case anybody should forget. Hearing the reverb, he objected to being put on the speakerphone until Carlyle explained that he needed his hands free for typing corrections, his ears were too sensitive to wear a headset, and he was alone in the apartment anyway. It was a fairly small lie, and the truth would not do. The editor never mentioned the speakerphone again; it was clear that he feared bruising the ego of such a prodigy.

Even when his young editor posed challenging questions, Fletcher Carlyle was never at a loss for words. From the finer points of Victorian etiquette and social mores to ships' logs and cuirass corsets, from the proper construction of a sawpit to the medicinal use of sulfur, Carlyle carried the minutiae in his head. It was as if he had *lived* in Venice in the nineteenth century. *Atlantis Requiem* pulsed with vibrant color and surefooted detail.

The book was released to great pomp and fanfare, aided more than a little by rave reviews and a timely announcement of Paramount's purchasing of the movie rights. Within a week of its release, *Atlantis Requiem* climbed into the Top Ten at both the *New York Times* and *USA Today*.

It was crunch time for the newly constructed Fletcher Carlyle.

Showtime.

The signing tour was a month-long blur of airplanes, taxis, rental cars, hotels, bookstore events, and local radio interviews, which was probably a good thing because for the most part they were relaxed, low-level public appearances. None of the radio people had actually read his book; they got their questions straight from the press kit. It was good practice for Carlyle. All he really had to remember was to stay in character, to use his professional speaking voice, to smile and say "Thank you" with heartfelt sincerity, and to shake hands with just his fingers in order to foster the slightly foppish image suggested by his clothes.

The only difficulty was that he couldn't take Crito with him. The chicken could take care of himself alone in the apartment, though they did find it necessary to purchase an automatic chicken feeder the size of a laundry hamper and stand it in a corner of his room like a great fat mushroom. While Carlyle was out of town there would be no fresh mangoes, no caviar. Crito's daily emails to Carlyle consisted largely of complaints about having to forego his exotic diet and eat "sawdust pellets" for a month.

By the time Carlyle got home from his whirlwind tour the publicist had lined up a couple of spots on local talk shows in the city. Crito warned him constantly to stay in character, and Carlyle followed the script. The PR snowball had begun to gather momentum by then; the New York literary establishment fell over themselves claiming him as their own, and all the morning shows courted him. During his first brief spotlight on *Big Apple This Morning*, the host only asked him a few questions, all taken verbatim from the press kit supplied by Crito. Carlyle's answers had been so relentlessly polished and rehearsed that they came off as utterly spontaneous.

Cameras loved the witty, urbane Fletcher Carlyle. In three minutes on the air, he stamped onto the public consciousness an indelible image of Mark Twain reincarnated. He charmed the city. Slowly but surely, requests from the big network talk shows trickled in.

"Authors enjoy the very best kind of celebrity," Carlyle said for the cameras. "They get the best tables in restaurants but, unlike movie stars, no one interrupts their dinner for an autograph."

While Fletcher Carlyle played the celebrity, basking in the spotlight and shaking hands with limp fingers, Frye withdrew deeper into the shadows. When Carlyle spun out droll answers to prepared questions and bowed his head demurely to the surprised laughter of those who knew no better, Frye found himself mildly disgusted. While Carlyle jetted from coast to coast playing the *bon vivant*, while

Crito ate chicken feed and pecked away at his next novel, Richard Frye atrophied.

Huntsman-Wisner's gamble paid off. Over the first six months their PR blitz and Carlyle's magnetism sold more books than their back-room prognosticators had projected even in their best-case scenario. As Crito had foretold, Fletcher Carlyle became a household name.

When Crito said it was time, Carlyle ditched his dingy, cramped flat and moved into a spectacular two-bedroom suite at the Dakota, the prestigious address on Central Park West where John and Yoko once lived, and whose entrance on West 72nd Street became famous when John died there.

It is an important address, Crito typed. **A statement. It says you have arrived, and you are here to stay.**

The suite at the Dakota was spacious, and positively regal in its appointments. High ceilings, polished hardwood floors, a grand fireplace, and old-world attention to detail all lived up to the reputation of the Dakota. When Carlyle made the leap from the Lower East Side to Central Park West, he brought everything he owned in one yellow cab: a couple of Vuitton garment bags, one large suitcase, a trunk containing all the computer stuff, and a battered cardboard box that he kept under his arm the whole time. The chicken had to remain out of sight; while pets were allowed, management at the Dakota would have frowned on the keeping of livestock.

As soon as they were alone Carlyle locked the door and let Crito out of his box. The chicken shook himself to air out his feathers, then waddled through every room, cocking his head and inspecting the new digs. After they'd both explored the place, Carlyle cranked up the laptop and sat Crito next to it on the black quartz countertop in the kitchen.

"So, what do you think? Nice place, but for the price I'da thought we owned the whole building." The apartment had cost millions—to a country boy an obscene, staggering sum.

It will suffice. The address alone is worth the price.

"What are we gonna do about furniture?"

The decorator will arrive at three, bedroom and dining pieces shortly thereafter.

"Man, I don't know nothing about this stuff. What am I supposed to say to him?"

I have outlined Fletcher Carlyle's rather sophisticated tastes in an extensive email to Mr. Delacroix. I suggest you read the email in case of emergency, but avoid answering questions altogether. Tell him you cannot decide and have him leave the swatches. Feign laryngitis if necessary. Swoon, if necessary, but do not be drawn into a discussion with this man.

"All right, I can manage that, but where are you gonna be?" This was starting to get complicated.

You will lock me in my room before he arrives. I informed him that the front bedroom is off-limits. He will not attempt to look in there.

"What makes you so sure? He sounded kinda, you know...*fussy* on the phone, the sort who'd want to see every last nook and cranny."

In Mr. Delacroix's world, everyone has at least one dark secret. I told him the front bedroom is where I keep my NASCAR memorabilia. He was suitably appalled.

The flamboyant Jules Delacroix and his white-gloved minions terrorized the new apartment for the better part of a month. Whenever they invaded, Carlyle was careful to lock Crito away and make himself scarce. They decorated the place in Nouveau Something-or-Other, all black and white with discreet splashes of brilliant red in the artwork. In front of a sleek white couch in the living room lay a solid black oval rug. This was anchored by a rectangular table of striped Marmara marble topped by a shiny, smooth, three-foot-high glob of onyx sculpture, like something out of a lava lamp, with a wide dribble of vivid red inlaid down one side of it. Carlyle thought the statue looked like a starving cormorant stabbed through the neck, but he never said so to Jules Delacroix; the man was too high-strung. A nine-foot ebony Bösendorfer piano ate a big chunk of the massive forty-nine-foot living room—Delacroix called it "the parlor"—though Carlyle couldn't play a note. On top of the piano sat a cylindrical glass vase as wide as a stovepipe, half full of black and white river rocks, with a spray of stark black twigs exploding out of it and one red silk bloom trumpeting from a lone black stalk, apparently a Nouveau Something-or-Other impression of a lily. The black-and-white chandelier hanging above the granite dining room table cost twelve thousand to create, and another two to install. When they were done there were rumors of a feature in *Architectural Digest,* but nothing ever came of it. Carlyle figured that during the month Delacroix and his white-gloved minions were raping his home and plundering his bank account, black-and-white Nouveau Something-or-Other probably went out of style.

The apartment overlooked Central Park. From the living room windows Carlyle could look down across the broad avenue of Central Park West, through the oak trees lining the street, past the sidewalk and the low stone wall, and down into the green depths of the park itself. Paved pathways lit by antique streetlamps curved gracefully under damp stone arches tinged with moss and age, between gently sloping greens and protruding rock formations. Joggers and dog walkers coursed along the lanes in a sporadic parade, held to the paths by low wire fences put there to preserve the grass and keep people from hurting themselves climbing the rocks.

Crito's bedroom—the one to which Mr. Delacroix had been denied access—faced out over the park as well. There was a tiny balcony outside his window, designed to hold three little evergreen shrubs, and when the weather was fine Crito insisted on having the window open so he could nestle between the shrubs and enjoy the view of the park. The little balcony became his sanctuary, a private place where he would go when he needed to be alone to think, and to breathe the outside air. The room became Fletcher Carlyle's office, designed by and for a chicken, and finished entirely by his pet human. The first thing Crito ordered was a thin sheet of dense neoprene that arrived on a roll, like carpet. For his feet, he said; the mahogany and cherry floors were too slick, and his claws tended to cling and stick in even the shortest of carpets. Neoprene was perfect. Carlyle rolled it out and trimmed the edges himself with a straightedge and a box cutter.

Next, he ordered a T-shaped perch made for a parrot, tall enough to put the chicken up near eye level, and then glued neoprene to a board to make a ramp up to the crossbar. Near the door hung a flat-panel sixty-inch monitor, so Crito could watch the news. The remote rested in a little raised mount fastened to one end of the perch, but he rarely touched it; the TV stayed on day and night, always tuned to CNN. Once in a while Crito would watch an old Marx Brothers movie, but only because he remembered S. J. Perelman with some fondness. To the left sat the desk, the top of which, along with the ramp leading up to it, was neatly trimmed in the same thin neoprene. Apart from a wide-screen monitor, wireless mouse, keyboard, and speakerphone, there was a heavy crystal ashtray and a bottle of scotch. It would be Carlyle's job to fill a fresh shot glass every evening.

Carlyle stood back and took it all in—the black neoprene office.

"Looks like the Batcave," he said. "Or Tim Burton's office. On the other hand, I reckon we both ought to feel at home in a rubber room."

It will do, Crito typed, then hopped down and loped across the black rubber floor into his own private bathroom where, per his instructions, even the toilet seat had been covered in neoprene.

Chapter 18

> A frost hard as an anvil lay across the battlefront, silvered under a full moon. On the other side of the valley enemy campfires burned low.
> "I wonder what they're thinking," the colonel mused.
> "Tha's no secret," the sergeant answered. "They'll be thinkin' of home."
>
> —*Daughters of the Nephilim*, Fletcher Carlyle

A scant eighteen months after the debut of the novel, Paramount rolled out the movie adaptation of *Atlantis Requiem*. A massive PR campaign put teasers and trailers everywhere in the public eye for two months before the release—*Coming Soon* spots on theater screens and DVDs, television ads, Internet trailers, even billboards in key cities. A team of techies kept Carlyle's name bubbling on Facebook and Twitter. On the night of the premiere, Fletcher Carlyle himself flew out to Hollywood to share the red carpet with an all-star cast.

Huntsman-Wisner hitched a ride on the publicity train by debuting Carlyle's second book the week after the movie premiered, and launching an ad campaign of their own. *Atlantis Requiem*, the movie, broke records in its first week, and so did *Daughters of the Nephilim*, the novel.

Fletcher Carlyle had become a star. Critics scrambled to find new adjectives to sing the praises of *Daughters of the Nephilim*, and they had to keep reminding themselves that it was fiction. The reviewer for the *Times* began the coronation with these words:

> *Daughters of the Nephilim* is a work of undiluted genius. Carlyle's thematic view of history and profoundly innovative approach to international diplomacy lend an astonishing geopolitical scope to his work, while an uncanny grasp of human nature imbues his priests and kings with heartbreaking humanity. Through Carlyle's singular alchemy, strikingly dissonant elements merge effortlessly into a soaring fable whose equal we have not seen in American literature in decades....

Meanwhile, the man-on-the-street interviews all spoke plainly of a completely engaging tale.

"A page-turner."

"Kept me up all night."

"Couldn't put it down."

"Flowed like water."

"What a ride!"

The Tonight Show wanted him. Fletcher Carlyle's face was all over the tabloids, and *Entertainment Tonight* couldn't get enough of him. The paparazzi stalked him. Strangers were suddenly interested in his love life.

It was only when they were pulling into his parking place at Weatherhaven that Anton Kohl realized he'd been so engrossed in Frye's tale that he'd made it through the ferry ride without even thinking about it.

"My first appointment is at nine," he said, getting out of the car. "Why don't you join me in my office and we can continue our conversation until then. I think I can skip the administrative business this once." He really wanted to hear more.

"Suits me. I got nowhere else to be." The jeans and T-shirt suited Frye as well. He seemed completely relaxed for the first time since he'd been there.

"Your nine o'clock canceled," Marlene said as they marched through the outer office. She winced when she said it, knowing how her boss felt about last-minute changes.

"Great!" Kohl chirped, clapping a hand on Frye's back as he ushered him into the office. "Hold my calls, and reschedule the ten o'clock with Dr. Friedrich. Tell him I'm busy."

Kohl settled into his chair, and Frye told him about the women. Nubile, young, beautiful women, fashion models and aspiring actresses, women who would never have granted Richard Frye a second glance threw themselves fawning and giggling like schoolgirls at Fletcher Carlyle.

It is essential to be seen with them, Crito said. **A different one every night, if possible. Fletcher Carlyle must become every woman's dream, every man's hero.**

"How did you handle all of that?" Kohl asked. "Your new celebrity and…popularity."

Frye grinned sheepishly. "About like you'd expect, at first. I went hog-wild. I wore women like cuff links. I bought a Maserati and dated a different girl every night, just like Crito said. Well, not *every* night. Maybe two or three times a week, but still. I'm here to tell you, I never even dreamed of a life like that. I was in heaven, for a while."

"For a while. Something changed?"

"Yeah, and I reckon it was me." There was a note of regret in his voice. "I don't know, maybe a man can get used to anything, but that's not really what I mean either. It just always seemed like there was a downside to Crito's heaven. Don't get me wrong—for a guy that grew up ugly and poor, having women hanging all over me was great, but it sure wasn't Dickie Frye they wanted. It wasn't even Carlyle, really. There was always a pitch. They wanted a career boost, every one of them—a contact, a movie deal, a little high publicity—always something. They were just networking."

"But surely, at least occasionally, you must have met someone you admired, someone with whom you might have had a genuine relationship."

Frye thought about it for a second. "Yeah, there was one. Do you remember Erin O'Rourke? She was famous for fifteen minutes a few years ago after she landed a role in a Bond flick. Tall Irish girl with red hair."

"Sorry, I'm not much on Bond films. You knew this girl?"

"Briefly. I met her in Letterman's green room. She was nervous about going on, so she talked ninety miles an hour to anybody that would listen. Kept squeezing my arm, and it made my heart thump, every time. After the taping she asked me if I wanted to go out to eat, so I took her to a nice little Italian restaurant in Brooklyn. Away from the lights she was different, kinda quiet and shy at first. Then she started talking about how hard it was, keeping up appearances in a world where everybody was crazy and nobody ever told the truth. Seems she was almost as lost as I was. In the candlelight there was something magic about that copper hair, those hazel eyes, that Irish lilt. I just sat there staring at her like a lovesick teenager. Looking into her eyes was like falling down a well. You can't imagine."

Kohl didn't answer, but he could, in fact, imagine.

"When we got done eating we decided to go to Stage 5, the new 'in' place on Broadway. There was a crowd outside, people lined up around the block trying to get in. We were both in the news right then, so when we got out of the car there were all these cameras flashing and stuff. The crowd parted and a couple muscle-bound guys ushered us past the velvet rope into this booming cavern of a place, full of thunder and lightning and people, like a storm at sea. Now I ain't never been a dancer, Doc—I hate it—but I danced half the night with Erin and loved every minute of it. I wish I could've got to know her a lot better."

"Why didn't you?"

A sad shrug. "I made the mistake of taking her back to my place. I hardly ever did that because of Crito, but that night at the club Erin kept handing me drinks—some kind of colorful thing in a skinny little glass. Never did find out what it was, but it must've had a kick to it because we ended up taking a cab home. When I woke up the next morning she was screaming her head off—standing next to the bed in one of my silk dress shirts, sleeves hanging off her arms and flapping up and down. Crito was perched up on the footboard, all reared up, wings spread, chest puffed out. Soon as she caught her breath Erin pointed at him and hollered, 'IT PECKED MA FESS! Tha' rooster o' yours was settin' on ma pillow—*rate there*—and it PECKED MA FESS!'

"I sat up too quick and the sunlight ricocheted around the inside of my skull like a .22 bullet. I told her it wasn't no rooster, it was a hen, and then I tried to apologize. I fed her a half-baked lie about how the chicken was research for my next novel. Pretty lame, but the truth wouldn't do and I wasn't in no shape to make up a proper lie. The last thing she ever said to me was, 'Your chicken stinks of cigarettes and scotch! And I thought *actors* were daft!' After she stormed out I went straight to Crito's office and asked him why he done that to her.

He said, **Do not get drunk in public, and do not bring your concubines here. There is more at stake than you know.**"

"You never saw her again after that?"

"No. I tried, but she wouldn't return my calls. She was *special*, Doc. I just had a feeling about her, and when Crito messed it up I couldn't take it anymore. I pretty much went celibate from then on."

"Really?"

"Oh, I'd still take a starlet to dinner now and then, grin for the paparazzi, but after Erin I always told them the truth—that it was just for show—and then I'd take them home and leave them at the doorstep. I reckon it finally hit me that I just didn't like Fletcher Carlyle. The whole thing was so...*deceitful*. I mean, it's one thing to cash royalty checks—at least people got their money's worth when they bought one of his books, you know? But the women who bought Fletcher Carlyle, they were getting scammed.

"And there was more to it than that, really. I guess I finally figured out that I didn't want women, I wanted *a woman*. I wanted to be somebody's hero. Somewhere out there was a woman that'd fall in love with *me*, Richard Frye—a real down-to-earth woman with some common sense. A woman that'd throw rocks at a phony like Fletcher Carlyle, but her eyes would light up when she saw Richard Frye and she'd want to have his babies. That's what I wanted, but it wasn't never gonna happen because Fletcher Carlyle wouldn't allow it."

Frye wandered over to the bookshelves as he spoke. Now he pulled down a book and flipped through it, looking at pictures.

"I was dying, Doc. All I ever did was play Carlyle. Dress me up, shove me onstage, pull my string, and I do my Fletcher Carlyle impression. Richard Frye didn't give a crap about the symphony or the latest Broadway musical. I'd a whole lot rather go bowling, bass fishing, or to a NASCAR race, but I couldn't do none of that stuff because it wasn't Carlyle. I couldn't even work on my own car— didn't even own any *clothes* raggedy enough for working on a car! Even when I was home alone I was always busy cramming for an interview—oh, and feeding the chicken, let's not forget that. Keep his Dunhills stocked, pour his scotch for him, sweep up the feathers, toss out the eggs, empty the ashtrays, and buy fresh fruit every day. Finicky little twit wouldn't even *touch* a mango if it was cut yesterday—it had to be fresh. And *caviar*! Crito had a major caviar jones, but he couldn't open the tin. At home I was nothing but a glorified butler. To a *chicken*. I was completely isolated, with nobody to talk to. Even as Carlyle, I couldn't afford any real friends because it was too risky. There was too many things that could go wrong, too many ways they could blow my cover."

"There was no one you were close to?"

"Not a soul." He paused for a second and said, "Well, there was this couple at the park. For a while. I used to go running in the mornings. Not a lot of phone calls then—I guess most folks knew better than to call a writer before noon. Weird, how nobody recognized me in sweats. It was like magic, like without the fancy suit and ruby cuff links I was invisible. I was cooling down after a run one morning, doing some stretches, and this young couple was there. I'd seen them before. Ted was always reading a book while Cory drew pictures, and *man* she was good. I got to know them on account of Tolstoy."

"The writer?"

"No, their dog. *Whew,* that dog was ugly—wouldn't do to cut up and make buttholes out of. Looked like a Chihuahua on chemo. Anyway, Tolstoy wandered off and came over to see me. I carried him back to them, and we got to talking. Turned out Cory was from Sand Rock, Alabama, not fifty miles from Squalor, and she's got this beautiful down-home Southern accent. I almost cried. Good people, instant friends. I swear, Doc, I didn't know how lonesome I was until that girl started talking. I got to be Richard Frye for a while, and it was like getting out of prison."

"You didn't tell them who you really were?"

"Well, see, that's the thing—they were the only people who *did* know who I really was. I just can't tell you how dear they were to me, Doc. The times I got to hang out with them in the park, that's all there was left of Richard Frye, the only time I could be *me*. I don't believe I ever even told them my last name.

"Ted was a big kid with a mop of kinky blond hair and cheap glasses with big black plastic rims. He worked maintenance for the Transit Authority at night, underground, and liked to get a little sun in the mornings. Always had his head in a book. Cory was a mousy little thing who didn't much care how she looked, but even I could see that she was gifted. She'd pull out a sketchbook, prop it against her backpack, and sit cross-legged on the green for two hours, reeling off pen and ink drawings of saucer-eyed cartoon figures, or a pencil sketch of somebody she saw in the park, or a close-up of Ted's eyes with those Drew Carey glasses. She worked quick. Whenever she finished something she didn't waste no time admiring it, she just flipped it and started another one. Most of the time she sketched in pen or pencil, sometimes pastels and, every now and then, watercolor. But she didn't sell any of it, far as I know—claimed it was all just practice. Her big dream was to get into the art program at NYU. Sweet kids, both of 'em. I don't know why, but they looked up to me."

Frye slumped into a chair and his whole body sagged, the unmistakable body language of defeat and regret.

"I'm getting the impression it didn't last," Kohl said.

"No. 'Bout six months, maybe."

"They moved away?"

"No, I reckon they're still around. Crito killed it. Somehow he found out about Ted and Cory and killed the whole thing graveyard dead."

"Why?"

"I wish to God I knew."

Chapter 19

> "Oh, go ahead, Judas. Who will know, or long remember?"
> —Mme. Dupree
> —*Of an Angry God*, Fletcher Carlyle

Carlyle's workload doubled when *Daughters of the Nephilim* came out. It was easy for Crito—he just moved on to the next project, pecking away at the keyboard day after day, taking a smoke break every hour or so and stopping for a gourmet meal two or three times a day. He only drank in the evenings, after he was done writing. Scotch dulled his words, he said. Around nine-thirty or ten he'd climb up on his roost and settle in for the night, but he was up every morning before daylight, hammering away.

By early afternoon the phone would start ringing. Frye—usually piled up in the living room, wearing sweats, listening to whatever god-awful highbrow music and reading whatever classic literature Crito had assigned him—always let the answering machine have it. If it turned out to be somebody wanting an interview or one of the screenwriters in Hollywood with a question, he'd pick up at Crito's desk and put it on the speaker. They had the routine down by then. Crito would save his work in progress and open a blank document, ready to type. Most of the time, before the interviewer finished asking a question, Crito already had the answer on the screen.

Frye never picked up the phone after Crito retired in the evenings. He couldn't risk having to answer questions without the bird's help, so he turned the ringer off and let the machine take calls. Half the time he had to go out for a TV appearance or book signing anyway.

Mornings were good. Frye would slip out to the park and try to be back by noon, content with two or three hours of freedom every day, sometimes hanging out with Ted and Cory and Tolstoy. He could have gone on like that indefinitely if it hadn't been for what happened that summer in Switzerland.

He heard about it on CNN late one afternoon. He'd just finished a telephone interview with *Newsweek Global* and was relaxing, kicked back in the office chair with his hands behind his head, watching Crito peck away at the keyboard. The workday was officially over when Crito clicked off the speakerphone and typed a command across the screen.

Scotch. Make it a double.

The chicken waddled to the end of the desk, plucked a Dunhill out of the box, lit it, squatted, and waited for his scotch.

Frye didn't move. Crito's black head tilted sharply, his little red comb jiggling as if to say, What are you waiting for?

"Why do you do this?" Frye asked. It had been bothering him lately. If his own existence seemed narrow and confining, how much narrower was this cramped and monotonous routine for a bird who could remember life as a condor? And what was Crito's percentage in all this? Scotch and cigarettes?

The chicken blew a V of smoke through his nose holes, stared.

"Seriously, Crito, you could jump off the balcony anytime you like, get run over by a car, migrate into a pigeon or whatever and blow this town. I mean, okay, you live pretty good for a chicken, but you could be a hawk, riding thermals over the Rockies. You could be a bald eagle in Alaska, but instead you sit here pecking at a keyboard day after day. Why do you do it?"

Crito propped his cigarette carefully in the crystal ashtray, then waddled over to the keyboard and typed.

I grow weary. After a few hundred lives, all is monotony. Every man, sooner or later, seeks redemption, absolution, peace. Most of all, at this moment in this life, I seek a double scotch.

"Coming up." Frye still didn't understand, but it was clear he wouldn't get any more of an explanation until Crito got his scotch.

The flat-screen TV on the wall was turned low, a CNN anchor with perfect hair and blinding white teeth talking earnestly into the camera. The sound was too soft for Frye to know what was being said, but when he got up to get a shot glass he thought he heard the name Carlyle.

He stopped and stared at the TV. In the background behind the anchor, a video displayed a large, old stone building on a picturesque hillside overlooking a river, and then switched inside to a cavernous arched-beam conference room with the longest table he'd ever seen.

Balding, gray-haired men in sedate blue or gray business suits lined one side of the table, while on the other side sat an equally long row of men, many of whom were deeply tanned and dressed in Middle Eastern robes.

Again, Frye thought he heard the name Carlyle in the muffled monologue of the anchor. He grabbed the remote from Crito's perch and turned up the volume.

"...talks made considerable progress today, thanks in large part to a work of fiction," the baritone voice of the anchor was saying. "Both sides at one time or another during the day made reference to Fletcher Carlyle's latest novel *Daughters of the Nephilim*, citing an ingenious approach to diplomacy taken by the characters in the book. This new paradigm is finding bilateral acceptance, even among the most hard-line factions. Said one Emir, 'Never before have we come to the table with such optimism. For the first time each of us is able to understand, perhaps even *sympathize* with the needs of the other. We are not so different, really.' Literary pundits have often praised Carlyle's novel for its unique insights into Middle Eastern customs and culture, but the conference in Bern marks perhaps the first occasion where principles and practices outlined in a work of fiction are being relied upon to effectively dissolve a real-world political impasse...."

———

Over the next two weeks the men around the conference table in Switzerland drafted a treaty that came to be known as the Bern Accords, a document virtually guaranteeing an ongoing dialogue with enough incentives and accountability built into it for even the most jaded political analysts to concede that it just might have a chance to forge a lasting peace in the Middle East.

As a result, Carlyle had a heavier load of interviews for a while, and a few extra requests for appearances, but as soon as the conferees went back to their countries and resumed a somewhat lower than usual level of bickering, the press moved on to the next big story and Frye's world returned to what passed for normal.

Or so he thought, until that cool, gusty day in mid-October when it all came crashing down. It was a spectacular fall day, a cool breeze rustling the trees, red and gold leaves slanting to the ground and skittering in little gangs across the grass. There was a magic anticipation in such days, almost like the first snowfall of winter. Frye ran for miles, ending up down by the lake, feeling better than he had in a long time, invigorated and wonderfully exhausted.

Cory was there, drawing as usual, but she was alone. She looked up, waved, and Frye sat down next to her.

"Where's the guys?" he asked, turning his Yankees cap backwards and wiping sweat from his face with a hand towel.

"They oughta be along d'rectly. Teddy had to make a run to the bank."

She sat cross-legged with her big sketchbook on her lap. There were pastel crayons scattered about her on the grass. Her fists were stained motley with the chalky powder and she bent over her work, barely looking up when Frye sat down. She was working on a fall landscape. The trees looked like the oak and poplar in the park, and the cool fall light was the same, but hers was a picture of a clearing in the woods. The way the light slanted through the trees and pooled on the ground captured the essence of autumn with a stunning clarity that filled Frye with a sense of loss, of ebbing life.

"Makes me homesick," he said.

She looked up. "What?"

"That picture. The color of the light. The woods."

"The woods make you homesick? We got trees *here*." She waved a hand at the oaks and poplars in the park. "I'm using them for models."

"Yeah, there's trees, but it ain't really woods. Grass, but no pasture. And the paths are all paved. Even the garden patches along the paths here—they're beautiful, but they're all planned, all man-made." He nodded toward the reservoir. "There's water here, but it ain't the same as the beaver pond in the woods down back of my uncle's place where deer come down to drink and you could catch supper with a cane pole and a can of worms. It just ain't the same. None of this is real." He looked up at the skyline towering over the trees. "It's all pretend."

She watched his face intently as he said these things, and a trace of silver gathered at the bottoms of her eyes. Without a word, she turned back to her drawing, picked up a different crayon, and swiftly sketched the outline of a girl in the foreground, walking, passing through the pool of light. It was a young girl, walking quickly with her hands in her pockets and her shoulders hunched, the collar of a light jacket turned up against the chill. As details emerged and the face came into focus, Frye saw that she was glancing back over her shoulder with a trace of fear, or regret, in her face. Something in it made his heart hurt.

"Girl, you are too gifted," he said softly.

"Tell that to NYU." She said this with a little smirk, still sketching.

"I would, if I thought the word of an art-challenged ex-mailman would mean anything to 'em." This was the cover he had given Ted and Cory, a story involving a vicious dog attack, ensuing lawsuit, large settlement, and therapy for post-traumatic stress. The sickle-shaped scar on his neck was actually from the handlebar of a bicycle he had wrecked when he was eleven, but the truth would not do.

Out of nowhere Tolstoy tore across the grass and jumped into Richard's lap, licking his face, lashing him with that whip of a tail. Ted was not far behind, strolling across the green, waving a handful of mail. He plopped down on the grass.

"Oh, that's *good*, Cory. Isn't she something, Richard?"

"Amazing."

"Oh, I almost forgot. There's a letter here from NYU for a Ms. Cory—"

She snatched the envelope from Ted's hand and clutched it in her lap, staring at it.

"I'm scared to open it."

Frye patted her shoulder. "Girl, they *gotta* say yes. You're brilliant. You got more talent in your little finger—"

"Lots of people can draw." Cory's mole eyes darkened with doubt. "And most of 'em got better transcripts."

"Open it," Ted said. "You'll see."

She stared at it for a few more seconds, that huge question mark in her lap, and then quickly tore the end off the envelope and blew it open. Pulling the letter out gingerly with two fingers, she unfolded it and sat reading, the breeze tugging at the corners of the paper. In a minute she looked up at the sky. She took off her glasses and palmed tears from both eyes, then folded the letter against the envelope, ripped both of them into pieces and flung the pieces into the air, where a gust of wind scattered them across the green. Jumping to her feet, heedless of the tablet and pastels raining from her lap, she stalked off with her arms wrapped tight about herself, her head down. Ted started to get up and go after her, but Frye put a hand on his shoulder to stop him.

"Give her a minute."

Ted sank back onto the grass, staring at him.

"I'm glad you're here, Richard. She really looks up to you. Trusts you like a father. The biggest problem she has with the city is that she's basically honest and she expects the same from everybody else. But here, she says everybody she meets is scamming or posing. Everybody but you. Just yesterday she told me, except for me of course, you're the only honest man she's met since she got here."

"She's a fine girl," Frye said quietly, swallowing a lump of guilt. "You need to build her a castle someday, with lots of wall space for pictures."

Ted wasn't listening. There was some kind of commotion behind them, up toward the trees, and Ted had turned around to look. Richard glanced back over his shoulder and saw a bunch of people, maybe twenty or thirty of them, headed in his direction. There were attractive young women in business attire and square-jawed young men in ties and jackets, most of them carrying microphones. There were also a lot of guys in jeans carrying video equipment, with headsets hung around their necks.

"*There he is!*" one of them shouted, pointing at Frye, and the throng picked up speed.

Rising, Ted glanced back and forth between Frye and the approaching gang of reporters.

"What's going on?"

"I gotta get out of here, that's what."

But it was already too late. The pond was at his back and there was nowhere to run. They closed around him, shouting questions, shoving cameras in his face, elbowing Ted aside. Frye saw him stumble, then saw him again on the outer edge of the crowd, putting his glasses back on, gaping, flustered.

"Mr. Carlyle, tell us what it was like when the call came!" a girl shouted, reaching around another reporter with her microphone. She was shouldered aside by a cameraman, and someone else's microphone filled the gap. Somebody, he could not tell who, pulled the Yankees hat right off his head, and it disappeared as a guy in a suit yelled over the commotion, "How does it feel, Mr. Carlyle?"

Frye was trying to make headway toward the path, but they closed ranks and moved with him, jostling, competing for his first words.

"HOLD IT!" he shouted, shoving them back and making a little space for himself. "Just hold on a minute, *please*!"

Ted was still there, on the edge, listening, not ten feet away.

"What are you people *talking* about?"

Again, they all started asking questions at once so that none of them could be understood. Richard raised his hands, palms out, and yelled, "SHUT UP!"

When they had quieted he said calmly, "One at a time. You." He pointed to a young blond woman right in front of him. She held up her microphone.

"Mr. Carlyle, where were you when the call came in?"

"What call?"

"Uh, from—well, you know, the call from the Nobel Committee."

He stared blankly, breathing heavily through his mouth. "I don't know what you're talking about. Clearly, there's been some kind of misunderstanding."

Again they closed in, shouting over each other. He waited, glaring, until they calmed down.

"You," he said, pointing to a young black guy in a power tie.

"Oh my god," the reporter said, sudden awareness widening his eyes. "You didn't know? Mr. Carlyle, you've been awarded the Nobel Prize in Literature."

By some miracle the hush held. Six bulbous black microphones and three digital recorders crowded into his face, hoping to catch the first word. They were dead serious. Frye glanced around and saw Ted, still out there watching, listening, his face twisted in confusion.

"*Fletcher Carlyle?*" his lips said.

"For *Daughters of the Nephilim*," the reporter prompted. "It was just announced about an hour ago. They always call the winner, wherever he is, a few minutes ahead of the announcement. You didn't get the call?"

"I…I wasn't home, and I don't carry a cell phone when I run. Are you sure about this?"

And how did you find me so fast?

A fresh wave of shouting broke out, and a crowd of gawkers began to cluster around the reporters, craning their necks to see what the fuss was about. Frye crossed his arms and looked up at the sky until the reporters ceased trying to shout over each other and quieted.

"You," he said, pointing to a tall redheaded woman in a beige suit, who had forced her digital recorder to the fore.

"Mr. Carlyle, what will you do with the prize money?"

He rolled his eyes. Reporters.

"Look," he huffed, beginning to let his exasperation show despite knowing from experience that it was a mistake, "I'm afraid you've caught me off guard. I need time to talk to my people about this—my editors, my publicist, my agent. I'm sorry, but this is not a good time."

The gaggle of reporters had loosened up a bit, and he sensed an opportunity. He shouldered his way through a gap and started edging toward the trees. They moved with him, but lagged behind just enough.

"I'll call a press conference this evening, I promise," he said, walking backward until he was in the clear, then turning and breaking into a run. The reporters, now behind him, were not dressed for the chase and were loaded down with equipment. They tried to keep up, raising their microphones and shouting their questions, but he outran them.

Up the slope at the edge of the trees, Richard Frye stopped once and looked back. Ted was watching him. Even from a distance he could see sadness in Ted's eyes and in the slump of his shoulders. He looked deflated.

Betrayed.

Chapter 20

> A well-told tale is like an ocean crossing. You may skim the surface and enjoy the trip; you need not plumb the depths. But for those who are of a mind, there must be depths to plumb.
> — *Atlantis Requiem*, Fletcher Carlyle

"Did someone call while I was out?"

Frye stood in the doorway of the Batcave, panting from the run, glaring at the chicken perched in front of the keyboard on the black-topped desk.

Crito looked up, nodded.

The phone rang. Both of them ignored it, man and chicken, locked in a stare.

"Did he leave a message?"

Another nod.

"About the Nobel Prize?"

Nod.

Frye had thought it through. It didn't take much; the possibilities were limited. There was only one way the reporters could have found him that quickly: somebody told them where he was. Crito was the only one who *knew* where he was, and whatever else he could do, Crito could not make a phone call.

Richard Frye never used the computer. Crito was on it all the time, writing and answering email. When Carlyle received an email it was read by Crito alone. The computer belonged to the chicken.

Richard Frye didn't *need* email because he didn't exist.

He jerked out the desk chair, plopped down in it, drew himself up to the desk, and swept the chicken unceremoniously to the floor with his arm. With a few clicks he closed Crito's manuscript, opened the email application, clicked on the Sent folder and read down the list.

The most recent forty-one emails were sent en masse to various media persons in Manhattan. They all bore the same subject line: Carlyle Interview Op.

He clicked on one of them, and the body of the message appeared.

Ladies and gentlemen of the press:

Mr. Carlyle is out of the office at present, but if you would like his thoughts on the Nobel you may find him in Central Park, near the west side of the reservoir. He is attired in navy sweat clothes and a Yankees baseball cap.

Thank you,
Office Mgr.
for Fletcher Carlyle

"*Office manager?*" He looked around at Crito.

The chicken was eyeing him cautiously from a half squat, his wings slightly flared—a defensive posture, ready to spring out of the way in case of attack.

"Baaaa-ack," he said.

"Do you know what you've done, you bastard? You *killed* me. You snuffed out the last trace of Richard Frye. You know how long it'll be before I can go to the park again? Everybody there knows who I am now. Is that what you wanted?"

"Baa-aaaack."

It was in that moment that Frye first thought of killing the chicken. He could just snatch him up by the neck the way he'd seen his mother do a hundred times when he was little, and crank him in quick circles until his body went flying off and left that black-feathered head gasping in his fist.

But what then? It was safe to assume there would be a lot of pomp and ceremony surrounding the Nobel Prize. At the very least, he would have to go to Scandinavia—was it Oslo or Stockholm?—and hobnob with a bunch of intellectuals, completely on his own and unprepared. If he decided to cut and run, the media circus would escalate six or seven notches—NOBEL LAUREATE MISSING! and there would be no hiding place remote enough.

Then there was the small matter of the prize itself. Something about twisting the head off of a *real* Nobel laureate gave him pause.

In the end, no matter how badly he wanted to kill Crito, he knew he couldn't do it. He just couldn't. Shoulders slumping, he got up and walked slowly out. Stopping in the door of the Batcave, he looked back at the chicken for a second.

"Why are you doing this?" he said softly, then he closed the door and padded into the living room. He didn't even want to look at Crito anymore.

After a while, when the calls started coming at greater intervals, he picked up the phone in the living room and ordered a case of beer.

———

Huntsman-Wisner had scheduled the release of Carlyle's new book for the first week of December because they wanted to get in on the Christmas rush, but after the Nobel was announced they moved it up a month. *Of an Angry God* came out in early November while the furor over the Prize was still white hot.

It was a complete shock, the Nobel. Nobody saw it coming. Mainly because Carlyle's books were immensely popular, no one pegged him as a serious contender for the Nobel, but the people who speculated about such things agreed that the Bern Accords had changed all that.

The next nine weeks were a complete blur, a whirlwind of banquets and public appearances, talk show spots and radio gigs. He even had to turn down a few product endorsements. The phone never stopped ringing. He never got a chance to read Crito's new book, though he had ample time in the back of assorted limousines to memorize the press kit Q&A. Always before, that had been enough. If a late-night talk show host ditched the script and ad-libbed a question that he couldn't answer easily, Fletcher Carlyle had always been able to rely on his wits to change the subject, and he usually got a laugh in the bargain. The pace of such interviews was always so fast and light that an offbeat one-liner was all it took to leave such a question behind, unanswered and forgotten.

It was bound to happen sooner or later. After Thanksgiving, right before he was to leave for Stockholm and the Magic Week of the Nobel, the stars aligned themselves against him and penciled the name Dennis Sinclair into his calendar. He didn't know Dennis Sinclair, didn't know anything about him, had never seen his show, and didn't even know until the limo pulled up in front of the building that Dennis Sinclair worked for PBS. He had just assumed it was another fast-moving, lightweight, late-night gabfest where celebrities went to plug their upcoming movies "right after this commercial break."

He was wrong.

They treated him like royalty at PBS. A cluster of bigwigs in suits met him at the front door and lined up to shake his hand, congratulate him, tell him how much they admired his work. Then they steered him through a labyrinth of hallways back to the studio, a large dark place that in the absence of a live audience felt more like a warehouse than a studio. In his colossal ignorance, even that didn't trigger any alarms. Everything was just fine until he saw the actual set: a round wooden table with a neat stack of notes on it. Two straight-backed wooden chairs.

This was altogether different from any talk show set he'd seen before. Waiting in the wings of the dark studio while a swarm of worker bees checked sound and lighting, Carlyle began to get nervous. That table and chairs, isolated in a little island of light, looked for all the world like something out of a police interrogation room.

Dennis Sinclair made him feel a lot better. As soon as he got word that Carlyle was in the studio, he came out to get acquainted. Sinclair was a young sixty-five with no gray in his sandy hair. He hadn't put on the jacket and tie yet, and his sleeves were rolled up.

"It's an honor, sir," he said, and Carlyle was convinced. The firm handshake, the eye contact, the warm smile, the rolled-up sleeves—Dennis Sinclair came across as intelligent, energetic, and sincere. A man of the people. A man of integrity. Carlyle's instincts were accurate, as far as they went. He just didn't think it through.

"I have to tell you, we really feel that we lucked out, booking you before the Nobel announcement and having you on before the actual award. What incredible timing! The brass are all saying this may be one of our highest-rated shows ever."

Carlyle could feel the blood draining from his face. Surely not.

"You mean, when it *airs*, right?"

Sinclair's eyebrows went up in surprise. "Oh, well, yes, but it airs live. I thought you knew. After all, the name of the show is *Dennis Sinclair Live*."

All Carlyle's calendar said was "Dennis Sinclair." His feet shifted involuntarily. He bit his lip, glanced back at the exit.

"Oh, but listen, Mr. Carlyle, it'll be fine. Really. We're just having a conversation, that's all. You and me. No surprises, no ambush—nothing like that. We want you to look *good*. We're very proud to have a Nobel laureate on the show, and I'll do everything in my power to make you comfortable. Trust me."

The worry in Carlyle's face must have been apparent, because Sinclair looked at his watch and said, "Listen, why don't you come on back to my dressing room while I finish getting ready and we'll just talk, get to know each other a bit. How's that sound?"

Smiling, concerned, he put a fatherly arm around Carlyle and guided him back toward the dressing room. "Can I get you anything? Cup of coffee? Glass of wine?"

He really wanted a cold beer, but Fletcher Carlyle didn't drink beer. Beer was Dickie Frye.

"Something light, perhaps—a White Zinfandel," he heard his Fletcher Carlyle voice say. Sinclair gestured to one of the long-haired young men who happened to pass by right then, and within a minute Carlyle was sitting on a sofa in Sinclair's dressing room with a glass of White Zin in his hand, watching his host tie a Windsor knot in front of a lighted mirror.

"Now tell me the truth," Sinclair said, his reflection making eye contact, "did you have any idea you might win the Nobel?"

"None whatsoever. As I recall, my editor did mention in passing that he thought the writing merited a Nobel nomination, but then he laughed and said it was highly unlikely because it had sold too well."

Sinclair chuckled. "I know exactly what he means. It seems the gap between popularity and excellence is only widening these days. It's a rare author who knows how to bridge that gap. So, when do you leave for Stockholm?"

And it went like that. Carlyle spent thirty minutes alone with Sinclair in his dressing room before they had to go out onto the set to get miked up and do a sound check. He made two mistakes during those thirty minutes. First, he drank three glasses of wine. Second, he got comfortable talking to Dennis Sinclair. The man was fascinated with Fletcher Carlyle because, although he'd interviewed two former recipients of the Peace Prize, he'd never actually gotten a crack at the Lit Prize winner. But because of the Prize, the conversation centered entirely on *Daughters of the Nephilim*. They never discussed the new book at all in the dressing room. It never came up.

By the time they cued the music and a smiling Dennis Sinclair looked into Camera One to deliver a glowing introduction of his guest, Fletcher Carlyle had gotten a little *too* comfortable.

The first twenty minutes of the hour-long show were all about the Nobel, and Sinclair stayed mercifully close to the conversation they'd already had in the dressing room. The next twenty minutes took them deeper into both *Atlantis Requiem* and *Daughters of the Nephilim*, and Carlyle found himself floundering once or twice, trying to keep up. It was the first time he'd ever encountered a talk show host who had actually *read* the books, and it caught him off guard. Dennis Sinclair had read all of them. Not only did he have an uncommon grasp of the nuances of the stories, but he also remembered things in great detail. By the time the show was in the home stretch, Carlyle was having trouble covering his ignorance of his own books, and he was starting to sweat.

Then disaster struck.

Copies of all three of Fletcher Carlyle's novels lay on the table between them. At a lull in the conversation Dennis Sinclair picked up Carlyle's new book, held it in front of him with both hands, looking at it, smiling benevolently, and said, "Tell us about *Of an Angry God*."

The press kit covered it well enough. There was a PR blurb, mostly a vague, poetic rhapsody on the grand theme of the book, and there were two pages of perfectly good interview questions to which Crito had already given him the answers—Carlyle had memorized all of those—but they were very specific questions. He was prepared to explain how Enoch Heinz captured a controlling interest in the silver market, or why Madame Dupree was willing to risk her life for a pocket watch, but when Dennis Sinclair dumped an impossibly broad "Tell us about the book" on him and then sat there waiting for an answer, he didn't know what to say. He started fumbling.

"Well, I, uh, let's see…a storm drives Enoch Heinz's ship into Marseilles, main mast broken, down by the bow, taking on water. The crew throws Heinz overboard in the harbor, he swims ashore penniless, with just the clothes on his back and—"

"Yes," Dennis Sinclair said, coming to the rescue, "and yet he manages within a year to gain control of the Eastern Mediterranean silver market." A sensitive man and the consummate professional, Sinclair had dived in as soon as he saw Carlyle floundering. He went on to give a succinct but very insightful summary of the plot, keeping the camera on himself for the next minute or two, allowing Carlyle time to regain his composure.

Then he came back with an easy one. He asked Carlyle a question straight out of the press kit. Just put it up on a tee for him.

Carlyle nailed the question. Trying to put him at ease, the host stuck to the press kit questions for a while, and it looked like Carlyle was back on an even keel until, with about five minutes of air time left, Dennis Sinclair inadvertently tossed a hand grenade. He didn't mean any harm; it was an honest question, one Carlyle might have been able to answer if he'd actually read the book.

"Listen," Sinclair said, holding *Of an Angry God* in front of him as he spoke, thumbing the pages lovingly, "I have to ask you one thing that's been keeping me awake at night. The one character I could never quite get a handle on was Féodor. Particularly his death scene in Milan."

Carlyle's pulse quickened. He tried hard to come up with a way to signal the man, or a quick song and dance to divert him, but Sinclair's eyes were on the book.

"I really felt I missed something significant in that scene." Sinclair was tapping the book's cover with a forefinger, lost in thought, completely oblivious to Carlyle's squirming. "Now, I know the pewter mug was symbolic of something because it turns up in critical scenes throughout the book, but I couldn't figure out what it was doing in Féodor's room. Please! For my own peace of mind, please enlighten me—what was the symbolism behind the pewter mug, and why did it figure so prominently in Féodor's death scene?"

Busted. Carlyle grew queasy and felt himself going pale, felt the sweat breaking out on his forehead and upper lip. He couldn't even guess. There were, by the producer's estimate, some nine million people watching, and he was utterly stumped. He didn't know the symbolism behind the pewter mug because he didn't know there *was* a pewter mug. He didn't know who Féodor was, or what he was doing in Milan, let alone how or why he died.

After ten pregnant seconds, the pressure grew unbearable and his eyes darted. His pulse pounded in his ears, and Carlyle suddenly became aware of the intense lights he'd been sitting under for an hour. His wool suit became a greenhouse, trapping all the heat inside and threatening to curdle the wine in his stomach. The queasy feeling tripled, and he deeply regretted not eating anything before coming to the studio. He glanced up at the lights, only vaguely aware that he was breathing in short, shallow gasps and his face had gone ash gray.

"Mr. Carlyle, are you all right?"

The voice seemed to come from the next room, or the next planet.

With great effort Carlyle forced his ashen face back down to try to focus on Dennis What's-his-name. The man looked worried.

And then the worried look disappeared, replaced by shock and disgust as the Nobel laureate threw up in Dennis Sinclair's lap in front of nine million viewers.

Chapter 21

> His station is nothing; how he *perceives* his lot is everything. One man's heaven is another man's hell.
>
> —*Of an Angry God*, Fletcher Carlyle

"Yes, I do remember seeing that on the news," Kohl said, "though I don't recall any speculation at the time about why it happened. I believe it was regarded as an unfortunate accident, an untimely illness."

Frye snorted. "Yeah. Accident. '*Carlyle Hurls*'—that was the title of the clip some snot-nosed punk posted on YouTube, which, by the way, is still there for everybody to horse-laugh."

"How did it make you feel?" Kohl had to ask the question, though the answer was obvious.

"How would you feel? How would *anybody* feel? At a time like that, right before the Nobel, with the whole world watching, to blow my groceries in Dennis Sinclair's lap on live TV? That's gotta be a once-in-a-lifetime experience, Doc, right up there with the most embarrassing moments of all time."

"I can imagine. I didn't realize the trip to Stockholm came right on the heels of that incident."

"Yeah, I flew to Stockholm two days later. I spent the whole two days pacing, trying to figure a way out of it, but it was the Nobel, you know? You can't just call in sick. I even asked Crito if there was any way I could pass on it. He wrote, 'I'm afraid not. Buck up, Dickie. In for a penny, in for a pound.'"

"Under the circumstances, I can imagine how the specter of such an embarrassment might have cast a shadow on your trip to Sweden."

Frye's shoulders shook with a low chuckle. "Cast a shadow. You got a gift for understatement, Doc. I don't know, though." He frowned, scrubbing at the fingers of his left hand with the thumb of his right, as if they were stained. "In a weird way, the Sinclair incident might have actually *helped* me in Stockholm."

"How so?"

"Well, the whole week in Sweden was one long gauntlet of highbrow Christmas parties—banquets, formal dinners, fancy china, solid gold flatware, concerts, balls, Christmas candles and holly. Seemed like every guy there was a hundred years old and had a pedigree longer than his beard—I swear, it was a steady stream of diamond-studded penguins. Even royalty, sometimes. I'm here to tell you, Doc, Stockholm is a long way from Squalor.

"I didn't know what I was getting myself into. First night there, I'm at this big party in this gilded hall with all these rich old farts rambling on about antiquity and tradition. Some coot with a mustache the size of a trout comes up to me with his fat wife on his arm—she's literally dripping in diamonds—and he starts talking to me in some other language. I had a gut feeling this was only the beginning, that it was gonna happen over and over because everybody knows Fletcher Carlyle speaks like nine languages, right? I'm compassed about with intellectuals, and ruin lies in every direction. So I shake my head, give the old coot a humble grin, and say, 'I'm terribly sorry but I would prefer to speak English. I have no wish to disgrace your beautiful language with my barbaric rendering.'"

He said this last in the inimitable genteel voice of Fletcher Carlyle, and carried it off perfectly.

"The old guy thought I was just being modest, so he kept on yammering in his mother tongue. I was holding a glass of red wine—I knew better than to drink it, I was just holding it—so I took a good long look at that wine, dropped my eyelids to half-mast and did this gag move. You know, just puffed my cheeks a little, like a hiccup. That backed him off. You could see it in his eyes. The old fart remembered Dennis Sinclair and pictured me blowing vintage cabernet all over his wife's designer evening gown. After that I kept a glass of red wine in my hands all the time, as a reminder. And it worked, slicker'n snot."

"What about the speech? You had to make a speech at the award presentation, right? How did that go?"

"Piece o' cake. You get to *read* the speech, except they don't call it a speech, they call it a lecture. You don't do it at the presentation, either. It's at a banquet earlier in the week. Crito wrote me a lecture and I stood up and read it, word for word. It was beautiful. You shoulda seen me. Pure Fletcher Carlyle—profound, yet accessible. Got a standing O. Kind of strange, though, all them white gloves clapping. Sounded like a covey of quail lighting out."

"That *is* impressive. So you managed to make it through the week without a major embarrassment?"

"Far as I know. Crito gave me a couple tips before I left—'Humility and grace. Nod, smile, deflect praise, brush the ladies' fingers with your lips and hold the fork in your left hand. Remember, Fletcher Carlyle is among the intellectual elite: silence will be interpreted not as ignorance but as introspection.' I made a lot of small talk and played bashful whenever they asked me about the books. It's an easy trick to steer a conversation away from yourself—just float a question about where the other guy's from, what he does for a living, or what he thinks about foreign policy. A guy in a tux ain't no different from a guy in overalls when you get right down to it. He don't really want to know about Fletcher Carlyle; he wants Fletcher Carlyle to know about *him*."

"It doesn't sound as though you enjoyed the experience very much."

"Nah. Not my kind of folks. Holding my breath the whole time, waiting for the train to go off the rails—it was all pucker factor and no fun. I just wanted to get it over with and go home."

———

The king of Sweden gave Fletcher Carlyle three things on December tenth as he stood and bowed before a crowd of over a thousand of the world's best and brightest in the gilded confines of Stockholm City Hall. The first was a twenty-three-carat gold medallion with Alfred Nobel on one side, and on the other an engraving of a naked writer under a laurel tree, listening while some woman in a toga played an autoharp. The name Fletcher Carlyle was engraved under their feet.

The second was a leather folder that opened to a signed, embossed, parchment diploma on the right and a piece of handcrafted art on the left. The artwork had been commissioned just weeks before the ceremony to reflect the book itself in some way. As best he could make out, it was a desert scene done in stark black and white with traces of red. Nouveau Something-or-Other.

The third was a check for ten million kronor, just over a million dollars.

He flew home first class. The flight attendants knew who he was and helped him drink too much. There was a crowd waiting for him when he touched down at JFK, most of them waving a copy of *Daughters of the Nephilim*. They all wanted an autograph, and he had to put the date on it too, so they could say their book was the first one signed after he won the Nobel. No telling what it would bring on eBay.

When he finally made it back to the sanctuary of his apartment, he went straight to the refrigerator and popped a beer. Fletcher Carlyle had walked in starlight and dined with kings. He had faced down the literati of the world and come away with a Nobel Prize, and yet the only thing Dickie Frye felt was a kind of empty relief on surviving the experience.

Surely this was not how things were meant to be.

With Crito watching from the footboard, he spread open his suitcase on the bed. He took out his little pile of trophies—the leather-bound diploma, the red leather box containing the medal, the envelope with the check—and carried them straight to the Batcave.

Crito followed him and trotted up the ramp onto his desk. Frye opened the leather folder with the big FC embossed on the cover and laid it out. Crito leaned close over it, with one eye examining the diploma, the painting. Next, Frye opened the red leather box containing the medal, then took the check from the envelope and placed it on the black rubber surface of the desk.

After Crito got his fill he turned to the keyboard.

Nice work, Dickie. Congratulations.

"They're yours," he said flatly, and took a slug of beer. "I got the free dinner—the baubles are yours. What you want me to do with them?"

Display them on the mantel, of course. Use a common book stand for the diploma, but call Newman Margolis and have them make a crystal mount for the medal. Something appropriately

heavy and impressive, a sandwich design so it can be seen from the front or back. As for the money, do with it as you wish. It is yours, Dickie.

"You sure?"

A nod.

"All right, then." Frye pocketed the check, then closed the box and the folder and took them to the mantel in the living room.

Chugging the last of his beer, he left the empty can sitting on top of the prize and went to get another. Then he spread the phone book on the kitchen counter, flipped over to N, and ran his finger down the columns, searching for Newman Margolis. He hadn't heard of them, but Crito was never wrong; if he said they could design and build the sort of crystal mount he wanted for the medal, they would do it.

But a boldface heading caught his eye as he scanned the page: NEW YORK UNIVERSITY. There was a long column of offices and departments listed under it.

NYU.

Cory.

He'd been so busy the last two weeks that he had only thought of her a hundred times or so. After what happened in the park, he wouldn't be able to go there again for a long time, if ever, and his last image of her was one of heartbreak. Ted and Cory had never given him a phone number, or even told him where they lived. As much as he hated it, he figured there was nothing he could do.

Then he spotted a subheading that gave him an idea. Without a second's hesitation he picked up the phone and dialed the number.

"Admissions," a woman's voice said.

"I'd like to speak to the Dean of Admissions."

A slight pause. "There's no such title. Perhaps—"

"Listen. I've no idea who does what at your school or what their titles are, but I wish to speak with a person of rank—*the* person of rank, whichever official is the final arbiter of admissions." He was careful to maintain his Carlyle voice despite bone-deep fatigue, jet lag, and a bit too much alcohol.

This time there was a lengthy pause. When the woman finally responded, her words were clipped, angry. "I'm afraid the *Director* of Admissions is in a meeting."

"Interrupt him. He'll thank you for it later."

"I'm sorry, sir, but that's just not—"

"I don't care. Get him."

Another pause. "I'd be happy to take your name and have him call you."

"My name is Fletcher Carlyle. Perhaps you've heard of me."

She must have recognized his voice at that point, because she didn't say another word. There was a click, ten seconds of Pachelbel's Canon, and then a man's voice.

"Mr. Carlyle?"

"Yes."

"Fletcher Carlyle, the novelist?"

"Yes."

"Well, this is a pleasant surprise indeed! I'm Dr. Michael Torrance, Director of Admissions. I'm honored to be speaking with you, Mr. Carlyle. Congratulations on the Nobel, by the way. I'm a big fan of your work. What can we do for you?"

There was no need to be coy. He decided to cut to the chase.

"Dr. Torrance, recently the NYU art program denied admission to one Cory Fincher—C-O-R-Y Fincher, just like it sounds. Female, twenty-two years old, from Sand Rock, Alabama, currently living in Manhattan. I would like the admissions department to contact Ms. Fincher and inform her that they made a clerical error, and that she is to be admitted with a full scholarship. I'm prepared to make a substantial donation to the university, to be used however you see fit so long as Ms. Fincher gets a full ride."

There was a long pause. Torrance cleared his throat twice before he finally answered, reluctantly, "Mr. Carlyle, of course I'd like to accommodate you in any way I can, but this is highly irregular. I'd be happy to meet with you and discuss the matter, or perhaps go over Ms. Fincher's transcript and see—"

"This is not a negotiation, Dr. Torrance, it's a simple donation with two conditions. One is a full scholarship for Cory Fincher, and the other is a guarantee of complete anonymity. No one beyond yourself is to know the particulars."

Torrance hesitated again, the natural caution of a career bureaucrat. There was a rustling as he switched the phone to his other ear, and his voice dropped. Very quietly he said, "Mr. Carlyle, I hope you won't take offense, but exactly how large a donation are we talking about?"

Carlyle took a slug of beer, smiled.

"Just north of a million dollars."

Chapter 22

> It is inevitable. The safeguarding of a great secret lie will carve away the edges of a man's world until he is left alone, with nothing but his lie to comfort him.
>
> —*Of an Angry God*, Fletcher Carlyle

"Interesting choice," Kohl said. "What an incredibly generous thing to do."

Frye shook his head, smirked. "It ain't generous if it ain't your money. Anyway, I did it mostly because I was mad."

"At Crito?"

"Yeah. And myself, I guess, for letting him trap me like that. I'm sure it was all his design, everything that happened. He walled me in one brick at a time so I didn't see what was happening, but in the end I was hog-tied. And scared."

"Of what?"

"Another Sinclair incident, mainly. In the back of my mind I always knew that was no accident. In Crito's world there *were* no accidents. He was a genius, a master manipulator—maybe he didn't know exactly when, but he knew I'd blow it someplace, sooner or later. If it hadn't been Sinclair it would've been somebody else, and it would've had the same effect. It was just a matter of time. I guarantee you, he had it all calculated out. All he had to do was turn up the heat and keep me hopping from one PR gig to another until I ran into one I couldn't handle. Right after Stockholm I had to do one more tour, a quick swing through the Southeast that we'd already booked, but nothing else till mid-January. So after that I quit. I got so gun-shy I canceled all interviews after the New Year and refused to do any more appearances. Just shut everything down."

"So you disappeared from the public eye after the Nobel because you were afraid there might be another Sinclair incident?"

"Wasn't no *might* about it, I *knew* something would happen. The interview requests coming in after the Nobel were mostly from NPR and PBS—people like Sinclair, serious people who actually read books. I'da been a lost ball in a wheat field and I knew it, so I called my publicist and canceled everything."

"You could do that?"

"What were they gonna do, fire me? The publicist got pretty hot over it, and Huntsman-Wisner wanted to send a shrink to see me because they figured I was having a nervous breakdown. I told them all to go to hell and quit returning their calls."

"And became a complete recluse."

"Yep. You know, it's taken me a while to figure it out, but things are finally getting clearer. Crito did this to me. All of it. I couldn't see it at the time because I was too busy feeling sorry for myself, but he set up every bit of it, didn't he? It's like he *wanted* me isolated and hemmed in."

Frye was staring at the carpet, his fist pressed against his teeth. Kohl let him stew for a while before priming the pump again.

"What are you thinking?"

With a deep sigh, Frye shook himself and straightened up, but the worried look remained.

"*Why?* I just can't figure out *why*."

"Why didn't you just ask him?" Kohl was sitting back in his chair, relaxed, chin propped in hand, a finger thrust alongside his cheek.

"I did. He always said the same thing, that he was granting my wishes—*bigger than Elvis, richer than God*."

"And you were. It seems to me he'd given you everything he promised. Everything you wanted."

"Oh, it was way beyond anything I ever wanted."

"Yet you were unhappy."

"To put it mildly. If there was ever a time I was clinically depressed, that was it."

"I think we should take a closer look at that. Can you tell me why you were depressed?"

Frye's eyes wandered and he shook his head. "Because it wasn't *me*, Doc! An author? Come on, Richard Frye was a ventriloquist's dummy. And fame? Fletcher Carlyle was all over the TV and the tabloids, in all the magazines—the Brad Pitt of the literary world—but when I took a girl out she wasn't with *me*, she was with Carlyle. I couldn't even go to the park anymore. And money? Yeah, there was a lot of money, but there's only so much you can do with it cooped up in an apartment, and in the end you can get tired of any lifestyle. It took me a long time to figure it out, but *style* ain't real. Life is. What matters is life its ownself, and what you do with it. I wasn't really doing anything with mine. I wanted out. I wanted out in the worst way, but there was nowhere to go. I found that out the hard way."

"What do you mean?"

"It's true what they say. You really can't go home again."

Kohl sat up straight. "You went back home? To Squalor?"

"Yeah. I did."

"When?"

"That last little signing junket, right after the Nobel. It was just a quick swing through the Southeast—Charlotte, Atlanta, Birmingham, Orlando, Jacksonville. Some kind of scheduling mix-up gave me a few hours of slack time on a Thursday afternoon in Atlanta, so I snuck away from my publicist, rented a car, and went back to Squalor."

———

Richard Frye hadn't heard a word from anybody around home since he'd left. He had no idea what he would find there, but the closer he got to Squalor the more he thought of Raye Anne, fantasizing about the look on her face when she found out he was alive, rehearsing for the moment when she and Buttface learned that he was Fletcher Carlyle.

Bigger than Elvis, richer than God.

But he hadn't reckoned on the nostalgic power of geography. Driving down the little two-lane macadam road past clapboard houses whose kitchens and porches he'd haunted all his life, where he'd eaten meals and swapped lies and worked and loved and played, past fields where he'd hunted rabbits and ponds where he'd caught catfish, he smelled once again the blue smoke of a spent shotgun shell and felt the urgent tug of a cane pole in his hands, and he was drawn inexorably back. Fletcher Carlyle had no memory of these fields and woods, or the people who grew from them, or the wealth of shared stories that lay waiting to be passed around a fire like a mason jar of home brew with a handful of friends as comfortable as old jeans. Fletcher Carlyle faded a little with every passing mile until he became a mere memory himself. The man who pulled into the convenience store parking lot in the heart of Squalor was almost all Richard Frye.

He had no real plan other than to go there and see what happened. The convenience store had changed some; they sold beer now, and there was a cappuccino machine. It wasn't until he sat a Styrofoam cup of cappuccino up on the counter that he realized the guy who took his twenty was Bo Huggins, a short, balding fireplug he'd known since the third grade, and who had apparently fallen on hard times of late, else he wouldn't be working the cash register at the convenience store. His eyes narrowed as he gave the English wool suit a once-over.

Sipping his cappuccino, Frye decided to mess with Bo's head. He went into Carlyle mode. "Pardon me, sir, but I don't suppose you'd know where I can find a decent haberdasher."

Bo squinted, his lips silently working over the first two syllables—*haber*.... He gave Frye a slightly sideways look of suspicion and said, "You ain't from around here, are you?" And then, without changing his puzzled expression, he added, "You look awful familiar."

"Really." Frye raised his nose just a touch, the merest hint of arrogance as Bo counted out his change.

"Reckon it's the eyes. Used to be a feller here that looked a bit like you, only shorter and fatter, with scraggly hair, rotten teeth and big ol' thick glasses. Uglier'n a mud fence. Went nuts and run off awhile back, God knows where. Good ol' boy, but crazier'n a shit-house rat."

"Mm," Frye said, smothering a smile behind his cup. "Well, it's been delightful."

Leaning against the double-door ice chest out front, Frye took his time with the cappuccino. It wasn't particularly good, but he had to look like he was doing something; a stranger in a Jacques Dumont suit couldn't just stand around in Squalor without some excuse for being there, something to occupy his hands. He just wanted to hang out and watch for a while.

Hal Teasley pulled in right in front of him, still driving the same old white-smoke-belching International Harvester pickup and wearing the same grimy overalls. The gangly pulpwooder tipped his cap to Frye as he passed, though the quick head-to-toe appraisal of Frye's clothes said Hal didn't know who he was. After he'd gone into the store, thinking the door had closed behind him, Hal called out, "Oooooo-WEE, Bo! Who's the pretty-boy? Got y'self a new girlfriend?"

Frye stood out there for twenty minutes while half a dozen people he'd known all his life walked right past him, in and out of the store. Not one of them recognized him—as Dickie Frye *or* Fletcher Carlyle. The Clip Joint was down at the other end of the strip from the convenience store, and he almost walked down there twice, but if the same bunch of girls still worked there they'd blow his cover in a minute. They had a sixth sense about such things. He didn't want to be recognized, but neither did he want to leave without at least a glimpse of Raye Anne.

He tried to imagine talking to her, though he knew it would be painful for at least one of them. But even if he didn't talk to her he wanted to see her, to look at her—if nothing else, to find out if he still wanted to kill her.

Or take her to Paris.

The remains of his cappuccino had gone cold, so he tossed the cup and was fishing for his keys when a big navy-blue van nosed into a parking place in front of the beauty shop at the far end of the strip. Frye didn't really pay any attention to the van until Raye Anne climbed out of it and sashayed inside. She looked good—looked like she'd lost weight, and she was dressed rich. Moving among New York society, he'd learned to spot cashmere sweaters and Italian shoes, expensive slacks. Someone else had been doing her hair, too. No more platinum. She looked classy. She couldn't have been in the beauty shop for more than a minute, but he changed his mind at least six times about whether or not to walk down there and confront her, just to see the expression on her face. While he was still arguing with himself she came back out, hopped up in the van and backed out.

The blue van passed right in front of him, not fifteen feet away. Raye Anne turned and looked straight at him, right at his face. Nothing. He knew she didn't recognize him because the van didn't wreck.

His heart pounding, he got in the rental car and just sat there for a minute, thinking. There was something not right about that van. Raye Anne hated driving anything that big; a full-sized van was just not her. Even odder, there was one of those blue-and-white handicap signs hanging from the rearview mirror.

Something didn't make sense. He had to know more. He searched his memory for somebody, *anybody* who could tell him what was going on, but there was no one he could talk to without the news spreading all over town in an hour.

Except maybe Odd Lester the Bird Man.

Lester kept to himself up there on that ridge and never talked to anybody. He drove all the way into Rome to the bulk food store once a month for supplies and, apart from that, never ventured out. Everybody in Squalor thought he was a complete wacko. His only known friends were a couple of falconers from a club somewhere up around Chattsworth.

And Dickie Frye.

Chapter 23

> This flat expanse of unbroken sea was once land, where mothers tended gardens and baked bread, where girls dreamed dreams and old men told tales, where tinkers and cobblers plied their trades. Memories haunt this place, great lost hordes of unfinished tales whispering in the deep.
>
> —*Atlantis Requiem*, Fletcher Carlyle

Fifteen minutes later Frye knocked on the door of an olive drab house set back in the woods at the far end of the ridge. No one answered, so he wandered around back.

Odd Lester was training one of his hawks. A sawhorse stood in the clearing, its entire top wrapped with heavy rope, and atop the rope sat a young hawk with a piece of twine tied to one leg. Thirty yards away, holding the other end of the twine, Lester held up a small chunk of red meat and called to the bird. The hawk leaned forward, spreading its wings tentatively, then leaped from the sawhorse and swooped in a low arc up to his gloved hand to take the bait.

Lester wore an old canvas farmer's jacket over jeans and boots, with what looked like a Russian army hat on his head, furry flaps hanging down loosely over his ears. A large revolver hung at his hip in a western holster. His bug eyes peered over the bird's head and spotted Frye standing by the corner of his house, watching.

"Go away!" he shouted. The hawk hopped up to his shoulder. The heavy leather glove fell to the ground as Lester shook it off, and his bare hand came to rest on the butt of the revolver.

Frye didn't move.

"Get out of here! Whatever you're selling, I don't want it. Leave! Now!"

Frye raised his hands, palms out. "I'm a friend. I just want to talk."

The Russian hat cocked to one side and Lester's bug eyes glared. He unhooked the twine from the hawk's foot and strode quickly across the yard, stopping an arm's length away, his hand still resting on the revolver.

Frye didn't budge. "I'm Dickie Frye. I used to deliver your mail."

Lester leaned close and looked him up and down. The hawk on his shoulder stared along with him.

"No you're not, you're Fletcher Carlyle. I'd know that face anywhere. It's on the back of your books, not to mention the six o'clock news."

Lester's growl held a trace of what Frye now recognized as a Boston accent—another reason the locals didn't trust him—but apparently even the appearance of Fletcher Carlyle wasn't enough to soften his tone. Odd Lester didn't entertain strangers and had little patience with a man who lied about his name, even if he was famous.

"Well," Frye said with a slightly embarrassed smile, "I *used* to be Dickie Frye. I been through some changes."

Those round eyes bored in and there was a flicker of surprise in them, of recognition.

"The voice is right, but the last I heard of Frye was four years ago, when he got pummeled for throwing a snake in Talbot Bonniface's black Lincoln."

"It was a red Cadillac. And it wasn't a snake; it was a bunch of Root Hollis's mice. You oughta know."

Lester let out a booming laugh then, and clapped his gun hand on Frye's shoulder. The test was passed.

"Dickie Frye, Nobel Prize-winning novelist!" He kept his hand on Frye's shoulder, steering him toward the back door. "Come in the house and I'll put on some coffee. I have *got* to hear this one." The hawk's head swiveled, keeping an eye on Frye.

Lester sat the hawk on the back of a kitchen chair while he hung his hat, coat, and gun belt on hooks by the back door. He didn't bother smoothing the shock of white hair that sprang every which way when he took off the Russian hat. Along with his bulging eyes, it gave him the look of a demented intellectual. Frye had seen his share of those in Stockholm.

He'd never been inside Lester's house before. It was surprisingly clean and neat, except for the books. The whole house was full of them, bookshelves everywhere and half-read books tented on every flat surface. Lester puttered around the kitchen making coffee, talking the whole time about Harris hawks like the one staring at Frye from across the table.

"Unlike me, they're very social animals," Lester was saying. "Not nearly as grumpy as a red tail. This one's a sweetheart." It was a largish hawk, mostly brown, not as colorful as a red tail but just as regal. The bird's head pivoted, watching Lester as he put coffee on the table and pulled out a chair to sit.

"So tell me, Dickie," he said, wiggling long fingers at the Fletcher Carlyle suit, "how did this happen?"

Frye didn't hesitate for a second. Maybe it was because Lester shared his reputation for being a fruitcake, or maybe it was only because there was a large bird sitting at the table with them and it appeared to be listening. Whatever the reason, he trusted the man, so he told him the whole truth—including the chicken. Frye talked for an hour while Lester listened, enchanted. He asked a question occasionally, but only for clarity; there was never the slightest hint of disbelief. In the end, his face was lit with wonder and admiration.

"Dickie, I'd give anything for a chance to sit down and have a long talk with this chicken of yours. Can you imagine what he could tell me about hawks?"

"I know. And I'd give anything to sit in on the conversation, but it ain't going to happen. Crito said if I ever told anybody about him he'd take off, and I think he meant it. I can't take the chance."

"Ah, well. Who'd believe it anyway? It's all right. Just hearing the story is enough for me—just knowing such things are possible. You know," he said, running a hand through that unruly mop of white hair, "I've read something like this before, somewhere. Something about a tribal lord in Mesopotamia, I think, whose chief advisor was an ibis. Birds have always loomed large in mythology, especially in Middle Eastern lore."

Frye stared at him for a second. "So you don't think I'm crazy?"

Lester cackled. "Of *course* you're crazy, Dickie! So was Galileo. You believe in something entirely outside other people's dogma— why, that's the *definition* of crazy. Listen, it's a verifiable fact that eleven percent of the known planets support intelligent life. *Eleven percent!* And even in the face of all those billions of suns out there, anybody who suggests we're not alone in the universe is crazy. Crazy just means you don't run with the herd."

Frye nodded thoughtfully. "We ought to start a club. But listen, I need to get back, and I never got around to my reason for coming up here in the first place."

"I'm listening. You want more coffee?"

"No thanks. I was wondering if maybe you could tell me anything about what happened with my ex-wife, Raye Anne. I saw her driving a handicap van."

Sadness came over Lester's face as he cradled his empty coffee cup on the table.

"She married Bonniface a few months after you disappeared. Of course, being Bonniface, he could never be content with just one woman. He didn't waste any time engaging in a dalliance."

"Where'd you hear that? I mean, you never talk to anybody."

Lester blushed a little. "They replaced you with a new letter carrier named Doris. I don't mind talking to *her*, if you know what I mean." The smile was almost bashful, but there was a lascivious gleam in his eye. "So anyway, Bonniface first had an affair with Shelly, a ditzy blonde who worked for him at the car dealership. Naturally, being the arrogant putz that he is, he forgot that he lived in a small town, so it wasn't long before Raye Anne found out and put a stop to it. Next thing you know, he's slipping around with Barry Coulter's wife. *Everybody* knows about that one because it made the newspaper when Barry caught them together and shot him."

Frye sat up straight, braced his forearms on the table. "Talbot Bonniface? Dead?"

Lester shook his head. "No, worse. Barry put two bullets in his back before he could make it to his car. One of them severed his spine and paralyzed him from the chest down."

"That's horrible." It was a low groan, from the heart. Though he may have even fantasized about it a time or two himself, it really was a shock for Frye to imagine Buttface paralyzed. Talbot Bonniface, the athlete. The peacock.

"Yeah, it was hard on everybody. He was kind of a god around here. Raye Anne wasn't the same after that. She coddled Bonniface, went with him to Shepherd and stayed by him round the clock until he got out. They bought that specially equipped van, and now she drives him and his wheelchair anywhere he wants to go. Dotes on him like a baby."

"Well, she's changed, then. I reckon it took something like that to make a whole human being out of her."

"Maybe so. Doris says it's almost as though Raye Anne had been waiting for this all her life, like all she wanted was someone to take care of. Someone worse off than her."

———

On his way out of town Frye went by the old garage and poked around. Somebody had stripped the copper pipes from the plumbing and hauled away the '57 Chevy, the computer, most of the tools, and the air conditioner, but the thieves were polite enough to roll the bay door back down. Shut up tight all this time, the place was full of spider webs, rat turds, and the heavy, musty smell of old dirt and mildew. The tires had gone flat on the Mazda, still sitting in the shadows under a thick blanket of dust. Rats had shredded the mattress from his old cot and scattered it all over the floor. Everything had fallen into shadows and cobwebs. Even half empty, the place seemed so much smaller now.

Leaving Squalor, somehow he didn't see the same things he had seen on the drive up. There was the tiny, white cinder-block Primitive Baptist Church, badly in need of paint, a pitiful little graveyard on the rise next to it with chipped headstones tilting, mossy and forgotten. And there was the stand of winter-bare shade trees where Sam and Ida Holt's house used to be—the house where they raised nine kids and upwards of sixty crops of cotton and corn. After their children scattered to the wind, Sam went to his reward, and Ida ended up in a nursing home where she didn't even know her own young'uns anymore. In no time at all the empty old farmhouse fell into ruin, and then delinquents burned the ruins for fun. All that remained was a tall brick chimney, a lonely sentinel between the oaks. Sam's well-tended fields had all gone to seed, the weeds even reclaiming the driveway, choking out Ida's beds of day lilies and irises. Life had a way of sweeping out a man's tracks as soon as he was gone.

Chapter 24

> "Only a fool enters the fray without fear, and such are cannon fodder. A hero is that rare soul who keeps his wits *despite* his terrors."
>
> —Uriah Rilke
> *The Forge*, Fletcher Carlyle

"So you really went back home. How did you feel afterwards?" Kohl asked.

Frye sighed, shook his head. "Seems like if you stay gone long enough, everything changes. I was back in Atlanta doing a radio interview by the time I figured out it wasn't Squalor that changed, it was me. I just didn't want the same things anymore. After what Lester told me I didn't even want Raye Anne anymore, but I didn't want to kill her no more, either. The thought of revenge just made me tired. I couldn't even dredge up spite for Buttface.

"So I quit playing the part. I mean, what was the point? I done got to where I hated Fletcher Carlyle anyway. The way he dressed, the way he talked, the way he wrote, the way he combed his hair—not one shred of it was me. Carlyle had way more in common with Talbot Bonniface than with me, so I up and quit. Fletcher Carlyle was still alive, but only in Crito's computer. He was still writing every day and firing off emails, but I was done with being his face."

Kohl straightened up, leaned forward. "Tell me about that time. After you became a recluse. What was that like?"

"I didn't do anything at first. The phone rang day and night after the Nobel, but I never answered it. I didn't even listen to the messages. They were all the same anyway—the top dogs at Huntsman-Wisner calling to make sure I was okay and asking if I needed anything, the publicist wanting to know when I was gonna end my 'sabbatical,' a reporter after a quote for a feature story, Micah checking up on me, all worried. I never returned any of the calls."

"That must have caused a few problems."

"Not as much as you'd think. You got to remember, all I ever did was public appearances. I told Micah from day one I wasn't fooling with all that online crap, so he and a couple interns at Huntsman-Wisner set up the website, played around on Facebook, wrote a blog twice a week, and kept up the chit-chat on Twitter. I never did any of that stuff anyway, so, far as fans were concerned, nothing changed. I quit taking phone calls, but by then most people just sent emails because Crito would answer those. Everybody figured the great Fletcher Carlyle was busy writing and didn't want to be bothered."

"No one came to visit you?"

"No. Micah came up once, but I saw him through the peephole and tiptoed away. After that I called security and told them not to let anybody else up. Ever."

"What about your neighbors in the building? Did you never speak to them?"

"Nah, I didn't have a whole lot to do with them. Folks at the Dakota were generally pretty bright. I couldn't risk casual conversations with them because I would've slipped up, sure as the world. I could fool an interviewer, but I never figured I could fool a neighbor for very long, so I steered clear of them."

"You must have gotten a lot of mail."

"Sacks full. All the way through Christmas there was bags of it, every day—fan mail, Christmas cards, gifts, letters from readers wanting to know when the next book would come out. For a while I read some of it, sitting on my white sofa in front of the wounded cormorant, growing a beard and swilling beer in my bathrobe. I opened the gifts, ate the chocolate and some of the fruitcake, but I never answered any letters, and in the end I fed it to the fireplace. All of it. After the New Year passed and the gift boxes petered out, I stopped opening mail and just kept a fire going.

"I drank my way through Christmas. Didn't go nowhere. Winter passed with the curtains drawn. I watched a lot of football, drank a lot of beer, gained weight, got a little more bored and a little more stir-crazy every day. After the Super Bowl even football abandoned me, and the baseball season was still two months away. Television's a wasteland. There were stock-car races to watch on weekends, but mostly I watched movies. I guess I've seen just about every movie ever made. The *Times* came every day, and I'd spend the afternoon fighting the crossword puzzle. Never finished one, though—the crossword in the *Times* is a bear.

"Sometimes I'd stand at the window for hours watching the park across the street. I liked when it snowed. The whole world slowed down, and everything got soft and quiet. I swear, Doc, I thought I was losing my mind."

Kohl knew depression was not an uncommon occurrence for someone who'd faced such an upheaval of life, and alcohol only exacerbated the problem. Particularly if he was pent up alone and isolated during the holiday season, after a man reached the pinnacle of his professional career it was quite common to succumb to feelings of disillusionment and depression. Nearly every one of his more affluent patients described it, sooner or later, with some form of the question, *Is this all there is?*

"It strikes me that you could have derived tremendous benefit from a good therapist during this time. Did you consider therapy?"

"No. I didn't go out."

"Well, given your name and resources, I'm confident Manhattan has a number of qualified psychiatrists willing to make house calls. If nothing else, they could have prescribed drugs. There are some very effective antidepressants out there."

"At the time I didn't know I was depressed."

"Did you get any physical exercise? That might have helped."

"No. The only exercise I got was looking after the chicken."

"You were no longer involved in the writing?"

"No. I didn't even *read* what he wrote anymore. After I quit doing interviews, I didn't see any point in keeping up with it. I done some reading, but not his books, and not the ones he wanted me to read. I didn't listen to no stinking opera, either."

"What did Crito have to say about all this? Surely he must have protested."

Frye's eyes narrowed. "No, now that I think about it, he didn't say much when I quit. I figured he thought I was just taking a break, that I'd get bored and go back to being Fletcher Carlyle sooner or later."

"But you had no intention of doing so."

"No."

Frye's demeanor had changed. He got up and paced, wringing his hands, then became conscious of them, stuck them in his pockets and sat down again, staring blankly. Clearly there was something he wasn't saying.

"What's wrong?" Kohl asked.

There was a new and profound worry in Frye's eyes, as if the axis of his world had shifted.

"*He knew.*" It was a mere whisper. "Crito knew everything. The man who lived inside that bird had the wisdom of the ages, Doc. It all looks different now, from a distance, now that he ain't here—now that I ain't having to wait on him hand and foot. I just didn't think it through at the time. He knew exactly what he was doing, didn't he? If he didn't get mad when I quit being Fletcher Carlyle, there can't be but one reason. *He knew it would happen.* So what was he thinking? It all comes back to *why*. Was he playing me?"

"Well, what do *you* think?"

"I don't know, Doc. It just don't make any sense."

"So tell me what happened next."

"I started spending a lot of time online, using the laptop. I had bought it for trips, mostly. I backed up all of Crito's files on it and hauled it around with me so if an editor or publicist needed something when I was out on the coast I'd have it, but it was also the only way I could talk to Crito—with email. Sometimes I'd link up with him and chat in real time, but either way the laptop was our only way of keeping in touch when I was on the road. If I got in a tight spot I could ask him questions. At home, I kept the laptop on the coffee table and he'd use it like a servant's bell. When he wanted something he'd send me an email from the other room and the laptop would *pling*.

"Anyway, I got hooked on the Internet. At first I just bought stuff. You can order anything and have it delivered right to your door. I bought books, movies, iPods, and more music than I could listen to in a lifetime. I ordered the biggest, newest, high-def TV on the market and hooked it up to the latest, greatest high-end surround sound. But all that stuff gets old, and after a while I found myself sitting there bored to death in a prison cell with a bunch of expensive toys. In the end a house is a house, no matter how fancy it is. If you're warm and dry at night, everything else is gravy. And if you can't *leave* your house, it's a prison. Life was better in the old days, back when I was living in Squalor and writing stories for fun. It finally occurred to me to look and see if they were still around."

"They who?"

"Section Eight—the little online forum where I used to post stories, 'bout a thousand years ago. Turns out they were still there, and my old password still worked. I saw some familiar names on the message board, so I logged on and posted a message as RaggedyRichard. I got nine replies. The old gang hadn't forgot me. They were glad to see my pixels again, wanted to know where I'd been, why I disappeared and what I been up to. I told them I had some personal problems, quit my job and ended up working in New York, all of which was more or less true. They wanted to know if I'd had any luck with my writing, and I said no. Not a lie, exactly, but the truth wouldn't do."

"That sounds like at least a fair remedy for your isolation," Kohl said. "It must have been a great relief to find there was still a place where you could share a sense of community with old friends."

"Yeah, they saved my life. There was no place else I could be myself. In Section Eight, I was just RaggedyRichard."

"So, did you start writing again?"

"Well, yeah, but at first it was just short stuff, stories about the old boys I grew up with—me and my cousin stealing Johnny Bunner's clothes while he was skinny-dipping with his girlfriend, and what he looked like walking home wearing her slip, and how amazing it was that he could still clear a cattle fence in that thing when her old man got after him with a 12-gauge full of rock salt. That kind of stuff."

There was bone-deep conviction in the warm Southern rhythm of Richard Frye's words.

"You're right," Kohl said. "Those don't sound like Carlyle stories."

"No. They're one hundred percent Frye."

Kohl noted the body language. Just talking about writing had been enough to relax Frye. His eyes were calm. His hands rested on the arms of the chair, unmoving.

"How did it feel to be writing again?"

Frye closed his eyes, smiled. "Like home. Like life before Fletcher Carlyle. Like I was me again."

The first time RaggedyRichard posted a new story in Section Eight, he checked the message board every fifteen minutes until finally, two days later, BikerBabe commented on it. He remembered her from the old days, a middle-aged wannabe romance writer with a penchant for heavy sex scenes.

Remarkable, she wrote. *Whatever you've been doing since you were here last time, keep it up. This is way better than anything you wrote before.*

Over the next few days he stayed glued to the message board as a flood of comments came in.

RoundMan, an aspiring playwright with an exuberant sense of humor, wrote, *The dialogue pops, the descriptive prose is spot-on, and I can hear your characters breathing. Quit your day job.*

JerseyGirl wrote, *Outrageously funny and poignant. I didn't know whether to laugh or cry.*

Breathtakingly beautiful, from OldRed, an aging member of Section Eight who wrote nostalgia intermittently. *A keeper, for sure. I knew these guys. Please tell me you're sending this out. Definitely publishable material.*

Most of these people had been contributing to the forum for years without ever making a serious effort to sell anything. They had no real ambitions for their writing; they wrote and uploaded and critiqued each other's stories as a hobby, and found in the forum a safe community where they could have someone read their stuff without fear of getting flamed. Feedback was reliably gentle, never more acerbic than a few kindly pointers, nudges in the right direction. But for Richard Frye, who in his isolation craved most of all a kind word from a friend, they were a godsend.

Frye poured himself into his stories. With no obligations and no place else to be, he worked day and night, writing, writing, writing. He carried the laptop with him when he went to the bathroom, ate his meals with it on the table in front of him, fell asleep at night with it glowing on his lap. When he finished a piece, he'd park it and work on the next one, then return to the first draft of the other one days later, when it was sufficiently cold, and sharpen it, strengthening verbs and eliminating adverbs, animating his descriptive prose and smoothing the syntax, cutting and slashing mercilessly, rewriting whole stories when he discovered at the end what he had really meant to say from the beginning. Before he would upload a piece to the forum, he polished it to a high shine.

He did it for the praise, and he knew it. He'd found a home, a place where he was appreciated, and he couldn't get enough. And then one afternoon, after two months of prodigious output, OldRed left him a message on the forum that shook him awake and changed his thinking.

Good grief, man, what are you doing here? Your stories are as good as anything I've ever read. Why are you not putting the time and effort into a novel? You could be published easily. Tell me the truth—are these pieces all part of something larger? Please tell me you're writing a book.

Richard Frye blinked when he read that. He was propped up in bed at the time, in the dark, the screen lighting his face. Closing the laptop, he put it on the nightstand, punched his pillow and pulled up the covers, but Red's question wouldn't let him sleep.

After an hour of tossing and turning he sat up, opened the laptop, and searched his hard drive for a file named *My Book*. But the search returned no results; the manuscript was not there. Setting it aside, he got up, went to the Batcave, and flipped on the light.

The chicken was asleep, telescoped into himself, hunkered down on his perch. As a rule, Frye never disturbed Crito while he was sleeping, but this would not wait.

"Hey!"

Crito's black head rose from his chest and his eyes blinked.

"Where's my book?"

The little head tilted, questioning.

"The manuscript I started, back home. Do we still have it someplace?"

The chicken shook himself. His feathers puffed out, then slowly relaxed into their normal smooth contour. Black legs emerged from under his white belly, and he stretched himself upward, wings and neck. Leaping, half flying down from his perch, he trotted up the ramp to the desk and tapped the keyboard. In less than a minute he had located the file and sent the manuscript through the ether to the laptop.

Done. It's about time.

When Frye went back to his bed the file was waiting for him on the screen, but the first thing he did was post a reply to OldRed on the message board.

Yep, you're just too sharp, Red. You guessed it—I'm working on a novel.

When the sun came up that morning and Crito started scratching around in the Batcave, Frye was almost done reading through the half-finished novel he'd begun so long ago in his garage. His eyes were red and heavy as he leaned over and laid the laptop on his nightstand for the second time. Pulling the covers over his head to shut out the dawn, Richard Frye smiled to himself as he drifted off.

His novel was a mess.

And he was elated. He was beside himself, and the thing that lit him up was simply that he could actually *see* that the manuscript was a mess. After years of looking over the shoulder of a master, by some alchemy or osmosis he now understood *why* it was a mess, and he knew how to fix it.

It was dark when he awoke. For the first time in months, he had slept soundly for twelve hours straight.

Chapter 25

> The goal of politics is, and ever has been, to peaceably resolve the tension between one man's desire for liberty and another's need for security. Neither is inherently evil. Balance is the goal.
> —*Daughters of the Nephilim*, Fletcher Carlyle

Colin Fenn kept a foosball table in his office because he specialized in adolescent boys, and he had learned from experience that a lot of them could not think unless they were moving. Some never loosened up at all until they found something for their hands and eyes to do. He'd grown up playing foosball so he was already good at it, and he got enough practice against his young clients to keep his reflexes razor sharp. Anton Kohl never had a chance, but he did his inept best whenever Colin challenged him. Standing opposite Colin, he pushed and pulled and twisted frantically at the handles, but Colin always dominated.

"Well, are you going to call her?" Colin asked.

"What is this, high school?"

"Come on, man, you just spent the last half hour talking about her, all about this dreamlike meeting in a hospital waiting room and how you passed out when you learned Emma wasn't indestructible. Now you're going to pretend it's not important?"

Kohl shuddered. "How can I call her? What would I say?"

Colin froze, leaning on the handles. An eyebrow went up. "Anton, you're a licensed psychologist. You're asking me what you should say to someone who's sick?"

"She could be dying. There's a difference. And it's *Emma*."

"All the more reason. You've been in love with the woman for most of your life. When were you planning on telling her, at the funeral?"

"I wasn't planning on telling her at all, actually. What would it change? What good would it do?"

Colin straightened, and for a moment his demeanor was deadly serious, a relatively rare event.

"It would make someone you care about considerably less alone, for one thing—at a time when she doesn't need to be alone. Don't take this the wrong way, Anton, because I honestly mean no disrespect, but sometimes there's nothing for you to do but suck it up, brass it out. Quake in your boots if you have to, but *be there*."

Kohl sighed. Easier said than done. "I'll think about it."

Colin dropped the little ball in the center of the table and grabbed the handles. He'd never been one to linger on a subject. "So, how was the *rest* of your day off campus with Carlyle?"

"I've never met anyone quite like him." Anton flicked his wrist, half missed the hard little soccer ball and watched it trickle down the table. "A day away from this place definitely did him some good, but in my opinion he's already recovered. He's got it together—runs three miles a day, eats like a lumberjack, gets along with everybody he meets. Apart from wanting out of here, Richard Frye is, to borrow his own phrase, 'happier than a buzzard after a flood.' If it weren't for his delusions I'd be asking *him* for advice."

"You know as well as I do, a happy fruitcake is still a fruitcake," Colin said, deftly stopping the ball, passing it to one of his forwards and smoking it past Anton's defense for another goal. "If he still buys into his delusions and operates from an alternate reality, then he's not well. He's the patient, you're the doctor."

Anton dropped the ball in the center of the table and gripped the handles for another round.

"Sometimes I wonder. I think he could teach me a thing or two. What would my life be like if I had *half* his courage?"

"Confucius say 'courage grow only from fear,'" Colin said, waving a flat hand as if he were bestowing a blessing. While he was doing this, his other hand scored another goal without him even looking. Then he leaned his palms on the edge of the table and turned serious again.

"Look, Anton, it's the truth. Your anxiety demands that you spend every waking minute backing the world down with a whip and a chair. It takes more courage for you to get up and come to work every day than it did for Carlyle to fly to Stockholm and make a speech, because he just doesn't have your fear. It isn't in him. Your problem is not a lack of courage but a superabundance of angst—that's why the drugs help. I mean, think about it. When Carlyle finally ran into something he was actually afraid of, he threw up all over Dennis Sinclair, right?"

"Maybe so." Kohl dropped the ball back onto the table and flailed at it in an attempt to score a goal while Colin wasn't looking. He missed. "But the man I spent the day with yesterday was remarkably brave. And by the way, he doesn't want to be called Carlyle anymore. He prefers Richard Frye. Oh, and we got the report from radiology at Southampton this morning. The MRI was negative. No lesion in Broca's area."

"And the good Dr. Fenn magnanimously refrains from saying, 'I told you so.'"

"I still can't justify the disparity between the man and his writing, Colin. Most of the time this fairy tale about a possessed chicken makes more sense than the reality in front of me."

"I'll say it again. There's nothing in his history that can't be explained by multiple personalities, Anton."

"Well, if that's the case, I've only met one of them. I don't see Fletcher Carlyle anywhere. Once in a while Frye *plays* Fletcher Carlyle, but he doesn't become him. The man sitting there talking to me is Richard Frye, and he knows exactly who he is."

Colin shrugged, dancing the ball back and forth between two rows of little wooden men, playing keep-away. "So rattle his cage. Find a way to shock him out of his equilibrium. Have you considered taking him back to the scene of the crime?"

Kohl blinked, looked up. He saw Colin's shoulders flinch and heard the little wooden ball smack into the goal.

"Why didn't I think of that?"

"Probably because you're not as smart as I am."

And possibly because the idea of an all-day trip into the city terrified him—two and a half hours driving down and two and a half back, with the insanity of Manhattan traffic sandwiched in between.

"Seriously, Colin, I should have thought of it a long time ago. A trip back to that apartment, under the watchful eye and stabilizing influence of his psychologist might force him to confront his delusions."

Late that afternoon, while Anton Kohl was bracing himself for the drive home, Marlene came in and laid a sticky note on his desk with the name Emma Lansing written across the top in Marlene's precise handwriting. Underneath that, a phone number.

"It wasn't hard to find," Marlene said.

Kohl was still uneasy about calling Emma, but at this point in his day he welcomed the distraction. He picked up the phone and dialed.

When she didn't answer, he was torn between dismay and relief. His watch said eight minutes to five. He would call back in precisely two hours and eight minutes.

After dinner that evening he settled into a comfortable chair with a glass of fine French cabernet—one glass, always, for his cholesterol. With two fingers he fished the sticky note from his pocket and stared at it. The clock on the mantel said three minutes before seven.

"Better finish the wine first," he mumbled, and laid her number on the table. But a minute later he caught himself rehearsing responses to what he imagined she would say—an internal dialogue he knew would spin out of control—and he realized he had to go ahead and dial the number before his anxiety made it impossible.

"I'm so glad you called," she said. "I was afraid I wouldn't hear from you again."

They made small talk for a while, catching up, but through it all he heard loneliness in her voice, something he'd never noticed before. Not what he expected from Emma.

"You sound a little down," he said. "What can I do for you?"

"Oh, I'm all right. I've just been alone in this house too long. I swear the walls inch closer when I'm not looking."

"Listen, why don't we take a day and go somewhere? A little fresh air and sunshine might do you good. We can have a picnic, just you and me." It sounded innocent enough when he suggested it, but it came back to bite him.

"We can go to the beach! Nobody's there yet—the crowds won't come for another three weeks. It may be a bit cold, but we'll have it all to ourselves!"

He didn't answer right away. "Emma, you know I—"

"I know, Anton. I haven't forgotten, really I haven't. But it's all right. I don't care if we don't go near the water. I just have to be there, to hear the surf and smell the air. There's just something about that infinite horizon."

He didn't answer at all this time. The infinite horizon was part of the problem.

"Seriously, it'll be fine, you'll see. I really, really need to recharge my batteries. Just this once, for me?"

"All right." Sigh. "This once." He wanted to accommodate her, but his palms were already sweating.

Chapter 26

> There are no new stories, only old ones seen through new eyes.
> —*Of an Angry God*, Fletcher Carlyle

Frye was practically bouncing when he came in for his next session. Dirt stains covered the knees of his jeans, his fingernails were black, and there was a new light in his eyes.

"I went for a run at dawn, then spent the rest of the morning helping Manolo plant new shrubs around the pine grove at the south end of the facility. I love this time of year, all sunshine and new green everywhere, a little snap in the air—it's invigorating."

Kohl smiled with him. "I'm glad to see you're feeling chipper. It seems to have done you a great deal of good, getting out and about. Oh, and by the way, you left your dirty clothes at my place. I had them cleaned, but I forgot to bring them with me today. I'll get them back to you in the next couple days."

"*Had* them cleaned? You're telling me you sent jeans and a T-shirt to the cleaners? I hope they didn't press my jeans—it's gonna take a few more years in the nuthouse before I'll wear jeans with a crease in 'em. So, what do we talk about today?"

It was time. His patient had grown strong—strong enough, perhaps, to face himself. Kohl wanted, finally, to get to the heart of the matter: it was time for Richard Frye and Fletcher Carlyle to confront each other at last.

"Richard, I feel I've come to understand you fairly well, and the only thing that still baffles me is the violence. The Richard Frye I've come to know is a decent, quiet, considerate human being." Kohl tapped his pen against his pad, gathering his thoughts. "So, what happened? We need to talk about what prompted the manic episode that brought you to us in the first place."

"It's complicated," Frye said quietly, picking at his dirty fingernails. "I still don't really understand it myself."

Kohl made himself comfortable in his chair, knowing by now that Frye would carry the conversation.

"It was because of the book," Frye said. "My book. I hadn't looked at that thing in five years. The manuscript had got cold enough so that I could read the words like they were somebody else's, and I saw it all in a whole new light. It just read clumsy. I mean, that stuff jumped out at me now, you know? There were lapses in point of view that I never noticed before, whole passages full of passive voice, watery adjectives, weak verbs, characters doing stuff without conviction or motivation.

"I guess the *main* thing is that five years of looking over Crito's shoulder taught me to think different, to stand back from the work and think bigger and broader. Life its ownself had taught me a whole lot about what I believe, what I really want to say, so when I read the manuscript this time I finally saw what was wrong with it. Thing is, it was a complaint, pure and simple, about my own sad little life. It was self-conscious and sniveling, just a way to blame somebody else for everything bad that ever happened to me."

"What was it about? Can you give me a synopsis?"

"It was about an old man named Isaac and his two sons. The older one joins the army and goes away to fight in the Middle East. He's a good kid, a serious kid—a patriot fighting for his country. The younger son stays behind and works in Isaac's contracting business, mainly because he's a hustler. He sees all kinds of ways to make money if he can just get around his daddy's ethics, so he sucks up to Isaac and takes over the reins when the old man gets sick. The younger son triples the business while the old man gets sicker, and before Isaac dies the kid talks him into signing over controlling interest in the company. When the older son comes home for the funeral, he finds out that not only has his kid brother gotten rich pillaging the family business, but his childhood sweetheart is in love with his just-rich kid brother and they're getting married. The righteous rage of that older brother was the meat of the story. It's probably a good thing I quit working on it halfway through."

"What you're saying is you think the novel was autobiographical on some level, but you had never realized this before."

"Not exactly autobiographical, but after five years of hanging around Crito I understood a lot more about where stories come from. It's so obvious I can't believe I missed it. I'm pretty sure that book was based on a story in the Bible that bugged me all my life. Drove me nuts. Every time I thought about it, it stuck in my craw. You heard of Jacob and Esau, right?"

"Yes, I know the story." And then it hit Kohl. "Ahhh, I see! Two sons, and the father's name was Isaac."

"There you go. No doubt, it's that Baptist upbringing again."

"Well, maybe the ancient stories stand the test of time because there's truth in them."

"Yeah, but sometimes you have to dig deep. In the Old Testament story, Jacob cheats Esau out of his birthright for a bowl of soup and then scams their blind old father out of his blessing while Esau's at work. The thing that always drove me nuts when I was a kid is that God picked Jacob to be the patriarch of a nation. Jacob the impostor, Jacob the liar, Jacob the con man. It just seemed like God favored the wrong people. So when I started working on a book in my garage, I aimed to turn that story around and fix it. If I'm God, I'm going to know better than to smile on an impostor."

"But later you began to see this as a mistake?"

"I finally saw the hypocrisy in it. See, in the five years since I started that manuscript, I *became* Jacob, the successful impostor. For the first time I saw straight through to the heart of my own book. Not only was it badly written; it was a small-minded, vindictive, self-righteous whimper. In that sense, I reckon it was autobiographical."

Kohl nodded slowly. Frye was analyzing himself, and doing a passable job of it.

"That kind of self-examination can be very productive. But a great deal depends on what you did next."

Frye's eyes were steady. "I rewrote it."

———

Richard Frye threw himself into his work with singular focus and total abandon. He worked on the laptop, sitting on the white couch, leaving Crito alone in the Batcave to do whatever he was doing.

His first order of business was research. If he owned a Bible he didn't know where it was, so he went online and Googled Jacob and

Esau. There had to be more to it than what he'd understood as a child.

He found reams of information, hundreds of articles from scholars and thinkers and theologians and skeptics, liberals and conservatives, true believers and peddlers of dogma, both Jewish and Christian. He read for hours. Tablets and pens gathered on the glossy white marble in front of him, torn pages and handwritten notes piling up and drifting unnoticed to the floor. At four in the morning he yawned and stretched, closed the laptop, and collapsed on the couch. Three hours later the morning sun peeked through the curtains and woke him up, a sliver of light falling precisely on the wounded cormorant.

He sat up, rubbed his eyes, opened a fresh document on the laptop, and typed a new title across the top.

Sons of Isaac.

This time he would get it right. The problem with his book was that he'd been writing about the wrong brother.

Lost in a world of his own creation, he'd been typing steadily for two hours when a movement caught his eye. Crito loped over to the marble table that now served as Frye's desk and hopped up next to the wounded cormorant, setting off a little landslide of loose papers.

Frye straightened up and arched his back, stretching while Crito crowded in over the keyboard. The chicken scrolled through what Frye had written, reading quickly. When he finished, his little black head jerked around and gave Frye a long stare. He pecked a few keys, then spread his wings, flapped himself backward off the table, scattering more notes, and trotted back to the Batcave. There was one word typed at the bottom of the page.

Yes.

The next six months flew by. Frye kept the curtains drawn and worked long hours, paying little attention to the time, losing track of what day it was. He still didn't go out, ordering meals at odd hours from the dining hall downstairs. Covered silver trays came directly up to his kitchen through a dumbwaiter, and the dirty dishes went back the same way. He went on the wagon, drinking only water and coffee, sleeping only when he could no longer stay awake. Whatever the hour when he awoke, he did push-ups and sit-ups to get the blood flowing to his brain, and put on more coffee. Sometimes when he was sitting at the computer thinking, he would pick up the cormorant and do curls with it just to keep his arms working. He was a man obsessed. For the first time in his life, he knew exactly what he wanted to say, and how to say it. Nothing else mattered.

Crito paid close attention. When Frye left the room for a bathroom or kitchen break, half the time he'd come back to find the chicken hunched over the laptop, reading. Occasionally he'd leave a comment, a critical remark, but this time Frye knew how to handle it. After years of working with Crito, Frye now understood his complaints and knew what to do about them. Only once did the chicken's critique cause a major argument. It happened when Frye was nearing the end of the manuscript, right after he had written the confrontation scene, where the brothers finally get down to business.

It is too big. Too much. Over the top.

"But it's the climax of the book. It's *got* to be big."

Perhaps, but he does not have to die. He MUST not die. Your premise—the entire manuscript up to here—points to atonement and reconciliation. The confrontation looms large, but the man cannot die. When this happens, the story changes, becomes something unintended. The strongest man wins, the man with the biggest weapon. A moron can write that story, and frequently does. You must reach deeper.

They fought for hours. Frye defended his choices fiercely because he felt the death scene, as written, was the most powerful, the most emotionally stirring scene in the book. Crito argued that yes, it was the most powerful scene in the book, but it was still a wrong turn.

Keep to the theme.

In the end, Frye gave in. He made the change, and the last chapter flowed from the climactic scene to a satisfying conclusion with a natural ease that convinced him Crito was right all along.

The minute he finished the manuscript he printed out a paper copy and sat reading through it, whole, while Crito marked up an electronic version. The chicken left a hundred notations scattered over the entire manuscript, but none of them amounted to anything, all dealing with minor technicalities of usage and syntax. Easy fixes. In the white space at the end of the book, he typed one word.

Bravo.

―――――

Kohl paced back and forth on the rug in front of his desk, listening. This was news.

"You mean to tell me you actually finished a book of your own? So *that's* what you were doing while you were out of circulation. That's truly remarkable, Richard!"

Frye nodded. "Yeah. And it was good, too."

"That's *fantastic*. What became of it?"

"Crito bypassed Micah and sent it straight to a publisher. Not Huntsman-Wisner, though. He sent it to a small press in New Jersey that does books with regional flavor. The book was wrong for Huntsman—too Southern—and anyway we didn't want it to cross paths with Fletcher Carlyle's work."

"So this was not to be a Carlyle book?"

"No, I told you, it was nothing like Carlyle. They used my real name."

Kohl stopped pacing, stared. "Wait. You mean they bought it?"

"Well, yeah. I'm pretty sure if a book's good enough for Crito, any acquisitions editor with one eye and half sense is gonna snap it up, but as it turns out I didn't even have to shop it. He had me send it to this one particular editor at Pirkle Press. Apparently Crito knew him—you know, from a previous incarnation. He said the old guy had been looking for this book all his life. I don't know how Crito knew these things, but those were pretty much the same words the editor used when he called me."

Kohl sat down heavily and leaned toward Frye. "You're telling me you *published* a novel—"

"*Sons of Isaac*."

"Under your own name. Richard Frye."

"Uh-huh."

Kohl sat staring at the carpet, clicking his pen, trying to put it all together in his mind.

"But that's extraordinary! I mean, for you to lift yourself out of a deep depression to produce a publishable novel—and in your own name, no less. Good for you!"

"It *felt* good. It felt right." Frye accented the words with a clenched fist. "Trouble is, I was starting all over again. Richard Frye was an unknown, and a little outfit like Pirkle didn't have any muscle in the market, so the book didn't do too well. They depended on the authors to promote themselves, and I couldn't do that because my face belonged to Fletcher Carlyle. But they put it in their catalog, and even without promotion *Sons of Isaac* sold a few thousand copies just by word of mouth. I was beside myself. Finally, I was a man again. More than that, I was a writer."

But this brought them back to the same question that had nagged Kohl from the beginning.

"It seems to me you were doing incredibly well, under the circumstances. I can certainly understand euphoria. In a sense, you had reclaimed control of your life, and yet it still leaves me wondering how you got from that place to this." He spread his hands, and his eyes swept the office. "How do you go from euphoria to murderous rage? What happened?"

Frye smirked. Anger flashed in his eyes, but only for a second. He rubbed a hand over his face and the anger faded into weariness and regret.

"The review," he said quietly. "The review happened."

"A book review?"

"Yeah. In the *New York Times*, no less. I got a call from the Pirkle editor on a Sunday morning, saying I should take a look at the *Times* and call him back. He sounded pretty mad. Unusual for him—he's a sweet old man.

"The Sunday paper was already there, outside my door. I tore it all apart and scattered sections everywhere, looking for the Book section. I remember Crito standing in the doorway of the Batcave, watching me. When I finally found it, sure enough, the lead story was a long piece on *Sons of Isaac*, with a cover shot and everything. I got all excited. I mean, it's unheard of for a first novel from an unknown author with a small press to even get mentioned in the *Times*, right? But it was a blistering review and, unless you happened to be Richard

Frye, outrageously funny. It started out, and I quote, 'If there is a God, if beauty is not gone from the earth, if there remains a shred of literary discrimination in America, Dickie Frye's first novel will be his last.'

"After that it got *really* nasty. It just went on and on, tearing me down brick by brick. The real killer was the last paragraph, where the reviewer blasted me for being 'coy and timid in the one place where a dash of boldness might have salvaged a modicum of dignity. The simpering confrontation between the brothers is anything but climactic, fittingly serving as the dying whimper of this cloyingly sweet nonsense.'

"I read every word of it, praying it was a joke, that it would end with a qualifier and a belated blessing, but it didn't. What it ended with was a byline—'Fletcher Carlyle.'"

"But *you* were Fletcher Carlyle—"

"Only his face. This review came from the *real* Fletcher Carlyle."

"Crito?"

"Now do you understand homicidal rage?" Frye seemed detached, gazing out the window at nothing. "I don't remember a lot after that, just flashes. I remember pulling the butcher knife from the block on the kitchen counter, and I remember him flapping across the Batcave, up into his window, lighting on the little balcony where he used to sit between the junipers sometimes and watch the park. I winged him there, I think, but then he jumped off and flapped his way down to street level. I took off down the stairs and caught up with him on the sidewalk." Frye paused then, his eyes narrowed in thought. "Now that I think about it, that seems kind of odd."

"What does?"

"That I caught up with him. He jumped off the balcony and fell three stories, straight down, flapping his wings the whole way. He was on the sidewalk in seconds. I had to run to the other end of my apartment, down the hall to the staircase, down three flights of stairs, across the courtyard, out the 72nd Street entrance, and then halfway around the building. All Crito had to do was make it across the street into the park and I never would have caught him. But he didn't. He was still on the sidewalk below the balcony when I got there, almost like he was waiting for me."

"I guess you have to ask yourself why the chicken didn't cross the road," Kohl said, a rare attempt at humor that Frye completely ignored.

"I chased him over a line of cars bunched up at the light. We were bouncing off yellow cabs left and right until I finally got ahold of that black foot in the middle of the street, on the hood of a white car. People were yelling, horns blaring. Tell you the truth, I was in such a state I don't even remember killing him—just little bits and pieces like snapshots—feathers flying, the sound of that knife point thumping into the hood, some woman screaming, a camera flashing, cops yelling, and getting body-slammed on the pavement. It all happened kind of fast. All I know is I didn't want to stop. I wanted to kill him some more."

Frye's jaw flexed and his breathing quickened. Even the memory brought murder to his mind.

Kohl shook his head. "I cannot fathom why he would do such a thing. Under those circumstances, perhaps homicidal rage *is* more or less understandable." Once again he'd forgotten himself, so caught up in the story that he became more participant than counselor.

Frye actually smiled at that. "I told you I wasn't crazy."

"We have to go back there," Kohl said, finally recovering his professional train of thought.

"What, to New York?"

"Yes. It's the only way to make sense of things. You have to go back there and walk through all of it. With *me*."

Frye thought for a moment, and a sly smile spread across his face. "All right, if you say so. When do we go?"

"As soon as possible. I have plans tomorrow, but I should be able to clear a day sometime in the next week."

Chapter 27

> "Suffer the slings and arrows? Pah! *Embrace* them, *revel* in them. Spit into the teeth of the gale and thrust laughter like a rapier into the belly of cruel fortune. Wear your scars like jewels!"
> —Uriah Rilke
> *The Forge*, Fletcher Carlyle

Anton Kohl stared into his closet for ten minutes, losing hope. Even the little things could paralyze him these days, like what to wear to a picnic. He didn't own any casual clothes because he never went out casually. There were two pairs of Dockers, both a little too snug from the ten pounds he'd gained in the decade since he'd bought them, and a Yale sweatshirt, even older, with wine stains on it—nothing he would want to be seen wearing. The Nike sneakers were fine, just a bit dusty and brittle.

Then he spotted the little pile of clothes Richard Frye had left behind when he stayed over. He pulled the jeans down from the shelf and tried them on. A perfect fit. He couldn't remember the last time he'd worn a pair of jeans, and he was confident he'd *never* worn anything with a tool pocket on one leg and a hammer loop on the other. They were surprisingly comfortable, and they didn't look half bad on him.

When he showed up at Emma's, she stood back and gave him a long appraisal.

"Wow! Anton, is that *you*?"

He had stopped and bought a rustic Sag Harbor fishing cap at a quaint little tackle shop on the way over. The edges of the long bill were pre-frayed, and there was even a large fish hook stuck in the end of it.

"I didn't know you even owned anything like—oh, wait. I've seen that outfit before." She snapped her fingers, pointed. "That guy, the one in the waiting room at the hospital. He wore jeans just like those, and if I'm not mistaken, the same T-shirt and hoodie. Didn't he?"

Kohl smiled, lifting a huge picnic basket from the kitchen floor. "You're too sharp for me, Emma. Yes, these are his. He spent the night at my place and left his dirty clothes there. I had them cleaned, but then I forgot to take them back to him. How do I look?"

"Well, they fit you. It's just that I've never seen you dressed that way. I like it. I like it a lot. I've always said you needed to loosen up a bit. Who was he, anyway?"

Kohl was bumping out the back door with the picnic basket and a beach bag when she asked him this. He started to say Fletcher Carlyle—she would have been impressed—but by the time he loaded the stuff into his trunk he'd changed his mind. Fletcher Carlyle, at least as far as Richard Frye was concerned, was dead.

"He's a writer," he said, meeting her at the back steps as she locked the door. "From the South. A good man. I expect he has a bright future."

"A writer! Have I heard of him?"

"I doubt it, but anyway I'm really not supposed to tell you his name."

"They called his name in the waiting room, but I can't remember anything these days, so you're safe. He seemed like a decent sort."

"He is. A very decent sort." Kohl reached out to help her down the steps. She seemed so doddery and fragile that he couldn't keep himself from treating her like an old lady.

Emma was dressed the same as she was when he saw her in the hospital waiting room, except that in place of the shawl she wore a heavy cable-knit cardigan so big she seemed lost in it. Her long, pleated skirt was different from the other one, but the same. She'd exchanged the scarf for a floppy white gardening hat, but she wore the same big gawky sunglasses.

"So he's one of your patients?"

"Yes."

"Actually, I already knew that, based on what little of your conversation I overheard in the waiting room. Something about a brain tumor?"

Opening the car door for her, he nodded. "Well, that's privileged information, Emma...but there doesn't appear to be anything wrong with your memory."

While he was fastening his seat belt she launched one more probe. "Well, is he okay?"

He paused for a moment, staring out over the steering wheel, and a wry smile played at his lips. "He's fine. No brain tumor, and psychologically I'm starting to think he may be sounder than I am. Speaking of which, are you absolutely certain we have to go to the beach? You know how I—"

"Yes, on both counts. Yes, we're going to the beach, Anton, and yes, I haven't forgotten how you feel about it. But don't worry. It's too cold for swimming anyway." She lifted the brim of her floppy hat and peered up at the sky through the windshield. Round white clouds hurried overhead, running down the wind. "I have to hear the waves rumble and feel the salt spray. I *need* it, Anton. Seriously. I just hope we don't get blown away."

They took the Montauk Highway east, toward the point, all the way out to where the South Fork narrowed so that from a high place in the road he could see water on both sides. The broad Atlantic fanned out to his right while Napeague Bay encroached from the left, the arc of Gardiners Island lying low in the blue distance. Remarkably, perhaps because Emma was sitting right there in the passenger seat, frail though she was, Kohl's anxiety didn't flare up. So far, there were no bees in his legs.

"Slow down," she said, and he took his foot off the gas. "It's coming up. Turn there." She pointed to an unmarked track off through the dunes on their right.

"I thought we were going out to Montauk." He slowed, switching on his turn signal, though no other car was in sight.

"Well, the beach out on the point is kind of rocky and narrow. I thought you'd like this place better." She did, after all, remember his embarrassment at Montauk years ago. Now she was being careful of *him*. "There's a nice wide white-sand beach here—lots of space between you and the water. And it won't be crowded this time of year."

She was right on both counts. This one stretch of dunes was on the edge of a state park, and isolated, with very few houses around. Anton turned in where she pointed, and followed a driveway between the dunes to a pretty little cottage with its shutters still bolted down for the winter. Between the dunes and drift fences and tall grasses, he could just make out the beach.

He looked to Emma for approval. "Park here?"

"Yes, we have permission, Anton. The owner is an old friend."

He glanced out his window at the sky. When they started out from Emma's house at North Sea, there had been a breeze blowing up from the southeast, but the sun was shining and it seemed pleasant enough, if a little cool. Now there was a broken line of low scud hurrying in from the ocean and the sun came and went, dodging behind clouds. The ocean breeze had strengthened.

"It'll be fine, Anton." Watching him watch the weather, she reached over and put a slender hand lightly on his forearm. A warm calm spread outward from her touch. He remembered this from his youth. It had always been so.

Kicking off her sandals, she left them in the car and walked barefoot over the dunes, her long skirt billowing in the wind.

"Look at us," she said, and then did just that, stopping and gazing with undisguised pity at her own gaunt frame. "We've become our own toys. Remember when we were in high school? Remember the Saturday it rained and we cleaned out our closets for that toy drive? Do you remember that, Anton?"

"Yes, I do." He smiled, reminiscing. "We dragged out your old toy box and it was all scuffed and scratched, the lid missing, the hinges gone off of it, part of a corner chewed off by a puppy. Everything in it was the same way—everything you ever owned was broken, beat up, abused. Naked dolls with arms missing, a Monopoly game without money, an inline skate missing a wheel—"

"Right, right, right. And then we went over to your house and you had this closet full of boxes. Anton, you still had the original boxes from every toy you ever owned, and everything was in its box! It was all brand-new!"

"I played with those things," he said defensively. "But I was brought up to believe it was important to take care of one's belongings, that's all. I think it's a fairly common characteristic among only children."

"But *look at us*, Anton! We've lived our lives the same way we played when we were kids. Here I am, spent, broken, my corners chewed off—but *you*! You're still in the original box, still brand-new."

"Well, if you're chiding me for not engaging in risky, self-destructive behaviors…"

She laughed gently, hugged his arm. "Come on, Anton, you don't engage in *any* behaviors! Eat a peach, for God's sake!" Her hands gripped his forearm, and despite the laughter and the light tone there was a rare urgency in her voice, a gentle nudge to someone who meant something to her.

He gave a defensive shake of the head. "There's nothing irrational about avoiding danger."

"I guess it all depends on what's important to you. I may have gotten the corners chewed off my toy box, but I did love that puppy. I might have busted my skates and skinned my knees, but by God I went down that hill! Ten years ago a bunch of us got caught in a gale sailing east from Madagascar and very nearly died, but I remember the wind on my face, Anton, and the Seychelles are mine to keep. Nothing can take that away from me. Even dying doesn't scare you if you've actually lived."

Her fingernails bit into the flesh of his arm for emphasis as she said these things. That was Emma—bloody, but unbowed. She waited while he spread a blanket on the sand up near the dunes, a good forty yards from the water's edge. Little things like that saddened him. The Emma he remembered would never have stood back and waited for anything; she was always in the middle of it.

She looked up at the roiling sky, one hand pinning her floppy hat to her head, and raised her voice to the clouds.

"'All I ask is a windy day with the white clouds flying, and the flung spray and the blown spume, and the sea-gulls crying.'"

Anton cocked his head, frowning as he took out a chipped plastic serving tray and carefully stood the wine bottle and the crystal goblets on it. "What is that? I've heard it before, haven't I?"

"It's from 'Sea Fever,' a little poem we learned in high school. I can't believe you don't remember—'All I ask is a tall ship and a star to steer her by'?"

"Oh yeah, right. I'd forgotten that."

"I haven't. I remember it word for word. It's always been my mantra."

And then she quoted the last few lines of the poem, looking out to sea with the wind in her skirts while he took out the crusty German rolls she'd always loved, and the Camembert, and poured a very fine wine into her glass. Her voice rang with a hard-won confidence, the mark of a life well used.

"'I must down to the seas again, to the vagrant gypsy life, to the gull's way and the whale's way where the wind's like a whetted knife; and all I ask is a merry yarn from a laughing fellow rover, and quiet sleep and a sweet dream when the long trick is over.'"

Precisely as she finished, as if she had conjured it, the cry of a gull came across the wind and fell perfectly into the silence between the rumble of the breakers. Sitting down beside him, she slid a hand inside Anton's arm and leaned her head against his shoulder, smiling quietly, the warmth of her hand spreading up the underside of his arm, and the two of them, together, stared out over an ocean the color of her eyes.

The poem, her voice, echoed in Anton's ears and fell in step with the thundering surf like the voice of God, a bolt of singular clarity that had lain waiting a hundred years for Emma and for this one perfect moment. *The vagrant gypsy life*. It seemed to Anton Kohl that she even looked like a gypsy, sitting there barefoot, hugging her knees in a painted skirt and a sweater that swallowed her, wearing a hat that would have looked silly on a lesser woman. In that moment, Anton Kohl saw Emma Lansing as he had not seen her since she was new. He saw her spirit whole, in all its excess and all its need, and he loved her completely, without reservation.

Without fear.

He would have died for her in that moment. He would have leaped cheerfully into a sea churning with snakes. He would have given everything he owned—handed over the keys to his house and car and 401(k) with a smile—for one merry yarn he could give to Emma Lansing.

But he didn't know one. He was no laughing fellow rover, and he had not lived a yarn. It was Emma who had been the swashbuckling, reckless, globe-trotting gypsy while Anton hid inside his house with the curtains drawn. It pained him deeply that he had no such gift to give. It was something he simply did not possess.

He hung his head in a small private grief, but then his eyes focused on the carpenter jeans and T-shirt and hooded sweatshirt he was wearing, the clothes of a spinner of yarns. When the thought flashed across his mind, he grabbed onto it. It did not require a decision, because in that moment he had no reservations.

"I will tell you a story," Anton Kohl said softly. "A merry yarn. It's the only one I know. It's privileged information and I could lose my position just for telling it to you, but right now I just don't care." He sighed heavily, and she snuggled tighter against his shoulder.

"I'm listening," she said, and the warmth spread through him.

"Once upon a time," he began, "on a very hot afternoon, on a winding macadam road in the north Georgia hills, there was a truck full of chickens."

———

They spent a golden afternoon on a blanket in the sand, Emma with her skirt tucked under her and that gargantuan sweater pulled close to keep the wind out of her brittle bones, sipping wine, tearing hard rolls into pieces and sharing them, spreading Camembert with a plastic knife. He told the story richly and well, adding his best imitation of the peculiar colloquialisms of Richard Frye, embellishing and polishing the tale at every turn. His only aim was to entertain her, to take her back to the edge of the unknown where she had spent so much of her life. She fell completely into the story, chortling till she got the hiccups over the tale of Root Hollis's dog, gasping in wide-eyed wonder at Crito's version of history, and gripping Anton's knee in despair at the slaughtering of the chicken on Central Park West.

She shook her head in amazement when he was done, her mouth hanging open, an empty wineglass dangling from her fingertips.

"Anton, the whole world is wondering what happened to Fletcher Carlyle—*Fletcher Carlyle!*—and you've been sitting on him the last six weeks? That's incredible! Good Lord, what a story!"

"Um, Emma, you know you can't—"

"Oh no! Of course I wouldn't write about this. I would never do that to you. If the story got out it would mean the end of your career, I understand that. It's just that this is the most incredible thing I've ever heard. I mean, *Fletcher Carlyle*! I've read everything he's written, and I'm telling you the man's a giant. So what do you think is really going on with him? Is he crazy or what?"

Kohl bit his lip, thinking. "Our best guess is dissociative identity disorder. But after spending time with him I just…"

"What?" She read his eyes, and her hand squeezed his knee. "You *believe* him?"

"Well, no, it's just that after spending so many hours listening to him I…well, apart from the sheer absurdity of his claims, I can't find a reason to—"

"But, Anton, there are so many things you could have done, so many ways you could have cross-checked his story. You people don't investigate at all?"

"No, not everybody is an investigative journalist, Emma. But come on, a chicken with human intelligence? It's clearly a delusion. If he believes it, then my job is not to prove or disprove, but only to try to understand *why* he believes it."

She shook her head, laughing. "But what if it's true?"

Then there would be powers in the world beyond human comprehension. Then there really might be demons in dark places, waiting.

"Don't be silly." He tried, unsuccessfully, to hide a touch of petulance.

Laughing, she threw her arms around him and kissed him playfully on the cheek.

"I just love you, Anton."

He wasn't looking at her; he was looking out at an angry sea with the warmth of her arms around him and her laughter ringing in his ears when the words fell out of him.

"I've *always* loved you." He didn't realize he'd said it out loud until it was too late.

She froze there for a moment, her cheek against his. Then her head backed away just a bit, enough to see his expression, and her mouth opened in a little quivering O. He might still have salvaged the situation if he'd thought to laugh, or at least smile, but he didn't, and she saw the naked truth in his eyes. She pulled away from him. A hand fluttered up to her chest.

"*Oh my God,*" she whispered. Her hand rose higher, thin fingers creeping up to her lips.

He looked away, down the beach. In the distance, a middle-aged woman in sweats threw a stick into the surf and sent her black Lab bounding through head-high breakers to fetch it. The wind had stiffened. A red flag pointed straight inland as if it had been starched, its tip buzzing, its fiberglass pole bending and twitching like a fishing rod.

Emma's fingertips touched his shoulder. "How could you not tell me this?"

He turned to face her. She'd taken off the glasses, and those sea-green eyes swallowed him.

"How could you not *know*?"

"How could…? Because I'm an *idiot*, Anton! Because I'm a spoiled, myopic, self-absorbed narcissist. *You!* Of all people, *you*, a psychologist, you didn't know that? Because the sea is bluer in Mykonos, and the wine is sweeter in Tuscany. YOU DIDN'T KNOW THAT?"

She was waving her arms in the air, railing, laughing, crying, and then suddenly she wasn't laughing anymore. Her face screwed up and strangled her words, her eyes spilled, and her arms flailed at him, slapping him about the head and shoulders. But hers was a weak and impotent fury that succeeded only in knocking the hat from her own head. The wind jerked it away and sent it rolling and flipping, hurrying into the waving dune grasses.

Anton shrank from the feeble blows, but he did not raise his arms to shield himself. She didn't last long. Her hands stopped hitting him shortly and fell away, their meager strength spent. Her fingers clutched at him and she pulled herself close, burying her face in his shoulder.

"How could you not tell me this? Why did you wait until I'm all used up and there's nothing left of me?"

What could he say?

How could he answer?

I thought you knew? That would be a lie, or at best a half-truth. The whole truth was that he hadn't the courage to tell her when he first had the chance, back in high school, and he'd been afraid ever since. He feared what she might say, what she might think, what she might do. As always, there were too many variables, and behind each and every one of them a worst-case scenario. Fear of failure nearly always became a self-fulfilling prophecy. There was only one thing he could say now, and it was not enough.

"I'm sorry."

He put an arm around her, felt her shoulders shake.

Out on the sea the wind tore the tops from the waves. Little mists of blown sand hurried over the dunes, running before the wind. Bits of sand and a fine salt spray stung his face. Tall breakers thundered against the beach, one after another, and spent their last bit of energy crawling up the sand to die.

"You're sorry," she said, pulling away, bracing her hands against his chest and giving him a little shove. He toppled softly, landing on his elbows. She palmed away tears and raised her face against the wind, red-rimmed eyes staring out to sea.

"The Azores are out there somewhere," she said, her chin nodding toward the gray horizon, and then pushed herself to her feet. The clouds had merged and driven out the sun. Now a solid bank of gray flannel scudded inland from the sea on a gusty wind that tore her sweater open and dropped it to her elbows, but she didn't seem to notice. Her silk blouse molded itself against her so that he could see her ribs. Her long skirt painted itself against hipbones and knees, fluttering and snapping behind her. She stepped off the blanket and stood facing the sea, holding her head with both hands and letting the wind beat against her. The wind, howling now, nipped at the edge of the red blanket, then slipped underneath it and lifted a large corner of it back on itself. Emma's picnic basket listed like a sinking ship and then capsized, knocking over the wine bottle and tipping the glasses.

Anton lunged for the basket, panic rising. He almost had it, but then Emma attacked from behind.

"LEAVE IT!" she shrieked. She grabbed the long basket by the handle and hurled it aloft. The wind caught it and separated it from the cloth she'd wrapped the rolls in, lifting basket and cloth in a high dance over the dunes, strewing rolls like a comet trail.

"Let it *go*, Anton!" She was screaming, pleading.

When she bent down and yanked at the red blanket, he crabbed backward and let her have it. She snatched up the blanket, heedless of the tumbling wine bottle, the sound of breaking crystal, and with both fists she flung it like a cast net onto the hungry wind. For a few seconds the blanket luffed and lurched upward like a magic carpet, then collapsed, twisting itself into a roll and plummeting into the tangled arms of a stand of shadbush.

Anton couldn't help it. He found himself crawling to the broken wineglass, genetically incapable of leaving shards in the sand for someone to find with a bare foot. The plastic tray still lay there, so he weighted it with the empty wine bottle and then carefully plucked all the tiny pieces of broken crystal from the sand and piled them on the tray. All of them.

When he looked up, she was gone. He shot a glance toward the trail through the dunes—the way back to the car—but she was not there. He looked down the beach the other way, where in the far distance he could still see the lady with the black Lab, but Emma was not there either. Reluctantly, he turned around and saw her standing knee-deep in the edge of the ocean, her face buried in her hands, nothing between her and the Azores but salt water. Her heavy sweater lay abandoned on the sand halfway between them. Waves plastered her hair to her head and painted her thin clothes against her frail body. When a wave hit her, chest-high, she staggered and almost went down, but caught herself. Flinging her arms about for balance, she waded deeper into the ocean.

He couldn't guess her intentions—whether she meant to drown herself, or swim to the Azores, or just stand there and let the surf beat her down while the riptide sucked the sand from under her feet—but it didn't matter. The big cat was toying with Emma, and Anton could not let it happen. He leaped to his feet and ran toward her. Toward the ocean.

A mountainous wave rose up in front of her, half again as tall as she was. She threw back her head and held her arms wide to greet it. The wave broke over her as he charged into the sea, and she disappeared.

He screamed her name, and then, high-stepping thigh-deep in the churning white water, felt her crash into his legs. He caught an arm and pulled her upright, hugged her to himself and moved to drag her out of the surf, but she resisted. Battling him with bony elbows, she twisted around to face the next wave. She didn't try to get away from Anton, but neither had she gotten her fill of whatever it was she needed from the cold seas breaking over her. He spread his feet, braced himself and hung on, his arms locked around her waist.

The next wave was as big as the last and it drove them backward, yet somehow he managed to keep his feet. Emma slung her hair, swiped water from her face and shouted something defiant, though the thundering surf drowned out her words. He was freezing, and he knew she had to be near collapse. With every wave he took a half step backward.

Something slimy and sinuous wrapped itself about his ankles. At first it only tickled, and then it tightened and began to pull, gently at first and then tugging hard, growing irresistibly heavy. His heart began to race and his breathing quickened, but he stood his ground. He would not allow himself to panic—not while he was holding Emma. Gritting his teeth, summoning courage he didn't know he possessed, he lifted his right foot to see what monster had taken hold of him.

It was only seaweed. The wet sand was littered with it, ropes and cords and tendrils of dead black seaweed, nothing more. It went slack when a wave came in and tightened with the surge of the undertow as the water rushed back out.

When Emma's legs finally buckled he caught her, hoisted her in his arms like a child, and carried her all the way back to the car. She weighed nothing, and even though she was bone thin, soaking wet, and borderline hypothermic, he felt the warmth spread outward from where her arms wrapped around his neck and her head lay against his shoulder.

He took her back to her house in North Sea and carried her up the steps. While she soaked in a hot bath, he built a fire, put on a pot of water for tea, and took a quick shower in the other bathroom. When she finally came out she was wearing a mauve satin robe with a rose-colored towel wrapped around her hair.

"Your color is back," he said. "You look positively radiant."

"It's the sea. I tried to tell you. Thank you for taking me, and I might add you look pretty dapper yourself. That's Enzo's robe, you know."

"It was all I could find. The kettle's hot—would you like a cup?"

"Ooh, yes. Earl Grey with a touch of milk, please."

They sat before the fire for a long time, neither of them speaking, or needing to. There was no sound except the gentle popping of the fire and the whine of the wind in the eaves. She leaned back against him, and that was enough. Once or twice he thought fatigue had finally caught up to her and put her to sleep, but it turned out that she had only been lost in her thoughts. She stirred, turning to him and bringing those eyes to bear.

"The thing is," she said quietly, setting aside her teacup and clinging to his arm, "a sailing ship only comes alive when it's breasting waves, when you can hear the groan of the ropes, the snap of canvas in the wind and the timbers creaking. But every ship needs a harbor, a safe place to come home to. If you can stand the strain, Anton…I need you."

Falling. He felt like he was falling.

Chapter 28

> Two immortals bar the way: one shrouded in darkness and seething with secret horrors, the other shimmering with beauty and promise, cruelly seductive. Deadly, both of them, yet there is no other path to Eden.
> —*Of an Angry God*, Fletcher Carlyle

Anton Kohl arrived at Weatherhaven a half-hour early on the day of the field trip—the drive down to New York to revisit Carlyle's apartment at the Dakota. Frye was waiting for him in the outer office when he got there.

"We best get cracking, Doc. It's like a two-hour drive, ain't it?"

"Three, if I'm driving."

Kohl made the ferry crossing to North Haven with surprisingly little angst and elected to bypass Sag Harbor. Taking the right fork at the turnabout, he drove the length of the narrow isthmus connecting North Haven to the South Fork. The public beach lay close on his right and the marshy reaches of Sag Harbor Cove on his left, where across the cove the McMansions of the *nouveau riche* lined Bay Point, their massive seagoing pleasure boats still tied up asleep in the morning mist. At the South Fork, he swung right onto Noyack Road, though he would not normally have gone that way because there was too much water, too many bridges. But he had traveled the same road last night, coming home from Emma's house in North Sea, and it had not bothered him in the least. This new courage was a gift from Emma, acquired through osmosis only yesterday, and he wanted to test it. So far, so good.

At Frye's insistence they stopped at a McDonald's for coffee and a McMuffin.

"You doing okay?" Frye asked as they crossed the parking lot to get back in the car.

"I'm fine," Kohl said, a bit surprised at himself. "Some days are better than others. But now comes the real challenge. I do not love driving on the expressway." From where they were, the fast track to Manhattan was the Long Island Expressway.

"You want me to drive?"

Kohl shook his head, putting on his seat belt, checking his rearview mirror. "No. I need to do this." Only then did it occur to him that in his rush to get an early start, he'd been thrown out of his routine that morning and forgotten his medication. But it was too late to turn back now. He felt fine. Surely he could make it through one day.

———

Neither of them spoke much for the first hour traveling west on the LIE. The heart of Long Island streamed past, a rolling sandy country populated by low-growing shrubs and grasses.

"Reminds me of Florida in places," Frye said. "Looks like it's been cleaned off by a hurricane some time or other."

"Twice, that I know of. Sandy, of course, and another one, I think, in 1938. A lot of people died in that one. Back then there wasn't much warning."

But Anton Kohl didn't really want to entertain thoughts of ravaged landscapes and mangled bodies while driving on the expressway. He'd gotten this far without a panic attack. No sense in tempting fate.

"I'm intrigued by something you said the other day," he said, in a clumsy effort to change the subject. "You told me you rewrote your manuscript because of a new perspective on the Jacob and Esau thing."

"Yeah, I did." Frye was looking out the window at nothing in particular.

"Can you elaborate on this new perspective?"

"It's kind of a long story."

"I'm not going anywhere." Kohl was doing a steady fifty-four miles an hour, other cars whooshing by at regular intervals.

Frye took a minute to gather his thoughts.

"The thing is, Jacob is a greedy, back-stabbing con man, right? He scams his old man, blows town to keep his big brother from killing him, then he moves in with some kinfolks out in the boondocks and gets scammed a few times himself. Over the years he settles down, gets married, has a mess of kids and does okay. In fact, he does great. Everything he touches turns to gold. Twenty years later he packs up all his wives and kids and goats and sheep and camels and goes home to make peace with big brother, and that's when things get weird."

"You mean the wrestling match."

"Right, but first you have to take a hard look at Jacob. See, when Jake gets close to home, he finds out Esau's coming after him with an army, so he sends his whole family on ahead with the flocks and herds, and he spends the night on the other side of the river, alone—like a coward."

"I don't understand. How is that cowardly?"

"Well, he puts his whole family out front and hides behind them. He even gives himself a river for a buffer, so if Esau starts slaughtering the wives and kids he'll hear the screaming and have time to haul ass. But then, out of nowhere, this guy shows up and Jacob wrestles with him. All night long. In the end, Jake gets his hip dislocated and his name changed to Israel, which means *struggles with God*. Out of the blue, this guy gives Jake his blessing and says, 'You have struggled with man and God, and you have overcome.' Now, that just never made any sense to me. First, a man don't outwrestle God, and second, it don't make sense to get God's blessing for being a cheat and a coward. So what, exactly, did he overcome?"

"Himself," Kohl said, white-knuckling the steering wheel as a semi roared past.

Frye's head backed away in surprise. "That's exactly where I ended up, except you're a lot quicker than I was."

"Not really. Jung pondered the same question. If I remember correctly, he said when a dream or a myth has someone wrestling with his god, it's fairly safe to assume it's a metaphor and he's actually grappling with some aspect of his own character."

"Seriously? Jung said that?"

"More or less, yes."

"Huh. I guess me and him think alike. Anyway, that's the same thing I finally saw. Something happens to Jake that night, all by himself on the other side of the river. He finally sees himself for who he is, and before daylight he overcomes his own rotten self, like you said. But that's still too vague, really, and it just leaves you with more questions. I mean, what was it? What was the thing inside himself that Jake had to overcome?"

Kohl shook his head, watching a motorcycle in his rearview mirror. "Do *you* know?"

"I think I do, now. I didn't understand it at the time, but Crito told me something way back in the beginning when he was trying to explain what makes a story tick, what makes a man do the things he does. He said when it comes to a character there's only two questions that matter: 'What does he want?' and 'What's he afraid of?' Crito'd been watching people for five thousand years, and in the end he said every bit of dirt anybody ever dished out was rooted in fear or desire. He said that's what keeps us down and stands between us, and the quality of a man's life is all about whether he can free himself from it."

Kohl kept his attention riveted on the car in front of him, devoutly wishing he hadn't forgotten his pills.

"That's impossible. No one is ever completely free of fear or desire...not while he's alive."

Frye turned to face him, animated now. "No, you're right. It comes with being human. You can't get *rid* of them, but you can *master* them—you don't have to let 'em tell you what to do. I went back and read Jacob's story from that angle, and this time I got it. Somehow, alone with God on the other side of the river, Jake finally conquers his own fear and desire. And you can see the difference in him, too, because when Esau shows up with an army behind him and every reason to put his brother's head on a pike, look where Jake's at. Now he's walking point, leading the way, and handing over a fortune as a peace offering. He bellies right up to his worst fear, and then gives away the produce of a lifetime of greed. In the end he makes things right in spite of himself, and that's what the story's really about. It's possible. In the right circumstances, a man can overcome himself. It ain't easy, but it's possible."

Kohl was silent for a long moment before he said, pensively, "That's rather profound...particularly for an avowed redneck."

Frye got a belly laugh out of that. They had become friends.

Chapter 29

> Their negotiations failed because they believed pure reason sufficient to the task at hand—a tragic arrogance.
> —*Daughters of the Nephilim*, Fletcher Carlyle

Even among the long row of impressive buildings facing Central Park, the Dakota was an imposing structure. Built in 1884, the façade was a complex mixture of European architectural influences with steep gables, dormers, balustrades, and balconies, all of which added up to an old-world intricacy reminiscent of a seventeenth-century French palace. Kohl got lucky and found a parking place a block from the Dakota—a good thing, as the traffic had already frayed the last of his nerves.

The doorman at the 72nd Street entrance did a double take when Frye walked up, then tipped his cap nervously and blurted, "Welcome back, Mr. Carlyle," as he swung open the wrought-iron gate to let him through.

Frye nodded curtly as he strode past the doorman, through the little tunnel and into the courtyard as if he had never left, as if he hadn't gone crazy and slaughtered a chicken in the street in broad daylight six weeks ago. Kohl was at his heels, watching. From the moment he got out of the car, Frye held his head high and assumed an imperiousness Kohl had not seen before. Switching roles. Becoming Fletcher Carlyle.

The apartment was on the third floor, far end. A grand mahogany-paneled entry hall led back to the living room. The drapes were drawn tight and the lights were still on, just as Frye had left them.

Kohl stood in the foyer and took it all in. This one room was almost as big as the entire downstairs of his own house—nearly fifty feet long and twenty feet wide, with a grand fireplace on the long inside wall, two tall windows on the park side, and a high ceiling. The room was appointed exactly as Frye had described it. Here was the nine-foot ebony Bösendorfer with the spray of twigs on top sporting one red lily, and there the white sofa with a large, tightly woven black rug in front of it. Atop the rug sat a rather simple but elegant white marble table, and atop the table a three-foot-tall piece of modern sculpture, onyx, with a streak of brilliant red coursing down one side.

Frye threw open the drapes and sunshine poured in.

"Astonishing," Kohl said, taking in the black-and-white Nouveau Something-or-Other décor. He touched a fingertip to the top of the statue on the marble coffee table. "It really does look like a wounded cormorant."

Frye made the rounds of the room, scooping up water glasses and coffee cups from nearly every flat surface. "Sorry for the mess. I left in kind of a hurry, and I didn't know I'd be bringing home company." With his hands full of stacked tumblers and cups, he disappeared through a swinging door into what Kohl assumed was the kitchen.

It was all as Frye had said, although Kohl didn't share his disdain for the color scheme. To him it appeared elegantly and tastefully done. A laptop computer sat open next to the cormorant on the marble coffee table, dead, amid a pile of scribbled notes. There were sections of a newspaper scattered all over the floor. Kohl picked up the sports section and noted the date—the very day Fletcher Carlyle had killed the chicken and ended up at Weatherhaven. He dropped the paper on the sofa and turned to look at the mantel over the fireplace. The Nobel diploma sat open on a book stand next to the medallion itself, which took center stage, sandwiched as Frye had said in a large, beautifully engraved slab of crystal. For a man whose life had been ruled by a delusion, Frye's memory and his powers of description were quite accurate.

Frye came back and, without a word, started gathering the newspaper into a pile, straightening up.

Kohl reached out reverently to touch the crystal-encased medallion. "Richard, this is a truly impressive achievement."

"It would be, I reckon, if it was mine." A large bundle of scrambled newspaper thumped down on the sofa, on top of the piece Kohl had put there.

"I love the mount as well. It's very nice."

"Looks like a crystal tombstone to me," Frye said flatly. "You want to see the Batcave?"

Like the living room, the converted bedroom overlooked the park across the street, with a ceiling as high and ornate as the one in the living room, but there was a surreal quality about Crito's office that spread a dark apprehension through Anton Kohl. Here, too, Kohl found everything precisely as Frye had described it. The walls were a dull brown; the air stank of stale cigarette butts and fermented fruit. A wide-screen, flat-panel television hung on the wall next to the door, still on, still tuned to CNN, the sound turned low. A T-shaped wooden perch sat shoulder-high in the far corner with a neoprene-covered ramp leading up to it. Kohl took a deep breath and forced himself across the room to the perch, his footsteps muffled by the layer of black rubber on the floor. There was a small wooden tray screwed to the top of the perch at one end, and in the tray lay the remote for the TV. There were a few downy feathers scattered on the floor underneath, but no droppings. Odd. Any ordinary chicken would surely have left a mess.

His toe nudged a shallow bowl on the floor under the perch and fruit flies swarmed up from it. Inside the bowl lay something black and shriveled and moldy. He bent down to look at it.

"A mango, I believe," Frye said, leaning against the doorframe with his arms crossed. "That's where the smell's coming from, I suspect."

A bulky, thigh-high, mushroom-shaped automatic feeder sat next to the perch, a handful of pellets spilling into an aluminum tray at its foot. Near the perch a tall window faced the park across the street, and it was ajar, unlatched. Outside the window was a small balcony on which sat three little spiral-shaped conifers of some sort, a scattering of white feathers on the soil between them.

Underneath the window a thin section of newspaper lay in a wad against the baseboard. Kohl picked it up, straightened it out, and stood with his back to Frye, looking at it—the book section of the *Times*. *Sons of Isaac*, by Richard Frye, was the lead review. He read the first paragraph, where the reviewer actually did refer to the author as "Dickie Frye," then skipped to the byline at the bottom of the column—Fletcher Carlyle. The bees were threatening to swarm, swelling up from his ankles, beginning to crawl in his forearms. He let the paper slip from his shaking hand and forced his attention elsewhere.

A dense trail of pinpricks in the black rubber carpet led from the perch, across the room to another neoprene-covered ramp, this one leading up onto the desk. It was a heavy, well-built cherry desk, its top covered with more neoprene. Kohl was no Daniel Boone, but those same little pinpoints dented the black rubber all across the top of the desk, with a particularly dense cluster in front of the keyboard, as if they'd been put there over a long period by the claws of a fairly heavy bird. In the middle of the space bar, where most keyboards were polished and shiny from long use, the finish was dulled by hundreds of little scratches. He could feel fear rising in his throat and caught himself holding his breath. When he exhaled, his breath sent a downy feather dancing across the desktop to fall down behind it.

The computer was still on, pinwheels of random color swirling across the screen. When Kohl hit the Return key, the screen saver disappeared and a cluttered desktop materialized. Fletcher Carlyle's mail icon showed upwards of two thousand unread emails.

Frye grinned at him from the doorway. "Find what you're looking for?"

Kohl didn't answer, but the truth was that he had not *at all* found what he was looking for—yet. This simply could not be. On the far end of the desk lay a blue box of Dunhill cigarettes, half empty, and a heavy crystal ashtray, half full. Frye's blood work had confirmed that he didn't smoke, but the tray full of butts proved that *somebody* did. Kohl put a finger on the edge of the brass hockey puck next to the ashtray and pressed. There was a click, and a neat blue flame sprouted from the center of it. The brass around the edges was frayed by a thousand little scratches. A spidery chill ran up the back of his neck.

On top of the computer tower sat a nearly full bottle of Aberlour scotch. A shot glass rested by the end of the keyboard. Kohl picked up the shot glass and eyed the rings of brown residue left in the bottom by some amber liquid having evaporated over the last six weeks. He sniffed. Scotch—faint but unmistakable.

Another haphazard trail of little pockmarks led from the desk to the open door in the corner, where the neoprene floor covering continued into the next room.

"Bathroom," Frye said. "Go ahead. Take a look."

The bathroom was spacious, and gorgeously appointed if one could ignore the odd black floor, but there were no towels in sight anywhere, no toilet paper in the holder. A neatly trimmed layer of the same black rubber was glued to the toilet seat, and it too was covered with pinprick tracks. Kohl bent down and looked closely at the gold-plated flush lever on the tank. Most of the gold was worn from the top of the lever, laid bare by scratches. As he turned to go he noticed a dusting of some kind of white powder on the neoprene floor outside the tub, and a few actual chicken footprints made with white dust. A one-inch layer of fine white powder covered the bottom of the tub, also full of chicken tracks.

"What's this powder?" he called out.

"Sevin Dust," Frye answered. "I forgot to tell you about that. He used to get in there and flop around sometimes. Said it kept the mites off him."

Kohl walked slowly out of the bathroom, pinching his eyes with a thumb and forefinger, his round glasses pushed up, his plans crumbling. This was not going the way he had expected. All he wanted was one scrap of indisputable hard evidence that he could use as a fulcrum to open a dialogue with Frye about the difference between fantasy and reality, but everything he saw corroborated the fantasy. His forearms itched fiercely.

Frye showed him the kitchen, but nothing there seemed out of the ordinary. Except for a layer of dust, the counters and sinks and stainless steel appliances were spotless. The dishwasher was full of drinking glasses and coffee cups.

"I never cooked," Frye said. "Like I said, I got my meals from the dumbwaiter."

Next, Frye led him to the master bedroom. It was larger than the Batcave, and carpeted—no black neoprene. Dirty clothes, socks, and shoes littered the floor, and a wrinkled shirt hung from a corner of the four-poster bed. The bedclothes were tossed about, hanging to the floor on one side.

The closet was nearly as big as the bedroom, and magnificent—cherrywood wardrobes with beveled glass doors, chests of drawers, and glass-covered shoe cases, mirrors perfectly placed on three sides, all of it amply but discreetly lit with pinpoint recessed lighting. A twelve-foot row of tailored suits and silk shirts hung evenly spaced behind glass, waiting for Fletcher Carlyle.

Kohl opened one of the doors and ran his hand down the shoulder of a dinner jacket. His hands shook a little less here, away from the Batcave.

"Fine fabric," he said. "You can't leave all this behind, Richard. There must be half a million dollars in—"

"I told you, I don't want this crap. I don't care what Crito said; clothes don't make the man."

"It just seems such a waste." Kohl lifted a gray suit from the rail and held it in front of himself, admiring it.

"If you like it, take it," Frye said. "It's yours."

"Oh no, I couldn't—"

"Look," Frye said curtly, producing a huge plastic shopping bag from one of the drawers and snapping it open, "I don't want anything from here, and I'm not coming back. After today it all goes to salvage." Before Kohl could protest, Frye snatched the gray pinstriped suit from his hand, folded it, stuffed it into the bag, and handed it to him.

He seemed agitated, and under the circumstances Kohl thought perhaps it was best, this once, to humor the man. Anyway, the gray suit did seem a bit drab for the flamboyant Fletcher Carlyle. Drab was Anton Kohl.

"Well…if you're sure. This is very generous of you."

"Psh. Generosity is when you give up something you'd rather keep."

They stayed another hour in the apartment, browsing Frye's impressive collection of books and vinyl recordings in the ebony cases in the parlor. There were tons of classics, both literary and musical. Many of the books were signed first editions. Kohl was blown away. Frye was unmoved.

As they were leaving, Kohl glanced up at the mantel once more and stopped.

"Wait. Richard, you at least have to take the medal with you."
"No."

Kohl pointed a finger. "That's the *Nobel Prize*, Richard. A thing like that happens once in a lifetime for a privileged few. You cannot just walk away from it."

Frye's eyes narrowed and he nodded once, angrily. "You hide and watch."

"You'll change your mind, you know. Trust me on this. One day you'll"—Kohl almost said *come to your senses*, but caught himself—"you'll get over your anger and...confusion, and you *will* change your mind. You'll regret leaving this behind, Richard."

"It's *his*!" Frye snarled, jabbing a finger toward the Batcave. "It ain't happening, Doc. After the way he stabbed me in the back?"

An ironic choice of words, but Kohl could see from his eyes that there was no point in trying to persuade him.

Frye glared. "*You* want it?"

"No." But Kohl reached for the crystal-encased medallion anyway. He took it down carefully with both hands, admiring it for a second, then tucked it under his arm and grabbed the diploma off its book stand for good measure.

"It's yours," he said, "but I'll keep it for when you change your mind. It'll be safe with me."

A steel-gray overcast had blanketed the city while they were inside, and a freshening breeze carried the scent of rain. It occurred to Kohl on the way back to the car that apart from salvaging the Prize, the entire trip had been a waste of time. He had brought Richard Frye back to his apartment to face reality, but what he found there had changed nothing. All the evidence corroborated Frye's story. The man was as adamantly delusional as ever, and even Kohl was beginning to wonder if there really were more things in heaven and earth than were dreamt of in his psychology. His hands wouldn't stop shaking, and he was so flustered that he crossed the street without looking, against the light. A yellow cab nearly hit him, the driver stabbing his brakes and screeching to a halt mere inches from Kohl's legs. He almost dropped the Prize. The driver blasted his horn, then stuck his head out the window and shouted a few choice obscenities.

They jogged the last few yards to the car as the first big drops of rain began to splat on the pavement. Kohl laid the diploma and the crystal tombstone flat in the floor behind the driver's seat so there was no way they could possibly be damaged, and then he placed the bag with the gray suit on top to protect them further. He was able to do this swiftly and without getting very wet because he had mentally rehearsed every move he would make before he reached the car.

Traffic had gotten worse, if that was possible—the beginning of rush hour. Cars brushed by uncomfortably close, all in a hurry, one after another, horns blowing. Kohl's hands shook so badly he had difficulty fastening his seat belt. Sweat beaded on his forehead, and he breathed sharply through his mouth. He inserted the key, but his hand wouldn't turn it. Any minute now, the bees would come.

"Let me drive," Frye said calmly. He'd been watching, and he'd learned to recognize the signs. "It's okay. I'll get you home safe, I promise."

Kohl forced himself to shake his head as huge raindrops thumped the roof, splattered on the windshield. "No," he gasped, wiping his face. "I have to do this."

He dreaded the drive back, especially in his current state of mind, but he had already crossed too many boundaries. No matter how he felt, there was no way he could allow a patient to drive him all the way from New York City to Shelter Island.

Chapter 30

> The best high-carbon steel is formed in a crucible, sealed and subjected to tremendous heat and pressure until disparate elements merge.
>
> — *The Forge*, Fletcher Carlyle

Kohl took 59th Street east to the Queensboro Bridge and promptly got lost in Queens. An hour and a half later, they were bogged down in traffic in Jackson Heights, windshield wipers slapping at a steady rain.

"Do you know where we are?" Kohl asked, his voice rising a notch. Sitting at a red light, he rubbed at his forearms and scanned unfamiliar buildings for something, *anything* familiar.

"No, but I don't see how it matters. The last sign I saw said we were heading east, right? That's all we need to know. It's a long skinny island, and home is on the east end. If we hit water we'll know we went too far. Relax, Doc."

That kind of thinking was foreign to Anton Kohl, though somehow Frye's easy confidence soothed his nerves.

"It may take us ten or twelve hours on the coastal roads, with all these red lights," Kohl said. "But you're right, we'll get home eventually."

"It's okay, Doc. If you want to take the scenic route, I'm down with it. There's no place I have to be." There was a note of sympathy in Frye's voice, and he stared a little too long. "Did I ever tell you about the time I tried to take Crito to the park with me?"

He launched into an outrageous tale involving a one-legged homeless man, an amorous Canadian goose, and a Schnauzer.

They were well out of the city before Kohl realized that Frye had been telling one story after another nonstop for an hour, and his yarns had a surprisingly calming effect. He took a hand off the steering wheel long enough to press a forefinger into the cleft under his jaw to check his own pulse. Almost normal. As best he could figure they were somewhere along the Gold Coast. Gatsby country.

As Frye rambled on about a dog he'd owned when he was a kid, they drove into open country, passing a cattail swamp on their left. Curtains of rain rolled over them, drumming hard on roof and windshield, like being inside a washing machine. Visibility dropped to almost nothing, and Kohl turned the wipers to high as they started up a slight incline. His nerves were frayed, but he kept going, doggedly determined not to chicken out and pull off the road.

"I swear," Frye was saying, "we didn't know what to make of it till one afternoon I was coming back from the spring and saw that mangy mutt in the garden with my own two eyes, digging up a turnip. I ain't making this up, Doc—he sat right there and ate the *whole thing*! Raw turnip! I mean, whoever heard of a dog—"

He didn't finish the sentence. Headlights pierced the curtain of rain, swelling and veering across the centerline, straight toward them. Kohl jerked the Volvo hard right to avoid a head-on collision, bounced off the guardrail like a pinball, and hydroplaned across oncoming traffic. An air horn blasted right on top of them as an eighteen-wheeler clipped the back bumper. The Volvo spun like a toy and vaulted into the air. A scream of grinding metal came from underneath them like the battle cry of some great dark cat, and then silence.

Kohl didn't even know they'd been on a bridge until he felt the car doing a slow-motion roll in that eerie quiet and his wide eyes got a glimpse of rain-pocked water rushing up to meet them.

Dark water.

The last thing he heard before the impact was a bone-chilling scream.

Awareness crept back into Anton a little at a time. He didn't know where he was or how he'd gotten there; he only knew his legs were freezing and there was a pitiful wailing coming from someplace. With a jolt, he recognized his own voice and ceased wailing.

Darkness. Disoriented, he lifted his face from the deflated airbag, and as his eyes adjusted in the blue glow of the dash lights he realized his legs were cold because they were underwater. The car rested nose-down, motionless. One of the headlights was still on, the eerie glow backlighting a cloud of brown silt hanging above the hood. River-bottom silt. Slowly, he turned his head and looked out the side window. A minnow appeared, inches from his face, pecked a tiny bubble from the glass, then turned tail and flashed away.

Into the dark.

The big cat had pounced, and Anton Kohl awakened in the belly of the beast.

His eyes went wide, his mouth flew open, and he shrieked, clawing in mindless panic at the door handle, banging on the window, wailing incoherently. The door would not budge, the window would not roll down. Crying like a child, he flailed with his fists until his battered knuckles left blood smears on the glass; then he stabbed at it with the door handle that had broken off in his hand.

And screamed.

Cold water inched upward into his lap.

He spun about, hyperventilating, and saw Frye hanging motionless against his seat belt. He shook Frye's shoulder, hard. The head lolled side to side, limp.

"RICHARD!" He shook harder, his shouts ringing in the shrinking capsule of air, but Frye was limp and heavy as a side of beef. "Wake *up*, Richard! NOW!"

Frye didn't move, didn't even twitch, his head slumped forward, his chin against his chest. Anton moaned and sprang away from him, recoiling in shock and horror from the realization that he was now completely alone.

The freezing sensation had faded from his legs, overpowered by the buzzing of bees. They moved and multiplied and swelled, crawling up through his hips and into the muscles of his lower back. Hives sprang up in both arms, swelling, growing. The bees grew angry and began to sting, separately at first, then in swarms. His vision narrowed—*my glasses, oh God, where are my glasses?*—and Frye's head slowly faded from view at the far end of a collapsing tunnel of darkness as the poison of stark terror consumed him. The bees filled his head.

Accompanied by the sound of insane shrieking, his childhood flashed across his mind at light speed, a flickering newsreel of half-remembered images, long-forgotten scents and sounds—a Cuban cigar, the drone of a lawn mower, his father's quiet laughter and the smell of Aunt Lyda's lasagna, a red plywood boat—all fleeting images, yet crystal clear and somehow connected. And then the newsreel froze abruptly, lingering on a sight he had not actually seen but only created in his head—the bloated white body of a boy clinging to a pine branch, alone in underwater darkness, his hair waving in the current and fat brown snakes wrapped around his arms. His eyes were open, staring at Anton, vacant and witless, uncaring.

He had no idea how long he grayed out that time, but his entire adulthood collapsed into a crevasse, and he returned to consciousness a helpless child. When the images faded, he was left with only the screams.

When the screaming abated, he began to beg.

"*Pleeease*," he cried, stroking Frye's long hair, snuffling, whining, keening, tears running down his face. "Please wake up, Derek, *pretty please*. You've got to get us out of here. If you don't, I'll *tell*!"

He hooked his hand under the chin and shoved the head up against the headrest to get a look at the face—an adult face with long hair plastered across it, jaw shaded by the stubble of a beard.

Richard Frye's face.

The face didn't move. The eyelids hung at half-mast, only whites showing. A thin line of drool swagged from the corner of his mouth. The mouth did not move either, and yet words came from somewhere and planted themselves in Anton's ears.

"It's possible," Frye's voice said, and then added, with a flippancy utterly out of place in hell, *"It ain't easy, but it's possible."*

Anton's hand began to shake from the strain of holding Frye's head against the headrest. He let go and the head lolled forward. He pressed a finger in the cleft of Frye's jaw.

A pulse. He's alive.

But Richard Frye, as resilient as he was, would not get them out of this. He was not going to save them. Richard Frye was going to hang there in his harness, oblivious, until the black water rose above his nose and mouth, and then he would not be alive anymore. He would be a bloated white thing with vacant eyes.

"*Someone will come.* They will, they'll come," Anton mumbled, chanting the words quickly, desperately, glancing upward in childlike hope, but the seed of a rational thought interceded. As ice-cold water rose to his chest, a pilot light flickered in the thinking part of his brain.

No one would come. Not in time. When they pulled the car from the water, there would be *two* bloated white things inside it.

The thought grew in him slowly, with a chill. If they were going to be saved, Anton Kohl was going to have to do it. There was no one else.

It's possible.

"No *time*," he whispered. His hands groped desperately in the black freezing water for his glasses, but he gave up quickly.

"No time. THINK, Anton!" This time it was a shout.

His hand found the seat-belt clasp. He released himself and fell against the steering wheel, his weight wedging him there for a few panicked seconds before he could worm free. But the shockingly cold water helped clear his head and, at least momentarily, held the bees at bay. His hand traced Frye's seat belt and his thumb punched the release. It was a struggle, but he managed to wrestle the inert body between the seats and into the back where there was more space above the rising waterline.

He swiped Frye's hair out of his face. Water and blood ran down from a gash on the right side of his head.

Anton tried the back door, gripping the handle and heaving his shoulder into it. Nothing.

Water pressure.

The words came to him as he stared through the window into blackness. A crack opened in his memory and reams of information began pouring in. Anton Kohl had not lived, but he had *read*, and he remembered everything he read.

Of course. To the best of his knowledge, none of the inlets in this area were over thirty or forty feet deep, depending on the tide, but a thirty-foot column of water weighed tons—more than enough to pin the door shut as long as there was air inside the car.

He would have to break the glass. Timing would be critical because as soon as he broke the window the car would flood and the remaining air would be expelled.

But what about his passenger? Even if he managed to get Frye out of the car, unconscious, he would drown before they made it to the surface. *If* they made it.

The top of the steering wheel disappeared. The water had crept up to the headrests on the front seats. The blue glow of the dash lights dimmed.

Anton screamed again, but this time in anger, through gritted teeth, exorcising the bees from his head.

"I'll hold his mouth and nose," he blurted, his voice tremulous and hoarse, but as soon as he said it he knew it was no good. He'd read it in the scuba book—thirty-three feet of water constituted the weight of an atmosphere. Air breathed in at that pressure expands as it rises so that, swimming up through thirty feet of water, a man's lungs would double in size before he reached the surface. The absence of light told Anton they were at least that deep, and if he clamped a hand over Frye's mouth and nose to keep him from drowning there was a good chance his lungs would burst on the way up.

The top of the headrests disappeared, and water began inching up the rear windows.

"WHAT?" Anton shouted, wild-eyed, gasping. *"What can I DO?"* There had to be a way.

A large white bubble bobbed in the water beside him like the tip of an iceberg.

The bag!

He grabbed at the shopping bag, wrestling with it until he found the open end. A completely incongruous bit of silliness popped into his head then, and he spoke the words out loud because it sounded like something Frye would have said.

"Custom-tailored, Jacques Dumont English wool suit—five thousand dollars. The plastic bag it came in—priceless."

The air pocket was still big enough so that he could snap the bag sideways and fill it with air, all the while pinning Frye upright with his knee. He managed to capture a sizable bubble, though he lost half of it as he pulled the bag down over Frye's head. It would have to do. There was no time.

It's possible!

Hugging Frye tightly in his plastic bubble, Anton kicked at the window with his heel. Nothing. He kicked again, harder. When his leg gave out he rolled over and stomped the window with the other foot. Snarling like an animal in the semidarkness, he slammed his heel into the glass over and over until he thought his ankle was broken, but the glass would not yield.

The heels of his shoes were too soft to break the window. Keeping a fist on Frye's bag, he tried the door again, ramming his shoulder against it in the hope that the dwindling air supply had allowed the water pressure to equalize enough for the door to open.

It still wouldn't budge.

He fell back, exhausted, dark water now up to his shoulders.

"I need a brick," he panted, gasping, and then remembered, suddenly, that he had one. Gathering Frye's bag tightly in one hand to keep the air trapped inside, he gulped a breath and dove down, groping on the floor behind the driver's seat for the slab of heavy crystal.

When the crystal tombstone smashed through the window, the inrushing water drove him backward and flushed out the last of the air pocket. But Anton's mind was clicking now, and he knew that once the air was gone the pressure would be equalized. He found the door handle. Now completely submerged, the back door swung open slowly and he slid Frye headfirst out into the darkness.

With his arms clamped tightly around Frye's waist and the bottom of the plastic bag gathered in his fists, he didn't need to kick. The bubble of air in the bag would fly them to the surface at the rate of about one foot per second.

Anton Kohl hummed on the way up, his ears popping as the darkness receded. He'd read it in one of his books— the best way to keep from bursting a lung was to let the swelling air out slowly, by humming. He kept humming until he and Richard Frye shot through the surface like a broaching whale.

A driving rain churned the face of the water, but through it he could see people on the bank forty yards away, waving and shouting in the twilight. He snatched the bag from Frye's head, rolled him onto his back, crooked an arm under his chin, kicked his shoes off, and side-stroked toward shore. Two men met them waist-deep in the water and drug both of them up into the tall grass on the rain-slick bank.

Kohl scrambled up next to Frye's inert body and checked his pulse.

Strong. Breathing steady.

Red lights strobed from somewhere above, emergency vehicles arriving at the bridge. Within minutes Frye was strapped to a gurney in the back of an ambulance with a foam brace around his head and Anton Kohl at his side.

On the way to the hospital, a paramedic lifted Frye's eyelid and shined a little flashlight into his eye. The author's arm rose up from the gurney. Knifing a drunken hand for emphasis, he mumbled, "—crazy dog dug up every last turnip, Doc. Beat anything I ever saw."

The paramedic shot a puzzled glance at Kohl.

"He's going to be fine," Anton said quietly, examining his own hands—the swelling, the bruises, the bloody knuckles, the torn fingernails. Emma would be proud.

Suddenly he felt very tired. He lowered his face into his battered hands and his shoulders shook. Laughing, crying—he wasn't sure which. It didn't really matter.

Chapter 31

> The universe distrusts inertia. Move, and the world moves with you.
>
> —*Atlantis Requiem*, Fletcher Carlyle

Frye's head moved. He opened one eye and peered unsteadily from under the gauze bandage around his head. Morning light slanted across his hospital bed.

"Doc?"

"I'm here." Kohl pulled himself upright in the corner armchair, rubbing sleep from his face. He had dozed in the chair rather than leave Frye's room during the night.

"How do you feel, Richard?" Rising cautiously, he made his way to the bedside, limping on an ankle sprained while kicking at a window.

Frye raised a hand slowly to his forehead, and Kohl could see the wince even without his glasses. "We wrecked, didn't we? We spun out and…aw man, my head's about to bust."

"You have a concussion. The headache is normal. It will pass, eventually."

Frye raised his head an inch or two and squinted at Kohl. "You look different."

Kohl was wearing green scrubs. A fresh white cast extended from the fingers of his left hand almost to the elbow. "Yes, I feel naked without my jacket and tie."

"And glasses. What's with the cast?"

"Oh, I, uh…I cracked a bone in my hand. In the wreck. It's nothing."

A small lie; it was far from nothing to Anton Kohl. Every time he looked at the cast, his heart swelled with pride. It was his first broken bone ever, and he couldn't wait to show Emma. Someone at the scene had called in the story of their escape, and a camera crew from a local television station came straight to the hospital to interview him, live, for the eleven o'clock news. Anton Kohl had stood in front of the hospital entrance with his arm in a sling, blinking mole-like at the lights while the reporter—a lovely girl as far as he could tell without his glasses—smiled into the camera and described his "harrowing ordeal," the heroic rescue of his passenger.

Then she'd stuck the microphone in his face. "Dr. Kohl, how did you manage to keep your composure in such horrifying circumstances? Weren't you afraid?"

"I...well, yes, it was somewhat stressful, but I didn't have any choice. Sometimes you just have to, you know, suck it up. Brass it out."

She called him a hero. Anton Kohl, a hero. Stifling a laugh, he glanced diffidently at his feet. He didn't plan it that way, but when he saw the film later it seemed to him that somehow it all came off very Errol Flynn.

"You should rest," he said to Frye. "Toma is on his way here to pick us up. The doctor said he'll examine you when he makes his rounds, but he felt sure you'd be ready to go."

The day nurse, just coming on duty, said good morning to both of them with a nauseatingly cheery smile. She was a young girl, a little plump, with hair a bit too big and a hint of Southern twang in her voice. Tapping on a touch-screen tablet, she pulled up Frye's chart and updated it, then peered over the tablet at his face. Her head tilted and she asked, rather timidly, "Are you the writer?"

When Frye glanced up in alarm, Kohl shook his head. He had filled out the hospital paperwork with the name Richard Frye, and he hadn't mentioned Fletcher Carlyle to anyone. A wave of panic washed over him as he envisioned a crane lifting the wrecked Volvo from the inlet, along with a Nobel medallion engraved with a name that would bring reporters and camera crews storming the hospital.

FLETCHER CARLYLE FOUND!

Neither of them knew what to say. They must have stared for ten or fifteen seconds without saying a word. She looked from one to the other, and that bashful grin melted, unnerved by the silence.

"Richard Frye," she said, apologetically, pointing at her touchscreen. "The name on your chart. I thought maybe you were the writer."

"Oh!" Frye's whole body relaxed. "Yeah, that would be me."

"Really?" She grinned, bigger than before, blushing. "I read your book. *Sons of Isaac*?"

"So *you're* the one."

"It was wonderful," she said, her eyes shining with excitement now that the tension was broken. "I'm a big reader and I grew up in Georgia, so I'm always looking for books about home. Those two old boys were so real, it's like I was there. I could smell the honeysuckle."

———

Two hours later they were heading east in the Weatherhaven van with the windows down, listening to reggae music. Toma was driving, rocking to the beat. Normally, Anton Kohl would never have tolerated Toma's reggae, but this was a new day. Marlene had even thought to send along the spare suit of clothes Kohl kept in his office, and his spare glasses. He could see again. The sky seemed a little bluer, the grass a little greener.

The hospital had taken the wraparound bandage off Frye's head, leaving only a square of gauze to cover the four stitches in his scalp. He was feeling a lot better, wide awake in the back seat. Toma had brought him a pair of Ray Charles sunglasses to cut the glare, and they suited him well. The sun was shining, the air crisp, and all was right with the world.

Kohl didn't hear Toma's cell phone ring, but the big Samoan suddenly flipped it open and put it to his ear.

"Sure, man," he said, and held the phone out to Kohl. "It's for you. Some lady." Before Kohl even said "hello," Toma had killed the reggae so he could hear.

It was Emma. She'd seen the story repeated in the morning news broadcast.

"Anton!" she shouted, breathless. "That's the most incredible thing I've ever heard! My God, are you okay?"

"Yes, I'm fine," he said, admiring his cast. "A few bumps and bruises, nothing major. I broke a skate, but I made it down the hill."

"Yes, you did. I'm so proud of you, Anton. I knew there was a lion in there someplace. How's Frye?"

"A mild concussion. He'll have to take it easy for a couple days, but he'll be fine once the headache wears off."

"Listen, is there anything I can do? Anything at all."

Kohl thought for a second. He did have a minor transportation problem. "As a matter of fact, if you could pick me up at Weatherhaven this afternoon, I could use a ride to the car rental place. I'll buy dinner."

Once he got Frye settled into his cottage at Weatherhaven, Kohl signed out for the rest of the day. Emma met him in the parking lot and gave him a hug that made him think she wasn't as frail as he'd imagined. In fact, she did appear to have put on a few pounds, and there was color in her cheeks.

When the car-rental guy tried to put Anton Kohl in something other than a Volvo, he balked.

"But, sir, we don't *have* a Volvo," the man said. "We can put you in a very nice Audi, or a Toyota—have you seen the new Lincoln?"

"No. Nor do I wish to."

Emma, who was holding on to his good arm, backed her head and raised her eyebrows as if to say, Look at *you*!

"Emma, are you up for a trip to Riverhead?"

"Okay. What's in Riverhead?"

"A Volvo dealership. I feel like buying a car." The flash in Emma's eyes was enough to tell him that the look on his face was, once again, a little bit Errol Flynn.

That evening he took her out for dinner in a newer model of the same car he'd left at the river bottom. It was even the same color. In Kohl's mind, the solidity of that car had saved his life, and Anton Kohl was nothing if not loyal. They ate at Beryl's, one of the finer seafood restaurants in the area. News of the rescue had made Anton Kohl a local celebrity, at least for a day, and the maître d' gave them the best seats in the house—a window table overlooking Shelter Island Sound, where tall-masted sailboats rested at anchor in the twilight and the lights of North Haven glittered across the water.

Ever the investigative reporter, Emma had been plying him with questions all afternoon, first about the wreck, the minutest details of his escape from the sunken car, and then about the trip to New York, what he'd found in Frye's apartment—and what he hadn't found. Her appetite had returned; she was halfway through her lobster salad when he told her about the nurse who had read Frye's book.

"That was quite a surprise," he said. "I've never even *seen* that book."

Emma's salad fork paused halfway to her mouth. "You haven't read Richard Frye's book?"

"Well, no. I only recently learned of its existence, and I just assumed it was such an obscure title that I wouldn't be able to find it anyway."

"You're hopeless!" She laughed when she said this, laid her fork down, and reached across the table to take his hands. "Anton, darling, nobody is that uninquisitive. How in the world could you treat a patient who'd written a book, and not think to read his book?"

"Well, I read the others—the Carlyle titles. But that one we just...we talked about it. He told me what was in it. And the way he tells it, Fletcher Carlyle strangled the book to death in its infancy. It's probably out of print already."

"But you never looked for it."

"No."

"Dear Anton," she said, shaking her head, "has it ever occurred to you just how much we need each other?"

"Once or twice." Warmth flooded through him. Looking out over the twinkling calm of Shelter Island Sound, he marveled at how the sight of the dark bay didn't trigger any alarm bells. He still had no desire to swim in the ocean, but the great gray cat was nowhere near.

"You know, I'm thinking about releasing him," he said quietly.

"Frye?"

"Yes."

"Soon?"

"Within the next week, perhaps."

"Is he ready?"

Kohl nodded. "The criterion, at least for me, is safety. The question I must always answer honestly is, *Is he a threat—to himself or anyone else?* If I don't feel he's a threat, then I cannot in good conscience detain him against his will. I can strongly recommend therapy, but I can no longer force it upon him. I've been through a lot with Richard Frye. I suppose the jury's still out on the dissociative identity disorder, but he's definitely no threat to anybody."

Emma looked like she was about to cry. "I was so hoping I'd have a chance to meet the man. I mean, *Fletcher Carlyle*."

"Richard Frye."

"All the more reason. What I wouldn't give just for the chance to sit down and chat with him for a while."

Kohl shrugged. "Then why don't you invite him over for dinner? Accompanied, of course, by his therapist. You *can* cook, yes?"

She thought about it for too long, squinting out the window at nothing in particular, searching her memory.

"Honestly? I don't know. But I'm certain I can find the phone number of an establishment whose employees cook dependably well. We can pretend. How about Friday evening?"

"Done. Red wine or...no, wait. I almost forgot he's a patient. I can't give alcohol to a patient."

Chapter 32

> "Dear boy, the father paid the greater price; the son was merely dead. But suppose the grieving Daedalus could have exchanged places as he wished, and Icarus thrived. What might the apprentice have become?"
>
> —Uriah Rilke
> *The Forge*, Fletcher Carlyle

Having missed one workday because of the trip to New York and another because of the wreck, Dr. Kohl's backlog kept him hopping that week. Friday was upon him before he knew it. Emma called at noon.

"Get here early," she said. "You know I told you I would do some digging? I did, and you're not going to believe what I found."

No matter how hard he pried, he could get no more than that; she was saving it for the sit-down with Fletcher Carlyle himself.

"But brace yourself," she said.

He and Frye went straight to Emma's house from Weatherhaven that afternoon. Kohl had already briefed Frye on Emma, but after the phone call he thought it might be a good idea to add a footnote.

"She's an investigative reporter," he said, "and a good one. Now, Emma is a very close, very old friend, and I trust her. Otherwise, as I said earlier, I would never have told her about you. She's just…well, outside of Weatherhaven she's the only person in the world with whom I discuss things like this, so I hope you don't mind. Anyway, she understands that anything I tell her is to be held in strictest confidence, and I've no doubt she will honor that. But that only means she won't repeat what she hears, or write about it. It does *not* mean Emma won't ambush you for her own amusement."

Frye shrugged. "Whatever. Long as I know the rules."

Emma's little house in North Sea was similar to Frye's cottage at Weatherhaven, a plain rectangle with a steep roof and almost no overhang, with cedar shingles all the way to the ground, like scales. A large silver maple shaded one corner of the house, and azaleas bunched against the walk, in full bloom.

Emma gave them both a big hug at the door, somehow managing to make a fuss over Frye without coming across like a starry-eyed Fletcher Carlyle groupie. Kohl had worried that it might be awkward. He should have known Emma better.

She looked good—stronger and more vibrant than the last time he saw her. She was still thin as a fashion model, but she'd done something different with her hair and added just a dash of makeup so that she *looked* like a fashion model. And those eyes were positively dangerous. Wearing a loose-hanging, lace-trimmed white skirt and blouse combination that looked like something out of the 1920s, she served them tea in the parlor from a silver pot and made the obligatory Thorazine wisecrack just to loosen things up. And, since it was Emma, it did in fact loosen things up.

"Dinner won't be ready for another hour or so," she said, setting the teapot on its tray. She pulled a book down from the shelf and settled herself gracefully on the end of the love seat, under the lamp. Kohl caught a glimpse of the title, the first time he'd actually seen *Sons of Isaac*.

"Mr. Frye—"

"Call me Richard, please."

She looked almost bashful for a second, pulling her hair back around a demure smile, and her hand fluttered the tiniest bit. "Okay—Richard. I'm sorry, but that face. I keep having to fight the urge to call you Mr. Carlyle."

"Fletcher Carlyle's dead."

Kohl noted that Frye said this with a kindly smile, more deferential with Emma than he had ever been with his counselor.

"Is it okay if we talk books?" She crossed one long leg over the other and, without waiting for an answer, added, "Because I'm dying to tell you how much I liked *Sons of Isaac*."

Frye chuckled, armpit deep in a wicker chair full of floral print pillows, sipping tea. "You actually read it?"

"Oh yes, and I loved it. The story is fantastic, Richard—moving, powerful, and scrupulously honest. There's a lovely agrarian rhythm in your prose, but more than that, when you talk about the places and people you know so well there's a respect, a genuine love of the characters that comes through between the words. It really is quite good."

"Thank you, you're very kind. Wow, two fans in one week. I could get used to this."

"You'd better."

"Well, it's nice of you to say that but—"

She raised a hand, cutting him off. "You haven't been to a bookstore lately, have you?"

"No. For one thing, there ain't that many of 'em left."

"We drove past one or two bookstores last week," Kohl said, "but when I suggested we actually stop in, Richard bowed up. Did I say that right? *Bowed up*?"

Frye nodded. "I ain't real fond of bookstores lately."

"Well," Emma said, "let me tell you about my trip to Bookhampton. As soon as Anton told me about *Sons of Isaac* I went into town to order it, hoping maybe they'd get it in time for tonight so you could sign it for me. Bookhampton is one of my favorite places, a big old creaky building right in the middle of Sag Harbor, with books piled on tables and crammed onto old wooden shelves. The air smells like dust and dry paper—oh, it's wonderful, I love it. Anyway, I went up to Mark, the tall clerk with the dark hair and the Clark Kent glasses, and told him I wanted to order an obscure small-press novel called *Sons of Isaac*. Mark's sipping on a latté, and he doesn't say a word, he just points toward the door. I thought he was throwing me out until he put the Styrofoam cup down and said, 'That rack over there. I think there are still a couple left.' So I go over and look at the big rack right inside the front door—the one with the best sellers lined up side by side, face out. And there sits *Sons of Isaac*, at number twelve."

Frye was leaning forward, so focused on Emma that he almost missed the edge of the coffee table when he put his cup down.

"*Sons of Isaac*? On the best-seller rack? How'd that happen?"

"I asked myself the same question. Unknown author, no promotion, no interviews or appearances and only the one review, which I also looked up and found to be as unkind as Anton told me it was. By rights, the book should have died on the vine."

Dumfounded, Frye shook his head and said nothing.

"It just didn't add up, so I came home and read the book, and then I read the *Times* review again. After reading the book, the review didn't make any sense, so I went online to see if there had been any feedback to it. As it turns out, because that merciless thrashing was administered by no less than Fletcher Carlyle—a Nobel laureate, bludgeoning a new author like a baby seal—it generated an instantaneous 'Why don't you pick on somebody your own size?' reaction from everyone who read it. The very next day, this glorious picture of 'homeless Fletcher' slaughtering a chicken caused such a stir that every major reviewer in the country felt compelled to read *Sons of Isaac* just to see if Fletcher Carlyle was as crazy as he looked."

She opened the little drawer on the face of the lamp table at the end of the couch and pulled out a sheaf of computer printouts.

"Since you've been at Weatherhaven there have been, by my count, twenty-three major reviews posted for *Sons of Isaac*—and that's just the big-league stuff. There are hundreds of others."

Frye picked up the stack of papers and leafed through it, skimming the articles. "These are not bad."

Emma chuckled, glancing at Kohl. "*Not bad*, he says. None of them are bad, and most of them positively glow. Great publicity, especially from major sources like these. The overwhelming consensus of those reviews is, 'Fletcher Carlyle has clearly lost his mind, because *Sons of Isaac* is wonderful.' But listen, I know a lot of good writers, and great reviews don't necessarily equate to success in the marketplace. What does mean something is buzz. That's what those two articles in the *Times* gave you. Buzz."

Frye's face registered only shock and confusion. He glanced at Kohl. "Can I borrow your cell?"

"Mine drowned," Kohl said. "I haven't had time to replace it."

"Here." Emma handed him the cordless.

"Oh, and can you look up a number for me? Sorry."

"The number for Pirkle Press?" Emma fished a slip of paper from a pocket in her skirt and held it out to him.

He smiled. "You're good."

"She's *amazing*," Kohl muttered, and picked up the stack of reviews.

Frye disappeared down the hall to call his editor. As soon as he left the room, Emma turned to Kohl.

"Anton, I need you to tell me this is okay, what I'm doing. I've uncovered some rather interesting things, but I need to know that he's strong enough to take it. Do I keep going, or should we talk about the Mets?"

"There's more?"

"Tons. I'm just getting warmed up."

"Keep going," Kohl said. "By all means, rattle his cage. But just for the sake of clarity, I need to know where you stand on this whole chicken issue."

"What do you mean?"

"I mean, sitting here listening to you, I can't tell what you believe. I don't know what else you've found in all your digging, but what I'm hearing so far sounds as if you've bought into his delusion. Do you really think *Daughters of the Nephilim* was written by a chicken?"

"I don't care!" She said this with a shake of the head and a wide-eyed, open-mouthed smile. "Listen, my perspective has changed a bit over the last two years. Shrapnel can do that to you."

He looked at her a little sideways, still not sure where she was coming from.

She took a deep breath. "Look, Anton, according to your own background check, Richard Frye is exactly who he says he is—an uneducated country boy, a high school dropout who lived his whole life in Squalor. Now, with that in mind, consider the possibilities, and there are only three. One, Crito was real, and a chicken really did write *Nephilim*, in which case my universe is wider and more magical than I ever thought possible. Or two, Crito was just an ordinary chicken that Frye's fractured mind, in self-defense, somehow imbued with incredible ability and then assigned it credit for writings he himself produced. But at the end of that story we have an uneducated country boy with multiple personalities winning the Nobel Prize for literature, and *again*, my universe is more magical than I thought. The third possibility is that all of this was carefully planned and orchestrated *consciously* by Richard Frye, who meticulously planted all the evidence to support his story, down to the minutest detail. Now, that wouldn't make sense for at least a dozen reasons, but just for the sake of argument let's say it's true. That makes our uneducated country boy the most brilliant con man in the history of the world *in addition* to being a literary prodigy—and yet again, my universe is wider and more fascinating than I ever imagined. Which scenario do I choose? It doesn't matter. *I really don't care!* After all I've been through and where it's brought me, I don't want to tell the world how to behave anymore; I just want to believe there's magic in it."

"I know exactly what you mean," Frye's voice said.

Kohl wasn't sure how long he'd been standing there, but the look of amusement on his face said it was long enough.

"Well," Frye said, "at least now all the cards are on the table." The wicker chair groaned when he dropped himself back into it, and then he leaned forward and returned the phone to Emma. "My editor tells me *Sons of Isaac* is already in its fourth printing. They're rolling out another fifty thousand next week, and they want to know when I can give them another book."

"Congratulations," Kohl said. "Maybe you won't have to go back to the post office after all."

"My wildest dream. The only problem I got now is I don't own a face. This one belongs to Fletcher Carlyle."

Emma chuckled. "Well, from what writers and publishers are telling me, you may not need one. Things are changing at light-speed in the publishing world. Most of the PR is done online now. These days—unless you're, you know, Fletcher Carlyle—public appearances are a thing of the past. All you need is some pictures for the Richard Frye Facebook page, and I'm guessing you can afford to hire a stand-in. It's been done before."

"Now *there's* a bit of irony," Kohl said.

"Yeah." Frye grinned. "And I know just the guy, too. Odd Lester's gonna love this. He can even pose with his hawk. Things couldn't have worked out better. Looks like my luck has finally turned."

Kohl watched Emma watching Frye. Sitting there in the lamplight with Frye's book on her lap, she was too poised and relaxed—a clear sign that she was about to drop a bomb.

She cleared her throat. "Richard, darling, luck had nothing to do with it. The whole thing was planned."

Frye studied her face for a moment, then shook his head slowly. "No way. Not even Crito could—"

"What, you don't believe he was capable of it? Don't you think he knew you'd come after him with a butcher knife as soon as you read that review?"

"Again," Kohl interrupted, "you're validating a delusion."

She gave Kohl a glance, but held her ground. "Richard, the thing about that review is, it's wrong. By any objective criteria, every detail of that review is dead wrong, and when a man of Fletcher Carlyle's prowess is wrong on every point, it cannot be an accident. That review got exactly the results he *meant* for it to get. He orchestrated the entire scene not to kill your book but to send it rocketing up the charts."

Frye raised a suspicious eyebrow. "His own execution?"

"Yes, all of it."

"I'm sorry, I just can't see it. There's too many variables, too many coincidences. The picture, for instance. If my editor hadn't called that morning I wouldn't have even known about the review. Sure, I would've seen it sooner or later, but then the photographer wouldn't have been there. No picture in the *Times*, no story."

"Yes, the same thing occurred to me. So I called the Pirkle editor myself, yesterday. He's a very nice man. In spite of that review, he was all worried about poor Fletcher Carlyle's state of mind, not to mention his whereabouts. He also mentioned getting a heads-up about the *Times* review, the day before it came out. An email from Fletcher Carlyle's office."

"Are you *serious*?"

"Crito needed you to play a role, and you played it perfectly. That's why he went out the window, and why he waited for you on the sidewalk. He wanted you in the street."

"Why?"

"For the pictures. The paparazzo didn't just *happen* to be there; he was invited."

Frye shook his head in disbelief. "How could you possibly know that?"

A shrug, as if it was all in a day's work. "I asked him. His name's Jimmy Falco. I worked with him a couple times on assignments in New York. Journeyman photographer—good, not great. Whenever Jimmy was hard up for cash, he haunted celebrity hangouts hoping for that million-dollar shot of a politician cheating on his wife or the Hollywood *bimbo du jour* falling down drunk, getting arrested. Jimmy told me that he got a tip the night before you killed the chicken—again, an email from Carlyle's office—telling him to wait in front of the Dakota on Sunday morning with his camera, promising him the shot of a lifetime. Since Carlyle hadn't shown his face in two years, Jimmy figured it was a hoax, but he went anyway, just in case."

Emma leaned forward, her eyes shining. "Crito choreographed the whole thing, and his timing was impeccable. He knew that picture would make a splash, and it would kill two birds with one stone...metaphorically speaking. It would completely destroy Fletcher Carlyle's credibility and, in conjunction with his review, the incident would catapult *Sons of Isaac* onto the best-seller lists. *That*, Richard, as any PR person will tell you, is pure genius."

Frye stared in silence for a moment, awestruck.

"That's gotta be the most twisted, convoluted...*exactly* the kind of Machiavellian crap Crito would come up with. Now that I think about it, Machiavelli himself.... Never mind."

"He didn't do it on the spur of the moment, either," Emma said. "He planned it months in advance, maybe even years, and there's proof. Richard, I have to ask you a rather odd question, considering who you are. Have you read *The Forge*?"

Frye bit his lip, thinking. "No, can't say I have. Who wrote it?"

This time she laughed out loud. "Fletcher Carlyle. It came out last week, and when I was standing at the best-seller rack at Bookhampton it was sitting in the number four spot. You didn't know about it?"

Kohl squirmed. Again, Emma was discussing Fletcher Carlyle—*with Fletcher Carlyle*—in the third person. She shot Kohl a sliver of a smile, and he envisioned the tail of a cat twitching.

Frye shrugged. "I remember signing off on some galleys a few months ago and sending them to the mail room. I never read a word of it. The release was on top of the pile, so I never even looked at the title page. I just signed the release, packed it up, and sent it back."

"You should read it. Crito left you a message." Letting the enigmatic phrase hang in the air for a moment, she leaned forward, focusing on Frye's face, and added softly, "In fact, he left a great many messages."

Leaving *Sons of Isaac* on the sofa, she went to the shelf, pulled down a bigger, thicker book, and handed it to Frye. The cover showed a stark silhouette of a chiseled blacksmith striking sparks from an anvil against a background of fiery red. The title THE FORGE dominated the top in raised metallic letters made to look like steel, and across the bottom in even bolder print, the author's name: Fletcher Carlyle.

"It's a period piece," she said, standing by Frye's chair with her arms crossed, watching him thumb through the book, "about a man named Uriah Rilke, a renowned swordsmith in England who, even though he's not of noble blood, has trained himself to be a world-class swordsman. He has a young apprentice, the orphan of a man he himself killed in a duel. The story draws you slowly, inevitably, to a place where you understand what Rilke understands—that his apprentice, whom he loves like a son, can only realize his own limitless potential by dispatching Rilke. Oh, here, let me read you something."

Lifting the novel from Frye's hands, she flipped to a dog-eared page near the end of the book and returned to her spot on the sofa under the lamp. A pair of half-glasses appeared from a pocket. Flicking a wrist, she snapped them open and slipped them onto her nose—a simple, natural, unselfconscious thing that Kohl found so adorable it almost brought a tear to his eye.

"This is a spoiler, but you really need to hear it," she said. "Listen."

She cleared her throat and read.

Uriah chose a September morning, the gray hour before dawn. A dense fog hung silent and somber in the tops of the cedars, a chill seeping into his clothes. Carriages waited at either end of the meadow, horses stamping and shivering, snuffling clouds of steam. Still under hat and cloak despite the swift approach of the agreed-upon hour, Uriah strolled unhurriedly through the dew-damp grass past the seconds, until he came face to face with Father Rupert.

"Good of you to come," Uriah said, his voice a murmur against the hush of the morning.

The priest made a noise like one of the horses. "Won't be any good a-tall if the bishop gets wind of it, but I'd be no kind of friend if I didn't try to stop this thing. Failin' that, someone's apt to need last rites."

"Aye, I expect so. I'd like that." Uriah breathed deeply, and his gaze drifted to the shrouded treetops from whence a flock of blackbirds launched themselves, fading ghostlike into the fog, as one. The truth was in his eyes.

"You've no intention of harmin' that lad," Father Rupert said. "And he means to run you through. You've seen to that."

"Aye." Uriah's eyes were still on the treetops. "Though I would like to have felt the sun one last time."

The priest gripped his friend's lapels, his eyes pleading. "Why are you doing this, Uriah? Can you at least tell me that?"

The lines in the blacksmith's leathered face framed a sad smile redolent of cold ashes and resignation.

"I owe a cock to Asclepius."

Emma closed the book slowly and, with her reading glasses dangling from her fingertips, looked calmly at Frye. "Do you recognize the line?"

"What line?" Frye's face registered only confusion.

Kohl suddenly smacked his forehead with a palm and flung himself against the back of his chair.

"*Gah!* Of course! *That's* where I've heard the name. How could I have missed that?"

Emma chuckled, enjoying Anton's momentary discomfort. It was an old and friendly competition.

Frye looked from one to the other. "What? Somebody want to let me in on this?"

Kohl sat up straight, raising a palm toward Emma. "Let me tell him. Richard, have you never read Plato's dialogues?"

"No. I *heard* of 'em."

"Well, at the end of one of his dialogues Plato describes, in some detail, the death of Socrates, who uttered his last words to a friend standing at his bedside, watching him die."

Emma nodded, a wry smile on her lips.

"He drank Hemlock," Frye said. "I do know that much."

"Well," Kohl continued, "Socrates' last words were, 'Crito, I owe a cock to Asclepius; will you see that the debt is paid?' or something to that effect."

"Close enough," Emma said.

Frye shook his head slowly. "No, that couldn't be him. Far as I know he never met Socrates, and the guy you're talking about was a man, not a—"

"No, no, no." Emma cut him off. "Follow the *metaphor*. Asclepius was the Greek god of healing. Socrates was asking his friend Crito to sacrifice a chicken to the god of healing. Don't you see? By putting this particular line in Uriah's mouth, your chicken has, in one stroke, associated the name Crito with the idea of the master sacrificing himself to the blade of his apprentice in order to bring about healing, and to set the apprentice free of his master's shadow."

Frye sat still for a minute, biting his thumbnail and staring at nothing. Finally, he sighed and said, "It still don't work, Emma. The thing is, he called himself Crito from the beginning. If what you're saying is true, then he would've had to know from the first day I met him what was gonna happen on Central Park West seven years later. That ain't possible, even for him."

"Really? Richard, when you write a story, do you know every detail before you start?"

"No."

"But you do have an idea how it's going to end, right? All you need is a character with a problem, and some idea of how to resolve it. Crito was writing the story of *Richard Frye*. From the very beginning he had a character, a problem, and a resolution. Everything in between was just details, a master craftsman manipulating his main character."

Frye sat staring at the floor for a long moment, searching his memory. A dawning realization crept over him, and when he finally looked up there was a new light in his eyes.

"It's all starting to make sense now. I didn't understand it at the time, but the night he laid out the whole Fletcher Carlyle scam, he said something about taking the long way around, an alternate route to my destiny. *My* destiny. This was never about Carlyle at all, was it?"

Gently, Emma reached across and placed her copy of *Sons of Isaac* into the author's hands.

"Fletcher Carlyle was a means to an end, a way to open your eyes to who you are—and who you're not. The goal was always Richard Frye. *This*," she said, touching a reverent fingertip to the name on the book jacket, "this was your dream. Crito understood that, even when you didn't. He brought you to your destiny in spite of yourself."

Kohl couldn't take it anymore. "An elaborate bit of reverse psychology, if you're inclined to believe in possessed chickens. My professional opinion, Richard, is that you're an extremely gifted man with a dissociative disorder—or at least it appears you *did* have a dissociative disorder until you destroyed Fletcher Carlyle."

Frye pondered this for a minute. "So you're saying I didn't go crazy when I killed the chicken; I went sane."

"I wouldn't put it exactly that way, but I wouldn't argue with it."

"Then, if you think about it, we all pretty much agree. Crito took me the long way around, but he got me there. In the end, he knew Richard Frye couldn't really live until he was ready to kill Fletcher Carlyle."

There was a flicker of surprise in Kohl's eyes. "I guess so! In essence we're saying the same thing, just from different perspectives. No matter what one believes about the chicken, his demise actually was the beginning of healing. To use your own metaphor, that was when you wrestled with yourself—and won."

"You should both read *The Forge*," Emma said. "It fills in a lot of blanks."

Rising from the couch, she handed the book to Frye.

"Do this, Richard. Read chapter three. One of the things for which the critics have taken *The Forge* to task is that chapter three seems out of place and superfluous. It appears to be an info dump about Sumerian religious practices, inserted into the middle of a rather lengthy history of sword making. But you're a writer, you decide for yourself. I must go put the finishing touches on our dinner."

She said this last while touching the back of a wrist to her forehead with a dramatic flourish, feigning exhaustion.

"Read it aloud!" she shouted, waving a finger in the air as she sauntered toward the kitchen. "I want to hear every word in Fletcher Carlyle's mellifluous baritone while I'm working my fingers to the bone in the galley."

But as soon as she left the room, Frye shifted to the edge of his chair, glancing at the door as if he wanted to escape.

"What is it?" Kohl asked. "What's wrong?"

The author leaned a little closer to Kohl.

"Do I really have to do this?"

Kohl completely understood the question. This was a watershed moment. Richard Frye had put Fletcher Carlyle behind him, and preferred to let him remain dead. Now Emma was asking him to play the part one more time. Anton Kohl caught himself glancing toward the kitchen to make sure Emma wasn't listening before he answered.

"No, you don't. You're free to choose, Richard, but our choices reveal what we believe. Given everything Emma has told you, how do you feel about Crito now?"

Frye sat back for a moment, his palm gliding reverently over the book cover. Nodding slowly, he opened *The Forge* and began to read chapter three, aloud, in the genteel Southern voice of Fletcher Carlyle.

Chapter 33

> Wisdom comes by ordeal, as a blade is tempered by fire. Plunge your secret dreams and terrors into the coals, pump the bellows with your own red hands, and watch the sparks fly to heaven like a prayer.
>
> —*The Forge*, Fletcher Carlyle

Kohl found himself closing his eyes and falling into the narrative, as if he himself were wandering the streets of ancient Sumer. The details—subtleties of color and scent, native plants and animals, nuances of obscure custom—might well have been perceived by critics as an unnecessary info dump, but Kohl had no objective in mind, no literary goal. He simply allowed himself to be transported, to bask in the textures of a long dead culture, guided by one whose words bore an unmistakable authority, the stamp of authenticity, as if the author had *been there*.

Sumerian kings, according to Crito, were little more than feudal barons, territorial and quarrelsome, iron-fisted and paranoid. The real power lay in the hands of the priestly class, for over the years they had been the prime engineers of Sumer's good fortune. It was they who devised ways to channel the rivers and raise the dry land, they who designed the tools and wheels and boats, they who discovered the paths of the stars and the secrets of bronze. Above all, the priests of Sumer gave birth to the written word, conceiving, nurturing and perfecting the craft. They were the first men of letters, and with their newfound literacy they recorded history and myth, wrote songs and epic poems. Their clay tablets made them the sole record keepers, and because of this they became guardians of the nation's storehouses. The priests of Sumer learned to wield the power of want and plenty with subtlety and finesse. In the gray dawn of civilization, their esoteric knowledge and artistry lent the priests a mystical air so that, inevitably, to the illiterate masses of earthbound farmers and wheelwrights and stonemasons and smiths, they became objects of worship themselves. It was also inevitable that the greatest of them would be consumed by pride.

"I see where this is going," Kohl said, interrupting the reading. "The man who would be a god. It's an old story, and it never ends well. He's talking about himself, isn't he?"

Frye grinned, answering in his own voice, "I reckon so. But what's got my attention is you, talking about him in third person. Do we have a convert?"

Kohl blushed. "Fiction requires a certain suspension of disbelief, that's all."

"READ!" Emma shouted from the kitchen.

The voice of Fletcher Carlyle picked up where he left off, describing the gleaming ziggurat in the heart of Nippur, rising seven stories on the highest point of land between the two great rivers.

The Temple of Nippur was the seat of power in the Sumerian Empire, and the High Priest the undisputed wielder of that power. It was he who presided over the Feast of the Summer Solstice, when tribes from the farthest corners of the empire gathered in Nippur. After a day of feasting and celebration, the priests lit bonfires on the temple grounds and the tribes gathered at the foot of the ziggurat to hear the words of the High Priest. The ceremonies would culminate at midnight with the sacrifice of a peacock, a priceless and regal gift, on the altar of the High Place as an offering to the Unknowable in the hope of a bountiful harvest.

Though there were many gods in those days, the Unknowable towered over the others. He was king of the earth, master of the universe, divider of the waters, father and protector of the first rivers, and bringer of storms. He it was who swelled the rivers and called forth the tender new-green shoots of grain in the spring. He it was who brought to earth the laws of the universe that all things obey, and He it was who pronounced judgment on Melkaz, the High Priest of Nippur.

When the High Priest appeared at the parapet wall on the lowest level of the ziggurat, the music and dancing ceased, and the crowds hushed. Melkaz began to recite an epic tale written for the occasion, a story of conflict and anguish among the gods and how the first rivers came to be, but in the middle of his oratory a peacock crowed.

As the honored guest of the Unknowable, the peacock roamed the temple unhindered but for a special guard assigned to keep him from harming himself or escaping. When he crowed, the crowd below murmured and smiled and tittered among themselves.

Melkaz waited for silence and resumed his recital, but again, at a particularly dramatic point in his tale, the peacock leaped to the parapet wall in sight of the people, threw back his head and crowed to the heavens.

For the second time the spell was broken, and Melkaz darkened with rage. Guards, fearing for their lives, rushed in to remove the peacock from the wall. Mistaking the scene for comedy, the masses roared in delight.

When the crowd finally hushed, the High Priest composed himself and continued. But at the very climax of his story, the peacock escaped the clutches of the guards once again, lofted himself onto the wall directly in front of the High Priest, and fanned his magnificent tail. Completely obscuring Melkaz, he swelled his chest and crowed lustily a third time.

Cheers and howls of laughter rose from the crowd below, but they melted into silence as Melkaz drew a sword from a temple guard, leaped upon the wall, and seized the bird. Heedless of the warning cries of his priests, in full view of his people, Melkaz slaughtered the peacock atop the wall. A little wind grew up in that moment, as Melkaz slashed and stabbed at his tormentor, and when he lifted the limp body to cast it from the wall, a cloud of iridescent blue feathers burst upward, scattering on the freshening wind.

The hush was broken only by the clattering of the sword as it fell from bloody hands.

A wail of anguish welled up from below, and grew. A great evil had been loosed upon them, so that even the priests were terrified. The time of the midnight sacrifice approached, but Melkaz, in his arrogance, had taken the gift reserved for the Unknowable and sacrificed it to his own wrath.

"So it wasn't just *any* peacock," Kohl said, mesmerized.

"Like the man said—justice is relative," Frye answered, and continued reading.

Desperate to salvage the situation, Melkaz ordered an ibis bound and brought to the temple.

The men of the tribes fell back, trembling. It was the women, nearly a thousand of them, who closed about the temple as the ceremony began, pressing themselves to the walls and crying out in despair. Some said it was the wailing of the women that awakened the Unknowable. Anguished, warbling cries mingled with the chanting of priests as the procession of white robes marched up stone steps to the High Place, led by Melkaz, who now carried a struggling ibis in his bloodstained arms.

The storm intensified, and a chill wind lashed the robes of the priests about them as they tethered the ibis and took their places, forming a complete circle of torchlight around the High Place. Raindrops the size of beetles spattered the stones and hissed against the torches.

The High Priest stepped forward in his formal headdress and breastplate, clutching the ceremonial blade before him, the wailing of the women and the chanting of the priests swirling on the wind, swelling to a crescendo. With both hands, Melkaz raised the bronze blade, and in that instant he was transformed.

A startling *snap!* preceded the murderous clap and flash. A searing streak of brightness drawn from the veins of the sun himself leaped from a low cloud and struck, like an adder, the upraised blade in the hands of the High Priest. For the briefest interval Melkaz became light, and his imprint lingered on the darkness.

The Unknowable had spoken.

In a driving rain the priests closed ranks and began, as one, to chant a strange incantation over the smoldering remains of their leader. The Incantation of Remembrance had never before been invoked; to a man the priestly class had always believed the words existed only as a looming threat against blasphemy, a way to impress upon the newly committed the importance of their vows. The words of the curse were said to capture the spirit of a man who would make himself a god, and imprison him in the body of a lesser animal. On the death of the animal, the mind and memory of the cursed would pass into the nearest animal of like kind, and would continue to do so until such time as he learned the error of his ways and found a way to make restitution to God and man.

The priests released the ibis, then bore the body of Melkaz down from the High Place, out onto the grounds, and flung it into the embers of a bonfire. The people of the tribes, thousands of them, brought branches and logs to heap upon the fire until a roaring flame rose high into the night sky. As the smoke of the pyre reached the clouds, the storm withdrew, shrinking and dissipating until the stars shined anew on the valley of the first rivers.

Emma reappeared at Frye's shoulder, wiping her hands on a dishtowel. He looked up at her.

"See what I mean?" she said. "The critics are right. This piece is completely out of place in *The Forge*, a mistake that a writer of Carlyle's talents would never make without a very good reason."

"And you think I'm the reason, that this chapter was just for me, like a letter of explanation."

"It has to be. Richard, when he wrote this, you were the only person in the world who would know it was autobiographical. Read the rest of it."

She took a seat and opened her laptop as Frye read the last few paragraphs.

No one could say for certain what happened to the spirit of Melkaz, but one by one the ibis in Nippur began to turn black about the extremities. Before long, all of them bore black beaks, black feet, black tail feathers; not a single solid white ibis remained in the land. The priests called it an omen, and, though the phrase was forgotten over time, for many years these black feathers were known as the "Mark of Melkaz." Within a generation the lowly ibis of the swamplands became known as the "Sacred Ibis" and was often sacrificed to appease the gods in times of pestilence and famine.

Frye closed the book reverently, and sat staring at it.

"I never knew any of this. I mean, yeah, he told me he killed a peacock, but...not like this. It kind of rings true, don't it."

Emma looked up from her laptop, reading glasses perched on her nose.

"Yes it does, especially after you do a little research. The Sumerian details are eerily accurate."

Again, Kohl felt compelled to play devil's advocate. "Emma, I'm sorry, but how can you possibly know? You're not an anthropologist—a writer of his skill could have made up the whole thing."

She smiled patiently and handed him her laptop. On the screen was a color photo of a large white bird with a long curved beak. Its head, legs, and tail feathers were black.

The caption underneath read, "Sacred Ibis."

"Dinner is served," Emma said.

Chapter 34

> "What them folks think of you ain't none of your business, young'un. You're the only one knows who you are, who God *meant* for you to be, and don't you forget that. Trust it, and someday you'll grow into it."
>
> —Isaac Brown
> *Sons of Isaac*, Richard Frye

They gathered around Emma's oak table in the dining room for a simple meal of spaghetti and salad, and for a while the dinner conversation centered on Emma. She was doing much better lately, partly due to a new drug her doctor had prescribed. But while the prescription had helped, she was convinced that her turnaround had been the product of something deeper than any drug.

"I was stuck inside these walls for too long—inside myself. I just couldn't see a way out. You changed that, Anton. Thank you."

Leaning across the table, Kohl lifted her hand and brought her fingers gently to his lips. "Believe me, the pleasure is all mine."

"Stop," she said, withdrawing the hand. "You'll make me cry."

Her eyes turned to Frye.

"And *you*. You gave me a mission, and it couldn't have come at a better time. I had almost forgotten what it was like to be an investigative reporter, to throw myself into a story in pursuit of the truth. Thank you, Richard Frye."

Frye actually blushed. "Dinner is wonderful, Emma. This salad—I ain't no expert, but this is just like what they serve in the finer restaurants. And the spaghetti sauce is enough to make you slap your granny."

"Thank you, I think." With a warning glance at Kohl, she added, "It's an old family recipe."

Frye peered over his shoulder at the kitchen. "Why is there smoke coming from the top of the oven door?"

"Oh," Emma said absently, "that would be the rolls."

"I've never been much of a bread eater," Kohl lied.

Frye chuckled. "Me neither. But you might want to toss 'em before the smoke alarm goes off."

While Emma threw out the pan of charred dinner rolls, switched on the fan and aired out the kitchen, Frye turned to Anton Kohl.

"You've been awful quiet, Doc. You all right?"

Kohl smiled, but he felt a small pang of guilt because he had almost come to depend on their occasional role reversals.

"I just can't help feeling that, on some level, I've failed you."

"Really?"

Kohl laid down his fork, wiped his mouth with a napkin, pushed his glasses up on his nose. "While you appear to be as sound and fit as anyone I know, Richard, we've made very little progress in resolving the disparity between your perception of the world and the actual reality."

Frye pondered this for a second, and shrugged. "So?"

Emma, who'd apparently been listening, returned to the table and sat sideways in her chair.

"He's right, Anton. 'So?' is a valid response, for him. He's perfectly comfortable in his world, but in the end it isn't Richard's world you're worried about; it's yours. He's not the one who needs order and certainty, conclusive answers and finality. You are."

Kohl sighed. "Yes. You're right."

She studied his face, her chin resting in her palm.

"Let me tell you a story," she said. "When I was young I went to Honduras to do a piece on Copán, and while I was there a very old indigenous woman named Rosa told me a story about an ancient ritual. She said when she was a child there was something wrong with her. Sickly and small for her age, her stomach was sour and she coughed constantly. The shaman told her mother there was nothing he could do, that she would never thrive and would die before she was old enough to have children. But every year at the same time, some of her tribespeople would travel two days to the slopes of the 'mountain of sleeping fire,' in the highlands where the clouds caressed the jungle and the trees were filled with bright orange flowers. They would gather there in the predawn darkness and wait, because they knew that on one certain morning, the jewel birds would come. At first light the birds started zipping through the trees by the thousands, and then, as the sun rose, by the millions. Magical little birds the size of a thumb, she said, who could hover and fly backward, and they shined like polished jewels."

"Hummingbirds," Kohl said.

"Yes, obviously, but I loved her mystical description. They dressed all the girls in their best hand-woven *huipiles* and stood them in a circle in the middle of a clearing, holding hands while their families watched from the tree line. Legend had it that if they truly believed, sometimes one of the birds would break ranks and come down to hover beside one of the girls for a moment, and it would touch her ear as if it were a flower. A buzzing, soft as the breath of God, Rosa said, and then it was gone. It was said that the kiss of the jewel bird would bring radiant health, long life, and a good man."

Emma smiled, remembering. "I was young then, and I so wanted to tell her that such myths had no effect whatsoever on reality. But Rosa believed it, and who was I to argue with her? She had long since buried her good man. When I spoke with her, as best her granddaughter could determine, Rosa was a hundred and eight years old."

Kohl let her words hang in the air for a moment, and then said, "A lovely story, Emma. Really. But there are alternative explanations—coincidence not least among them."

Emma spoke softly, patiently. "Yes, Anton, there are always other explanations. And yet, at the end of the day, what does it matter? No one can ever prove or disprove such things, but Rosa believed it, and that alone was enough to change her life."

Frye chuckled. "Brother Emmet would've said her faith made her whole."

Kohl raised an eyebrow. "But even you have to admit that a Nobel Prize-winning chicken is a fairly broad leap of faith."

"Despite the evidence." Frye's head tilted and his eyes narrowed, distracted by a brand-new question. "I wonder if he made it."

"Who, dear? Made what?" Emma asked.

"Crito. I wonder if he got what he was after. Absolution, redemption. If everything you told me is true, then I'd say he made restitution, wouldn't you? If nothing else, he made restitution with men at the Bern Accords, not to mention what he did for me. As for appeasing the gods, seems like that always required blood."

Emma nodded. "He did that, too."

"So, you think he freed himself from the curse?"

There was a faint, curious smile in Emma's eyes. "Maybe. Let me show you something. I really didn't know what to make of it...until now."

She got up and disappeared into the back of the house. They could hear her stirring around in her office for a few minutes before she returned with a stack of four-by-six pictures and laid them on the table in front of Richard Frye. He picked up the stack and leafed through them.

"These are from that day. On Central Park West."

Emma sat sideways at the table, watching his face. "Jimmy didn't just take one picture that day, he took a hundred. He sent me a twenty-shot sequence, starting with the killing."

Frye went through them one by one, beginning with the infamous photo of a wild-eyed Fletcher Carlyle, sunlight glinting from the butcher knife in his raised hand. Two shots later showed a policeman grabbing him, and the next a scuffle between the two of them. This was the policeman who ended up with nine stitches. Then two more uniforms joined him, and the next few pictures documented the ensuing melee—three cops, eventually joined by a fourth, grappling with Carlyle, slamming him to the pavement and flipping him onto his face. In the last photograph, all that could be seen of him was his bare legs, toes down, protruding from under a pile of blue-clad policemen.

"So what am I looking for?"

"Look closely at the last picture, upper right," Emma said.

Frye picked up the photo and studied it for a minute. Suddenly his eyes widened and his mouth opened. His hand shook as he laid the picture on the table and looked up at Emma.

"Well, I swear," he whispered.

"What?" Kohl reached for the photograph, held it close to his face and squinted. The camera was focused on Carlyle and the pile of policemen in the middle of the street, but in the slightly blurred upper right corner he could see the front wheel of a white BMW, and in its shadow lay what appeared to be the body of the chicken, where it had fallen in the scuffle.

Kohl shrugged. "I don't get it. What is it you want me to see?"

"Look closer," Emma said. "Compare it to the first one." She handed him the first picture in the sequence, the one with the butcher knife poised to strike, and Carlyle's left hand pinning the chicken against the hood of the BMW. He was holding it by the legs, and the feet stuck out of his fist.

The claws and feathers of the legs were black.

Kohl looked again at the last picture, the one of the chicken on the pavement. It was out of focus, and much of the bird lay in shadow, but sunlight fell across the legs. Squinting, Kohl adjusted his glasses.

"Oh, now I see it. His legs appear to have changed color." The claws were yellow, the leg feathers white.

Frye nodded, still looking at Emma. "The Mark of Melkaz is gone."

"That would be my guess," Emma said.

"It could be a trick of the light," Kohl said. "It's not terribly clear, in the shadow of the fender like that. Some animals' colors fade when they expire, and anyway, how do we know it's not an entirely different bird—maybe a white pigeon struck by a car?"

Emma smiled patiently. "Anton, those are not the legs of a pigeon. And chickens, black *or* white, are relatively uncommon on Central Park West."

Capturing him with those eyes, she reached across and laid her hand on top of his cast. Warmth spread up his arm from his exposed fingers. He picked up his fork with his right hand and began tapping the tines nervously against his plate, but Emma's warmth washed through him. Something in him relaxed, and a hint of a smile crept onto his face.

"I guess in the final analysis, all I can say is, Richard Frye is two of the most interesting people I've ever met." He laid the fork down gently. "What we need now is a glass of wine."

Emma cut her eyes toward Richard. "I thought you said—"

"What I said was, I can't serve wine to a patient. But *you* can if you like. Furthermore, as of tomorrow morning he will no longer be a patient. I'm releasing him."

"Ooh," Emma said, rising, "this calls for a *special occasion* wine. I'll be right back."

In a moment she returned from the cellar, wiping down a dark bottle with a dish towel. She glanced at the cast on Kohl's wrist and presented the bottle to Richard Frye, along with a corkscrew.

Frye peered down his nose at the label.

"Emma, this is a Château Margaux 2000, a very fine Bordeaux." Then, as if to compensate for slipping into Fletcher Carlyle mode, he added, "It ain't no third-rate table wine."

"Special occasion, special wine," she said, putting three long-stemmed glasses on the table.

Frye stood up to pour, being careful not to spill a drop. After he sat down, none of them said a word for what felt like a long time. Three glasses of Bordeaux waited while each of them contemplated a proper toast.

It was Frye who raised his glass first.

"To Crito."

Kohl raised an eyebrow, then his glass.

"To overcoming," he argued.

Emma laughed, a great big hearty one-syllable "Hah!" Then she lifted her own glass, and the three of them touched.

"To life," she said.